DESMOND BAGLEY was born in 1923 in Kendal, Westmorland, and brought up in Blackpool. He began his working life, aged 14, in the printing industry and then did a variety of jobs until going into an aircraft factory at the start of the Second World War.

When the war ended he decided to travel to southern Africa, going overland through Europe and the Sahara. He worked en route, reaching South Africa in 1951.

He became a freelance journalist in Johannesburg and wrote his first published novel, *The Golden Keel*, in 1962. In 1964 he returned to England and lived in Totnes, Devon, for twelve years. He and his wife then moved to Guernsey in the Channel Islands. Here he found the ideal place for combining his writing with his other interests, which included computers, mathematics, military history, and entertaining friends from all over the world.

Night of Error was written in 1962. It was withheld from publication by the author as he wished to make certain revisions. As other ideas took precedence this task was postponed. Now, twenty years later incorporating the author's revisionary notes, *Night of Error* takes its rightful place in Desmond Bagley's list of novels.

DESMOND BAGLEY

Night of Error

FONTANA/Collins

First published by William Collins Sons & Co. Ltd 1984
A continental edition first issued in Fontana Paperbacks 1984
This edition issued in Fontana Paperbacks 1985

Copyright © Brockhurst Publications Ltd 1984

Made and printed in Great Britain by
William Collins Sons & Co. Ltd, Glasgow

The publishers and author wish to thank
William Robinson for kindly granting his
permission to quote from his book
The Great Southern Sea.

And when with grief you see your brother stray,
Or in a night of error lose his way,
Direct his wandering and restore the day.
To guide his steps afford your kindest aid,
And gently pity whom you can't persuade:
Leave to avenging Heaven his stubborn will,
For, O, remember, he's your brother still.

JONATHAN SWIFT

For
STAN HURST,
at last, with affection

Preface

The Pacific Islands Pilot, Vol. II, published by the Hydrographer of the Navy, has this to say about the island of Fonua Fo'ou, almost at the end of a long and detailed history:

> In 1963, HMNZFA *Tui* reported a hard grey rock, with a depth of 6 feet over it, on which the sea breaks, and general depths of 36 feet extending for 2 miles northwards and 1½ miles westward of the rock, in the position of the bank. The eastern side is steep-to. In the vicinity of the rock, there was much discoloured water caused by sulphurous gas bubbles rising to the surface. On the bank, the bottom was clearly visible, and consisted of fine black cellar lava, like volcanic cinder, with patches of white sand and rock. Numerous sperm whales were seen in the vicinity.

But that edition was not published until 1969.
This story began in 1962.

Chapter One

1

I heard of the way my brother died on a wet and gloomy afternoon in London. The sky was overcast and weeping and it became dark early that day, much earlier than usual. I couldn't see the figures I was checking, so I turned on the desk light and got up to close the curtains.

I stood for a moment watching the rain leak from the plane trees on the Embankment, then looked over the mist-shrouded Thames. I shivered slightly, wishing I could get out of this grey city and back to sea under tropic skies. I drew the curtain decisively, closing out the gloom.

The telephone rang.

It was Helen, my brother's widow, and she sounded hysterical. 'Mike, there's a man here – Mr Kane – who was with Mark when he died. I think you'd better see him.' Her voice broke. 'I can't take it, Mike.'

'All right, Helen; shoot him over. I'll be here until five-thirty – can he make it before then?'

There was a pause and an indistinct murmur, then Helen said, 'Yes, he'll be at the Institute before then. Thanks, Mike. Oh, and there's a slip from British Airways – something has come from Tahiti; I think it must be Mark's things. I posted it to you this morning – will you look after it for me? I don't think I could bear to.'

'I'll do that,' I said. 'I'll look after everything.'

She rang off and I put down the receiver slowly and leaned back in my chair. Helen seemed distraught about Mark and I wondered what this man Kane had told her. All I knew was that Mark had died somewhere in the Islands near Tahiti; the British Consul there had wrapped it all up and the Foreign

13

Office had got in touch with Helen as next of kin. She never said so but it must have been a relief – her marriage had caused her nothing but misery.

She should never have married him in the first place. I had tried to warn her, but it's a bit difficult telling one's prospective sister-in-law about the iniquities of one's own brother, and I'd never got it across. Still, she must have loved him despite everything, judging by the way she was behaving; but then, Mark had a way with his women.

One thing was certain – Mark's death wouldn't affect me a scrap. I had long ago taken his measure and had steered clear of him and all his doings, all the devious and calculating cold-blooded plans which had only one end in view – the glorification of Mark Trevelyan.

I put him out of my mind, adjusted the desk lamp and got down to my figures again. People think of scientists – especially oceanographers – as being constantly in the field making esoteric discoveries. They never think of the office work entailed – and if I didn't get clear of this routine work I'd never get back to sea. I thought that if I really buckled down to it another day would see it through, and then I would have a month's leave, if I could consider writing a paper for the journals as constituting leave. But even that would not take up the whole month.

At a quarter to six I packed it in for the day and Kane had still not shown up. I was just putting on my overcoat when there was a knock on the door and when I opened it a man said, 'Mr Trevelyan?'

Kane was a tall, haggard man of about forty, dressed in rough seaman's clothing and wearing a battered peaked cap. He seemed subdued and a little in awe of his surroundings. As we shook hands I could feel the callouses and thought that perhaps he was a sailing man – steam seamen don't have much occasion to do that kind of hand work.

I said, 'I'm sorry to have dragged you across London on a day like this, Mr Kane.'

'That's all right,' he said in a raw Australian accent. 'I was coming up this way.'

14

I sized him up. 'I was just going out. What about a drink?'

He smiled. 'That 'ud be fine. I like your English beer.'

We went to a nearby pub and I took him into the public bar and ordered a couple of beers. He sank half a pint and gasped luxuriously. 'This is good beer,' he said. 'Not as good as Swan, but good all the same. You know Swan beer?'

'I've heard of it,' I said. 'I've never had any. Australian, isn't it?'

'Yair; the best beer in the world.'

To an Australian all things Australian are the best. 'Would I be correct if I said you'd done your time in sail?' I said.

He laughed. 'Too right you would. How do you know?'

'I've sailed myself; I suppose it shows somehow.'

'Then I won't have to explain too much detail when I tell you about your brother. I suppose you want to know the whole story? I didn't tell Mrs Trevelyan all of it, you know – some of it's pretty grim.'

'I'd better know everything.'

Kane finished his beer and cocked an eye at me. 'Another?'

'Not for me just yet. You go ahead.'

He ordered another beer and said, 'Well, we were sailing in the Society Islands – my partner and me – we've got a schooner and we do a bit of trading and pick up copra and maybe a few pearls. We were in the Tuamotus – the locals call them the Paumotus, but they're the Tuamotus on the charts. They're east of . . .'

'I know where they are,' I interrupted.

'Okay. Well, we thought there was a chance of picking up a few pearls so we were just cruising round calling on the inhabited islands. Most of 'em aren't and most of 'em don't have names – not names that we can pronounce. Anyway we were passing this one when a canoe came out and hailed us. There was a boy in this canoe – a Polynesian, you know – and Jim talked to him. Jim Hadley's my partner; he speaks the lingo – I don't savvy it too good myself.

'What he said was that there was a white man on the island who was very sick, and so we went ashore to have a look at him.'

15

'That was my brother?'

'Too right, and he was sick; my word yes.'

'What was wrong with him?'

Kane shrugged. 'We didn't know at first but it turned out to be appendicitis. That's what we found out after we got a doctor to him.'

'Then there was a doctor?'

'If you could call him a doctor. He was a drunken old no-hoper who'd been living in the Islands for years. But he said he was a doctor. He wasn't there though; Jim had to go fifty miles to get him while I stayed with your brother.'

Kane took another pull at his beer. 'Your brother was alone on this island except for the black boy. There wasn't no boat, either. He said he was some sort of scientist – something to do with the sea.'

'An oceanographer.' Yes, like me an oceanographer. Mark had always felt compelled, driven, to try and beat me whatever the game. And his rules were always his own.

'Too right. He said he'd been dropped there to do some research and he was due to be picked up any time.'

'Why didn't you take him to the doctor instead of bringing the doctor to him?' I asked.

'We didn't think he'd make it,' said Kane simply. 'A little ship like ours bounces about a lot, and he was pretty sick.'

'I see,' I said. He was painting a rough picture.

'I did what I could for him,' said Kane. 'There wasn't much I could do though, beyond cleaning him up. We talked a lot about this and that – that was when he asked me to tell his wife.'

'Surely he didn't expect you to make a special trip to England?' I demanded, thinking that even in death it sounded like Mark's touch.

'Oh, it was nothing like that,' said Kane. 'You see, I was coming to England anyway. I won a bit of money in a sweep and I always wanted to see the old country. Jim, my cobber, said he could carry on alone for a bit, and he dropped me at Panama. I bummed a job on a ship coming to England.'

16

He smiled ruefully. 'I won't be staying here as long as I thought – I dropped a packet in a poker game coming across. I'll stay until my cash runs out and then I'll go back to Jim and the schooner.'

I said, 'What happened when the doctor came?'

'Oh sure, you want to know about your brother; sorry if I got off track. Well, Jim brought this old no-good back and he operated. He said he had to, it was your brother's only chance. Pretty rough it was too; the doc's instruments weren't any too good. I helped him – Jim hadn't the stomach for it.' He fell silent, looking back into the past.

I ordered another couple of beers, but Kane said, 'I'd like something stronger, if you don't mind,' so I changed the order to whisky.

I thought of some drunken oaf of a doctor cutting my brother open with blunt knives on a benighted tropical island. It wasn't a pretty thought and I think Kane saw the horror of it too, the way he gulped his whisky. It was worse for him – he had been there.

'So he died,' I said.

'Not right away. He seemed okay after the operation, then he got worse. The doc said it was per . . . peri. . . .'

'Peritonitis?'

'That's it. I remember it sounded like peri-peri sauce – like having something hot in your guts. He got a fever and went delirious; then he went unconscious and died two days after the operation.'

He looked into his glass. 'We buried him at sea. It was stinking hot and we couldn't carry the body anywhere – we hadn't any ice. We sewed him up in canvas and put him over the side. The doctor said he'd see to all the details – I mean, it wasn't any use for Jim and me to go all the way to Papeete – the doc knew all we knew.'

'You told the doctor about Mark's wife – her address and so on?'

Kane nodded. 'Mrs Trevelyan said she'd only just heard about it – that's the Islands postal service for you. You know, he never gave us nothing for her, no personal stuff I mean. We

17

wondered about that. But she said some gear of his is on the way – that right?'

'It might be that,' I said. 'There's something at Heathrow now. I'll probably pick it up tomorrow. When did Mark die, by the way?'

He reflected. 'Must have been about four months ago. You don't go much for dates and calendars when you're cruising the Islands, not unless you're navigating and looking up the almanack all the time, and Jim's the expert on that. I reckon it was about the beginning of May. Jim dropped me at Panama in July and I had to wait a bit to get a ship across here.'

'Do you remember the doctor's name? Or where he came from?'

Kane frowned. 'I know he was a Dutchman; his name was Scoot-something. As near as I can remember it might have been Scooter. He runs a hospital on one of the Islands – my word, I can't remember that either.'

'It's of no consequence; if it becomes important I can get it from the death certificate.' I finished my whisky. 'The last I heard of Mark he was working with a Swede called Norgaard. You didn't come across him?'

Kane shook his head. 'There was only your brother. We didn't stay around, you know. Not when old Scooter said he'd take care of everything. You think this Norgaard was supposed to pick your brother up when he'd finished his job?'

'Something like that,' I said. 'It's been very good of you to take the trouble to tell us about Mark's death.'

He waved my thanks aside. 'No trouble at all; anyone would have done the same. I didn't tell Mrs Trevelyan too much, you understand.'

'I'll edit it when I tell her,' I said. 'Anyway, thanks for looking after him. I wouldn't like to think he died alone.'

'Aw, look,' said Kane, embarrassed. 'We couldn't do anything else now, could we?'

I gave him my card. 'I'd like you to keep in touch,' I said. 'Perhaps when you're ready to go back I can help you with a passage. I have plenty of contacts with the shipping people.'

'Too right,' he said. 'I'll keep in touch, Mr Trevelyan.'

I said goodbye and left the bar, ducking into the private bar in the same pub. I didn't think Kane would go in there and I wanted a few quiet thoughts over another drink.

I thought of Mark dying a rather gruesome death on that lonely Pacific atoll. God knows that Mark and I didn't see eye to eye but I wouldn't have wished that fate on my worst enemy. And yet there was something odd about the whole story; I wasn't surprised at him being in the Tuamotus – it was his job to go poking about odd corners of the seven seas as it was mine – but something struck a sour note.

For instance, what had happened to Norgaard? It certainly wasn't standard operating procedure for a man to be left entirely alone on a job. I wondered what Mark and Norgaard had been doing in the Tuamotus; they had published no papers so perhaps their investigation hadn't been completed. I made a mental note to ask old Jarvis about it; my boss kept his ear close to the grapevine and knew everything that went on in the profession.

But it wasn't that which worried me; it was something else, something niggling at the back of my mind that I couldn't resolve. I chased it around for a bit but nothing happened, so I finished my drink and went home to my flat for a late night session with some figures.

2

The next day I was at the office bright and early and managed to get my work finished just before lunch. I was attacking my neglected correspondence when one of the girls brought in a visitor, and a most welcome one. Geordie Wilkins had been my father's sergeant in the Commandos during the war and after my father had been killed he took an interest in the sons of the man he had so greatly respected. Mark, typically, had been a little contemptuous of him but I liked Geordie and we got on well together.

He had done well for himself after the war. He foresaw the yachting boom and bought himself a 25-ton cutter which he chartered and in which he gave sailing lessons. Later he gave up tuition and had worked up to a 200-ton brigantine which he chartered to rich Americans mostly, taking them anywhere they wanted to go at an exorbitant price. Whenever he put into England he looked me up, but it had been a while since last I'd seen him.

He came into the office bringing with him a breath of sea air. 'My God, Mike, but you're pallid,' he said. 'I'll have to take you back to sea.'

'Geordie! Where have you sprung from this time?'

'The Caribbean,' he said. 'I brought the old girl over for a refit. I'm in between charters, thank God.'

'Where are you staying?'

'With you – if you'll have me. *Esmerelda*'s here.'

'Don't be an idiot,' I said happily. 'You know you're welcome. We seem to have struck it lucky this time; I have to do a bit of writing which will take a week, and then I've got three weeks spare.'

He rubbed his chin. 'I'm tied up for a week too, but I'm free after that. We'll push off somewhere.'

'That's a great idea,' I said. 'I've been dying to get away. Wait while I check this post, would you?'

The letter I had just opened was from Helen; it contained a brief letter and the advisory note from British Airways. There was something to be collected from Heathrow which had to clear customs. I looked up at Geordie. 'Did you know that Mark is dead?'

He looked startled. 'Dead! When did that happen?'

I told him all about it and he said, 'A damned sticky end – even for Mark.' Then he immediately apologized. 'Sorry – I shouldn't have said that.'

'Quit it, Geordie,' I said irritably. 'You know how I felt about Mark; there's no need to be mealy-mouthed with me.'

'Aye. He was a bit of a bastard, wasn't he? How's that wife of his taking it?'

'About average under the circumstances. She was pretty

broken up but I seem to detect an underlying note of relief.'

'She's best remarry and forget him,' said Geordie bluntly. He shook his head slowly. 'It beats me what the women saw in Mark. He treated 'em like dirt and they sat up and begged for more.'

'Some people have it, some don't,' I said.

'If it means being like Mark I'd rather not have it. Sad to think one can't find a good word to say for the man.' He took the paper out of my hand. 'Got a car I can use? I haven't been in one for months and I'd like the drive. I'll get my gear from *Esmerelda* and go out and pick this stuff up for you.'

I tossed him my car keys. 'Thanks. It's the same old wreck – you'll find it in the car park.'

When he had gone I finished up my paperwork and then went to see the Prof. to pay my respects. Old Jarvis was quite cordial. 'You've done a good job, Mike,' he said. 'I've looked at your stuff briefly and if your correlations are correct I think we're on to something.'

'Thank you.'

He leaned back in his chair and started to fill his pipe. 'You'll be writing a paper, of course.'

'I'll do that while I'm on leave,' I said. 'It won't be a long one; just a preliminary. There's still a lot of sea time to put in.'

'Looking forward to getting back to it, are you?'

'I'll be glad to get away.'

He grunted suddenly. 'For every day you spend at sea you'll have three in the office digesting the data. And don't get into a job like mine; it's *all* office-work. Steer clear of administration, my boy; don't get chair-bound.'

'I won't,' I promised and then changed tack. 'Can you tell me anything about a fellow called Norgaard? I think he's a Swede working on ocean currents.'

Jarvis looked at me from under bushy eyebrows. 'Wasn't he the chap working with your brother when he died?'

'That's the man.'

He pondered, then shook his head. 'I haven't heard anything of him lately; he certainly hasn't published. But I'll make a few enquiries and put you in touch.'

21

And that was that. I didn't know why I had taken the trouble to ask the Prof. about Norgaard unless it was still that uneasy itch at the back of my skull, the feeling that something was wrong somewhere. It probably didn't mean anything anyway, and I put it out of my mind as I walked back to my office.

It was getting late and I was about ready to leave when Geordie returned and heaved a battered, ancient suitcase onto my desk. 'There it is,' he said. 'They made me open it – it was a wee bit difficult without a key, though.'

'What did you do?'

'Busted the lock,' he said cheerfully.

I looked at the case warily. 'What's in it?'

'Not much. Some clothes, a few books and a lot of pebbles. And there's a letter addressed to Mark's wife.' He untied the string holding the case together, skimmed the letter across the desk, and started to haul out the contents – a couple of tropical suits, not very clean; two shirts; three pairs of socks; three textbooks on oceanography – very up-to-date; a couple of notebooks in Mark's handwriting, and a miscellany of pens, toiletries and small odds and ends.

I looked at the letter, addressed to Helen in a neat cursive hand. 'I'd better open this,' I said. 'We don't know what's in it and I don't want Helen to get too much of a shock.'

Geordie nodded and I slit the envelope. The letter was short and rather abrupt:

Dear Mrs Trevelyan,
  I am sorry to tell you that your husband, Mark, is dead, although you may know this already by the time you get this. Mark was a good friend to me and left some of his things in my care. I am sending them all to you as I know you would like to have them.
       Sincerely,
       P. Nelson

I said, 'I thought this would be official, but it's not.'

Geordie scanned the short note. 'Do you know this chap, Nelson?'

'Never heard of him.'

Geordie put the letter on the desk and tipped up the suitcase. 'Then there are these.' A dozen or so potato-like objects rolled onto the desk. Some of them rolled further and thumped onto the carpet, and Geordie stooped and picked them up. 'You'll probably make more sense of these than I can.'

I turned one in my fingers. 'Manganese nodules,' I said. 'Very common in the Pacific.'

'Are they valuable?'

I laughed. 'If you could get at them easily they might be – but you can't, so they aren't. They lie on the seabed at an average depth of about fourteen thousand feet.'

He looked closely at one of the nodules. 'I wonder where he got these, then? It's a bit deep for skin-diving.'

'They're probably souvenirs of the IGY – the International Geophysical Year. Mark was a physical chemist on one of the ships in the Pacific.' I took one of the notebooks and flipped the pages at random. Most of it seemed to be mathematical, the equations close-packed in Mark's finicky hand.

I tossed it into the open suitcase. 'Let's get this stuff packed away, then we'll go home.'

So we put everything back, higgledy-piggledy, and carted the case down to the car. On the way home Geordie said, 'What about a show tonight?' On his rare visits to a city he had a soft spot for big gaudy musicals.

'If you can get tickets,' I said. 'I don't feel like queueing.'

'I'll get them,' he said confidently. 'I know someone who owes me a few favours. Look, drop me right here and I'll see you at the flat in half an hour, or maybe a bit longer.'

I dropped him and when I got to where I lived I took Mark's suitcase first because it came handiest, then I went back to the car for Geordie's gear. For some time I pottered about estimating what I'd need for a trip away with him, but I had most of what I needed and the list of things I had to get was very short and didn't take long to figure out.

After a while I found myself looking at the suitcase. I picked it up, put it on the bed and opened it and looked at the few remnants of Mark's life. I hoped that when I went I'd leave more than a few books, a few clothes and a doubtful reputation. The clothing was of no particular interest but, as I lifted up a jacket, a small leather-bound notebook fell out of the breast pocket.

I picked it up and examined it. It had obviously been used as a diary but most of the entries were in shorthand, once Pitman's, but adapted in an idiosyncratic way so that they were incomprehensible to anyone but the writer – Mark.

Occasionally there were lines of chemical and mathematical notation and every now and then there was a doodled drawing. I remembered that Mark had been a doodler even at school and had been ticked off often because of the state of his exercise books. There wasn't much sense to be made of any of it.

I put the diary on my dressing table and turned to the larger notebooks. They were much more interesting although scarcely more comprehensible. Apparently, Mark was working on a theory of nodule formation that, to say the least of it, was hare-brained – certainly from the point of view of orthodox physical chemistry. The time scale he was using was fantastic, and even at a casual glance his qualitative analysis seemed out of line.

Presently I heard Geordie come in. He popped his head round the door of the bedroom and said triumphantly, 'I've got the tickets. Let's have a slap-up dinner first and then go on to the theatre.'

'That's a damned good idea,' I said. I threw the notebooks and the clothing back into the case and retied the lid down.

Geordie nodded at it. 'Find anything interesting?'

I grinned. 'Nothing, except that Mark was going round the bend. He'd got hold of some damn fool idea about nodules and was going overboard about it.'

I shoved the case under the bed and began to get dressed for dinner.

3

It was a good dinner and a better show and we drove home replete with fine food and excellent entertainment. Geordie was in high spirits and sang in a cracked and tuneless voice one of the numbers from the show. We were both in a cheerful mood.

I parked the car outside the block of flats and got out. There was still a thin drizzle of rain but I thought that by morning it would have cleared. That was good; I wanted fine weather for my leave. As I looked up at the sky I stiffened.

'Geordie, there's someone in my flat.'

He looked up at the third floor and saw what I had seen – a furtive, hunting light moving at one of the windows.

'That's a torch.' His teeth flashed as he grinned in the darkness. 'It's a long time since I've had a proper scrap.'

I said, 'Come on,' and ran up into the foyer.

Geordie caught my arm as I pressed for the lift. 'Hold on, let's do this properly,' he said. 'Wait one minute and then go up in the lift. I'll take the stairs – we should arrive on your floor at the same time. Covers both exits.'

I grinned and saluted. 'Yes, sergeant.' You can't keep an old soldier down; Geordie was making a military operation out of catching a sneak thief – but I followed orders.

I went up in the lift and stepped out into the lighted corridor. Geordie had made good time up the stairs and was breathing as easily as though he'd been strolling on the level. He motioned me to keep the lift door open and reached inside to press the button for the top floor. I closed the door and the lift went up.

He grinned in his turn. 'Anyone leaving in a hurry must use the stairs now. Got your key?'

I passed it to him and we walked to the door of my flat, treading softly. Through the uncurtained kitchen window I could see the flash of a torch. Geordie cautiously inserted the key into the lock. 'We'll go in sharpish,' he whispered, gave the key a twist, threw open the door and plunged into the flat like an angry bull.

As I followed on his heel I heard a shout – '*Ojo!*' – and the next thing I knew was a blinding flash in my eyes and I was grappling with someone at the kitchen door. Whoever it was hit me on the side of the head, it must have been with the torch because the light went out. I felt dizzy for a moment but held on, thrusting forward and bringing my knee up sharply.

I heard a gasp of pain and above it the roar of Geordie's voice from further in the flat – possibly the bedroom.

I let go my grip and struck out with my fist, and yelled in pain as my knuckles hit the kitchen door. My opponent squirmed out from where I had him pinned and was gone through the open door of the flat. Things were happening too fast for me. I could hear Geordie swearing at the top of his voice and the crash of furniture. A light tenor voice called, '*Huid! Huid! No disparéis! Emplead cuchillos!*' Then suddenly someone else banged into me in the darkness and I struck out again.

I knew now that this assailant would certainly have a knife and possibly a gun and I think I went berserk – it's wonderful what the adrenal glands will do for a man in an emergency. In the light from the corridor I caught a glimpse of an upraised knife and I chopped viciously at the wrist. There was a howl of pain and the knife clattered to the floor. I aimed a punch at where I thought a stomach was – and missed.

Something was swung at the side of my head again and I went down as a black figure jumped over me. If he hadn't stopped to kick at my head he would have got clean away, but I squirmed to avoid his boot and caught his leg, and he went sprawling into the corridor.

I dived after him and got between him and the stairs, and he stood in a crouch looking at me, his eyes darting about, looking for escape. Then I saw what he must have swung at my head in the flat – it was Mark's suitcase.

Suddenly he turned and ran, towards the blank end of the

corridor. 'I've got him now,' I thought exultantly, and went after him at a dead run. But he had remembered what I'd forgotten – the fire escape.

He might have got away then but once again I tackled him rugby-fashion so that I floored him just short of the fire escape. The fall knocked the breath out of me and he improved the shining hour by kicking me in the face. Then, as I was shaking my head in dizziness, he tossed Mark's case into the darkness.

By the time I regained my feet I was between him and the metal staircase and he was facing me with his right hand, now unencumbered, darting to his pocket. I saw the gun as he drew it and knew the meaning of real fear. I jumped for him and he side-stepped frantically trying to clear the gun from his pocket – but the foresight must have caught on the lining.

Then I hit him hard on the jaw and he teetered on the top step of the fire escape. I hit him again and slammed him against the railing and, to my horror, he jackknifed over. He didn't make a sound as he fell the three floors into the alley and it seemed a long time before I heard the dull thump as he hit the ground.

I looked down into the darkness and saw nothing. I was conscious of the trembling of my hands as they gripped the steel rail. There was a scurry of footsteps and I turned to see Geordie darting down the stairs. 'Leave them,' I shouted. 'They're armed!'

But he didn't stop and all I heard was the thud of his feet as he raced down the staircase.

The tall thin man who lived in the next flat came out in a dressing gown. 'Now, what's all this?' he asked querulously. 'A chap can't listen to the radio with all this racket going on.'

I said, 'Phone the police. There's been an attempted murder.'

His face went white and he looked at my arm. I looked down and saw blood staining the edges of a slit in the sleeve of my jacket. I couldn't remember being knifed and I felt nothing.

I looked back up at him. 'Well, hurry,' I yelled at him.

A gunshot echoed up the stairwell and we both started.

'Christ!'

I clattered down the stairs at top speed, all three flights, and came across Geordie in the foyer. He was sitting on the floor staring at his fingers in amazement – they were red with welling blood.

'The bastard shot me!' he said incredulously.

'Where are you hit, for God's sake?'

'In the hand, I think. I don't feel anything anywhere else, and he only fired one shot.'

I looked at his hand. Blood was spurting from the end of his little finger. I began to laugh, an hysterical sound not far from crying, and went on until Geordie slapped my face with his unwounded hand. 'Pull yourself together, Mike,' he said firmly. I became aware of doors slamming and voices upstairs but as yet nobody had ventured down into the foyer itself, and I sobered suddenly.

'I think I killed one of them,' I said emptily.

'Don't be daft. How could you kill a man with your fist?'

'I knocked him off the fire escape. He fell from the third floor.'

Geordie looked at me closely. 'We'd better go and have a look at that.'

'Are you all right?' We were both bleeding freely now.

He was wrapping his finger in a handkerchief which promptly turned bright red. 'I'm okay. You can't call this a mortal wound,' he said dryly. We went out into the street and walked quickly round to the alley into which the fire escape led. As we turned the corner there was a sudden glare of light and the roar of an engine, together with the slamming of a car door.

'Look out!' yelled Geordie and flung himself sideways.

I saw the two great eyes of headlamps rushing at me from the darkness of the alley and I frantically flattened myself against the wall. The car roared past and I felt the wind of it brush my trousers, and then with a squeal of hard-used tyres it turned the corner and was gone.

I listened to the noise of the engine die away and eased

myself from the wall, taking a deep shaky breath. In the light of the street lamp on the corner I saw Geordie pick himself up. 'Christ!' I said. 'You don't know what's going to happen next.'

'This lot aren't ordinary burglars,' said Geordie, brushing himself down. 'They're too bloody persistent. Where's this fire escape?'

'A bit further along,' I said.

We walked slowly up the alley and Geordie fell over the man I had knocked over the edge. We bent down to examine him and, in the faint light, we could see his head. It was twisted at an impossible angle and there was a deep bloody depression in the skull.

Geordie said, 'No need to look any further. He's dead.'

4

'And you say they were speaking Spanish,' said the Inspector.

I nodded wearily. 'As soon as we went into the flat someone shouted, "Look out!" and then I was in the middle of a fight. A bit later on another man shouted, "Get out of here; don't shoot – use your knives." I think it was the man I knocked off the fire escape.'

The Inspector looked at me thoughtfully. 'But you say he was going to shoot you.'

'He'd lost his knife by then, and I was going for him.'

'How good is your Spanish, Mr Trevelyan?'

'Pretty good,' I said. 'I did a lot of work off south-west Europe about four years ago and I was based in Spain. I took the trouble to learn the language – I have a flair for them.'

The doctor tied a neat knot in the bandage round my arm and said, 'That'll hold it, but try not to use the arm for a while.' He packed his bag and went out.

I sat up and looked about the flat – it was like a field dressing station in a blitzed area. I was stripped to the waist with a bandaged arm and Geordie sported a natty bandage on his little finger. He was drinking tea and he held out his finger like a charlady at a garden party.

The flat was a wreck. What hadn't been broken by the burglars had been smashed during the fight. A chair with no legs lay in the corner and broken glass from the front of my bookcase littered the carpet. A couple of uniformed constables stood stolidly in the corners and a plain clothes man was blowing powder about the place with an insufflator.

The Inspector said, 'Once again – how many of them were there?'

Geordie said, 'I had two on my hands at one time.'

'I had a go at two,' I said. 'But I think that one of them had a bash at Geordie first. It's difficult to say – it happened so fast.'

'This man you heard – did he say "knife" or "knives"?'

I thought about that. 'He said "knives".'

The Inspector said, 'Then there were more than two of them.'

Geordie said unexpectedly, 'There were four.'

The Inspector looked at him with raised eyebrows.

'I saw three men in the car that passed us. One driving and two getting in in a hurry. With one dead in the alley – that makes four.'

'Ah yes,' said the Inspector. 'They would have one man in the car. Tell me, how did you come to get shot?'

A smile touched Geordie's lips. 'How does anyone get shot? With a gun.' The Inspector recognized a touch of over-excitement and said dryly, 'I mean, what were the circumstances?'

'Well, I chased the little bastard down the stairs and damn nearly caught him in the foyer. He saw he was going to be copped so he turned and let me have it. I hadn't reached him yet. I was so surprised I sat down – then I saw all the blood.'

'You say he was little?'

'That he was. A little squirt of not more than five foot four.'

'So two men went down the stairs, there was one in the car – and one went over the fire escape,' the Inspector summarized.

He had a blunt, square face with watchful grey eyes which he suddenly turned on me like gimlets. 'You say this man threw a suitcase into the alley.'

'That's right.'

'We haven't found it, Mr Trevelyan.'

I said, 'The others must have picked it up. That's when they nearly ran us down.'

He said softly, 'How did they know it was there?'

'I don't know. They may have seen it coming over. I guess the car was parked in the alley waiting for the others to come down that way.'

He nodded. 'What was in the suitcase – do you know?'

I glanced across at Geordie who looked back at me expressionlessly. I said, 'Some stuff belonging to my brother.'

'What kind of – er – stuff?'

'Clothing, books – geological samples.'

The Inspector sighed. 'Anything important or valuable?'

I shook my head. 'I doubt it.'

'What about the samples?'

I said, 'I only saw the specimens briefly. They appeared to be manganese nodules of the type which is often to be found on the ocean bed. They're very common, you know.'

'And valuable?' he persisted.

'I don't think that anyone with knowledge of them would regard them as valuable,' I said. 'I suppose they might be if they were generally accessible, but it's too hard to get at them through two or three miles of water.'

The Inspector seemed at a loss. 'How do you think your brother will regard the loss of those specimens, and his other things?'

'He's dead,' I said.

The Inspector sharpened his attention. 'Oh? When did he die?'

'About four months ago – in the Pacific.'

He looked at me closely and I went on, 'My brother, Mark, was an oceanographer like myself. He died of appendicitis a few months ago and I've just received his effects today. As for the specimens I would say they were souvenirs of the IGY survey in which he was engaged. As a scientist he would naturally be interested in them.'

'Um,' said the Inspector. 'Is there anything else missing, Mr Trevelyan?'

'Not that I know of.'

Geordie clattered his cup. 'I think we were too quick for them,' he said. 'They thought they were on to a good thing, but we didn't give them enough time. So one of them grabbed the first thing he saw and tried to make a getaway.'

I carefully didn't mention that the case had been hidden under my bed.

The Inspector looked at Geordie with something approaching contempt. 'This isn't an ordinary burglary,' he said. 'Your explanation doesn't account for the fact that they went to a lot of trouble to retrieve the suitcase, or why they used so many weapons.' He turned to me. 'Have you any enemies in Spain?'

I shrugged. 'I shouldn't think so.'

He pursed his lips. 'All right, Mr Trevelyan, let's go back to the beginning again. Let's start when you say you first saw the light on in your flat. . . .'

It was after three a.m. before we got rid of the police, and they were back again next morning, to recheck the premises and to hear the whole tale yet again. The Inspector wasn't satisfied but neither he nor any of his colleagues could pin down what was wrong. Come to that – neither could I! It was a great way to start my leave. His last word to me that morning was, 'There's been a fatality here, Mr Trevelyan, and that's a very serious matter. I shall expect both of you to hold yourselves in readiness for the inquest. You are not under arrest,' he added in such a way as to make me feel that I was. He strode out of the flat with his myrmidons trailing behind.

'In other words – don't leave town,' I said. 'There goes a very unhappy policeman.'

Geordie said, 'He'll be burning up the wires looking for an expert on manganese nodules. He think there's something fishy there.'

'By God, so do I! But he won't find much. He'll phone the

Institute of course, and speak to Jarvis or some other big noise and get exactly the same story I told him.'

I got up, went into the kitchen and got a couple of bottles of beer from the refrigerator and took them back into the living room. Geordie eyed them and said, 'You have some good ideas, sometimes. Tell me, these nodules – are they really valueless?'

'I told the coppers the plain truth,' I said. 'But Mark seemed to have some curious ideas about nodule formation – still, the notebooks are gone and I can't check up on his theories without them.'

Then suddenly I remembered something. 'Wait a minute,' I said and went into the bedroom. Sure enough, there it was – the little leather-bound diary, still lying on my dressing-table. The police would have had no reason to think it wasn't mine, and hadn't touched it.

I went back and tossed it to Geordie. 'They didn't get that. I meant to tell you – I found it in a pocket of one of Mark's suits. What do you make of it?'

He opened the book with interest but I watched the enthusiasm seep out of him as he scanned the pages. 'What the hell!'

'That's Mark's patent Pitman variation,' I said. 'I doubt if old Isaac himself could make anything of it.'

'What are all the drawings?'

'Mark was an inveterate doodler,' I said. 'You'd have to apply psychological theory to make anything of those.'

I sat mulling over the events of the previous day, trying to piece them together.

'Geordie, listen to this,' I said. 'Mark dies, and Norgaard, his colleague, disappears. Jarvis keeps his ear close to the ground and knows all the gossip of the profession, and if he says he hasn't heard anything of Norgaard then it's unlikely that anyone else has either.' I held up a finger. 'That's one thing.'

'Do you know anything about Norgaard?'

'Only that he's one of us oceanographers. He's a Swede, but he was on an American survey ship during the IGY. I lost sight of him after that; a lot of comradeship went for a bust when the operation closed down.'

'What's his speciality?'

'Ocean currents. He's one of those geniuses who can dredge up a bit of water and tell you which way it was flowing a million years ago last Wednesday. I don't think there's a name for his line yet, so I'll call it paleoaquaology – there's a mouthful for you.'

Geordie raised his eyebrows. 'Can they really do that kind of thing?'

I grinned. 'They'd like you to believe so, and I've no reason to doubt it. But to my mind there's a hell of a lot of theory balancing uneasily on too few facts. My line is different – I analyse what I'm given and if anyone wants to build any whacky theories on what I tell 'em, that's their affair.'

'And Mark was like yourself – an analytical chemist. Why would he team up with Norgaard? They don't seem to have anything in common.'

I said slowly, 'I don't know; I really don't know.' I was thinking of the highly unlikely theory indicated in Mark's missing notebooks.

'All right,' Geordie said. 'Norgaard's disappeared – you think. What else have you got?'

'The next thing is Kane. The whole thing is too damn pat. Kane turns up and we have a burglary. He knew the stuff was coming – I told him.'

Geordie chuckled. 'And how do you tie in the four Spanish burglars with Kane? Speaking as a non-theoreticist, that is?'

'I'm damned if I know. There's something odd about that too. I couldn't place the accent; it was one I've never heard before.'

'You don't know them all,' said Geordie. 'You'd have to be born Spanish to be that good.'

'True.' There was a long silence while I marshalled my thoughts. 'I wish I could get hold of Kane.'

'You think there's something odd about him, don't you?'

'I do. But I don't know what it is. I've been trying to bring it to the surface ever since I saw him.'

'Mike, I think this is all a lot of nonsense,' Geordie said decisively. 'I think your imagination is working overtime. You've had a shock about Mark's death and another over the burglary – so have I, come to that. But I don't think Norgaard has mysteriously disappeared; I think he's probably sitting somewhere writing a thesis on prehistoric water. As for Kane, you've got nothing but a blind hunch. But I'll tell you what I'll do. If Kane is a seaman he'll probably be down somewhere in dockland, and if you want him that bad I'll put my boys on to nosing around a bit. It's a pretty hopeless chance but it's all I can do.'

'Thanks, Geordie,' I said. 'Meantime, I'd better ring Helen and tell her I've been burgled. She's not going to like hearing that Mark's stuff is gone but there's no hope for it. I can only play it down, tell her it was all worthless anyway.'

'Are you going to pass on the notebook to her?'

I shook my head thoughtfully. 'What notebook? As far as she's concerned, it was all stolen. She could never make anything of that stuff of Mark's – but maybe I can.'

5

I had nightmares that night.

I dreamed of a lovely Pacific island with white beaches and waving palm fronds where I wandered quite happily until I became aware that the sky was darkening and a cold, icy wind had arisen. I started to run but my feet slipped in the soft sand and I made no progress. And I knew what I was running from.

He caught me at last with my back to a palm trunk, and came nearer and nearer, brandishing a rusty kitchen knife. I knew it was the Dutch doctor, although he was screaming in Spanish, '*Emplead cuchillo – cuchillo – cuchillo!*'

He was drunk and sweaty-faced and as he came nearer I felt powerless to move and I knew he was going to stick me with the knife. At last his face was close to mine and I could see the individual beads of sweat on his shiny forehead and his lean dark face. It was the face of Kane. He drew back his arm and struck with the knife right into my guts.

I woke with a yell.

I was breathing deeply, taking in great gulps of air, and I could feel a slick film of sweat all over my body. The knife-scratch in my arm was aching. And I knew at last what was wrong with Kane's story.

The bedroom door opened and Geordie said in a low voice, 'What the devil's going on?'

I said, 'Come in, Geordie; I'm all right – just a nightmare.'

I switched on the bedside light and Geordie said, 'You gave me a hell of a fright, Mike.'

'I gave myself a hell of a fright,' I said and lit a cigarette 'But I discovered something – or remembered something.'

'What?'

I tapped Geordie emphatically on the chest with my forefinger. 'Mark had his appendix out years ago.'

Geordie looked startled. 'But the death certificate . . .'

'I don't know anything about the death certificate. I haven't seen it yet, so I don't know if it's a fake. But I know that Mr Bloody Kane is a fake.'

'Are you sure about this?'

'I still know the doctor who operated on Mark. I'll give him a ring and check on it – but I'm sure.'

'Perhaps this Dutch doctor made a mistake,' offered Geordie.

'He'd be a damned good doctor who could take out an appendix that wasn't there,' I said acidly. 'Doctors can't make mistakes like that.'

'Not unless he was covering up. Lots of doctors bury their mistakes.'

'You mean he was incompetent?' I thought about that, then shook my head decisively. 'No, Geordie, that won't wash. He'd see the old operation scar the moment he made his examination, and he'd know the appendix had already been removed. He wouldn't stick his neck out by signing a certificate that could be so easily disproved – no one is as incompetent as that.'

'Aye. If he wanted to cover up he'd put down the cause of death as fever or something like that – something you couldn't prove one way or another. But we don't know what he put on the certificate.'

'We'll soon find out. They sent it to Helen. And I want to find Kane more than ever – I want to nail that lying bastard.'

'We'll do our best,' said Geordie. He didn't sound too hopeful.

Chapter Two

1

I had no more dreams that night, but slept heavily and late. It was Geordie who woke me by shaking my shoulder – and incidentally hurting my arm once again. I groaned and turned away, but he persisted until I opened my eyes. 'You're wanted on the phone,' he said. 'It's the Institute.'

I put on my dressing gown and was still thick-headed with sleep when I lifted the receiver. It was young Simms. 'Dr Trevelyan, I've taken over your old office while you're away and you've left something behind. I don't know if it's valuable or if you want it at all. . . .'

I mumbled, 'What is it?'

'A manganese nodule.'

I was jolted wide awake. 'Where did you find it?'

'I didn't. One of the cleaners found it under your desk and gave it to me. What should I do with it?'

'Stick tight to it. I'll pick it up this morning. It's got some – relation to work I'm engaged on. Thanks for calling.'

I turned to Geordie. 'All is not lost,' I said, 'we've got a nodule. You dropped some on the floor of my office, remember, and you left one under the desk.'

'I don't see what all the fuss is about. All along you've been insisting that the damn things are worthless. What's so exciting about this one?'

I said, 'There are too many mysteries connected with this particular lot to suit me. I'm going to take a closer look at this one.'

As I breakfasted on a cigarette and a cup of strong coffee I rang Helen and asked her to read out Mark's death certificate. It was in French, of course, and she had some difficulties over

38

the hand-written parts but we got it sorted out. I put down the phone and said to Geordie, 'Now I want to talk to that doctor as well as Kane.' I felt full of anger and frustration.

'What was the cause of death?'

'Peritonitus following an appendectomy. And that's impossible. The doctor's name is Hans Schouten. It was signed in Tanakabu, in the Tuamotus.'

'He's a hell of a long way from here.'

'But Kane isn't. Do your damndest to find him, Geordie.'

Geordie sighed. 'I'll do my best, but this is a bloody big city, and no one but you and Helen can identify him for sure.'

I dressed and drove down to the Institute, retrieved the nodule from Simms and then went down to the laboratories – I was going to analyse this lump of rock down to the last trace elements. First I photographed it in colour from several angles and took a casting of it in latex – that took care of the external record. Then I cut it in half with a diamond saw. Not entirely unexpectedly, in the centre was the white bone of a shark's tooth, also neatly cut in two.

One of the pieces I put in the rock mill and, while it was being ground to the consistency of fine flour, I polished and etched the flat surface of the other piece. Then the real work began. By early afternoon everything was well under way and luckily I had had the place almost to myself the whole time, but then Jarvis walked in. He was surprised to see me.

'You're supposed to be on leave, Mike. What's all this?'

He looked at the set-up on the bench. I had no worries about that – I could have been analysing anything, and the identifiable half-rock was out of sight. I said lightly, 'Oh, just some homework I promised I'd do when I had the chance.'

He looked at me out of the corner of his eye. 'What have you been up to, young feller? Saw something about you in yesterday's press, didn't I? And I had a chap in from Scotland Yard asking questions about you – and about manganese nodules. And he said you'd *killed* someone?'

'I had a burglary two nights ago and knocked a chap off the

fire escape,' I said. I hadn't seen the papers myself and it hadn't occurred to me that the story would be public. From Simms' lack of reaction, however, it seemed not to be exactly front-page news.

'Um', said Jarvis. 'Very unfortunate. Place is getting like Chicago. Nasty for you. But what's it got to do with nodules?'

'A couple were nicked from my place, with other stuff. I told him they weren't of much value.'

'I made that plain to the Inspector,' growled Jarvis. 'And I take it he's now convinced that your burglars were surprised and took the first things that came to hand. I gave you a reasonable character, by the way.'

I had my doubts about the Yard's acceptance of the front story. The Inspector had struck me as being full of deep suspicions.

'Well, my boy, I'll leave you to it. Anything interesting?' He cast an inquisitive glance at the bench.

I smiled. 'I don't know yet.'

He nodded. 'That's the way it is,' he said rather vaguely and wandered out. I looked at the bench and wondered if I was wasting my time. My own knowledge, backed by that of an expert like Jarvis, told me that this was just an ordinary Pacific nodule and nothing out of the ordinary. Still, I had gone so far, I might as well carry on. I left the glassware to bubble on its own for a while and went to take photomicrographs of the etched surface of the half-nodule.

I was busy for another couple of hours and having to use my bad arm didn't help. Normally I would have used the services of a laboratory technician but this was one job I wanted to do myself. And it was fortunate that I had taken that precaution because what I finally found astounded me. I looked incredulously at the table of figures that was emerging, breathing heavily with excitement and with my mind full of conflicting conjectures.

Then I became even busier, carefully dismantling the glassware and meticulously washing every piece. I wanted no evidence left of what I'd been up to. That done, I phoned the flat.

Geordie answered. 'Where the devil have you been?' he demanded. 'We've had the cops, the press, the insurance people – the lot.'

'Those are the last people I want to be bothered with right now. Is everything clear now?'

'Aye.'

'Good. I don't suppose you found Kane.'

'You suppose rightly. If you're so suspicious of him why don't you take what you've got to the police? They can do a better job of finding him than I can.'

'I don't want to do that right now. I'm coming home, Geordie. I've got something to tell you.'

'Have you eaten, boy?'

I suddenly realized that I hadn't eaten a mouthful all day. I felt very hungry. 'I've been too busy,' I said hopefully.

'I thought so. I'll tell you what; I'll cook up something in this kitchen of yours – one of my slumgullions. Then we won't have to go out and maybe get tagged by one of the newspaper blokes.'

'Thanks. That'll be fine.'

On the way home I bought some newspapers and found that the story had already sunk with no trace. A local shop produced me a copy of the previous day's press and the story was a short one, buried in the body of the paper, lacking in detail and with no mention of what had been stolen, which suited me very well. I didn't want to be questioned on anything concerning manganese nodules. I'm not naturally a good liar.

When I entered the flat I found Geordie busy in the kitchen surrounded by a mouth-watering aroma, and a remarkably well cleaned up living room. I made a mental note never to have glass-fronted bookshelves again – I didn't much like them anyway. Geordie called out, 'It'll be ready in about an hour, so you can get your news off your chest before we eat. I'll be out in two ticks.'

I went to the cabinet for the whisky bottle and two glasses, then picked my old school atlas off the bookshelf. Ink-blotted and politically out-of-date as it was, it would still suit my purpose. I put it on the table and turned to the pages which showed the Pacific.

Geordie came out of the kitchen and I said, 'Sit here. I want to tell you something important.'

He saw the glint of excitement in my eye, smiled and sat down obediently. I poured out two whiskies and said, 'I'm going to give you a little lecture on basic oceanography. I hope you won't be bored.'

'Go ahead, Mike.'

'At the bottom of the oceans – particularly the Pacific – there is a fortune in metallic ores in the form of small lumps lying on the seabed.' I took the half-nodule from my pocket and put it on the table. 'Like this lump here. There's no secret about this. Every oceanographer knows about them.'

Geordie picked it up and examined it. 'What's this white bit in the middle?'

'A shark's tooth.'

'How the hell did that get in the middle of a piece of rock?'

'That comes later,' I said impatiently, 'in the second lesson. Now, these lumps are composed mainly of manganese dioxide, iron oxide and traces of nickel, cobalt and copper, but to save time they're usually referred to as manganese nodules. I won't tell you how they got onto the seabed – that comes later too – but the sheer quantity is incredible.'

I turned to the atlas and moved my forefinger from south to north off the shoreline of the Americas, starting at Chile and moving towards Alaska. 'Proved deposits here, at the average of one pound a square foot, cover an area of two million square miles and involve twenty-six *billion* tons of nodules.'

I swept my finger out to Hawaii. 'This is the mid-Pacific Rise. Four million square miles – fifty-seven billion tons of nodules.'

'Hell's teeth,' said Geordie. 'You were right about incredible figures.'

I ignored this and moved my finger south again, to Tahiti. 'Fourteen million square miles in central and south-eastern Pacific. Two hundred billion tons of nodules. Like grains of dust in the desert.'

'Why haven't I heard about this before? It sounds like front page news.'

'There's no reason why you shouldn't have, but you won't find it in the newspapers. It's not very interesting. You'd have to read the right technical journals. There's been no secret made of it; they were first discovered as far back as 1870 during the *Challenger* expedition.'

'There must be a snag. Otherwise somebody would have done something about it before this.'

I smiled. 'Oh yes, there are snags – as always. One of them is the depth of the water – the average depth at which these things lie is over fourteen thousand feet. That's a good deal of water to go through to scoop up nodules, and the pressure on the bottom is terrific. But it could be done. An American engineer called John Mero did a post-graduate thesis on it. He proposed dropping a thing like a giant vacuum-cleaner and sucking the nodules to the surface. The capitalization on a scheme like that would run into millions and the profit would be marginal at one pound a square foot of ocean bed. It's what we'd call a pretty lean ore if we found it on land.'

Geordie said, 'But you have a card up your sleeve.'

'Let me put it this way. The information I've given you is based on the IGY surveys, and the one pound a square foot is a crude approximation.'

I stabbed my finger at the eastern Pacific. 'Zenkevitch, of the Soviet Institute of Oceanology – the Russians are very interested, by the way – found 3.7 pounds a square foot right there. You see, the stuff lies in varying concentrations. Here they found five pounds a square foot, here they found eight, and here, seven.'

Geordie had been listening with keen interest. 'That sounds as though it brings it back in line as an economic proposition.'

I shook my head tiredly. 'No, it doesn't. Manganese isn't in short supply, and neither is iron. If you started picking up large quantities of nodules all that would happen is that you'd saturate the market, the price would slip accordingly, and you'd be back where you started – with a marginal profit. In fact, it would be worse than that. The big metals firms and mining houses – the only people with the massed capital to do anything about it – aren't interested. They already run manganese mines on land, and if they started anything like this they'd end up by wrecking their own land-based investments.'

'It seems that you're running in circles,' said Geordie acidly. 'Where is all this getting us?'

'Have patience. I'm making a point. Now, I said there are traces of other metals in these nodules – copper, nickel and cobalt. You can forget the copper. But here, in the south-east Pacific, the nodules run to about 1.6 per cent nickel and about .3 per cent cobalt. The Mid-Pacific Rise gives as much as 2 per cent cobalt. Keep that in mind, because I'm going to switch to something else.'

'For God's sake, Mike, don't spin it out too long.'

I was and I knew it, and enjoyed teasing him. 'I'm coming to it,' I said. 'All the figures I've given you are based on the IGY surveys.' I leaned forward. 'Guess how many sites they surveyed.'

'I couldn't begin to make a guess.'

I took a sip of whisky. 'They dredged and photographed sixty sites. A lousy sixty sites in sixty-four million square miles of Pacific.'

Geordie stared at me. 'Is that all? I wouldn't hang a dog on evidence like that.'

'The orthodox oceanographer says, "The ocean bed is pretty much of a piece – it doesn't vary greatly from place to place – so what you find at site X, which you've checked, you're pretty certain to find at site Y, which you haven't checked."'

I tapped the atlas. 'I've always been suspicious of that kind of reasoning. Admittedly, the ocean bed is pretty much of a piece, but I don't think we should rely on it sight unseen. And neither did Mark.'

'Did Mark work together with you on this?'

'We never worked together,' I said shortly. 'To continue. In 1955 the Scripps expedition fished up a nodule from about – here.' I pointed to the spot. 'It was two feet long, twenty inches thick and weighed a hundred and twenty-five pounds. In the same year a British cable ship was grappling for a broken cable here, in the Philippines Trench. They got the cable up, all right, from 17,000 feet, and in a loop of cable they found a nodule 4 feet long and 3 feet in diameter. That one weighed 1700 pounds.'

'I begin to see what you're getting at.'

'I'm trying to put it plainly. The orthodox boys have sampled sixty spots in sixty-four million square miles and have the nerve to think they know all about it. I'm banking that there are places where nodules lie fifty pounds to the square foot – and Mark knew of such places, if I read enough of his notes correctly.'

'I think you had a point to make about cobalt, Mike. Come across with it.'

I let my excitement show. 'This is the clincher. The highest assay for cobalt in any nodule has been just over 2 per cent.' I pushed the half-nodule on the table with my finger. 'I assayed this one today. It checked out at *ten* per cent cobalt – and cobalt, Geordie, is worth more than all the rest put together and the rocket metallurgists can't get enough of it!'

2

We ate Geordie's stew and very good it was, and by midnight we had just about talked the subject to death. At one stage I said, returning to a sore point, 'I wish I still had those notebooks. They were only rough working notes and Mark seemed to have gone up a lot of false trails – some of the assumptions seemed completely cockeyed – but I wish they hadn't been pinched.'

Geordie sucked on his pipe, which gurgled. 'I could do with knowing why they were pinched – and who pinched them.'

'Then you agree that it has something to do with Mark's death?'

'It must do, boy. He got hold of something valuable. . . .'

'And was murdered for it,' I finished. 'But who killed him? Kane? That's unlikely – it's an odd murderer who travels halfway round the world to inform the family.'

That was a good conversation-stopper. We were quiet for some time, then I said tentatively, 'If only we could get hold of Schouten.'

'He's on the other side of the world.'

I said softly, 'I think Mark came across a hell of a big deposit of high-cobalt nodules. He wasn't a bad scientist but, being Mark, he was probably more interested in the worth of his discovery – to himself. His theories were a bit startling though, and they intrigue me.'

'So?'

'So I'd like to do something about it.'

'You mean – organize an expedition?'

'That's right.' Saying it aloud began to jell all the ideas that had been bubbling up in me since the assay.

Geordie knocked the dottle out of his pipe. 'Tell me, Mike, what's your interest in this – scientific or personal? You weren't particularly friendly towards Mark. Is it that you feel that Trevelyans should be free to go about their business without being murdered, or is it something else?'

'It's that and a lot more. For one thing, someone is pushing me around and I don't like it. I don't like having my home burgled, being knifed, or having my friends shot at. And I don't appreciate having my brother murdered, if that's really what happened, no matter what I thought of him as a person. Then, of course, there's the scientific interest – I'm fascinated. A find like this would hit oceanography like evolution hit biology. And then there's the money.'

'Yes,' said Geordie. 'I suppose there would be money in it.'

'You suppose damn right. And if you're thinking in millions, stop it, because you're thinking small – it could be billions.'

He wasn't ready to be enthusiastic. 'So you think it's as good as that?'

'As good as that,' I said firmly. 'There's enough at stake for quite a few murders.'

'How much would such an expedition cost?'

I had already been thinking about that. 'A ship – plus about fifty thousand for special equipment – plus stores and running expenses.'

'Running expenses for how long?'

I smiled wryly. 'That's one of the jokers – who knows in a thing like this?'

'It's a lot of money. And there's over sixty million square miles of Pacific, you said.'

'I know my job,' I said. 'I wouldn't be going entirely blindfold. I know a hell of a lot of places where there aren't any high-cobalt nodules. And there's what I can recall of Mark's theories – perhaps they're not so fantastic after all. Plus there's this – I'm sure we can make something of it.' I held up Mark's little diary, which I was keeping on my person.

Geordie slapped his hands together suddenly. 'All right, boy. If you can find the capital and the running expenses – and God knows where you'll find money like that – I can provide the ship. Would old *Esmerelda* do?'

'My God, she'd be perfect for running on a small budget.' I looked at him closely, trying not to show my excitement too much. 'But why should you come into this? It's a chancy business, you know.'

He laughed. 'Well, you did mention a few billions of money. Besides, some little bastard shot off the top of my little finger. I'm not particularly interested in him, but I would like to get my hands round the neck of the man who paid him. And chartering tourists isn't very much fun after a bit. I suppose you have some ideas about finance? I mean, without a tame banker it's a non-starter.'

I had been thinking about it, for the last hour or two in between our bouts of conversation. The pieces seemed to be dropping into place nicely, so far.

I said musingly, 'I saw Clare Campbell the other day – she's in town with her father, attending some conference or other. He's my goal.'

'Who is Campbell?'

'Jonathan Campbell – never known as J.C. A Scottish-

Canadian mining man. Mark worked for him for a while after the IGY – something to do with a mining venture in South America. . . .' I trailed off and Geordie cocked his head enquiringly. Something about that statement teased at me but I couldn't identify it and let it go with a shake of my head.

'So he's got money.'

'He's loaded with it,' I said, back on the track. 'He's got the reputation of being a bit of a plunger, and this thing might appeal to him. He lost a packet in the South American business not long ago – something to do with mines being nationalized – but I think he's got enough left to take a gamble on something new.'

'How do you know all this about Campbell, Mike? I didn't know you studied the financial pages.'

'I was thinking of getting out of pure research after the IGY. The pay's small compared with industry, so I thought I'd look about for a job compatible with my expensive tastes.' I waved a hand around my modest flat. 'Lots of other chaps did it – Mark was one – so I did a bit of investigating and Campbell cropped up.'

'But you didn't take the job.'

I shook my head. 'He'd already signed Mark on, you see, and I didn't fancy having Mark as a colleague. Anyway, I was asked to go to the Institute about that time – less pay, but a more interesting job. Mark left the IGY programme early and got out of pure research. I never actually met Campbell but I did once meet his daughter – in Vancouver. Mark had her in tow. They seemed to be pretty close – they would, she being the boss's daughter.'

Geordie's voice had become as cold as mine. 'Poor stupid cow.'

I thought that she didn't look like his description at all, and wondered how long it had taken for her to read Mark's character. She hadn't struck me then as the sort of girl to be taken in for long. But I hoped that nothing much had happened between them, lest it colour Campbell's attitude towards me when I came to approach him.

'How long did Mark work for Campbell?'

'Not very long – about a year and a half. Then he pushed off into the South Pacific and teamed up with Norgaard, last I heard of it. I don't know exactly what they were doing – they had neither a decent boat nor the right equipment for proper research, as far as I could tell.'

'But if Campbell's a mining man, what makes you think he'll finance a deep sea adventure?'

'I think he might,' I said. 'Metals are his business. Never gold or silver, nor the other end of the scale, the base metals. He's dabbled in tin and copper and had a go at platinum once. Now it seems he's concentrating on alloy metals – titanium, cobalt, vanadium and stuff like that. Now that rocketry is big business there's a boom in these metals.'

Geordie asked curiously, 'How does he go about it – his investing, I mean?'

'He takes advantage of us scientific types. He employs a few good men – people like Mark, for instance – and the number varies from time to time. Most of them are geologists, of course. He organizes field expeditions into remote parts, spots a body of ore, puts a million or so into proving and development, then pulls out and sells to the real big boys at a profit. I heard that in one of his recent ventures he put in two million dollars and a year of his time, then sold out at a net profit of a million and a quarter. Not bad for a year's work, eh, Geordie?'

'Not bad at all. But I'd say it needs experience and a hell of a lot of cold nerve.'

'Oh, he's a canny Scot, all right. I hope he's still in town – I'll find out tomorrow.'

'What about Kane – why not put the coppers on to him?'

I shook my head vigorously. 'Not now. All they'd do would be to pass on a query to Tahiti and I've no positive faith in the activities of the French Colonial Police, especially when there's a convenient legal death certificate handy. The delays would be awful, for one thing. No, I'll see for myself – if I can get Campbell interested. I would dearly like to talk to Dr Schouten.'

Geordie rubbed his chin meditatively. 'I'm thinking of

making one or two changes in the crew if we go on this caper. I'd like a couple of blokes I know from the old days. I wonder what Ian Lewis is doing now? When I met him a few months ago he said he found life a little tedious.'

I vaguely remembered a tall, gangling Highlander. 'What was he doing?'

'Oh, he had a place in the Scottish wilderness that he said he'd be glad to leave. You know, I reckon I could get you half a dozen good chaps, all trained fighters and some of them seamen. I've got a couple anyway that I'd keep on for this trip.'

I had a dawning suspicion of what was in Geordie's mind. 'Hold on – what's the idea?'

He said, 'I'd like to see the bunch of thugs who'd stand up against some of your dad's old mob. They may be getting older, but they're not that old and they're all trained commandoes. They're not all settled down and married, you know.'

'What do you think you're doing – setting up a private army?'

'Might not be a bad idea,' he said. 'If the other night is a sample of what to expect we might need a bloody army.'

I sighed. 'All right, Sergeant Wilkins. But no one who's married or has other responsibilities, and you'd better hold your hand until we get Campbell tied up. We can't do anything without money.'

'Ah yes, the money,' said Geordie, and looked very sad.

3

The following morning, quite early, I had a visit from the Inspector and one of his men. Geordie was already out and I was impatient to begin my search for Kane, but tried not to show it. The Inspector was cagey and suspicious, but very casual. I think his trouble was that he didn't really know what to be suspicious of.

He asked, 'Know anyone in South America?'

'Not off hand. No, I don't,' I said.

'Um. The man you killed may have been a South American. His clothes were labelled from Lima, Rio and Montevideo. He could be from almost anywhere except Brazil.'

'I think that answers one question. I couldn't place the accent. What was his name?'

The Inspector shook his head. 'That we don't know, Mr Trevelyan. Or anything else about him, yet. Are you quite sure you don't know any South Americans?'

'Positive.'

He changed tack. 'Wonderful thing, this science; I've found out everything there is to know about manganese nodules.'

I said dryly, 'then you know more than I do – they're not really my line. Did you find it interesting?'

He smiled sourly. 'Not very – they're about as valuable as road gravel. Are you sure there wasn't anything else in that suitcase that might have been of value?'

'Inspector, it was just junk. The kind of stuff that anyone might carry in a case, apart from the nodules, that is.'

'Looks as though Mr Wilkins might have been right, after all. You surprised the burglars before they could pinch anything else.'

I didn't fall for that one – the Inspector didn't for one moment believe it was an ordinary break-in. I said noncommittally, 'I think you're right.'

'The inquest will be next Wednesday,' he said. 'You'll get an official notification, both of you.'

'I'll be there.'

Then they were gone and I thought about South America. That was nearer the Pacific than Spain, but apart from that it made no particular sense to me. And then, belatedly, I thought of Mark's connection with Jonathan Campbell, and Campbell's reputed connection with some South American mining venture, and I had something else to chew on. But it still made no sense, and for the time being I gave up.

Finding a rich Canadian in London's millions was a damn sight easier than finding a poor Australian. The rich are circumscribed in their travelling. The Institute gave me the address of the conference centre, and they gave me the address of the hotel Campbell was staying at, and I had him at the third phone call. Campbell was blunt and curt to the point of rudeness. Yes, he could give me half an hour of his time at eleven that morning – it was already nine-thirty. His tone indicated that if he thought I was wasting his time I'd be kicked out in the first two minutes. The telephone conversation lasted only that long.

At eleven I was at the Dorchester and was shown up to Campbell's suite. He opened the door himself. 'Trevelyan?'

'Yes, sir.'

'Come in.'

He led the way into a room once a luxury living-room but now fitted out as a temporary office, complete with desk, files and secretary; he sent her out and seated himself behind the desk, gesturing me to sit opposite. He was a broad, stocky man of about sixty with a square, tanned face lined with experience. Somebody once said that after forty a man is responsible for his own face; if that's so then Campbell had had a lot of responsibility in his time. His eyes were a frosty blue and his hair iron grey and grizzled. His clothes were expensive and only the slightest accent indicated his transatlantic origin.

I decided that attack was the best policy. I produced the half-nodule and put it on his blotting pad. 'That assays at ten per cent cobalt,' I said without preamble.

He picked it up and looked at it carefully, masking any curiosity. 'Where did it come from?'

'The bottom of the Pacific.'

He looked up and stared at me, then said, 'Are you any relation of the Mark Trevelyan who worked for me a while back?'

'He was my brother.'

'Was?'

'He's dead.'

Campbell frowned. 'When and where did he die?'

'About four months ago – in the Pacific.'

'Sorry to hear it,' he said but perfunctorily. 'A good scientist.'

I detected the careful note in his voice, and thought that here was someone else who had seen through Mark, or had had some example of how my brother went about his affairs. I wondered if it was a business problem, or if it had had anything to do with his daughter's relationship with Mark. I couldn't assess whether it was going to make things harder or easier for me.

He carried on looking at me rather than at the specimen. 'Trevelyan – I've heard the name more recently. Oh yes!' He turned and produced a tabloid newspaper from a shelf and shook it out. 'Are you the Trevelyan mentioned here? The one who killed a man defending his home? An Englishman's castle and all that stuff?'

I caught a glimpse of the headline: SCIENTIST KILLS BURGLAR. Quite mild, considering the paper. I nodded. 'That's right.'

He pursed his lips and put aside the paper, and then came back to business. 'This is a manganese nodule. There are billions of them lying on the bottom of the Pacific. There are quite a few in the Atlantic too.'

'Not many there,' I said. 'And the quality's poor. Too much sedimentation.'

'True.' He tossed the stone and caught it. 'The highest cobalt assay so far is a fraction over 2 per cent. That one came from the central Pacific. Where did this one come from?'

I looked at him blankly and shook my head. He smiled suddenly and it transformed his face – he had a very charming smile. 'All right, I tried,' he said. 'You'd be surprised how often it works. Do you know why I am able to reel off facts about manganese nodules?'

'I was wondering.'

'Your brother told me,' he said. 'He wanted me to fit an expedition a couple of years back. I must say I was tempted.'

'Why didn't you?'

He hesitated, then said, 'I lost a packet in South America. It caught me off balance and until I reorganized I didn't have

53

any fluid capital. About that time your brother left my company, and he hadn't left me enough to go on by myself.'

'I hope you're better placed now,' I said dryly. 'Because that's why I've come to you – now it's my turn to ask you to fund an expedition.'

'So I gathered,' he said, equally dryly. He touched the nodule. 'I must say you brought more than your brother did. He talked a good story but he never showed any concrete evidence. You say this assayed at ten per cent cobalt?'

'I assayed it myself yesterday afternoon – the other half, that is.'

'Mind if I have this assayed – independently?'

'Not at all,' I said equably.

He laughed, showing his charm again. 'All right, Trevelyan, I won't need to. I'm convinced of this anyway.'

'I'd prefer it if you did,' I said. 'I could do with corroboration. But I must tell you that what you've got in your hand is *all* the evidence I have to show.'

His hand clenched around the nodule. 'Now you do begin to interest me. I think you have a story, Mr Trevelyan. Why don't you tell it and quit beating around the bush?'

I had already decided that if we were to work together at all I must hold nothing back. It was only moderately risky. So I told him everything, and when I'd finished we were well past my original half hour. He listened in absolute silence until I was done and then said, 'Now let's see if I've got all this straight. One, your brother died out in the Pacific; two, a man called Nelson whom you have never heard of sent you a case which contained notebooks and nodule samples; three, Kane shows up and pitches what you think is a cock-and-bull yarn; four, the suitcase is stolen by presumed South Americans with additional violence including one killing; five, you retain *one* nodule, analyse it and find a fantastic percentage of cobalt; and six, you also retain a diary of your brother's which you can't even read.'

He looked at me for a long time and then said gently, 'And on the basis of this you want me to invest maybe a million dollars.'

I got out of my chair.

'Sorry to have wasted your time, Mr Campbell.'

'Sit down, you damned fool. Don't give up without a fight. I haven't said I won't invest, have I?' He saw the look on my face and added, 'And I haven't yet said I will, either. Have you got that diary here?'

Wordlessly I took it from my breast pocket and handed it over the desk. He flicked it open and turned rapidly from page to page. 'Who taught your brother to write shorthand?' he asked disgustedly. 'St Vitus?'

'Basically it's Pitman's,' I said. 'But Mark adapted it.' I could have gone on to say that Mark had always been secretive, never liking anyone to know what he was doing. But I kept my mouth shut.

Campbell tossed the diary aside. 'Maybe we can get something out of it somehow – maybe a cipher expert can sort it out.' He turned in his swivel chair and looked out of the window towards Hyde Park, and there was a long silence until he spoke again.

'You know what really interested me in this improbable story of yours?'

'No, I don't.'

'Those South Americans,' he said unexpectedly. 'South America has been unlucky for me, you know. I lost nearly ten million down there. That's when Mark's expedition went down the drain, along with a lot of other things. And now Mark has come back – in a sense – and more South Americans are involved. What do you make of that?'

'Not a thing,' I said.

'I don't believe in coincidence. Not when it happens like this. What I do have to consider lies outside your domain, perhaps – the complications of international law regarding mining, especially offshore, undersea stuff. International relations – so I have to know more about the areas you want to research. Financing. Distribution. Markets.'

I was a little taken aback. Perhaps I was too much of the research scientist – the hard facts of commercial dealing had hardly occurred to me. But on reflection I could hear no note of doubt or dismay in Campbell's voice, only the sound of a man mulling over the forthcoming ramifications of the deal he was being offered – and liking it. There was undoubtedly the faint note of challenge in his attitude, and this encouraged me. I guessed that he, like Geordie's old pal Ian Lewis, may be finding life a little boring at present and was attracted by the novelty of my proposition.

He poked the nodule with his finger. 'There are two things necessary for industrial civilization – cheap power and cheap steel. What's the iron oxide content of this?'

'Thirty-two per cent by weight.'

'That does it. The cobalt will make it economically feasible and the result is a cheap high-grade iron ore, a hell of a lot of manganese, plus some copper, vanadium and anything else we can pick up. Cheap metals, billions of dollars' worth and cheaper than anyone else can produce. It can be tied into one neat, strong package – but it needs careful handling. And above all it needs secrecy.'

'I know. I've already been stalling off a police inspector who thinks there's more to the burglary than meets the eye.'

Campbell appeared satisfied. 'Good. You've got the point.'

'Then you're willing to finance an expedition?' I asked. It was almost too easy, I thought, and I was right.

'I don't know yet. I want to make some investigations of my own, enquiries which I can make and you can't. And maybe I can find Kane for you. Besides, you may not be in a position to undertake anything for some time – you killed a man, remember.' His smile this time was more grim than charming. 'Not that I blame you for it – I've killed men myself – but let's wait for your inquest before deciding anything.'

4

It was six days to the inquest, the longest six days I've spent in my life. To fill in the time I got down to writing the paper that I was supposed to turn out. It wasn't a very good paper as it happened; I had too much else on my mind to concentrate really well.

By the end of the week Geordie still hadn't found Kane, though he'd got a lot of other things moving. 'It's hopeless,' he said to me. 'A needle in a haystack would be easier – this is like trying to find one particular wisp of hay.'

'He may not be in London at all.'

A truism which didn't help. But on the morning of the inquest Kane was found – or rather, he found me.

He called at the flat just as I was leaving for the court – Geordie as usual was out ahead of me and would meet me there. Kane was looking a little the worse for wear with bloodshot eyes and a greying stubble on his cheeks. He coughed raspingly and said, 'Sorry to trouble you, Mr Trevelyan, but you did say I was to keep in touch.'

I looked at him in astonishment and choked back the questions that were on the tip of my tongue. I invited him inside and did a bit of fast thinking as I poured him a cup of coffee. Geordie and Campbell had as much at stake in this as I had, and besides I wanted witnesses when I questioned Kane. I decided to play it softly, though I could hardly bear to speak to him without losing my control.

I made myself smile pleasantly at him. 'Had enough of England, Mr Kane?'

'It 'ud be a nice country if it wasn't for your bleeding weather. We could do with some of this rain back in Queensland, my word.'

'But you've enjoyed your stay?'

'I've had a bonzer time,' he said. 'But my stay's over, Mr Trevelyan. I got to gambling again. I'll never learn.'

'I'm sorry to hear that,' I said.

He looked at me hopefully. 'Mr Trevelyan, you said you might be able to arrange a passage for me. I wondered. . . .'

'Do you have to get back to the Pacific immediately?'

For some reason that didn't please him. 'Not specially, no. But I've got no boodle. If I had some cash or a job I'd like to stay around a bit. I thought maybe you could. . . .'

I said, 'I have a friend who has a yacht which he's fitting out. He and I hope to get in some sailing together, and I think he needs crew. How would that suit you?'

He took the bait eagerly. 'That 'ud be just fine, Mr Trevelyan!'

I put an opened writing pad in front of him, trying to hold back my own eagerness. 'Write down the name of wherever you're staying so that I can get the owner to contact you,' I said. 'He'll want to interview you but I'll make it all right with him. And I'll let you have something ahead of your pay, to cover your rooming costs. How's that?'

He wrote an address down. 'I'll do that. Thanks a whole lot, Mr Trevelyan.'

'That's all right,' I said generously. 'You've earned it.'

I gave him a head start and then left for the court hearing. The encounter had been good for me, giving me something else to think about and making a vital connection in my story for Campbell. I had no time to tell Geordie about it, however, but savoured telling him afterwards.

The inquest was simple and straightforward. A doctor gave evidence of death, then I went on the stand, followed immediately by Geordie. We stuck to straight facts and didn't elaborate but I noticed that Geordie kept his bandaged finger prominently in view of the coroner. My neighbour spoke and then the police had their turn.

As Geordie was giving evidence I glanced round the courtroom and saw Campbell sitting at the back. He nodded to me, then turned his attention to the proceedings.

The Inspector made an appearance and confirmed that he

had found a gun, a Beretta automatic pistol, hanging from the right-hand coat pocket of the deceased. The foresight was caught in the torn lining. I felt a lot better after this because it had been one of the points I had made myself. I looked the coroner straight in the eye and he didn't avoid my glance – a good sign. The lack of identity of the dead man was briefly discussed.

There was a surprise witness, at least to me – old Jarvis appeared to give expert testimony. He told the coroner what manganese nodules were and even produced one to show what the things looked like. The coroner prodded him a bit about their value and Jarvis responded in his downright, damn-your-eyes way. But that was just for the record.

Then suddenly it was over. The coroner took little time to decide that death was due to justifiable manslaughter. He wound everything up with a pontifical speech to the effect that while an Englishman's home may be his castle, no man had the right to take the law into his own hands and that if a little more care had been taken, in his opinion, a death could have been averted. However what was done was done, and Mr Michael Trevelyan was free to leave the court without a stain on his character.

We all stood up when he swept out and there was a general drift to the doors. An official elbowed his way up to me and gave me a note. It was brief and to the point. '*See you at the Dorchester. Campbell.*'

I passed it to Geordie as he reached me to slap me heavily on the back. 'I hope this means what I think it means,' I said. 'I've got a lot to tell you.'

We drifted out with the crowd and were eventually deposited on the pavement. A lot of people I didn't know congratulated me on killing a man and getting away with it, some reporters had a lot of questions to ask, and at last I caught sight of the man I was looking for. I ran to catch up with him, Geordie behind me. It was Professor Jarvis.

He saw me coming, waved his stick and waited for me to join him.

'Well, that went off all right, my boy,' he said.

'You did your bit – thank you.'

'Damned fools,' he grumbled. '*Everyone* knows that those nodules are basically worthless – not an economic proposition at all.'

'I wondered if you had a moment to talk to me – here, rather than at the Institute,' I asked him. There seemed to be no difficulty and we sat down on the low stone wall outside the courthouse, enjoying the thin watery sunshine.

'I have nothing to tell you, young man,' the Professor said. 'I made a few enquiries about that chap, Norgaard, but there's nothing doing. The feller seems to have disappeared off the face of the earth.'

'When was the last you heard of him?'

'About six, seven months ago – when he was with your brother. They were fossicking about in the islands round Tahiti.'

'When did Norgaard start working with Mark?' I asked.

'Now let me see. It must have been nearly two years ago, after Mark left that Canadian firm he was working for. Yes, that was it – after he had to leave the IGY project he went to Canada and was with that chap Campbell for over two years, then he left to join up with Norgaard. What they were doing I don't know; they didn't publish anything.'

His grasp of events was remarkable, I thought, and then seized on something he had said. 'What do you mean – *had* to leave the IGY?'

Jarvis actually looked embarrassed. 'Oh, I shouldn't have said that,' he mumbled.

'I'd like to know. It can't hurt Mark now.'

'It's bad form. *De mortuis* – and all that, don't you know.'

'Out with it,' I said. 'After all, it's all in the family.'

Jarvis regarded the tip of his highly polished shoe. 'Well, I never did get to the bottom of it – it was hushed up, you know – but apparently Mark fudged some of his results.'

'Faked his figures?'

'That's right. It was found out by sheer chance. Of course he had to leave. But we – the IGY agreed not to make any more of it, so he was able to get the job in Canada, after he resigned.'

'So that's why he left before it was over. I wondered about that. What was he working on at the time?'

Jarvis shrugged. 'I don't recall, but it certainly had to do with the underwater surveys. Manganese nodules, perhaps?' Not too shrewd a guess, all things considered; but I didn't like it. He went on, 'I never did like your brother. I never trusted him and the fact that he cooked his books didn't surprise me a bit.'

I said, 'That's all right – lots of people didn't like Mark. I wasn't too keen on him myself. And it wasn't the first time he rigged his results. He did the same at school.' And at university. Not to mention his personal life.

Jarvis nodded. 'I'm not surprised at that either. Still, my boy, I don't mistrust the whole Trevelyan family. You're worth ten of your brother, Mike.'

'Thanks, Prof.,' I said warmly.

'Forget all this and enjoy your leave now. The South Atlantic is waiting for you when you return.'

He turned and strode away, jauntily waving his stick. I looked after him with affection; I thought he would be genuinely sorry to lose me if the deal with Campbell came off and I went to the South Pacific instead of the South Atlantic. He would once more angrily bewail the economic facts of life which drew researchers into industry and he would write a few acid letters to the journals.

I turned to Geordie. 'What do you make of that?'

'Norgaard vanished just about the same time that Mark kicked the bucket. I wonder if. . . .'

'I know what you're thinking, Geordie. Is Norgaard still alive? I do hope to God Campbell comes through – I want to do some field work in the islands.'

'You had something to tell me,' he reminded me. But I had decided to save it up.

'I'll tell you and Campbell together. Come with me to see him.'

5

Campbell was less crusty than at our first meeting. 'Well,' he said, as we entered his suite, 'I see you're not entirely a hardened criminal, Trevelyan.'

'Not a stain on my character. The coroner said so.' I introduced Geordie and the two big men sized one another up with interest. 'Mr Wilkins is willing to contribute a ship – and skipper her, too.'

Campbell said, 'I see someone has faith in your crazy story. I suppose that getting hurt added to your conviction.'

'What about you?' I asked.

He ignored this and asked what we would drink. 'We must celebrate a successful evasion of the penalty of the law,' he said, almost jovially. He ordered and we got down to business. I decided to keep the Kane episode to be revealed at the proper moment and first hear what Campbell had to say.

'I knew my hunch about your South Americans would work out,' he said. 'I've got a pretty good intelligence system – you have to in my line of work – and I find that Suarez-Navarro are fitting out a research ship in Darwin right at this moment. It's new business and new territory for them, so my guess is that they are heading your way.'

I looked at him blankly. That didn't mean a thing to me.

I think he enjoyed my lack of comprehension because he left me dangling for a while before elucidating. 'Suarez-Navarro is a South American mining house, active in several countries,' he said. 'I've tangled with them before – they're a crowd of unscrupulous bastards. Now, why would a mining house be fitting out an oceanographical research ship?'

'Nodules,' said Geordie succinctly.

'How unscrupulous are they?' I asked. 'Would they stoop to burglary?' I didn't mention murder.

Campbell folded his hands together. 'I'll tell you the story and let you judge for yourself. Once I had a pretty good set-up in South America, never mind just where. The mines were producing well and I ploughed a lot back in the interests of good labour relations. I had a couple of schools, a hospital and all the civilized trimmings. Those Indian miners never had it so good, and they responded well.

'Suarez-Navarro cast an eye on the operation and liked the look of it. They went about things in their own smelly way, though. They had a trouble-shooter, a guy called Ernesto Ramirez, whom they used for that type of operation. He pitched up, got at the government, greased a few palms, supported the Army, and then suddenly there was a new government – which promptly expropriated the mines in the interests of the national economy – or that's what they said. Anyway, I never got a cent out of it. They just took the lot and Ramirez vanished back into the hole they dug him out of.

'The next thing that happened was that the government wanted somebody to run the mines, so Suarez-Navarro offered to take on the job out of the kindness of their hearts and a hefty percentage of the profits. I had been paying 38 per cent tax but Suarez-Navarro got away tax free since they claimed it was really government property anyway. They had a sweet set-up.

'They closed the schools and the hospital – those things don't produce, you see. Pretty soon they had a strike on their hands. If you treat a man like a man he kind of resents going back to being treated like a pig – so there was a strike. That brought Ramirez out of his hole fast. He called in the Army, there was quite a bit of shooting, and then there was suddenly no strike – just fifty dead Indians and quite a few widows.'

He smiled grimly. 'Does that answer your question about the scruples of Suarez-Navarro?'

I nodded. It was a nasty story.

Campbell seemed to go off at a tangent. 'I'm attending a conference here in London, a conference on mineral resources.'

'That's how I found you,' I murmured, but he took no notice.

'It's a Commonwealth deal really but various other interested parties have been invited to send observers. Suarez-Navarro have two – you can't keep them out of anything – but another one arrived last week. His name is Ernesto Ramirez.' Campbell's voice was hard. 'Ramirez isn't a conference man, he's not a negotiator. He's Suarez-Navarro's muscle man. Do I make my point?'

We both nodded, intently.

'Well, I'm going to hammer it home really hard. I've found Kane for you.'

'Well, I'll be damned!' I said.

'You were going about it the hard way. I put someone on to watch Ramirez and was told that a man called Kane had a two-hour talk with him yesterday. We had Kane followed to where he's in digs and I have the address.'

I reeled it off.

It was effective. Campbell said, 'What?' disbelievingly, and Geordie gaped at me. I enjoyed my moment.

'Kane came to visit me this morning,' I said, and told them both what had happened. 'I suggest you get him down to the docks and have a serious talk with him,' I said to Geordie.

Campbell frowned and then his great smile broke on his face. 'No, you don't,' he said. 'Don't ask him a damn thing. Don't you see what's happening?'

Geordie and I shrugged helplessly. We weren't quick enough for Campbell in matters like this.

'Ever heard of industrial espionage? Of course you have. Every big outfit runs a spy system. I do it myself – don't much like it, but I've got to keep up with the hard-nosed bastards in the business.' He actually looked as if he enjoyed it very much. 'Now let's reconstruct what's been happening. You got hold of something you shouldn't have – from the point of view of Suarez-Navarro. Ramirez hotfoots it to England – he arrived the day before Kane came to see you, so it's a cinch they came together. Kane comes to you to find out if Mark's stuff has arrived yet, and he knows it has because you tell him

64

so yourself. He spins you a yarn as cover – it doesn't really matter what it is. Then Ramirez tells his boys to snatch the stuff but you surprise them in the middle.' He lifted his eyebrows. 'Does that make sense so far?'

Geordie said, 'It makes sense to me.'

I said nothing. I was a little more doubtful, but if this served to keep up Campbell's interest I was all for it.

He continued, 'But something goes wrong – they leave the diary and one nodule. Ramirez doesn't know this, but he does know you've contacted me and that all sorts of enquiries are out – including questions in court about nodules. Oh yes, I bet he was there – or someone for him. He must have had a shock when you came to see me. You see, he'd keep a tail on you as a matter of routine just to see if you did anything out of the ordinary – and you did. So what does Ramirez do now?'

'I'll buy it,' I said. 'What does he do?'

'He lays Kane alongside you again,' said Campbell. 'You gave him the perfect opportunity – you practically invited Kane to come back. It's Kane's job to find out what, if anything, is in the wind. But what Ramirez doesn't know is that you were suspicious of Kane right from the start, and this gives *us* a perfect opportunity. We string Kane along – employ him, feed him any information we want him to know and keep from him anything we don't want him to know. We also keep him underfoot and don't lose him again. That's why you mustn't ask him any awkward questions – not right now, anyway.'

I thought about it for a long time. 'Does this mean you're coming in with us? Putting up the finance?'

'You're damn right it does,' snapped Campbell. 'If Suarez-Navarro are going to all this trouble they must be on to something big, and I'd like to stab them in the back just for old times' sake. I'll put up half a million dollars – or whatever it takes – and I ask only one thing. That we get there, and do it, before they can.'

Geordie said gently, 'It *was* a good idea of mine, wasn't it?'

'What's that?' asked Campbell.

'Geordie's recruiting a private army,' I explained. 'As he gets older he gets more bloodthirsty.'

A look passed between them for the second time that made me feel like the outsider. Without saying a word they were in full accord on many levels, and for a moment I felt very inexperienced indeed.

Campbell said, 'There's another thing. My doctor is troubled about my health, the goddam quack. He's been pestering me to take a sea voyage, and I'm suddenly minded to accept his advice. I'm coming along for the ride.'

'You're the boss,' I said. I wasn't surprised.

He turned to Geordie. 'Now, what kind of a ship have you, Captain?'

'A brigantine,' said Geordie. 'About two hundred tons.'

Campbell's jaw dropped. 'But that's a little sailing ship! This is supposed to be a serious project.'

'Take it easy,' I said, grinning at Geordie who was already bristling at any slight to *Esmerelda*. 'A lot of research vessels are sailing ships; there happen to be a number of sound reasons.'

'All right. Let's hear them.'

'Some of the reasons are purely technical,' I said. 'For instance, it's easier to make a sailing ship non-magnetic than a powered ship. Magnetism plays hell with all sorts of important readings. But the reasons you'll appreciate are purely economic.'

'If you're talking economics you're talking my language,' he growled.

'A research ship never knows exactly where it's going. We might find ourselves dredging a thousand miles away from the nearest land. Station keeping and dredging take power and fuel, and an engine powered ship would need a hell of a lot of fuel to make the round trip.

'But a sailing ship can make the journey and arrive on station with close on full tanks, given careful management. She can keep on station longer and no one need worry about whether there'll be enough fuel to get back. You *could* use a powered ship to do the job but it would cost you – oh, a million pounds plus. Geordie's boat will be fine.'

'The day's not been wasted,' Campbell said. 'I've learned something new. I reckon you know your job, Trevelyan. What will you need in the way of equipment?'

So we got down to it. The biggest item was the winch, which was to be installed amidships, and storage space for 30,000 feet of cable below it. There was also to be a laboratory for on-the-spot analysis and all the necessary equipment would take a lot of money, and a lot of refitting.

'We'll need a bloody big generator for this lot,' said Geordie. 'It looks as though it'll take a diesel bigger than the main engine. Lucky, isn't it, that charter tourists take up so much space with luxuries.'

Presently Campbell suggested lunch, so we went down to the dining room to do some more planning over grilled steaks. It was arranged that I should concentrate on collecting equipment while Geordie prepared *Esmerelda* and got his crew together. Very little was said concerning the location, or the availability, of the strange treasure we were after, and I knew that I alone could come up with anything of use there. I had some heavy studying ahead of me as well as all the rest.

'If you take on Kane it'll mean we've got him in our sights,' said Campbell, harping back to his favourite subject. 'Not that it makes any difference. Ramirez is sure to have other scouts out. I'll be watching him too.'

I'd been thinking about Kane.

'Your review of the situation was very well in its way, but it was wrong on one point.'

'What's that?' said Campbell.

'You said that Kane spun me a yarn as cover, and that it didn't matter what it was. That's not entirely so, you know – we have independent evidence. The death certificate states the cause of death as appendicitis. Kane and Schouten both told the same lie and I'd like to know why.'

'By God, you're right,' said Campbell. 'We'll get it out of Kane as soon as he's served his purpose.'

Geordie grunted. 'We're going into the Pacific,' he said. 'Maybe we'll get it out of Schouten. At all events, we'll be at the root of it.'

Chapter Three

1

It was nearly three months before we got away. You can't begin a scientific expedition as though you were going on a picnic. There were a million things to do and we were kept busy on a sixteen hour day, seven days a week. The first thing I did was to hand in my resignation from the Institute. Old Jarvis didn't take it too well, but there wasn't anything he could do about it so he accepted the situation with reluctance. I wished I could have told him what I was doing but that was impossible.

Geordie assiduously recruited his crew and soon they began to turn up. He had kept on four of his own lads and had of course taken on Kane in place of one of the men he let go. Of the other six that he added, all were faces that I hadn't seen since I had been a boy during the war, tagging around after my dad's gang.

Ian Lewis detached himself from his croft with alacrity and Geordie made him first mate; he'd had years under sail and was almost as good as a professional. Ex-corporal Taffy Morgan came along; one night during the war he had killed six Germans with a commando knife in utter silence, earning himself the M.M. Danny Williams had also won the M.M., although I never found out what for since he was reticent about it. There was the burly bulk of Nick Dugan, an Irishman from the Free State. Bill Hunter turned up – he had made a name for himself as an underwater demolitions expert and was the only other regular sailing man among the team. And there was Jim Taylor, another explosives wizard – he had been very near my father when he was killed.

They were now all into their forties, like Geordie, but seemed as tough as ever. Not one had lost his fitness and there wasn't a paunch among the lot of them. Geordie said he could have recruited twenty-five but he'd picked the best of them, and I almost believed him. I was confident that if we ran into trouble we could handle it.

Geordie was confident too, of welding them into a good sailing crew. What any of them lacked in knowledge they'd soon pick up and the enthusiasm was certainly there – although for the time being they knew nothing of the complications in which we were entangled. It was a straight research and survey trip to them all, including Kane, and any hints Geordie may have given his special team they kept strictly to themselves. As Campbell had predicted, Kane was sticking as close to us as a leech; Geordie had simply told him that there was a berth for him if he cared to cross the Atlantic with us, and Kane had jumped at the opportunity.

Campbell had gone back to Canada. Before he left he had a long talk with me. 'I told you I had a good intelligence service,' he said. 'Well, so have Suarez-Navarro. You'll be watched and they'll know everything you do as soon as you do it, even apart from Kane's spying. It can't be helped. We're deadlocked and we know it. So do they. It's a case of we know that they know that we know, and so on. It's a bastard of a position to be in.'

'It's like a game with perfect information – chess, for example. It's the man who can manoeuvre best who wins.'

'Not quite. Both sides have imperfect information,' he corrected me patiently. 'We don't know how much they really know. They might have the exact location of the nodules we're after, and only have to drop a dredge to prove their case, but perhaps they're behind us in planning and need to stop us somehow first. On the other hand, they don't know how much *we* know. Which is precious little. Maybe as much as, or no more than them. Tricky, isn't it?'

'It would take a logician to sort it out. Talking of knowing, have you made any progress with the diary?'

Campbell snorted. 'I gave it to a top-flight cipher expert and he's having his troubles. He says it isn't so much the peculiar shorthand as the sloppy way in which it's written. But he says he can crack it, given time. What I wish I knew was how Suarez-Navarro got on to this in the first place?'

My own thoughts were that Mark, cheated out of Campbell's involvement – I guessed that's how he would see Campbell's loss, only in terms of his own disappointment – had approached them himself. But I still didn't know enough about how Campbell viewed Mark to say so. It hung between us, a touchy subject that we both carefully avoided.

So he went off to Canada to further his own progress, we speeded up ours as much as possible, and it was with great relief that I heard Geordie announce one day that we were at last ready for sea. All he needed to know was where to head for.

I said, 'Do you know the Blake Plateau?'

'Never heard of it.'

'It's just off the coast of Carolina. We'll test the winch and the rest of our gear there, and it's a long enough voyage for you to pull your crew together. I don't want to go into the Pacific to find that anything doesn't work for some reason or other. If there's anything wrong we can get it fixed in Panama – they've got good engineering shops there.'

'Okay. But why the Blake Plateau?'

'There are nodules there. I've always wanted a closer look at Atlantic nodules.'

'Is there any place where there aren't any?' he asked.

I nodded. 'They won't form where there's heavy sedimentation, so that cuts out most of the Atlantic – but the Blake Plateau is scoured by the Gulf Stream and nodules do form. But they're poor quality, not like the ones in the Pacific.'

'How deep?'

'Not more than three thousand feet – deep enough to test the winch.'

'Right, boy. Let's go and scoop up some poor quality wealth from the bottom of the sea. We should be away in a few days now.'

'I can't wait,' I said. I was in fact boiling with impatience to be gone.

2

We made a fair and untroubled crossing of the Atlantic. Geordie and Ian, together with the regular crew members, soon got the others into a good working pattern and spirits ran high. Kane, we were pleased to notice, fitted in well and seemed as willing and above-board as the others. Knowing that they were all curious as to our purpose I gave occasional rather deliberately boring lectures on oceanography, touching on a number of possible research subjects so that the matter of manganese nodules got lost in the general subject. Only two people retained an interest in what I had to say, and to them, in semi-private, I spoke at greater length about our quarry. One was Geordie, of course, and the other, not too surprisingly and in fact to my satisfaction, was Bill Hunter. Already our diving expert, his interest and involvement might well be crucial.

One afternoon they both joined me in the laboratory, at my request, to learn a little more. A quiet word from Geordie to Ian made sure that we weren't going to be interrupted.

Geordie picked up a nodule which I'd cut in half – I had brought a few on board to help my explanation along.

He pointed to the white central core.

'I suppose you'll tell me again that it's a shark's tooth in the middle of this rock. You never did get around to explaining that, did you?'

I smiled and held up the stone. 'That's right, it is.'

'You're kidding.'

'No I'm not – it happens often. You see, a shark dies and its body drifts down; the flesh rots or is eaten, the bones dissolve – what bones a shark has, it's cartilage really – and by the time anything reaches the very bottom there's nothing left but the teeth. They are made of sodium triphosphate and insoluable in water. There are probably millions of them on any ocean bottom.'

I opened a small box. 'Look here,' I said and gave him a larger white bone. It was as big as the palm of his hand and curiously convoluted.

'What's this?'

'It's a whale's earbone,' said Bill, looking over his shoulder. 'I've seem 'em before.'

'Right, Bill. Also made of sodium triphosphate. We sometimes find them at the core of larger nodules – but more often it's a shark's tooth and most frequently a bit of clay.'

'So the manganese sticks to the tooth. How long does it take to make a nodule?' Geordie asked.

'Estimates vary from one millimetre each thousand years to one millimetre each million years. One chap estimated that it worked out to one layer of atoms a day – which makes it one of the slowest chemical reactions known. But I have my own ideas about that.'

They both stared at me. 'Do you mean that if you find a nodule with a half-diameter of ten millimetres formed round a tooth that the shark lived ten million years ago? Were there sharks then?' Geordie asked in fascination.

'Oh yes, the shark is one of our oldest inhabitants.'

We talked a little more and then I dropped it. They had a lot to learn yet and it came best in small doses. And there was plenty of time for talk on this voyage. We headed south-south-west to cut through the Bahamas and the approach to the Windward Passage. Once in the Passage we kept as clear as possible of Cuba – once we came across an American destroyer on patrol, which did us the courtesy of dipping her flag, to which we reciprocated. Then there was the long leg across the Caribbean to Colon and the entrance to the Panama Canal.

By then we had done our testing. There were minor problems, no more than teething troubles, and generally I was happy with the way things were going. Stopping to dredge a little, trying out the winch and working out on-station routines, was an interesting change from what we had been doing and everyone enjoyed it, and we remained lucky with the weather. I got some nodules up but there was a lot of other material, enough to cloud the issue for everyone but Geordie. Among the debris of ooze, red clay and deposits we found enough shark's teeth and whale's earbone to give everyone on board a handful of souvenirs.

Both Geordie and Bill were becoming more and more interested in the nodules and wanted to know more about them, so I arranged for another lab. session with them one day. I'd been assaying, partly to keep my hand in and partly to check on the readiness of my equipment for the real thing.

'How did the Atlantic nodules turn out?' Geordie asked. On the whole he did the talking – Bill watched, listened and absorbed.

'Same old low quality stuff that's always pulled out in the Atlantic,' I said. 'Low manganese, low iron and hardly anything else except contaminants, clay and suchlike. That's the trouble in the Atlantic; there's too much sediment even on the Blake Plateau.'

'Why does manganese behave this way – why does it lump together?'

I laughed. 'You want me to give you a course of physical chemistry right now? All right, I'll explain it as simply as I can. Do you know what a colloid is?'

Two headshakes.

'Look. If you put a teaspoon of sugar into water you get a sugar solution – that is, the sugar breaks down right to the molecular level and mixes intimately with the water. In other words, it dissolves. Right?'

'Right.'

'Now what if you have a substance that won't dissolve in water but is divided into very fine particles, much smaller than can be seen in a regular microscope, and each particle is floating in the water? That's a colloid. I could whip you up a colloid which looks like a clear liquid, but it would be full of very small particles.'

'I see the difference,' Geordie said.

'All right. Now, for reasons that I won't go into now, all colloidal particles *must* carry an electric charge. These charges make the colloidal particles of manganese dioxide clump together in larger and larger units. They also tend to be attracted to any electrically conductive surfaces such as a shark's tooth or a bit of clay. Hence the nodules.'

'You mean,' said Bill slowly, 'that having broken down a long time before, the manganese is trying to get together again?'

'Pretty well just that, yes.'

'Where does the manganese come from in the first place – when it starts clumping, that is?'

'From the rivers, from underground volcanic fissures, from the rocks of the sea bottom. Fellows, the sea out there is a big chemical broth. In certain localized conditions the sea becomes alkaline and the manganese in the rocks leaches out and dissolves in the water. . . .'

'You said it doesn't dissolve.'

'Pure metallic manganese *will* dissolve as long as the conditions are right, and that's what chemists call a "reducing atmosphere". Just believe me, Geordie. Currents carry the dissolved manganese into "oxidising atmospheres" where the water is more acid. The manganese combines with oxygen to form manganese dioxide which *is* insoluble and so forms a colloid – and then the process goes on as I've described.'

He thought about that. 'What about the copper and nickel and cobalt and stuff that's in the nodules?'

'How does the milk get into the coconut?'

We all laughed, taking some of the schoolroom air out of the lab. 'Well, all these metals have certain affinities for each other. If you look at the table of elements you'll find they're grouped closely together by weight – from manganese, number twenty-five, to copper, number twenty-nine. What happens is that as the colloidal particles grow bigger they scavenge the other metals – entrap them. Of course, this is happening over a pretty long period of time.'

'Say a hundred million years or so,' said Geordie ironically.

'Ah well, that's the orthodox view.'

'You think it can happen faster than that?'

'I think it could happen fast,' I said slowly. 'Given the right conditions, though just what these conditions would be I'm not sure. Someone else doing research thought so too, though I haven't been able to follow his reasoning. And I have seen pecularities that indicate rapid growth. Anyway that's one of the objects of this trip – to find out.'

What I didn't say in Bill's hearing was that the 'somebody' was Mark, nor that the peculiarities I had seen were contained in the prize nodule left from his collection. And there was something else I didn't talk about; the peculiarities that led to high-cobalt assay. I was beginning to grope towards a theory of nodule formation which, though still vague, might ease the way ahead. I was becoming anxious to know how Campbell's cipher expert had made out in translating Mark's diary.

3

Ten days after leaving the Blake Plateau we warped into the dockside at Panama. At last we were in the Pacific, all my goals a step nearer. Campbell was waiting for us, jumped spryly aboard and shook hands with me and Geordie, waving genially at the rest of the crew.

'You made a good fast trip,' he said.

'Not so bad,' said Geordie complacently.

Campbell looked about the *Esmerelda* and at the crew who were busy stowing sail and clearing the decks. 'So this is your crew of cut-throats and desperadoes,' he said. He was in a jocular mood – a mercurial man. 'I hope we won't need them.' He took my arm and walked me along the dock, amused at my wobbling land-legs.

'I've booked you into my hotel for a night or so; there's no reason why you shouldn't have a last taste of luxury before the big job. Geordie too, if he wants it. I'll expect you both to dinner – you can't miss the hotel, it's the Colombo, right on the main street. You can tell me all about the trip then. Meantime I want to talk to you in private, now.' He steered me into one of the waterfront bars that always seem to be handy, and I sat down thankfully in front of a large glass of cold beer.

Campbell wasted no time. He produced a biggish envelope from his jacket. 'I had photostats made of the diary pages,' he said. 'The original's in a bank vault in Montreal. You don't mind? You'll get it back one day.'

'Not at all,' I said.

He shook out the contents of the envelope. 'I got the translation done. My guy said it was a bastard of a job – he only hopes he's got the scientific bits right.'

'We'll soon find out.' I was stiff with eagerness.

Campbell handed me a neatly bound booklet which I flicked through. 'That's the stat of the original diary. This one's the translation. There are reproductions of all the drawings at the back. The whole thing looks screwy to me – it had better make sense to you or this whole thing is a bust already.' His good humour had already evaporated, but I was getting used to his changes of mood.

I glanced through it all. 'This is going to be a long job,' I said. 'I'm not going to be able to make any snap judgements here and now; I'll look at this lot this afternoon, in the hotel room. Right now I want to go back to *Esmerelda* and sort out procedures with Geordie, pack my gear and go and take a shower and a clean-up.'

If he was disappointed he didn't show it – clearly what I said made sense. And so it was not until I was lying, damp and half-naked in the blessedly cool hotel room a couple of hours later that I finally opened the envelope. The translation of the cipher was pretty well complete except for a few gaps here and there, but it didn't improve matters as much as I'd hoped. The thing was disappointingly written in a kind of telegraphese which didn't make for easy reading. It was a true diary and evidently covered the last few months of Mark's life, from about the time he left the IGY, although there were few dates and no place names written in clear at all.

I wondered if he'd always kept such a diary, and decided that he must have done so – diary-keeping is a habit as hard to break as to develop. As to where the earlier volumes had got to, there was no guessing, nor did I think they would have helped me much anyway. This was the vital period.

It was, on the whole, an ordinary enough diary; there were references to shore leave, films seen, people mentioned by initials only in the irritating way that people have when confiding to themselves, and all the other trivia of a man's life, all in brusque lack of detail. Mark had kept a brief record of his amours which wasn't pleasant to read, but otherwise it was fairly uninteresting on the surface.

Then there were the entries made at sea. Here the diary turned professional with notes of observations, odd equations roughly jotted, analyses of bottom material, mostly sea ooze. Occasionally there were analyses of nodules – nothing very startling, just run of the sea stuff.

I waded on feeling that I might be wasting my time, but towards the end I was pulled up with a start. I had run my eye down the typewritten sheet and was aware that I was at last looking at something remarkable. It was an analysis of a nodule, though it didn't specifically say so, and the figures were startling.

Translated from symbols, they read: *'Manganese – 28%; iron – 32%; cobalt – 8%; copper – 4%; nickel – 6%; other 22%. Wow!'*

'Wow,' indeed.

There followed analyses of four more nodules, all equally rich.

I did some calculating and found the average cobalt in the five nodules to be a fraction under nine per cent. The copper and nickel weren't to be laughed away either. I didn't yet know much about the economics of recovery but it was evident that this might be a paying proposition even with relatively primitive methods of dredging, depending on the depth of water. And I had reason to believe that this was not too great to be worked in. With more sophisticated equipment it would be better than owning a gold mine.

But there was always the snag – nowhere in the diary did Mark say where these riches were to be found. In the whole notebook there was not one place name mentioned. So we weren't really any better off than we were before, except that scattered through the typewritten pages was the phrase, '*Picture Here*', with a number attached, and at the end was a sheaf of reproductions and a brief account by the cipher expert of these doodled drawings.

It is possible and indeed probable that these drawings are of the nature of pictograms or rebuses. A study of the pictograms leads me to believe that they must indicate place names, and of the 32 drawings, I believe I have successfully identified 24.

To illustrate: the rough sketch of the gas mantle with the word GRATIS beneath may well refer to the Australian town of Fremantle; the bearded man with the sword and the baby is probably Solomon, referring to the biblical story, and may indicate the Solomon Islands; the bearded man looking at a monkey may be a reference to Darwin in the Australian territory; the straight line neatly bisected may refer to either the Equator or Midway Island.

The fact that all these names occur in the same quarter of the globe is a further indication that one may be on the right track in such surmising. Other names tentatively identified are also to be found in the same geographical area.

Tracings of the drawings, together with possible identifications are attached. Of the eight drawings unidentified all I can say is that to solve these one would need to have a more precise knowledge of these geographical areas, together with the need to know a great deal more about the 'artist', since it is obvious that an idiosyncratic mode of thought is here employed, involving a person's training, experience and interior feelings; in fact, a total life.

I looked up the analyses of the two non-standard nodules again. Coming immediately after them were two of the drawings, numbers 28 and 29. I checked them against the tracings. One was of a busty wench wearing a Phyrgian cap with underneath it the words, '*The Fair Goddess*'. The other was a rather bedraggled-looking American eagle with the inscription, '*The Disappearing Trick*'. Neither was identified.

I leaned back and thought about it all. I knew that Mark's ship had been based on Australia during the IGY – hence, possibly, the Australian references. Mark had probably been in the Solomons and might well have gone as far as Midway – he would certainly have crossed the Equator anyway. Did he go as far as Easter Island? I checked the tracings and found it – a rabbit apparently trying to hatch an egg, the traditional fertility symbols of Easter. That was one the expert had spotted too.

It was a hell of a big area in which to find *The Fair Goddess* or *The Disappearing Trick*.

I thought about Mark and his 'idiosyncratic mode of thought'. The expert had been dead right there; Mark's mode of thought had been so damned idiosyncratic that there had been times when I thought it wasn't human. He had a strangely twisted, involute mind which delighted in complexity and deception, never taking a straight course but always heading ultimately for one goal – the eventual well-being of Mark Trevelyan.

All my life I had watched him cheat and scheme his way towards the things he wanted, never realizing that if he'd gone about his business in a straightforward way it would have been more efficient. He had a first-class brain, but he was lazy and always looking for short cuts – but you don't find many short cuts in science and thus he tended to lag behind in his work.

I think he was envious of me for some odd reason of his own. I was two years older than he and when we were children he nearly beat himself to death trying to keep up, physically and mentally. The psycho boys have a term for it in their tasteless jargon – 'sibling rivalry' – but with Mark it took an unhealthy turn. He seemed to see his whole life in terms of competition with me, even inventing apparent parental favouritism towards me where I could see none. The only reason that I know for his having elected to study oceanography was because I had done so and not, like me, out of any burning interest in the subject. He once said that he would be famous when I had been forgotten.

It was ironic in a way that he should have said that, because he had the makings of a first rate scientist with a theoretical bent and if he'd lived I'm sure he could have surprised us all – provided he wasn't looking for a short cut at the time.

For years I'd avoided him, physically and professionally, but now I had to match my mind against his. I had to ferret out the meanings of his cryptic scrawls and it wasn't going to be easy. Mark had almost certainly been up to something fishy – no high-cobalt results had come out of the IGY investigations, and Mark had such results. I thought about what Jarvis had said about Mark faking figures during that period, and about Mark trying to persuade Campbell into an expedition to look for nodules. It was beginning to add up.

I was interrupted by Geordie, banging at my bedroom door.

'Aren't you ready yet?' he demanded. 'We've got a dinner date with the boss.'

'My God, the time's slipped away.'

'Found anything?'

I looked up wryly. 'Yes, I've found something but I'm damned if I know what it is. It looks as though we still have to play children's games against Mark's tortuous mind. I'll tell you about it when we're all together. Give me ten minutes to get dressed.'

'There's just one thing first,' Geordie said, hovering in the doorway. 'Kane went ashore and sent a cable.'

'Where to?'

'We were lucky. I detailed Danny Williams to trail him – don't worry, he'll keep it dark – and he managed to hear Kane asking about cable rates to Rabaul.'

'Rabaul! But that's in New Britain – in the Bismarck Archipelago. Why in hell would he send a cable clear across the Pacific? Do you know who he sent it to?'

'Danny couldn't find that out. He should have bribed the counter clerk, but he didn't. The boss says come to the lounge first – it's early for a meal. He wants to talk to us there – about that, I guess.' He pointed to the diary pages lying on my bed.

4

The Colombo was a modern American style hotel. We went to the reception desk where I had signed in earlier and asked for Campbell, and were told that he was in one of the lounges. It was discreetly lighted and in one corner a trio was playing soft music. It was all very civilized and pleasant and a definite change from life on board *Esmerelda*. Over drinks I asked Campbell to bear with me in setting aside for the moment the matter of the diary, and instead listen while I brought him up to date concerning manganese nodules, to which he reluctantly agreed. He was at his most churlish but I knew that mood would wear off as his interest sharpened. He had already done some homework so I was able to cover the matter of nodule formation and distribution fairly quickly, feeling pleased that I had already brought Geordie up to that point as well. I came at last to the matter of nodule dating.

'I've come to the conclusion that our nodule isn't very old,' I said, producing it from my pocket.

'How old?' Campbell demanded.

'He always talks in millions,' said Geordie wisely, but he was wrong.

'Not more than fifty thousand years,' I said flatly. 'It could be between thirty thousand and fifty thousand but not more than that, I'll stake my reputation on it. Somewhere in the Pacific these things are growing at an explosive rate.'

'Explosive,' said Geordie incredulously. 'Do you call fifty thousand years explosive?'

'From a geological standpoint it's very fast. It's damned unusual, though, and it's very important.'

'Why so?' Campbell asked.

'Look, the whole damn Pacific is covered with these things which have been growing slowly over millions of years. Now we have one which has grown in a fraction of that time. There must be a specific reason for it. My guess is that it's the result of a purely local condition, and if it is the chances are that this condition still exists – in other words, these nodules are growing at the same rate even now.'

'I can't see that that helps us much.'

'It helps us this much. It means we can cut out vast areas – millions of square miles – where I *know* that no peculiar conditions exist in the sea. I'll go along with orthodoxy on that one; the seabed is pretty regular, there are few changes of climate for one thing. What we've got to watch for is the oddity.'

'Got any idea what kind of oddity?'

I nodded. 'I have vague ideas that I'm not prepared to put into words just yet,' I said. 'Maybe I'll get something from the diary translation. It may only need one word to make the whole picture clear – like the last piece in a jigsaw puzzle.'

'We'll come back to that later,' Campbell said. 'Meanwhile I've been keeping tabs on Suarez-Navarro. Ramirez left London and joined that ship of theirs.'

'Where are they now?' Geordie asked.

'Still lying in Darwin – doing nothing. I don't quite get it.'

He glanced up as he spoke and then got to his feet. Coming through the lounge towards us was a young woman whom I recognized as his daughter, and Geordie and I both stood up as she joined us. Campbell introduced us. 'Clare, this is Michael Trevelyan and this is our Captain, George Wilkins.'

Geordie shook hands gravely and corrected his name. As I took her hand she looked at me very carefully but did not react to my name at all. I was on the point of reminding her that I had met her once long before, with Mark, but took my cue from her and made my greeting noncommittal. We all sat down once again, and during the few minutes while drinks were being ordered I assessed her, as a man assesses any woman.

When I had seen her in Vancouver I hadn't been particularly interested. I couldn't be bothered with Mark or any of his affairs. But now I saw that she was really beautiful and wondered why I hadn't noticed it before. She was tall, with black hair and straight brows over grey eyes. Her mouth was generous with mobile corners, a mouth made for laughter but presently in tight control, as though she had learned not to laugh. She was dressed with that deceptive simplicity which means money, not surprising considering that she was Campbell's daughter. She wore, I noticed, no jewellery apart from a small ruby brooch.

We all chatted for a short time about this and that, and I saw that there was something wary and watchful about her, and felt that it concerned me. I wondered how Mark had got on with her. When I saw her with him she had seemed to have a lot more sparkle, and this present introversion wasn't Mark's style at all – he always liked his women to have some animation.

Presently Campbell brought us to the matter in the forefront of all our minds. I was not altogether surprised when he said, 'Gentlemen, you had better know that I've told the whole story – so far as I can – to Clare. She's my right hand, you know, doubles as secretary sometimes, and she's always been involved in my affairs. This one is no different.'

I thought that burglary, forgery, espionage and murder would certainly make it different in my eyes, but perhaps she'd seen all that already, on other missions with her father.

'What's more, when I join ship she's coming along as well,' he continued. He was the boss after all, but he seemed just a little truculent as he said it, as if daring our opposition. Geordie looked faintly dismayed and glanced at me for his cue.

'Why not?' I said evenly. 'Lots of room – and we could do with an extra hand in the lab from time to time. And if you can cook, Miss Campbell—'

'Clare, please. Are you Michael or Mike?'

'Mike, always.'

She smiled. 'I can cook, but I wouldn't want to be chief cookie. I'll spell whoever it is, though.'

84

Geordie was on the edge of his chair, and finally had his say. 'Have you been to sea before, Miss – er, Clare?' he asked sternly. Clare bore it equably.

'Yes, Geordie, I have – for quite long trips too. I've got all my gear and you'll believe me when you see how worn out it all is. In fact I'm much more familiar with what we're going to do than Pop is.'

Geordie was routed.

Campbell broke in impatiently at this point. 'What about the diary, Mike? You've read through it, I suppose.'

'There are interesting possibilities opening up.'

'How come?'

'The diary was written partly while Mark was with the IGY survey. Now, *he* made a record of those high-cobalt nodules, but the fact never came out in the open scientific record. In other words, he suppressed the evidence.'

Campbell seemed perturbed. 'I shouldn't think your brother would do a thing like that,' he said stiffly. And that told me that any reservations he may have about Mark stemmed from Mark's personal affiliation with Clare, and that he had never plumbed the depths of Mark's personality. I would have to be careful, but it was time to bring things out into the open.

I said, 'Can you think of any other explanation?'

He shook his head. 'I'm at a loss what to make of it – I have been giving it some thought already. Are you serious when you said your brother would do a thing like that? He struck me as a very fine scientist.'

'Mark was never too scrupulous,' I said. 'He wanted something from you and he was showing his cleanest face.'

Campbell didn't like that. My open distrust of Mark offended his sense of fitness. Brothers should be brotherly and blood is thicker than water. I suspected he had a strong puritan streak in him, inherited from his no doubt calvinistic ancestors. He said, almost hostilely, 'There's nothing to be gained by running down your brother – especially as he can't answer back.'

I said softly, 'You should study the Bible, Mr Campbell.

There are a few stories in the Book that are very illuminating. Read about Cain and Abel, or Esau and Jacob. There's no hard and fast rule that brothers should like one another – and lots of villains have innocent kinfolk.'

He was acid. 'Well, I suppose you knew him best. I never had any reason to doubt him while he was in my employ.' He caught Clare's eye and faltered just a little. 'Must admit that personally. . . .'

Clare's face was calm, showing only a polite interest, but her jawline caught my notice.

I said, 'We must discuss this. We're faced with a problem put to us by Mark and we can only solve it by understanding him and the way he worked. Geordie can support some of what I may have to tell you.' I had them all riveted now. 'Let me tell you something that I'll bet you don't know – Mark was kicked out of the IGY for falsifying figures. That was just before he joined your company.'

'I didn't know that and I don't think I believe it.'

'It's true,' I said. 'Professor Jarvis, my old boss at the Institute, told me about it – and Geordie heard him too. I think he got hold of those nodules at the time, found out their value, and decided to keep the knowledge to himself. Then he moved in on you – and he was using you.'

Campbell was affronted. 'Using *me*!'

'You had the money he wanted for an expedition. He couldn't show you the nodules because you'd want to know where he got them. And that was by stealing them from the people who paid his salary.'

Campbell began to look baffled. 'He never showed me anything. He talked a good story though.'

'That's right. He had a lot of theory and you nearly fell for it. If you had, he'd have wasted his time and your money fossicking round the Pacific for six months and then his "theory" would have led him to a spectacular find. You see, he knew where those nodules came from. Anyway you'd be in the chips and he'd be both rich and vindicated – the great scientist.'

Campbell nodded unwillingly.

I said, 'But something went wrong. You had your run-in with Suarez-Navarro and found yourself strapped for ready funds. You couldn't finance his expedition, and so he left you flat because you were of no further use to him. Isn't that so?'

There was silence while Campbell digested all that.

'All right, you've made your point – don't drive it into the ground. Assuming something like that is possible – what do you suggest we do now?'

'First, another point. You wondered how Suarez-Navarro came into the nodule hunt. I think Mark may have tried the same ploy on them. In fact I think he and Norgaard were waiting in Tahiti for the ship that's being fitted out right now, and that ties everything in squarely together.'

'All right, let's assume that too. We're safer the more we can see into the forest, I suppose.' Campbell was still shaken by what I'd said about Mark. 'What do we do next?'

'Well, we could find out where Mark's IGY ship dredged and drop ours in the same places. But I don't think it will be any of the sites they actually surveyed or this would have come out already – Mark wasn't the only one doing assays. No, I think it was a trial site, one they weren't serious about, and probably didn't even make a record of, though we could check it out.'

We all sat in gloom for a while. The faint drift of music changed tempo and a woman began to sing with the trio, and I turned to watch her. Her voice was nice but she was no world-beater. Her body was better than her voice and set off admirably by a revealing gown. For a moment, lost in something not at all of our troubled world, I relaxed and only caught the end of a sentence directed at me by Clare Campbell.

'. . . to ask you a question – if I'm not distracting you, Mike?' Her voice was calm but when I turned back I saw an ironic sparkle in her eyes.

'Sorry, yes?' I said.

'You say that Mark was kicked off the ship for falsifying figures – but which figures? Not the high-cobalt nodule assay because, as you said, that news hasn't broken yet. So he must have falsified *other* figures which caught him out. What were they and why did he cook them – could they matter?'

That was something I hadn't thought of, and it was a stopper. I said, 'Mark was always a fast boy with a red herring. He cheated once in his school exams, and this is how he did it. He was called into the headmaster's office just before an exam and the master happened to be out of the room. On the desk was a pile of question papers. Mark played it cleverly – he didn't take one, he took six. Then he made a copy for himself and passed the six papers to other boys – anonymously.'

Campbell said, 'I don't get it.'

'It's simple. He told me about it afterwards – he always knew *I* wouldn't tell tales. He reckoned that if the thing blew up in his face he'd see to it that the six papers were all found – in the possession of other boys. He'd be in the clear. It wasn't found out and he got away with it. Now what if he's done something like that here?'

Campbell looked frustrated. He was supposed to be a man with acumen, after all. 'I may be dumb, but I still don't get it.'

'Look,' I said patiently. 'Mark has located a deposit of high-cobalt nodules and he's busy suppressing the information. He knows that if he's found out he's not only in disgrace but he's lost a potential fortune. So – knowing Mark – I'd guess that he'd toss out a few red herrings. He'd falsify some more figures to confuse the issue, and he'd probably revise all estimates upwards. It would add slightly to the risk of discovery, but if it was found out, as it evidently was, he'd be only another glory-hunting scientist, rather too optimistic and looking for professional praise. No one would suspect that one set of figures was wrong for another reason. They may not ever have caught it.' I laughed humourlessly. 'I'll bet that *all* Mark's findings were junked, anyway. None of his colleagues would trust his figures after that.'

'Why didn't they tell the world about it – to protect people like Pop?' asked Clare a little bitterly.

'I think they would feel that commercial folk like your dad can take care of themselves,' I said. 'They're mostly too gentlemanly.'

Campbell was looking at me in wonder, Geordie in silent assent of my assessment. 'Did Mark really have a mind like that?' Campbell said.

I saw that he was hurt; his pride in his judgement of men had been badly undermined. But then, he'd been taken in by an expert. 'He had a mind that would make a corkscrew look like a straight edge. You don't have to take my word for it, either. Geordie can tell you some tales.'

Geordie nodded. 'Aye, the boy was a twister. He caused the family a lot of grief.'

'All right. Supposing that Mark was as machiavellian as you make him out to be, it seems we're back where we started – all we have to go on is the diary.'

'And that's going to be a devil of a job, sorting out his scribbles. I can make a fair stab at the science, but the rest is a teaser.'

'We'll discuss it over dinner,' Campbell decided, to my secret relief.

We chewed over the diary and the dinner together. The dinner was digestible which was more than any of us could say for the diary. Clare asked if she could have it for bedside reading. 'I like that sort of thing,' she said. 'Puzzles, jigsaws.' And I also thought that she might have felt that her own knowledge of Mark's odd mind might be useful.

'You're welcome,' I told her. 'I want a break from it.' I was pleased that as the evening wore on she seemed to lose some of her reserve and her mouth began to lose its tight-locked caution. We were at the coffee stage when a waiter came up to the table. 'Are one of you gentlemen Mr Trevelyan?'

'I am.'

'There's a lady in the foyer asking to see you.'

I looked around blankly. 'I don't know anyone in Panama.'

Campbell looked up at the waiter. 'An old lady or a young lady?'

'Oh, a young lady, sir.'

Campbell's eyes twinkled. 'If I were you I'd be in the foyer now. What's stopping you?'

I got up. 'It's probably a mistake,' I said, thinking that it almost certainly wasn't. 'Excuse me.'

There were several people in the foyer including more than one young lady, but no one approached me. I crossed to the desk and said, 'My name's Trevelyan. I understand someone wants me.'

The clerk pointed with his pen, indicating that I should come into the office behind the desk. The young lady was waiting all right, and I did know her, in a way; she was the singer who had been entertaining us in the lounge.

'I'm Trevelyan. You wanted to speak to me?'

She was nervous, I could see that. She was rather slight and looked, at close quarters, a trifle undernourished, with hollows under her dark eyes and a skin more weathered than tanned. There was an appealing quality about her – I think the best word would be winsome. I was intrigued.

'I'm sorry to trouble you – I saw your name in the register – but I wondered if you were any relation of Mark Trevelyan? From Tahiti?'

'He was my brother,' I said. 'I'm Michael. Obviously you know Mark.' I didn't know if she knew of his death and I felt it would be unkind to throw it at her without warning.

She nodded, gripping her hands together. 'Yes, I knew him, very well. Have you just come from England?'

'Yes.'

'Do you know his – wife?'

'Yes.'

'Did she get the suitcase I sent?'

I stared at her now. 'Well, I'm damned! I thought you were a man. So you are P. Nelson.'

She smiled and some of the tension left her. 'Yes – Paula Nelson. Then the case did arrive all right?'

'It arrived, thank you,' I said. I didn't say that it had been stolen immediately afterwards because I didn't know just where this girl stood in the complexity of Mark's affairs. But I could try to find out.

'Miss Nelson, what about coming into the lounge and having a drink with me and my friends? We're all of us interested in Mark and in what he was doing out here.'

She shook her head. 'Oh, I couldn't do that, Mr Trevelyan. I'm one of the hired help around here – we're not supposed to drink with the customers. The manager says this isn't a clip joint.' Her nervousness now seemed to include a fear of the manager's imminent wrath.

I said gently, 'Perhaps we could go somewhere else, if you've the time. I would like to talk to you.'

She looked at her watch. 'I could spare half an hour. Then I've got another stint in the lounge. If you'll wait while I get my wrap?'

'It'll be a pleasure.'

I thought of sending a message back to the others but decided against it. I didn't have to account to them for all my actions. We went to a small bar a little way down the street, I bought a couple of drinks and we settled down in an alcove. The bar was deserted except for a solitary drinker. I said, 'You're an American, aren't you?'

'Yes. And you're from – Cornwall. You talk the same way Mark did. I used to tease him about that sometimes.'

Which of course put their relationship on a firmer footing.

'Where did you meet him?'

'In Tahiti. I was working a little joint in Papeete. Mark used to come in with his sidekick, and we got pretty – friendly.'

'Who was his sidekick?'

'A Swedish guy, Sven someone. But this was, oh, maybe two years ago when we first met.'

About the time he left Campbell, I calculated. I said, 'I'm interested in how Mark came to die. Can you tell me anything about it – if it doesn't distress you too much.'

'Oh, that's all right,' she said, but it was a tremulous voice. 'I can't tell you a lot. He died of appendicitis out in the Paumotus – didn't you know that?'

'Yes – but how did you know?'

'I didn't believe it at first, but they let me see the death certificate.'

'Who are "they"? Who told you in the first place?'

'A schooner came in with the news. And I went down to the Government bureau to see the proof. You see, I thought he might have – just – gone away.'

'Did the doctor come to Papeete himself, the one who operated on Mark?'

She shook her head. 'Not much point, was there? I mean, it's over two hundred miles and he's the only doctor out there. He wouldn't leave just to bring the news back.'

This clashed with Kane's story; according to him the doctor had dealt with the certificate and the authorities. Or had he? I thought back to what Kane had said – that he and his partner, Hadley, had left it all to the doctor. Perhaps it only meant sending the papers back on the next convenient transport.

I said, 'Did you know the men on the schooner?'

She was silent for a bit and then said, 'Why are you asking me all these questions, Mr Trevelyan?'

'I could say out of natural interest in the death of my only brother, but I won't,' I said deliberately. 'I think there's something very odd about the whole affair.' As I said it I suddenly wondered if she was a plant – one of the spies of Ramirez of whom Campbell so often warned me. If so I'd already dealt a hand I should rather have hidden, and I felt cold at the thought. But it was very hard to imagine this girl as a crook's agent.

'You think he was murdered, don't you?' she asked flatly.

I tightened my lips. Time for a quick decision, and I thought that I may as well continue. It was already too late to do otherwise. 'You think so too, Miss Nelson?'

There was a long pause before she nodded. 'Yes,' she whispered, and started to cry. I felt better, for some reason – she was ruining her makeup, and surely no spy would do that, not just before making a public appearance?

I let her run on for a little while, then took her hand in mine.

'You were living with Mark, weren't you?'

'Yes, I was. Oh God, I *loved* him,' she said. She was so intense, her grip tightening, that I felt I must believe her.

92

'Were you happy with him?' I asked. 'Was he good to you, Miss Nelson?'

Amazingly, a smile appeared. 'Oh, I was. Please – don't call me Miss Nelson. My name is Paula.'

'And I'm Mike.'

We were silent for a few moments, then I said, 'What really happened, Paula?'

She said, 'I suppose it all started when Sven was killed—'

'Norgaard? Killed!'

'Yes. He was found out on the reef, outside Papeete, with his head bashed in. At first everyone thought it was the sea – it comes in with tremendous force against the reef. They thought he'd been washed off his feet and had his head smashed on the rocks. Then – I don't know exactly how – they decided he'd been murdered. It was something to do with what the police surgeon found.'

I nodded grimly. 'Then what happened?'

'The police were asking questions and they came to Mark. He said he knew nothing about it, but it didn't seem to worry him.'

I took a deep breath. 'Paula, do you think that Mark killed Sven?'

She hesitated, then shook her head violently. 'No, it *couldn't* have been Mark. I know he could get very angry – even violent – but he couldn't have killed Sven. They were partners.'

I had experienced some of Mark's violence, in my younger days.

'Paula, did he ever hit you?'

She looked down at the table, nodding. 'Sometimes – but I'm hell to live with. I'm untidy and sloppy about housework. I'm—' She laughed, but the laugh broke off on a sob and tears rolled down her cheeks. I was appalled.

'What happened then?'

'Mark ran away. He ran from the police. I don't mean literally, not the day they spoke to him, but that night he disappeared from Tahiti. And then we heard that he was dead – I've already told you exactly how that was.'

'Who brought the news of his death – in that schooner?'

'It was a man called Hadley – he brought the news. He said that he and his partner had found Mark dying out in the islands.' She had the look of nervousness back, and I thought that it may have been caused by her mention of Hadley.

But I had more important things to think about. This was the break – this was the evidence that showed Kane to be a downright liar. There could have been an honest mistake about the death certificate, but not about this. Kane had told me that he and Hadley had left things to the doctor. This was the crack in his story.

I said, 'Hadley's partner – was it a man called Kane?'

'I don't know, I never met him. I knew Hadley, though; he came to visit Mark often.'

'The devil he did!' I ejaculated. This was a new development.

'Oh sure. Mark and Sven used to hire Hadley's boat and go off for weeks at a time with him.'

'You've no idea where they went, I suppose?' I said casually.

'Mark never talked to me about what he did,' she said.

'There's just one more thing, but it's very important. You said you thought Mark had been murdered. What led you to think that?'

'It was Hadley,' she said. 'He came to my place and said he wanted Mark's things. The way he talked about Mark – he was so triumphant. I didn't see any reason why he should have Mark's stuff so I gave him the air. He was mad about it but he couldn't do anything then because I had friends with me. But he scared me – he's a bad bastard. I looked at Mark's case and there wasn't anything there that would do me any good, so I sent it home to his wife. Mark talked about her to me.' There was pain in her voice. 'He talked about you too – he wasn't very nice about you.'

'I can imagine. Did Hadley try again?'

'Yes. He came and beat the living daylights out of me and searched my place but of course there wasn't anything there.'

'You mean – he beat you up?'

'Oh brother, you ought to have seen the shiner I had.' She looked at me gravely. 'You don't know much about men like Hadley, do you?'

'Not yet,' I said grimly. 'But I soon will. I'm going to catch up with that bastard.'

She laughed scornfully. 'He'd tear you in half, Mike. Be careful of him – don't come at him from the front, club him down from behind. He'd do the same to you. He's an uncivilized savage.'

I looked at this girl who talked of brawls and beatings so matter-of-factly. No wonder she had that permanently shrinking air – or perhaps it was her manner which attracted violence in the first place. 'I'll remember that.'

She sighed. 'Well, then I got real scared because I said too much. You know what I said? I said I had proof that he was lying – that Mark hadn't died the way he said. He looked at me in a real funny way and said he'd be back – with friends. So I packed a few things and got out. I stayed with someone else the rest of the night and next morning there was a trading schooner leaving for Panama at five o'clock and I was aboard by four. I kept below deck until Papeete was out of sight.'

'What was your proof, Paula?'

She said what I guessed she was going to say. 'Mark already had his appendix out. I saw the scar. He couldn't have died that way.'

'I knew about that too. Mark had his appendix out years ago.'

Paula looked at her watch and jumped to her feet. She still looked ravaged but she seemed a little calmer now. 'I have to get back.'

'Thanks, Paula. You've helped me a lot. Do you think that Hadley killed Mark and Sven Norgaard?'

'I do,' she said intensely.

'Have you any idea why he should?'

She shrugged. 'No idea – but I'm sure he did it.'

'Paula, before I leave here – will you write down what you know for me?'

'I – I guess so, Mike. I – have to be careful.'

She wouldn't come into the hotel lounge with me so I went in alone ahead of her and found Geordie sitting talking to Clare. 'Pop's gone to bed,' she said. 'It's late and he gets tired.'

'I hope Geordie's been entertaining you all right.'

'Oh yes, he's been telling me more about Mark – and you.'

I said lightly, 'I thought I felt my ears burning.'

I saw Paula join the trio. In the dim lounge lighting one could not see any trace of disarray and she began to sing in the same pleasant, husky voice. 'Nice voice she's got,' said Clare casually.

I saw they were both looking at her.

'How was your assignation?' asked Geordie.

'Interesting.'

A mischievous smile played briefly on Clare's mouth. 'We saw you escorting her out of the foyer.'

'Her name is P. Nelson,' I said. Geordie choked over his coffee.

I put Clare in the picture regarding the name, then said, 'She's had a lot to tell me, all fascinating. She thinks that Mark was murdered, and his partner Norgaard too – oh yes, he's dead. And she thinks they were both killed by Hadley, this mystery partner of Kane's. But the concensus of opinion in Tahiti seems to be that Mark killed Norgaard – that's the official police view – and that Mark died by accident while on the run. It's a hell of a mess.'

'Good God,' said Geordie. 'What's she doing here?'

'Ran away from Hadley. I'll fill you all in in the morning. I'm tired.'

It seemed an age since we had come sailing into Panama, only that morning.

Clare looked over towards Paula, who was still singing.

'How well did she know Mark?'

'Pretty well,' I said unthinkingly. 'She was another of Mark's popsies.'

And could have bitten my tongue out the moment I spoke.

5

Next morning at breakfast Campbell came down with a cable. He frowned as he read it. 'Suarez-Navarro have started to move,' he said. 'Their ship has left Darwin, bound for New Guinea.'

Geordie said, 'The Bismarck Archipelago is up that way too.'

'What's that got to do with it?'

'We forgot to tell you,' I said. 'Kane sent a cable yesterday, to Rabaul, which is in the Archipelago.'

'Kane – maybe to Ramirez, telling him where you are. Would your nodule deposit be anywhere up near Rabaul?' asked Campbell.

'There's nothing against it and a few things for it,' I said. 'Though personally I think Mark wouldn't have been so far away from where it is. But from what I could gather from the notebooks Mark was linking nodule formation with vulcanism, and there's a hell of a lot of volcanoes in that part of the world.'

'Not here?'

'Oh yes, all over the Pacific. I'm going to explain that to you when my own ideas are clearer.'

'Do you think he was right in that theory?' said Campbell.

'I don't know,' I admitted. 'It's all very theoretical. There's nothing against it in principle.'

Campbell muttered, 'When I get an unqualified answer from a scientist I suppose the world will be coming to an end. Now, what's all this about the girl last night? Clare's told me a little.'

So I filled them all in and we sat back, aghast and disturbed by the implications in Paula's story. We were running into something which got steadily nastier. Campbell approved of my wanting her evidence written down, preferably legally

97

attested, though I wasn't sure if she would commit herself so far.

Clare said, changing the subject, 'Mike, I've been giving the diary some thought and especially the drawings, and I think I've come up with something. Can we all go up to Pop's suite after breakfast?'

Geordie assented reluctantly. He was anxious to get back to his ship, but we persuaded him that all would be well for a couple of hours more. 'They're good lads, plenty to do and they know where you are if they want you,' I said firmly. So after breakfast we found ourselves seated round a coffee table in the suite, already sweating gently in spite of the air conditioning, and with the sunshine of Panama calling to us through the open windows. Clare laid out the diary and tracings in front of us.

'I've been working backwards, from where we know Mark was, to see if we can identify any more of the drawings. The very last one is what looks like a monocle, and I think I know what it is – but only because we *do* know where Mark was. I think it means Tahiti.'

'How the hell can it mean Tahiti?' said Campbell.

'They're also known as the Society Islands. And a monocle is the epitome of the uppercrust, the "society" bloke. It's lean, but could it do?' She looked anxiously for my opinion.

I laughed. 'As well as anything. Crude but effective. Go on.'

'Numbers 31 and 30 I can't see at all – perhaps Geordie might, if he knows the area well. One's a cow and one's a – well, it's this.' She pointed to an object like an irregular, flattened semicircle standing on a flat base. It was connected to the cow with the word '*OR*', and made no sense at all to any of us.

'Then we come to these. *The Fair Goddess* and *The Disappearing Trick*, a woman and an eagle.'

I interrupted her. 'They are the two that come immediately before his high cobalt assay figures. I think they may be crucial.'

'Good,' she said briskly. 'Because there are lots more

possibilities. I've been thinking about the woman. I think she could be La France – you know, Uncle Sam for America, John Bull for Britain and this female – Marianne – for France. You see her in newspaper cartoons.'

Campbell looked at the drawing intently. 'You may have something there. This thing on her head is the Cap of Liberty, isn't it? What's the extent of French territory in the Pacific?'

'French Oceania – about a million square miles of it, including Tahiti, Bora-Bora, the Tuamotus, the Marquesas, the Austral Islands. You'd have to get it down much closer than that.'

'The Marianas Islands,' said Geordie and he sounded very glum. 'The Marianas Trench.'

Clare looked thrilled. 'Where are they?'

'A long way off, too far for comfort. Almost alongside the Philippines,' I said. 'It just can't be there, or else why was Mark so far away from it? I don't believe it.'

But Geordie had thought of something else. 'Suarez-Navarro's ship is heading that way.'

We looked at one another in dismay. 'Just doesn't feel right,' I said, only because I didn't want it to be. 'We want something down this way.'

Campbell said, 'What's this about a goddess? Marianne isn't one.'

'Let's go through a list of goddesses,' I suggested. 'There's Venus for a start. Is there a Venus Island?'

Geordie grinned. 'I've heard of the Good Ship Venus, but not an island. Wait a minute, though – there's a Venus Point in Tahiti.'

'That sounds promising,' said Campbell.

'It's too close ashore – and all round there has been dredged.'

'Not so promising,' said Campbell glumly, 'but we'll keep it in mind.'

'Let's carry on with the goddess list,' said Clare. 'What about Aphrodite?'

We all thought about that. 'Nothing doing,' said Geordie finally.

'It could be a French name,' said Campbell.

I was brutal about it. 'Or a Polynesian name. Or a Polynesian goddess.'

'Good grief,' said Campbell, 'we're getting nowhere fast.'

We ran through the pantheon and couldn't even make a start on the Polynesian tribal deities without a single degree in anthropology amongst us. We switched our combined brains to the problem of the eagle, got nowhere, and came back to La France. Clare gazed fiercely at the drawings. 'All right, one last try. Let's go through it all once more.'

We all groaned.

'Venus.'

'Tahiti,' muttered Campbell, whose attention was waning.

'Demeter.'

Still nothing doing.

'Athena.'

Campbell said, 'I think this whole whacky idea is wrong. Let's pack it up.'

Clare gave a shout of laughter. 'I've got it – she's not La France at all, she's Athena, the goddess of justice. Mark used "fair" in the sense of "fair play".'

'Not that he knew much about that,' Geordie said.

'What about the Cap of Liberty?' I asked.

'It's not – it's a Roman helmet. She ought to have a spear too.'

'But Athena wasn't a Roman,' objected Campbell. 'She was a Greek goddess.'

I said, 'The Roman equivalent was Minerva – what about that?'

Geordie thumped the table and burst out laughing. 'My God! I think that's it – I should have seen it before. *Récife de Minerve*, of course!'

Campbell said, 'You mean there is such a place?'

I was struggling with a memory. I'd read about the place and there was something very out of whack about it, but I couldn't recall what it was. Geordie couldn't stop laughing. 'There's been a shipwreck on it. Oh, this is too damn funny.'

Campbell rubbed his hands, his interest rekindled. 'Now

we're getting somewhere – where is it? Obviously down this way?'

'Down south of the Tuamotus,' said Geordie.

'Is it worth a trip?' Campbell asked me. 'You're the expert here.'

I thought that it was only a remote possibility that we'd hit on the right spot on our very first guess, and that there'd probably be a lot of false alarms on the way, unless some much more concrete evidence came up; but on the other hand I didn't want the expedition to founder through lack of either activity or enthusiasm – and we had to start somewhere. 'It could have possibilities,' I said, voicing a little of my reservation. 'It partly depends on where it is, which is what Geordie's going to tell us.'

'Are you kidding?' said Geordie, still spluttering over his private joke. 'Nobody – not even the Royal Navy – knows where Minerva is.'

There was a dead silence. Campbell broke it. 'What the hell do you mean by that?'

'I mean this,' said Geordie, suddenly sober. 'The Navy looked for it but couldn't find it. I suppose it's all in the Pacific Islands *Pilot* – I'd have to look – but there's an account of it in a book I've got on board.'

'But what is it?' Clare asked.

'Just what it says. *Récife de Minerve*. Minerva Reef. It's a hidden shoal.'

Geordie left us to go down to *Esmerelda*. Apart from fetching the book he was anxious to know if all was well, and to supervise the beginning of the restocking for sea. He also had to arrange for a cabin for Clare, which I knew would mean a little crowding up for someone else. We agreed that we might as well get on with things, and that all being well we should be able to sail within a day or so; impatience was in the air. I decided to try and have another word with Paula, who had left a note for me, containing her address. I had another idea that I wanted to try out on her.

I used the phone in the foyer and got her at once. 'Paula, it's Mike. I'd like to talk to you again.'

'Sure,' she said sleepily, and I guessed that late nights singing meant late mornings lying in. 'When – now?'

'If I can.'

'Okay. I'll see you in that little bar up the street.'

She was waiting for me, sitting at the same table. 'Hi,' she said. 'What's on your mind?'

I ordered coffee for both of us. She looked fresh and decidedly less tense this morning, and had obviously decided that I was an ally – as I had concluded about her.

'Hadley and people like him are on my mind. You're sure you don't remember a man called Kane?'

She shook her head firmly.

'Or Ramirez – ever hear of him?'

That drew a blank too. I said, 'Look, how well do you know Tahiti – especially Papeete?'

'Pretty well. I was there a long time, Mike.'

I rubbed my chin. 'I don't know it well at all. And I certainly don't know Hadley. I could pass him on the street without a second glance. What I need is a pair of eyes.'

She said in a small voice, 'You want me to go back to Papeete?'

I nodded. 'But not without an escort or a backup. Scared of Hadley?'

'I'll say I am. I don't mind admitting it.'

I said, 'Paula, I'm here on a small ship crewed by the toughest mob outside of the Mafia – but straight. Most of them are ex-Commandoes and anyone of them could take Hadley with one arm tied behind his back. We're leaving tomorrow, most likely, to sail to Tahiti. If you come with us I'll assign two of them as your permanent bodyguard when we get there. If Hadley tried anything he'll learn something he never knew about dirty fighting, and probably end up with a broken back, or in gaol.'

I thought that having her on board would be tricky with Kane around, but she said they had never met and it was worth the risk. If I left her behind I might never have another chance to use her.

'You'll have company, by the way – female company, if

you're thinking about that. The girl we were with last night – she's coming too.'

She bit her lip. 'Oh Mike, I'd be scared. Besides, I'm on contract here, though it's up in a couple of weeks. I don't want to run out on a contract. Things like that get about in my business.'

I said, 'If it's money you're worried about, we'll pay all your expenses and you'll get a bonus too. Hell, we can buy out your contract.'

'I'm not thinking of money. You're really going to find out what happened to Mark, aren't you?'

'I am,' I said definitely.

She thought for a moment, then sat back and looked determined.

'Then I'll come. Mark was the only man I've ever loved – and I think he loved me, a little. If he was killed I'd like to see his killer caught.'

'Good girl! Look, why not come over on a cruise ship – do they go from here to Tahiti? Can you find out?'

'Wait a minute – I'll see if I can find out anything.'

It was five minutes.

'There's a smallish cruise ship, the *Eastern Sun*, coming through here but not for a few weeks. It'll stop at Papeete. I can get a cabin – and I might even get a job for the trip, which would save you cash. But it's a long time off yet.'

That would suit me. I thought we would be a few days before we could really be sure of leaving, and then might be dredging or searching for several weeks around Minerva Reef, wherever that was. I got the date of the *Eastern Sun*'s arrival in Papeete and promised Paula that we would be there before her, so that she would not be alone. 'I don't want to see you out of pocket,' I went on. 'I'll pay your fare and expenses. If you get a paid job you can let me have it back. Do you have a bank?'

She told me and I said, 'I'll transfer enough to your account. I'm grateful, Paula. I'm glad to have you on our team; and you don't have to break your contract.'

'There's more to this than just Mark's death, isn't there?' she said shrewdly.

'A lot more. I'll tell you about it in Papeete, perhaps after we've found out more still.' A girl like Clare Campbell would have demanded a much greater share of knowledge before committing herself, but Paula seemed accustomed to playing subsidiary roles. As we said goodbye I wondered how in hell Mark could have attracted such widely disparate women, though they had one thing more than their sex in common. Both seemed determined and courageous, and they were both worthy of a better man than Mark in their lives.

I went back to the hotel slowly, looking at shops and enjoying the exotic street scenes around me. I lunched alone, not finding any of the others in, but presently I saw Clare and her father arriving, and soon after we were joined by Geordie carrying a book. Over cold drinks we got down to business once more.

The book Geordie had brought from the ship was a copy of Bill Robinson's *To The Great Southern Sea*.

'Here's the bit. I've looked up the *Pilot* too, but I left that on board for later. I've been rereading Robinson, knowing that we'd be sailing down this way. He sailed from the Galapagos to Mangareva in his schooner, and here is what he has to say about Minerva. This was published in 1957, not long ago, by the way.'

He passed the book to Clare, indicating a paragraph. She started to read silently but her father said, 'For God's sake read it aloud so we'll all know what's going on.'

So Clare read to us:

'Approaching Mangareva we passed close to Minerva, one of those shoals of doubtful position and uncertain existence known as "vigias". Vigias are the bane of navigators, for one is never sure where they are, or if they are there at all. According to the Sailing Directions, which neglect to state how she got her name, there seems to be no doubt about Minerva's authenticity. A ship named the *Sir George Grey* was assumed lost there in 1865, although the British Navy failed to locate a reef there a few years later. In 1890 the German bark *Erato* saw the shoal. It was again seen breaking heavily in 1920 ten miles from the position reported by the *Erato*.

'To my great disappointment, the *maraamu* spoiled our chances of looking for Minerva. For although the wind had gone down to a fresh breeze and we arrived at the vicinity at midday, there was still a big sea running, which broke in an unruly fashion. It was impossible to distinguish breakers caused by a shoal from those left in the wake of the *maraamu*. We steered a course that took us ten miles to the north of the northernmost reported position of the errant shoal, kept a vigilant look-out, but saw nothing.'

Clare stopped reading and Campbell said, 'Well, I'm damned. Do you mean to tell me that while spacemen are whirling round in orbit and we're on the verge of going to other planets that there's a piddling little shoal like this that hasn't been located?'

'That's right,' said Geordie. 'There are lots of them.'

'It's disgusting,' said Campbell, more accustomed to precise locations on land. 'But if Mark found it we can find it.'

'If he did. I doubt it,' I said. 'If an IGY survey ship had found Minerva they'd have reported it, and they didn't. But it doesn't mean they didn't dredge around there,' I added hastily into three disappointed faces. 'You heard what Robinson said about it. You'd probably only be able to see it in a flat calm, with the tides right.'

'Robinson took damn good care to steer well clear of it,' snorted Campbell. 'Ten miles north of its reported position, indeed.'

'He was a wise man and a good seaman,' said Geordie. 'He didn't want to lose his ship. It might be a shifting shoal and if you can't see where it is it's a good idea to keep clear of it. I'll do the same, believe me.'

Once again they all looked at me – the reluctant expert.

'The conditions I'm thinking of are possible,' I said. 'We

have to make a start somewhere, and it would be fun to find it, if we can. Why not?'

One more thing happened before we left Panama. Kane came to see me.

We had ostensibly treated him as just one of the crew, and he'd done his work well and was not a bad seaman. But Geordie had only agreed to take him as far as Panama and now we were waiting to see what his next step would be.

He came down to my cabin one morning and said, 'Mr Trevelyan, could I have a word?'

'Come in.' He looked fit again. Without trying to show it, I had kept clear of him on the voyage, finding it intolerably creepy to have the possible murderer of Mark underfoot, but I couldn't avoid some contacts and this was one I had almost been hoping for.

'What is it?'

'You're carrying on this research stuff, aren't you?'

'That's right. As you know, we're leaving in a day's time.'

'There was a message waiting for me here in Panama from my partner, Jim Hadley. Jim's down in New Guinea and he says he can't come up this way for a while. Now, I know you only promised to bring me as far as here, and I'm grateful, my word I am. But I wondered if I could stick with her a bit longer – you'll need a man in my berth, anyway. Maybe you'll be putting in some place that's nearer for Jim – Tahiti, maybe? That 'ud suit us both.'

I said, 'I don't see a problem. You're welcome to stay on as far as I'm concerned, if it's all right with the skipper.'

'Gee, thanks, Mr Trevelyan. I know I keep asking favours and you help out every time.'

'There's no favour. We will need a man – you work well and you earn your keep. But it's up to Mr Wilkins, mind.'

'Too right. I'll check with him. Thanks again.'

I passed the word to Geordie to accept the expected offer, and told Campbell about it. 'Right, we'll keep him under our thumb,' he said. 'Not much chance of him knowing where we're going if *we* don't know, and he can't pass the word on from out there.'

So friend Kane stayed on with us. And the next day we sailed on a voyage of uncertain duration to an unknown destination which might, or might not, exist.

Chapter Four

1

According to local knowledge the *Récife de Minerve* was nothing but a legend, and not an uncommon one at that. The *Pilot*'s preface on vigias showed that there were probably masses of them around, but certainly it said that in 1880 HMS *Alert* had searched the area in which it was said to lie, without any success. And she wasn't the only one – several ships had looked for it, some had found it – but it was never quite in the same spot twice.

We left Panama and made good time at first but in a day or so found ourselves becalmed in a sea of glass. We stuck it for twenty-four hours and then went ahead under power. Campbell didn't like clichés about painted ships on painted oceans, especially after I told him another legend concerning the ship that had floated in the Gulf of Panama for forty years until she rotted and fell apart.

Using the engines was a pity because there would be so much less fuel for station-keeping and dredging, but in Campbell's view time was as precious as fuel, and I couldn't disagree with him. I had Paula to think of. Campbell had sent a spate of cables to his ferrets, advising them that they must keep their eyes on the movements of Suarez-Navarro's ship, and once we were at sea he became nervous. I think he was unused to being cut off from the telephone. He haunted the radio, but though he needed news he half didn't want to get it, and he certainly didn't want to answer. We had a powerful radio telephone that he had insisted on installing; it was an electronic shout that could cover the Pacific. But he didn't want us to use it for fear the Suarez-Navarro would monitor the broadcasts.

News did finally come that they had dropped anchor in Port Moresby, in Papua, and, as in Darwin, were sitting tight and doing nothing. Campbell was as worried by their inactivity as he would have been if they had been constantly on the move.

We all felt better when *Esmerelda* surged forward under the impact of her engine. She forged through the placid seas at a steady nine knots to where we would catch the southeast trade wind and find perfect sailing weather. It wasn't long before we picked up a southerly wind and we headed south-west under fore-and-aft sails only, *Esmerelda* heeling until the foaming sea lapped at the lee rail. As the days went by the wind shifted easterly until the day came when we knew we were in the true trade winds. We hoisted the big square sails on the foremast and *Esmerelda* picked up her heels.

These were Kane's home waters and, while we didn't depend on him, he was free with his advice on weather conditions to be expected. 'A bit further on we'll get revolving storms,' he said. 'Not to worry – they're not very big – but my word they're fast. On you like a flash, so you've got to keep your eyes peeled.'

Campbell turned out to be a poor sailor and spent a great deal of time on his bunk regretting that ships were ever invented. It was unusual for him not to be the master of the situation, and he said he felt like a spare wheel on deck, surrounded by men who were doing all sorts of mysterious things fast and well without his guidance. He must have been hell to his mining engineers on land.

Clare, on the other hand, was a good sailor. She worked hard on deck, wearing the battered sailing gear she had promised us and a healthy tan, and was greatly appreciated by all the crew, who had found her an unexpected bonus on this leg of the voyage. She did help cook and kept watch like the rest of us, but she also absorbed the books in our small library like blotting paper, becoming especially interested in Geordie's collection of small boat voyages, many of which dealt with the Pacific.

One evening she and I talked together and I got another look at my brother, through Clare's eyes.

It was one of those incredible nights you find in the tropics. There was a waning moon and the stars sparkled like a handful of diamonds cast across the sky. The wind sang in the rigging and the water talked and chuckled to *Esmerelda*, and a white-foamed wake with patches of phosphorescence stretched astern.

I was standing in the bows when Clare joined me. She looked across the sea-path of the moon and said, 'I wish this voyage would go on forever.'

'It won't. There's a limit even to the size of the Pacific.'

'When will we get to Minerva?'

'Perhaps never – we've got to find it first. But we'll be in the vicinity in a week if the weather keeps up.'

'I hope we were right about that drawing,' she said. 'Sometimes I wish I hadn't tried interpreting them. What if we're wrong?'

'We'll just have to think of something else. Figuring out Mark's mental processes was never an easy job at the best of times.'

She smiled. 'I know.'

'How well did you know Mark?'

'Sometimes I thought I knew him pretty well,' she said. 'In the end I found I didn't know him at all.' She paused. 'Pop doesn't think much of what you've said about Mark – about his honesty, I mean. Pop thought well of him – mostly.'

I said, 'Mark had many faces. He was working for your father and he wanted something out of him so he showed his cleanest, brightest face. Your father never really knew Mark.'

'I know. Speaking figuratively and with due respect to your mother, Mark was a thorough-going bastard.'

I was startled and at the same time unsurprised. 'What happened?'

She said reflectively. 'I was a bit bitchy the other night and then you pulled me up with a jerk when you called that singer "just another of Mark's popsies". You see, I suppose I could be regarded as "just another of Mark's popsies". It

110

was the usual thing. It must happen a thousand times a day somewhere in the world, but when it happens to you it hurts. I went overboard for Mark. I was all wrapped up in rosy dreams – he was so damned attractive.'

'When he wanted to be. He could switch the charm on and off like a light.'

'He let it happen, damn him,' she said. 'He could have stopped it at any time, but the devil let it happen. I was hearing the distant chimes of wedding bells when I discovered he was already married – maybe not happily – but married.'

I said gently, 'He was using you too, to get at your father. It's not surprising behaviour from Mark.'

'I know that now. I wish to God I'd known it then. Mark and I had a lot of fun in those days, and I thought it was going to go on forever. Do you remember—?'

'Meeting you in Vancouver? Oh yes.'

'I wondered then, why you didn't seem to get on. You seemed so cold. I thought you were the rotter, and he said things. . . .'

'Never mind all that. What happened?'

She shrugged. 'Nothing – nothing at all. And I found out at about the same time that Pop was having his troubles with Suarez-Navarro, so I didn't tell him, or anyone – though I think he guessed something. Have you noticed that he only praises Mark as a scientist, not as a person?'

'And then Mark vanished.'

'That's right. He'd gone and I never saw him again.' She looked ahead over the bows. 'And now he's dead – his body lies somewhere out there – but he's still pushing people around. We're all being pushed around by Mark, even now – do you know that? You and me, Pop and the Suarez-Navarro crowd, your friend Geordie and all your commando pals – all being manipulated by a dead man with a long arm.'

'Take it easy,' I said. She sounded terribly bitter. 'Mark's not pushing anyone. We all know what we're doing, and we're doing it because we want to. Mark is dead and that's an end to him.'

It was time to change the subject. I used the standard approach.

'Tell me about yourself, Clare. What do you do? When did your mother die?'

'When I was six.'

'Who brought you up? Your father was away a lot, wasn't he?'

She laughed. 'Oh, I've been everywhere with Pop. He brought me up.'

'That must have been some experience.'

'Oh, it was fun. I had to spend a lot of time at boarding schools, of course, but I always went to Pop during the vacations. We weren't often at home though – we were mostly away. Sometimes on a skiing holiday, sometimes to Europe or Australia or South America during the longer vacations. I was always with Pop.'

'You're well travelled.'

'It was tricky at times though. Pop has his ups and downs – he hasn't always been rich. Sometimes we had money and sometimes we didn't, but Pop always looked after me. I went to good schools, and to college. It was only last year that I found out that once, when Pop was on a crest, he'd put aside a fund for me. Even when he was busted he never touched it, no matter how much he needed money.'

'He sounds a fine man.'

'I love him,' she said simply. 'When the Suarez-Navarro mob put the knife into him it was the first time I was old enough to understand defeat. I got down to studying stenography and so on, and he made me his confidential secretary when he couldn't afford to hire one. It was the least I could do – he'd lost faith in everybody and he had to have someone around he could trust. Although I didn't feel too trusting myself just about that time.'

'He seems to have survived.'

'He's tough,' she said proudly. 'You can't keep Pop down, and you can bet that in the end Suarez-Navarro will be sorry they ever heard of him. It's happened to him before and he's always bounced back. I still work for him. I—'

'Whatever it is, say it.'

'I had you checked out in London, when you were preparing for this trip. I didn't want Pop stung again. Besides. . . .'

'My name was Trevelyan?'

'Oh, I'm so sorry,' she said. 'But I had to. You checked out fine, you know.' For the first time since I'd known her she was a little shy. She went on. 'That's enough about the Campbells. What about the Trevelyans – about you?'

'What about me? I'm just a plodding scientist.'

We both laughed. Plodding certainly didn't describe this airy swooping progress, and it eased her tension.

'Most scientists seem to be looking up these days, not down.'

'Ah, space stuff,' I said.

'You don't seem very enthusiastic.'

'I'm not. I think it's a waste of money. The Americans are spending thirty billions of dollars to put man into space; in the end it could cost ten times that much. That works out at about twenty thousand dollars for every square mile of airless lunar surface. You could get cheaper and better land on earth and if you poured that much money into the sea the returns would be even better. I think the sea is our new frontier, not space.'

She smiled at the missionary note in my voice. 'So that's why you became an oceanographer.'

'I suppose so – I was always in love with the sea.'

'And Mark? What made him one? I don't think I've ever known two brothers more different.'

I said, 'Mark was eaten up with ambition. How he got that way I don't know – I think some of it was jealousy of me, though God knows what he had to be jealous about. When my father died Mark seemed to go wild; mother couldn't control him. Since she died I've had nothing to do with him – he went his way and I mine. It hasn't always been easy having a brother like that in my line of work. People sometimes confuse us – to my detriment.'

'And his advantage.'

'Why, thank you, lady,' I said and bowed; and our relationship suddenly took a step forward.

'Trevelyan; that's Cornish, isn't it? Are you Cornish?'

'Yes. We're descended from the Phoenician and Carthaginian tin traders. Hannibal is still a popular name in Cornwall, though not in our family, thank God.'

'You're kidding.'

'No, I'm not. It's a fact.'

We had a long, relaxed and easy conversation that night, talking about everything under the sun and moon, and by the time she went back to her cabin I had a better idea about both Clare and her father. Campbell was a difficult man to assess, not very forthcoming about himself and sticking to business most of the time. This talk with Clare had given me something of his background and I felt more than ever that he was a man to be trusted.

And then there was Clare herself. I found myself wondering if she could bring herself to trust another Trevelyan, or whether Mark had soured her on Trevelyans for life. I mentally chalked up another stroke against Mark. I spent a long time thinking about Clare before I turned in.

And then I suddenly thought of what she had said about Mark – of his dead hand pushing people around like pawns on a chessboard. It was true; everything we had done or were doing stemmed from Mark and his character. It was as though Mark had been a showman and we were his puppets as his skeletal hands pulled the strings. It was a shuddery thought to go to sleep on.

2

We entered a region of small revolving storms as Kane had predicted. They ranged from mere waterspouts, ten yards across, to monsters fifty feet in diameter. These squalls provided exhilarating sailing as long as care was taken. *Esmerelda* would be foaming along beneath a brilliant blue sky when the horizon would darken and within minutes the water would be dark and wind lashed, and when the storm had gone there would be rainbows plunging into the sea and the faithful trade wind would pick up again, driving us deeper into the heart of the Pacific towards the south-east corner of French Oceania.

Sixteen days after leaving Panama Geordie figured out the midday sights and announced, 'We're nearly there. We'll enter the search area this afternoon.'

We had decided not to tell the crew too much, and so Geordie gathered them and merely said that I wanted to stooge about looking for a particular sort of water condition, but that everyone was to be on the watch for shoals. Everyone knew there wasn't much land out here and his request may have sounded strange, but they willingly organized for extra eyes on each watch, and we had a man up the foremast with binoculars a lot of the time. To my mind that was just a token that a search was in progress as I didn't think they'd spot anything, but for everyone else it perked up interest. We arranged for some dredging, to give the teams practice as we went along.

I was in the chart room early the next morning with Campbell and Geordie, going over the chart and the *Pilot*.

I said, 'The *Erato* spotted Minerva here – that was in 1890. In 1920 another ship placed Minerva here, stretching east-north-east for two miles. As Robinson points out, there's a difference of ten miles.'

Campbell said, 'It's strange that there should only have been two sightings in thirty years.'

'Not so strange,' said Geordie. 'These waters are pretty quiet, and they're quieter now that power has taken over from sail. There's no need for anyone to come here just for commerce.' He put his hand on the chart. 'There are several possibilities. One of these sightings was right and the other wrong – take your pick of which was which. Or they were both wrong. Or they were both right and Minerva is a moving shoal – which happens sometimes.'

'Or they were both wrong – and Minerva is still a moving shoal,' I said dubiously.

'Or there are two shoals,' offered Campbell.

We all laughed. 'You're getting the idea,' said Geordie. He bent to the chart again. 'Now, we'll put each of these sightings into the middle of a rectangle, ten miles by twenty. That'll give us two hundred square miles to search, but it'll be sure. We'll start on the outside and work our way in.'

Campbell said, 'Let's get to the heart of the matter. Let's go right to each of these positions and see what's there.'

But Geordie decided against that. 'It depends on the weather. I'm not going anywhere near those two positions unless the sea is pretty near calm. You read what Robinson said about not being able to distinguish breakers from storm waves. We might find her too quickly and rip the bottom out of *Esmerelda*.'

'We've got the echo sounder,' I said. 'They should tell us where the water's shoaling.'

'Damn it, you're the oceanographer,' said Geordie. 'You should know that these islands are the tops of undersea mountains. There'll probably be deep water within a quarter of a mile of Minerva. And we could be sailing in twenty fathoms and a spire of coral could rip our guts out.'

'You're right, Geordie. Minerva's probably a budding atoll. Give her another million years and she'll be a proper island.'

'We can't wait a million years,' said Campbell acidly. 'All right, you're the skipper. We'll do your square search.'

So we got on with it. Geordie estimated that we'd have to pass within a mile of Minerva in order to see it. That meant we'd have to cover about 100 miles in order to search a 200 square mile area. We used the engine as sparingly as possible, confined our speed to about five knots and less, and that way a daylight search would take about two days.

The first leg of the search gave us nothing and in the evening we hove-to, knowing that it would be the devil of a job to assess our actual position the next morning because of the rate of drift in this area, and an uncertainty factor of at least one knot. Geordie pointed this out to Campbell to make him realise that this wasn't like searching a given area of land which, at least, stays put. Campbell hated it.

That evening, relaxing on deck, I was bombarded with questions by the crew as we ate our evening meal. They were all curious and I thought that this was not a satisfactory way to deal with them – they'd be more use and have more enthusiasm if they were in the know, of one piece of the story at least. And I was also curious myself as to Kane's reaction, and he happened to be among the off-watch members.

'What is all this, Mike?' Ian Lewis asked.

'Yes, what are we poking about here for?'

I glanced at Geordie, caught his eye and nodded very slightly. 'All right, chaps, we're looking for something a bit offbeat here.'

They were intent, and I knew I was right to share this with them.

'Ever hear of Minerva?' I asked.

It brought no reaction but murmurings and headshakes from all but one. Kane raised his head sharply. '*Récife de Minerve*!' he said in a barbarous French accent. Everyone turned to look at him now. 'Are you looking for that? My word, I wish us all luck then.' He chuckled, enjoying his moment of superiority.

'What is it?'

I told them briefly what we were after, and its tantalising history.

'What's the idea anyhow?' Danny Williams wanted to know.

I said, 'Well, this is an oceanological expedition and chaps like me are always interested in mysteries – that's how we make our living. The waters round a newly-forming island are fascinating, you know.'

They accepted this, though I did hear Danny saying softly to his nearest companion, 'I've always thought there was something crazy about these scientific types, and this isn't making me change my mind.'

Presently everyone fell silent, if a little more alert to the night sea around them, and it was then that Kane came over to join me, dropping his voice very slightly to address me alone.

117

'Er – this got anything to do with your brother, Mr Trevelyan?' he asked as though idly.

I was wary. 'Why do you ask?'

'Well, he was in the same line of business, wasn't he? And he died not very far from here. Wasn't he looking for something with another bloke?'

I looked into the darkness towards the north-east where the Tuamotus lay a hundred miles on the other side of the invisible horizon. 'Yes, he died near here, but I don't think that he had anything to do with this. I'm not the boss, you know. This is Mr Campbell's party.'

Kane chuckled derisively. 'Looking for Minerva! That's like looking for a nigger in a coal-black cellar – the little man who wasn't there.' He stayed on for a bit but, getting nothing more from me, he moved away and I could hear him chuckle again in the darkness. I realised that my fists had been clenched at my sides.

Next day we were up before the sun, waiting to take a sight and hoping there would be no clouds. Taking a dawn sight is tricky and a bit uncertain, but we had to know if possible how far we had drifted during the night, or the search would be futile.

I was with Geordie, holding the stopwatch, as I told him about Kane's query. 'Becoming inquisitive, isn't he?' he commented.

'I don't know, it was a natural question.'

'I'm not sorry you told the lads, by the way. Otherwise they'd be getting edgy. If you were on board a ship that suddenly started to go in circles in the middle of the Pacific you'd like to know why, wouldn't you? But I wonder about Kane – he tied it up with Mark pretty fast.'

'He tied it up in a natural way. Damn him, he makes a good case for himself as an innocent, doesn't he?' I heard the bitterness in my voice and was glad to be distracted. 'Ah, here's the sun.'

Geordie shot the sun and then said, 'Well, let's find out where we are.' We went into the chartroom and he worked out our position which he then transferred to the chart.

'We've drifted about seven miles in the night. There's a set of just over half a knot to the south-east. Right, now that we know where we are we can figure out where we're going.'

We started on the search. Geordie had the man up the foremast relieved every hour because the glare from the sea could cause eyestrain. He stationed another man in the bows with strict instructions to keep a watch dead ahead – he didn't want Minerva to find us. That might be catastrophic.

The day was a dead loss. It had its excitements as when Minerva was sighted only to turn out to be dolphins playing over the waves, to the delight of Clare and the other landsmen. Otherwise there was nothing. We hove-to again and waited out another night.

And the next day was largely a repetition. The last leg of the search took us directly over both reported positions, and we were anxious about it because the wind had veered northerly and the waves were confused, showing white caps. In the evening we held a conference in the chart room.

'What do you think?' asked Campbell. He was at his most brusque and edgy.

'We could have missed it in the last three or four hours. Those white horses didn't make things any easier.'

Campbell thumped the table. 'Then we do it again. Not all of it – the last bit.' He was very dogged about it.

Geordie looked at me. 'Tell me something; when you find Minerva what are you going to do with her?'

'Damn it, that's a silly question,' I said, then immediately had second thoughts as I saw what he was getting at.

'We're probably within five miles of Minerva right now. You said that the conditions that created our prize nodules were local, in your estimation. What exactly did you mean by "local"?'

'I won't know until I find it. It could be an area of ten square miles – or it could be fifty thousand.'

'I think you should drop your dredge around here and see what you can find. We could be right on top of your "locality".'

I felt very foolish. In the mixture of anticipation and

boredom that had gone into our two-day search so far I had actually forgotten what we were really here for – and I'd made plans for action earlier in the trip. 'You're right, Geordie. We've wasted some time and it's my fault. Of course we can dredge and keep a lookout for Minerva at the same time.'

Campbell and Clare cheered up visibly. The prospect of doing something other than cruise gently back and forwards was enticing, and I wondered how long it would be before their fresh interest waned once again. I didn't have any hopes of a great find.

So I started to get the winch ready for operations. The seas were choppy and flecked with white and *Esmerelda* was lurching a bit as the dredge went over the side. As we'd done the drills before things went fairly smoothly, though I'd had to take the Campbells aside with a strong suggestion that they should not appear too eager – to the others this was to be a standard research procedure. The recording echometer was registering a little under 15,000 feet.

We dredged two sites that day and five the next. On two occasions operations were interrupted when something was sighted that looked very much like a coral reef, lying some twenty feet under the water, but on both occasions this turned out to be masses of a greenish algae floating on the surface, and we had our share of false alarms when fish shoals were seen. I was kept very busy in the lab analysing the stuff we had brought up, which often included volcanic particles amongst the other material – this pleased me as it bore out some of the theories I was turning over in my mind. We recovered many nodules but test results were poor and disappointing to the others, if not to me. I hadn't expected anything.

I showed a sheaf of papers to Campbell at breakfast, away from the crew. 'Just the stuff you might expect from round here. High manganese, low cobalt. In fact the cobalt is lower than usual – only .2 per cent.'

Geordie said, 'We've only been dredging west of where we think Minerva is – how about a stab at the eastern side?'

I agreed and he said, 'Right, we'll go there today.'

There wasn't much point in pulling the winch down and

making sail for such a short trip so we motored across the few miles, starting immediately after breakfast. The sea was calm again with just the trade wind swells and no whitecaps, which would make the search easier.

It was Ian Lewis's watch and he had given me a spell at the wheel. I wasn't much of a practical seaman and I wanted to learn while I could, during periods of calm weather, under the watchful eyes of Ian or Geordie.

Clare was sitting talking to me. 'Isn't this the life,' she said. 'I had flying fish for breakfast this morning. Taffy saved them for me – I think he's falling for me.'

'Your dad isn't enjoying it,' I observed.

'Poor Pop, he's so disappointed. He's like this on every new project though, Mike. As long as it's going well he's on top of the world, and when it isn't he's down in the dumps. I keep telling him he'll get ulcers.'

'Like gout, it's supposed to be the rich man's ailment. That should cheer him up,' I said. 'It's only—'

Danny Williams's voice soared up from the bows, cracking with excitement.

'Go left! Go left! Go to port!'

Someone else started shouting.

I spun the wheel desperately and *Esmerelda* heeled violently as she came round. Hanging on, I had only time to see a jumble of white waters in the sunshine, and then to my intense relief Ian was with me, taking over at the wheel. I fell away from him, cannoning into Clare who was also off balance. Shouts and the thud of bare feet told me that the whole crew was tumbling up on deck to see what was happening. I noticed the echo sounder and in one incredible second I saw the indicator light spin round the dial. It looked as though the bottom was coming up to hit us.

Ian let *Esmerelda* continue to go about until the foaming area in the sea was well behind us, then straightened her out and the indicator light of the echo sounder spun the other way just as fast. He throttled the engine down and I took a deep breath to steady myself. Geordie came running along the deck.

'What the hell was that?' he shouted.

'I think we damn near speared ourselves on a reef – I think we've found her,' I gasped, still winded. Everyone was crowding to look astern at the jumble of white waters, but from where we were it was already impossible to see anything underneath it. 'Unless it's more fish—'

Ian said, 'No, it was a reef. I saw it – about a foot sticking out. And we shoaled bloody fast just then too.'

Campbell came up from below, looking startled and groggy. He may have been asleep. 'What's happened?'

'I think we've found Minerva.'

He looked aft and saw what we were all trying to get a better glimpse of. 'What, that?' he asked incredulously.

'Is that all?' Clare asked. Some of the crew, the non-sailors, looked equally baffled.

'What did you all expect – the Statue of Liberty?' I asked.

'We've got it, boys, wherever it is we're there!' Geordie was exultant and relieved, and more nervous for the safety of his ship than ever.

Danny Williams came aft to a little storm of back-patting. 'Good job you kept your eyes open,' I told him, and he looked very pleased.

'God, I was never so scared in my life,' he said. 'It came out of nowhere – now you see it, now you don't. I thought the bloody boat was going to ride up on it. You were pretty handy with that wheel.'

There was another murmur of assent and it was my turn to look pleased.

Geordie said to Ian, 'I want you to keep her just where she is. I'll bet that if we lay off a couple of miles we'll never find it again. Christ, it's lucky it's almost low water, it wouldn't show at all otherwise. It'll only dry out to about three feet at this rate.'

'There'll be coral clusters all round,' I said, reinforcing Geordie's warning. 'And deep water between them and the actual reef. There'll be a lagoon beyond that. An atoll is forming.'

I saw that they were all taking an interest, apart from Iar

and the on-watch lookouts, so I expanded a little. 'This rock spear that was underneath us can't have been there very long, or it would have been higher – you'd have an island here. But this coral has only just started to form.'

Geordie said suspiciously, 'What do you mean by "only just"?'

'Within the last five or ten thousand years – I'll know better when I can take a closer look at it.'

'I thought you'd say that. But you're not going to look at it. Do you think we could get to the middle of that little lot?'

We all looked back towards Minerva, if Minerva it was. 'No,' I said dubiously. 'No, perhaps not.'

Campbell had a question on his lips that he was dying to ask, but not in public. Headshakes and heavy gestures indicated his desire for a private word, so I extricated myself from the still excited crew and followed him below together with Clare.

Campbell said, 'I'm sorry to interrupt the course of pure science, but how does this tie in with the nodules? Do you think we're going to be luckier now?'

I said soberly, 'That's just the trouble; I don't see how we can. Most nodules are very old, but Mark's was comparatively young. He had a theory which I'm beginning to grasp, to do with them forming very fast as a result of volcanic action. Now there's been volcanic action here all right but much too long ago for my taste. There's been time for a long slow coral growth and it doesn't quite tie in.'

'So this is another goddam false alarm,' said Campbell gloomily.

'Maybe not. I could be wrong. We can only find out by dredging.'

3

So we dredged.

As soon as he could Geordie had taken careful sightings of the reef. 'I'm going to nail this thing down once and for all,' he said. 'Then we'll cruise around it carefully and not too closely, keeping an eye on the depth, and take soundings and chart everything we can see. And then we'll decide what to do next.'

After we had satisfied him we got started. Geordie took *Esmerelda* in as close as he dared and the dredge went over the side. I could imagine it going down like a huge steel spider at the end of its line, dropping past the incredible cliffs of Minerva, plunging deeper and deeper into the abyss.

The operation was negative – there were no nodules at all.

I was unperturbed. 'I was expecting that. Let's go round and try the other side again.' So we skirted the shoal and tried again, with the same result – no nodules.

I thought that there probably had been nodules in the area, but the upthrust of our friendly reef had queered the pitch. We were all calling it Minerva by now, although Geordie and I were aware that it might be a different reef altogether – the seas hereabouts were notorious for vigias. I decided to try further out, away from the disturbance.

This time we began to find nodules again, coming in like sacks of potatoes. I was busy in the lab once more but becoming depressed. 'This is standard stuff,' I told my small audience. 'High manganese – low cobalt, just as before. And it's too deep for commercial dredging. But we'll do it thoroughly.' And day after day the dredging and the shifting of position went on, with the results of my assays continuing to be unfruitful.

Then one evening Geordie and I consulted with one another and decided to call it off. We had been out from

Panama for over two weeks, nearly three, and I was anxious to carry on to Tahiti to be there before the *Eastern Sun* arrived. Geordie wasn't anxious over stores or even water – thanks to his careful planning we could stay at sea for up to six weeks if we needed to – but he felt that the activity, or lack of it, would begin to irk a crew which was after all partly made up of people to whom he'd virtually promised action and excitement. Campbell was quite ready to chuck the whole thing in – on a land search he would be more tenacious, but then he was seldom out there himself during the early exploratory days, usually only coming in at the kill, so to speak. And so we decided to call a halt to the proceedings and to turn towards Tahiti the next morning. The news was greeted with relief by everyone, the excitement of finding the reef we were searching for having palled. Campbell walked heavily across the deck towards the companionway, his shoulders stooped. I realized for the first time that he wasn't a young man.

'It's hit him hard,' I said.

'Aye,' said Geordie. 'What do we do now – after Papeete?'

'I've been thinking a lot about that. If it hadn't been for that damned diary then Minerva Reef would be the last place I'd go looking for high-cobalt nodules, but Mark's scribbling has hypnotized us.'

'We don't even know if he meant Minerva. Do you think he was on the wrong track?'

'I don't know what track he was on – that's the devil of it. I only leafed through those notebooks of his before they were stolen, and I couldn't absorb anything much in that time. But one thing did keep cropping up, and that was the question of vulcanism.'

'You mentioned that before,' said Geordie. 'Are you going to put me in the picture?'

'I think another little lecture is in order – and I'll deliver it to Campbell and Clare as well. It'll give him something else to think about. Get the three of you together in here after dinner, Geordie, and put a lad on watch, to keep Kane away. They'll be expecting a council of war anyway.'

And so later that same evening I faced my small class, with

a physical map of the seabeds of the world unrolled on the chart table.

'You once asked me where manganese came from and I told you from the rivers, the rocks and from volcanic activity. And I've been doing a bit of serious thinking about the latter class. But to start with, the Pacific is full of nodules while the Atlantic hasn't many. Why?'

The professorial method, involving the class in the answers always works. 'You said it had something to do with sedimentation,' Geordie recalled.

'That's the orthodox answer. It's not entirely wrong, because if the sedimentation rate is high then the nodules stop growing – they get covered up and lose contact with the seawater – the colloidal medium. The sedimentation rate in the Atlantic is pretty high due to the Amazon and Mississippi, but I don't think that's the entire explanation. I want to show you something.'

We all bent over the map.

'One fact about the Pacific stands out a mile; it's ringed with fire.' My pencil traced a line, beginning in South America. 'The Andes are volcanic, and so are the Rockies.' It hovered over the North American Pacific coast. 'Here's the San Andreas Fault, the cause of the San Francisco earthquake of 1908.' My hand moved in a great arc across the North Pacific. 'Active volcanoes are here, in the Aleutians and all over Japan. New Guinea is very volcanic and so are all the islands about there; here is Rabaul, a town surrounded by six cones – all active. There used to be five, but things stirred up a bit in 1937 and Vulcan Island·built itself up into a major cone in twenty-four hours and with three hundred people killed.'

I swept my hand further south. 'New Zealand – volcanoes, geysers, hot springs – all the indications. South again to the Antarctic and you have Mount Erebus and Mount Terror, two bloody big volcanoes. And that completes the circle – a round trip of the Pacific.'

I turned my attention eastward. 'The Atlantic is pretty quiescent, volcanically speaking, except perhaps for the Icelandic area. There was the enormous Mount Pelée eruption down here in the Caribbean but as you can see that's only just off the Pacific ring – and Krakatoa is in it, over Java way. The only place you find nodules in any quantity is on the Blake Plateau – and the interesting thing about that is that the Plateau is exactly where the current runs from the Caribbean, which I've already mentioned as being volcanic.'

Geordie straightened up from the map.

'You've got a hell of a lot of places to choose from.'

'That's the problem. And there are vents in the Pacific seabed which we don't know about – hell, we're almost on top of one now. But I know that high-cobalt area exists and I'll stake my reputation that we find it in a volcanic area.'

Campbell said, 'As I understand you correctly, the nodules in the Pacific, the ordinary ones which occur in the greatest number of places, have been slowly growing through millions of years as a result of long-ago volcanic activity. But you think there are places where certain nodules might grow faster due to specific and recent volcanic activity.'

'That's it – and they'll be high-cobalt, high-nickel and so on because of the fast growth. The metals will be entrapped while they're still around, before they're dispersed into the general waters of the Pacific.'

'Um. That still doesn't tell us where to look.'

'I want to stick around the Western Pacific,' I said intensely. 'There are plenty of known undersea vents here, and it's better fossicking round here than wasting our time.' I had other reasons, of course – I wanted to begin my investigation into my brother's death, but I was only too well aware that in Campbell's eyes the commercial venture was the main, perhaps the only reason for our carrying on. He had some personal stake but not necessarily enough.

There was a lot to think about, and talk fell away. Presently Geordie spoke up. 'All right, let's get on to Papeete and see what we can decide on the way,' he said with finality.

4

We sailed for Tahiti, first heading south to skirt the Tuamotus, and then on a direct course. Geordie didn't want to sail through the Tuamotus unless he had to; the name, he told us, meant 'The Dangerous Isles' and they were every bit as dangerous as the name implied, a vast area of coral atolls and sharp-toothed reefs, not all of them charted.

I judged we should arrive in Papeete just about the same time as the *Eastern Sun*, if she kept to her published schedule. I certainly hoped we would arrive first – I didn't relish leaving Paula there without protection.

Campbell perked up on this leg of the voyage, gradually returning to his old aggressive self, abetted by Clare. We had talked further about the possibilities ahead of us and I had tried to persuade him that I wasn't taking him on any wild-goose chases, but in fact I had nothing much to go on myself, and was feeling very bothered by this. Clare was back to poring over Mark's diary, trying to unravel a few more mysteries. I almost hoped she wouldn't – we'd had enough trouble over the *Récife de Minerve*. She had hidden the transcript and the photostatted drawings, but had first made copies of these into her own notebook, and studied them covertly from time to time.

It was pleasant enough sailing but not as invigorating as the first part of the trip out from Panama. In spite of the decision to make a new beginning we were all a little depressed, and had all been at sea for a long time. We felt the urge to tread firm ground again.

So it was with relief that everyone heard Geordie's announcement that Tahiti was within easy reach and would be sighted at any time. We were having lunch on deck and conversation was relaxed and easy. Clare sat a little way from the rest of us, still studying those damned drawings.

'Land – dead ahead!' Taffy Morgan hailed, and we all scrambled to our feet to get our first sight of Tahiti. There was only a small smudge on the horizon and we had a long while to go before we would see any more detail. We praised Geordie's navigation and then stood lounging at the rails watching the smudge gain sharpness when Kane came over to Clare.

'You left this on deck, Miss Campbell. It could blow over the side.'

And he held out her open notebook, with many of Mark's drawings in full view. We were all very still, looking at it.

Clare said coolly, 'Thank you, Mr Kane.'

'I didn't know you could draw, Miss.'

'I can't, not very well.'

Kane grinned and flicked at the open pages. 'Doesn't look like it,' he agreed. 'That's a pretty cow, mind you, but it's a pretty scraggy-looking falcon.'

Clare managed a smile as she took the book from him. 'Yes, I'll never be an artist,' she said.

Geordie said harshly, 'Kane, have you spliced that new halliard yet?'

'Just going to, skipper, no sweat.' He walked away briskly and I let my breath out. Clare said in a soft voice, 'God, I'm sorry.'

Campbell watched Kane out of sight and made sure we were out of anyone else's hearing. 'Clare, of all the damn silly things to do.'

'I said I was sorry.'

'I don't think it matters,' I said calmly. 'It's not the actual diary – none of Mark's handwriting shows. And for all we know Kane isn't aware that the diary ever existed.'

'Somebody might,' said Clare. 'That man Ramirez, he sent people to steal Mark's things – he may have known about it.'

'If Kane is a low man on the totem pole then he wouldn't know everything. I don't think it makes a bit of difference what Kane saw. Forget it.'

Clare looked at the drawings again, and suddenly a smile

displaced her air of tension. 'Now that he's mentioned the cow, I think I may have one of Mark's awful puns figured out. Don't get excited though, Pop – it's only a wild guess.'

She pointed to the cow and its companion, the squashed semi-circle.

'I've been reading things, and I read somewhere that another name for the Tuomotus is the Low Islands. That's what this flattish object is, a low island on the sea. Then he's put *OR* – and drawn the cow. It's two drawings for the same place – the Tuamotus.'

'For God's sake, why?' Campbell demanded.

'Cows go moo – they low.' And she burst out laughing. I had to join her and even her father started to smile as he saw the joke. If true, it was a good one. We put the incident with Kane out of our minds.

As *Esmerelda* drew nearer to Tahiti the sea gave place to mountains, hazy green, and then we began to see the surf breaking on the beaches as we sailed along the coast. We all turned our thoughts to cold beer ashore.

Papeete, the Pearl of the Pacific, is a pleasant town with all the usual offices – banks, a hospital, shops and so forth, but it is also a collection of tin huts set down on a tropical island and therefore a trifle squalid; but the setting is magnificent. Arriving there we tied up almost in the main street and there are not many ports in the world where you can do that. Looking over the harbour you can see the island of Moorea nine miles away, a volcano which exploded in the far past leaving a jumble of spires and peaks leaning at impossible angles, one of the most splendid sights in the world, and one which must go a long way to compensate for any inconveniences occasioned by living in Papeete.

I looked around the harbour for the *Eastern Sun* but there was no sign of her, so I tried to relax as we waited for customs clearance. Campbell was fretful, anxious to go ashore and see if there was anything for him at the post office. He was too much in the dark concerning the Suarez-Navarro expedition. I wasn't any too patient myself. I had questions to ask and I wanted to try and see the Governor. I believe in starting at the top.

At last a customs officer arrived, gave us a leisurely scrutiny and departed, leaving us free to go ashore. I had asked him when the *Eastern Sun* was due, and one of life's rare miracles occurred.

'The cruise boat, m'sieur? She come any time, I 'ave 'eard on ze radio. She is due tomorrow.'

I spoke to Geordie before everyone vanished. 'Who are the two toughest chaps you have?'

'Ian Lewis for one,' he said promptly. 'Then it's a toss-up between Taffy and Jim Taylor.'

'Whoever it is must be good at unarmed combat.'

'Then it's Ian and Jim. Taffy's the knife expert. Who do you want laid out?'

'Paula Nelson will be in tomorrow, on the *Eastern Sun*. And this place is unhealthy for her. When it comes in I want you to go and meet her, because she'll recognize you, and I want you to take the others along, collect her and bring her back here – unhurt. Anyone who tries anything is to be stepped on hard.'

He listened carefully and then nodded. I knew she'd be in good hands.

'Right. I'll leave you to your own filthy devices, Geordie. We'll want to get refitted so that we could leave almost any time, so warn the crew not to stray. Anyone who ends up in gaol stays there. I'm going to try for an interview with the Governor.'

There was a lot of mail for Campbell at the main post office. He was back even before I went ashore, clutching a sheaf of papers and disappearing below with Clare. I hoped he'd let her out some time, and it occurred to me to ask her to dine with me that night. It would be nice not to eat surrounded by the others, but nicer still with Clare along. I collected a file from my cabin and set out for Government House, and discovered it to be a rambling edifice in Late Tropical Victorian set in a large garden.

I had, as I expected to have, a royal tussle with batteries of underlings, secretaries and so forth, but I was persistent and was at long last shown to a room to await a summons for a brief meeting with the Governor. He was a tall, cadaverous man with a thin hairline moustache, sitting behind an imposing desk cluttered with papers. He did not rise but stretched his hand out to me across the table.

'M. Trevelyan, what can I do for you? Please sit down.'

I said, 'Thank you for seeing me, Monsieur – er—'

'My name is MacDonald,' he said surprisingly, and smiled as he saw my expression. 'It is always the same with you English – you cannot understand why I have a Scottish name – but you should know that one of Napoleon's Marshalls was a MacDonald.'

It appeared that this was one of his usual opening gambits with English visitors, so I said politely, 'Are you any relation?'

'My father thought so, but many Scots settled in France after the abortive revolutions in the eighteenth century. I, myself, do not think I am descended from a Marshall of France.' He became more businesslike. 'How can I help you, M. Trevelyan?' His English was fluent, with hardly a trace of accent.

I said, 'About a year ago my brother died in the Tuamotus, on one of the smaller atolls. There appears to be some mystery about his death.'

MacDonald raised his eyebrows. 'Mystery, M. Trevelyan?'

'Do you know anything about it?'

'I am afraid I have no knowledge of the death of your brother. For one thing I am new here, and am merely the Acting Governor; the Governor of French Oceania is away on leave. And also one would not recall the details of every death, every incident in so large a jurisprudence as this one.'

I wouldn't describe my brother's death, possibly his murder, as an incident myself; but no doubt the Governor would see it differently. I managed to express my disappointment without actually dismissing myself from his office, which had clearly been his wish, and he settled back to hear me out.

'We will have something on the files,' he said, and picked up a telephone. While he was speaking I opened my own file and sorted out documents.

He replaced the receiver. 'You spoke of some mystery, M. Trevelyan.'

'Mark – my brother – died on an unnamed atoll. He was treated by a Dr Schouten who lives on an island called Tanakabu.'

MacDonald pulled down his mouth. 'Did you say Dr Schouten?'

'Yes. Here is a copy of the death certificate.' I passed a photostat across the desk and he studied it.

'This seems to be quite in order.'

I said sardonically, 'Yes, it's a well filled-in form. You note that it states that my brother died of peritonitus following an operation to remove a burst appendix.'

MacDonald nodded. I was going to continue but I was interrupted by the appearance of a clerk who put a file on MacDonald's desk. He opened it and scanned the contents, pausing halfway through to raise his head and look at me thoughtfully before bending his head again.

At last he said, 'I see the British Foreign Office asked for details. Here is the letter and my superior's reply.'

'I have copies of those,' I said.

He scanned the papers again. 'All seems in order, M. Trevelyan.'

I pushed another photostat across the desk. 'This is an attested copy of a statement made by an English doctor to the effect that he removed my brother's appendix several years ago.'

It didn't take for a moment and then suddenly it sank in. MacDonald started as though I'd harpooned him and picked up the photostat quickly. He read it several times and then put it down. 'It looks as though Dr Schouten made a mistake then,' he said slowly.

'It seems so,' I agreed. 'What do you know about him?'

MacDonald spread his hands. 'I've never met him – he never comes to Tahiti, you understand. He is a Dutchman and

133

has lived in the Islands for about twenty years, administering to the people of the Tuamotus group.'

But I remembered his wry mouth and sensed that he knew more.

'He has a problem, hasn't he? Is he an alcoholic?'

'He drinks, yes – but everyone does. I drink myself,' said MacDonald in mild rebuke. He was not going to commit himself.

'Is he a good doctor?'

'There have never been any complaints.'

I thought about Schouten, living in a remote group of islands far from the administrative centre of Papeete. Complaints about his professional capacity would have a way of dying on the vine, especially if most of his clientele were local people.

I said, 'Did Dr Schouten come to Papeete to report my brother's death?'

MacDonald consulted his file. 'No, he didn't. He waited until there was a convenient schooner and then sent a letter together with the death certificate. He would not leave his hospital for so long a journey for one death – there are many, you understand.'

'So no one saw my brother except Dr Schouten and the two men who found him – and no one has made any investigation, no one has questioned Kane or Hadley or the doctor?'

'You are wrong, M. Trevelyan. We are not standing in Hyde Park Corner in the midst of a modern civilized metropolis. The Tuamotus are many hundreds of miles away and we have but a small administrative staff – but I assure you that questions were asked. Indeed they were.'

He leaned forward and asked coldly, 'Are you aware, M. Trevelyan, that at the time of your brother's death he was suspected of murder, and a fugitive from the police?'

'I did hear that cock-and-bull story. It must have been convenient for your police department to have such a tidy closing of the case.'

He didn't like that and his eyes flickered. 'Here in French Oceania we have a peculiar problem. The islands have an enviable reputation, that of an earthly paradise. Consequently, men are drawn here from all over the world, hoping to live in ease and comfort. They think they can live by eating the fruit from the trees and by building a little thatched hut. They are wrong. The cost of living here is as high as anywhere else in the world.

'These men who come here are often, not always, the failures of civilization. Most go away when they find that the islands are not the paradise of reputation. Others stay to cause us trouble. Our work here is not to aid the degenerate sweepings, but to maintain the standard for our own people. And when an unknown white who is already in trouble dies we do not make too much fuss.'

He tapped the file. 'Especially when there is a valid death certificate, apparently in order, especially when we think he may be a murderer, and very especially when he evaded the Tahiti police and ran away to die on some atoll two hundred miles from here.'

I kept my self-control with some difficulty. 'Yes, I understand all that, but will you make an investigation now? My brother, as you will see in there, was a scientist, not a beachcomber. And you will admit that there is something wrong with the death certificate.'

MacDonald picked up the doctor's statement. 'True, a man cannot have appendicitis twice. Yes, we will certainly interview the doctor again.' He made a note on his pad. 'I will appoint an officer to interview him personally, rather than send a message to the local authorities. It will be done as soon as he next goes out to the Tuamotus.'

He leaned back and waited for my thanks.

'When will that be?' I asked.

'In about three months' time.'

'Three months!'

'Your brother is already dead, M. Trevelyan. There is nothing I can do to bring him back to life. We also are busy men; I administer an area of over a million square miles. You must realize that the government cannot come to a stop while we—'

'I am not asking you to stop the government. All I'm asking is that you investigate the death of a man!'

'It will be done,' he said levelly. 'And we will find that the doctor has made an honest mistake. Perhaps he confused two patients on the same day. That is nothing new, but it would be a pity to ruin him for one mistake. We need doctors in the islands, M. Trevelyan.'

I looked into MacDonald's eyes and realized I was up against a stone wall. Nothing would be done for three months and then the whole affair would be hushed up, covered in a web of red tape.

I wrote my lawyer's address on a piece of paper. 'I would be obliged if you would let me know the results of your investigation. You can write to that address.'

'I will let you know, M. Trevelyan. I am sure there will be a simple explanation.' He half stood up, clearly dismissing me.

I went immediately to the British Consul and got no joy. He was urbane and civil, pointing out that everything MacDonald had said was true and that the only thing to do was to wait. 'They'll investigate the matter, don't you worry, Mr Trevelyan. If old Schouten has made a mistake they'll find out.'

But he didn't sound convincing even to himself.

I said, 'What kind of man is this Schouten? I gather you know him.'

The consul shrugged. 'An old Islands type – been here for years. He's done some good work in the past.'

'But not lately?'

'Well, he's getting old and—'

'Hitting the bottle,' I said viciously.

The consul looked up sharply. 'Don't blame him too much for that. He lost his entire family when the Japs invaded New Guinea.'

I said bitterly, 'Does that excuse him for killing his patients?'

There was no reasonable answer to that, and I pulled myself together and changed the subject slightly.

'Have you heard of a man called Jim Hadley?'

'A big Australian?'

'That's the man.'

'Of course he's never been in here,' said the consul. 'We've no official connection, but I've seen him around. He's well known here as a rather hard-headed type, not a man to be crossed I'd say. Your brother chartered his schooner for a while.'

'Is he really that tough?'

He frowned. 'Very much so. Not a consular tea party type at all. I wouldn't recommend him.'

'What about a man called Kane?'

'Is that the other Australian? His partner, I think – I've seen him with Hadley. It's the same answer, I'm afraid; I've never spoken to him.'

'Tell me honestly – do you think the administration is dragging its heels in this matter?'

He sighed. 'I'll have to speak bluntly, Mr Trevelyan. When your brother died he was on the run from the police. He was suspected of murder.' As I was going to interrupt he raised his hand. 'Now, don't tell me that's ridiculous. Most murderers have brothers, like yourself, who refuse to believe anything ill of their kin, especially at first hearing.'

That wasn't what I was going to say, but I kept my mouth shut.

'When he died, complete with death certificate signed by a qualified medical man, the police called off the hunt, and quite naturally so in my opinion. At the present time the administration has a hell of a lot on its plate, and they had no reason to suspect anyone else. But they'll get around to investigating the new evidence you've brought them sooner or later.'

'When the trail is totally cold.'

'I do see your point,' he said. 'I don't think I can do anything about it. But I'll try.'

And with that I had to be content.

When I reboarded *Esmerelda* I felt blue. I think I had expected my news to come with a devastating shock, and it had been dismissed as a hiccup. Clare was on deck and she said sunnily, 'Isn't this a beautiful place?'

'It stinks,' I said sourly.

'What are you mad at? You look as though you wouldn't care if the whole island sank into the sea.'

'It's these damn colonial French. Justice – but at a snail's pace. The British here aren't much better either.'

'No dice with the Governor?'

'Oh, they'll make a new investigation in three months – or three years. He doesn't want to lose his precious Dr Schouten. If he looks too closely he might have to arrest the doctor for unprofessional conduct and he doesn't want to do that, so he's going easy on the whole thing – sweeping it under the carpet in the hope that it'll be forgotten. He's got much more important things to do than to find Mark's killer.'

She was sympathetic and I began to loosen up a little. After a while I even felt cheerful enough to ask her to dine with me, and to my delight she agreed at once. I excused myself and went in search of Geordie, whom I found tinkering with the engine in company with two of the crew. Everyone else had vanished ashore. I took Geordie aside and told him what had happened.

He wiped the oil from his hands and said, 'Then you're stymied.'

'Looks like it, as far as authoritative aid goes.'

'Now's the time to put some pressure on Campbell. You won't get anywhere without him if you want to see Schouten. It's a pity you can't interpret one of those drawings to read Tanakabu – or perhaps you can scare up some good scientific reasons for going there.'

'As well there as anywhere,' I said morosely. 'I'll work on it.'

I spent the rest of the day wandering around the town and picked out a restaurant for the evening, and when it came Clare and I took ourselves off for an enjoyable time during which we both avoided any of the subjects concerning the voyage, and got to know each other better. Campbell had booked himself and Clare into a hotel for the time we were to stay in Papeete, but I had declined his suggestion that I too make such an arrangement, so at the end of the evening I escorted Clare to her new temporary home and came back to the ship feeling weary but reasonably happy.

Early the next morning I saw the *Eastern Sun* enter harbour. Geordie disappeared with Ian and Jim, and I wandered on deck to find Danny Williams just reboarding.

'Morning, Mike,' he said. 'Just back from me detective stint.'

'What's all this?'

'The skipper arranged for some of us lads to keep an eye on Kane. Yesterday he was at the post office and suchlike, and then he holed up in a spot called Quin's Bar. I had Nick follow him today, and I've sent Bill down to hang around Quin's again – we think it's his meeting-place. Yesterday he was asking for someone there.'

'Good enough,' I said. 'Why not yourself, though? Tired of playing copper?'

'I thought I'd better pull out. I followed Kane all over Panama and I thought that if I did the same here he might twig.'

I nodded in satisfaction. Danny was using his brains. After a while Campbell and Clare came on deck, clearly rested and ready for a fresh start, and I decided that this was as good a time as any to work on him. But he anticipated me.

'Clare's been telling me that you want to go and see this Schouten.'

I looked at Clare. I hadn't told her that but she must have been reading my mind, and I was grateful. I said, 'Under the circumstances, I thought it might be a good idea.'

Campbell frowned. 'I don't know about that.' He dug into his pocket and produced a letter. 'Suarez-Navarro are on the move again – heading towards Rabaul. They should be there by now.'

'Do you know if they're doing any dredging?'

He shook his head. 'My man doesn't say, but I don't think he could know without a flyover.'

'Do you want to follow them?'

Campbell shook his head again irritably as though shaking flies away. 'It's not what I want to do. You don't seem to know where to go next, and apparently Ramirez does. Maybe we should follow him.'

I looked up and saw a small party coming on board, Paula Nelson diminutive between Ian and Jim, Geordie shepherding her with her suitcase. 'Miss Nelson's here,' I said. 'Let's see where this leads us. If she can identify Hadley for me here we may not have to go and see Schouten.'

Campbell and Clare had been told that Paula was coming to Papeete and were both full of curiosity about her. I went over to greet Paula, who looked frankly delighted to see me, and introduced her. I cocked an eye at Ian, who grinned easily. 'No trouble,' he said. 'No one tried anything.'

'Thanks, fellows. We're glad to see you, Paula. Did you have a good trip?'

'It was wonderful! I've never been on one of those big cruise ships before. And say – I hope you don't mind but I didn't work my passage. It was kind of fun to be one of the tourists for a change.'

'That's great,' I told her. Before I had a chance to say anything more I saw Nick Dugan coming up and speaking urgently to Geordie, who then levelled a pair of binoculars at the harbour mouth. I left Paula with the Campbells and joined Geordie at the rails.

Nick said, 'There's the man who was talking to Kane in Quin's Bar.' He pointed. 'He's just gone on board a schooner – and they're getting under way.'

I took the glasses and focused them on the schooner. A big bull of a man was standing at the wheel, apparently bellowing orders to his native crew. They were getting under way very smartly and there wasn't much time to lose. I had a sudden intuition and called Paula over sharply, thrusting the glasses into her hands.

'Look at that ship and tell me if you can identify anyone.'

She had a bit of difficulty focusing at first but then she got it and gave a shuddering gasp. 'It's Jim Hadley,' she said. 'And that's his ship, the *Pearl*.'

Campbell snatched the binoculars and had a look himself.

'Where's Kane?' I asked urgently.

'Still at the bar, last time I saw him,' Nick said. 'Bill's on his tail.'

Ian Lewis had joined us and seemed eager and willing to go on an immediate chase. 'How soon can we get under way, skipper?' he asked Geordie.

'Too long, and half the crew isn't here,' said Geordie. 'But there's no need to go chasing after him – I saw that schooner in Panama. He's following us, damn his eyes.'

I said, 'So Kane lied again in Panama. I wonder what he'll say this time?'

'He'll say that his chum Hadley is nowhere around and he'll ask if he can stay with the *Esmerelda* a bit longer,' Geordie guessed.

Ian looked at him and nodded thoughtfully. 'Skipper, I think it's time we all knew what was going on,' he said gently. 'Who is yon lad, anyway?'

Geordie and I exchanged glances. It was indeed high time. He said, 'Ian, gather the lads together – just our bunch, that is, not my regular crew. We'll put you all in the picture sometime later today – somewhere ashore I think. I'll be happier with you lot in the know, anyway.'

'Come to my hotel,' said Campbell, taking over as he liked to do. 'I'll arrange for a room big enough for all of us, and we'll pool information. You too, Miss Nelson. I want a word with you, Mike.'

He led me aside.

'I feel as though we're losing out on this thing. I thought we could use Kane to feed Ramirez phoney information, but it's not working out that way. Kane is reporting our every movement, and we're learning nothing.'

I laughed. 'I bet his report puzzles Ramirez. He'd have a hell of a job trying to find the last place we dredged.'

Campbell watched the schooner *Pearl* going out through the pass in the reef. 'What do we do now?'

'We can't go after Hadley; we don't know where he's going and he has too big a start for us to follow. Besides these are his home waters; he could easily give us the slip. If we do anything through government channels we get wrapped in red tape. That leaves Schouten. . . .'

'I thought you'd say that. But Ramirez is in Rabaul. What's he *doing* there?'

'Waiting to follow us, at a guess; when he thinks we've hit pay dirt. I'm sure Suarez-Navarro don't know any more than we do, or they'd be there. But this all started with Mark's death and Schouten was present. I think we should talk to him, if only to clear up some unanswered questions.'

He nodded. 'Clare had that idea too. She came up with the idea that perhaps all of Mark's gear wasn't returned to England – that Schouten might have some stuff stashed away. How about that?'

'I'd have to ask Paula – she might know something.'

Campbell drummed with his fingers on the mast tabernacle. 'I tell you – I'm split in two on this thing. After all, we did pull a boo-boo at Minerva, and that was a month wasted. We'll spend nearly a fortnight back-tracking to go and see Schouten and that fortnight might be precious. And God knows what Ramirez will be doing.'

He fell silent and I let him ruminate for a few minutes.

'I suppose we may find something that'll short-circuit the whole damned affair. All right, it's worth the risk. We'll go. But if we get no answers there I'm calling the whole thing off.'

I was too delighted with his decision to worry about the threat. I could take care of that later, if necessary. We went over to rejoin the two girls, who had been chatting together with Geordie.

'We're going to Tanakabu,' I told them briefly and Geordie looked very pleased, while Clare cheered softly. Paula, of course, only looked puzzled.

'Paula,' I asked, 'do you know if the stuff of Mark's that you sent home was everything of his – could he have had more elsewhere?'

'I really don't know for sure, Mike. But I don't think so. He never had much stuff while he was with me.'

I had an idea. 'Paula, you're going to join in the briefing this afternoon, which I'm sure you've realized is going to be very confidential. After all, you have a lot to contribute. But we may be going off soon after that and as I've brought you here I can't just leave you. You're my responsibility now, you know. Would you like to come along with us?'

I watched them all for their reactions. Campbell had already put on an avuncular act towards her and looked smug, as if it was his idea. Geordie merely looked resigned – now he had two women on board, and even less space to spare. Clare was the problem, but I saw that while she was being rather formal with Paula she wasn't showing any overt hostility, and she appeared to take my suggestion calmly enough, even adding a civil rider of her own.

'Why not? It would be nice for me too, I think.'

Paula looked dumbfounded. Her big dark eyes swept all of us and came back to me, and I could see that she was almost unable to conceive of the notion.

'Think about it. Have you sailed before?'

'Yes, a little. Just locally hereabouts. I was on the *Pearl* once, with – with a friend.'

'You can buy what you need here. It's not too rough, we eat well and you won't have to sleep in a hammock,' I said encouragingly. I also felt that she was probably the only one of us who had faith that Mark wasn't an utter bastard. It would be good to have someone along who was completely on his side.

'What do we do about Kane?' Geordie asked.

'Keep him on ice – we take him with us, if he asks to go. Which he will. Then after I've talked to Schouten we ask him some pointed questions. Until then you just watch him, Geordie.'

'That'll be easy,' Geordie said. 'It's not too big a boat, you know.'

Chapter Five

1

We sailed the next day for the Tuamotus, after announcing that we were heading for Indonesia in slow stages. This was not only for the benefit of Kane, who had reacted as predicted by asking to come along on our next leg, but lest MacDonald get wind through the harbour officials that I was going to interview his precious Dr Schouten – he might have objected.

We sailed through the pass in the reef and out into the open sea, continuing west until we were out of sight of land. Then Geordie gave the order to change course northwards. Kane happened to be on the wheel and accepted the order without comment, but a couple of hours later when relieved and with the new helmsman setting a course easterly, he said to me, 'We're going the wrong way for New Britain, Mr Trevelyan.'

'Who said we were going to New Britain?' He had slipped up; New Britain specifically had never been mentioned in his hearing, but I knew he was probably thinking of Ramirez.

He covered it up well. 'Oh, I thought you'd drop anchor in Rabaul for refuelling. It's a prime spot for it,' he said easily.

'The boss has some unfinished business here,' I said briefly, and he left it at that, although I could see he was thinking hard.

I couldn't help goading him. 'I thought your pal Hadley was going to be waiting in Papeete.'

'Yair, he's a fine cobber now, isn't he? But he left a message for me – said he couldn't wait. Anyway, I don't mind giving you a hand,' he said with an air of largesse.

Kane certainly had a nerve – now he was helping us!

Geordie was careful in going through the Tuamotus, careful to the point of keeping Kane off the wheel. We still didn't know what his game was, but we didn't feel like being run ashore deliberately. Geordie kept a sharp eye on the charts and picked a way through the thousand and one islands in the archipelago, always heading for Tanakabu, away on the further side.

Clare liked the Tuamotus. 'It's just like a movie,' she said happily as she viewed an atoll on the horizon. 'Couldn't we go in closer, and have a look?'

I took her elbow. 'Come here. I'd like to show you something.' In the chartroom I pointed out our position. 'Here's that atoll – you see the marks here, extending out about three miles from the island. Do you know what they are?'

'Oh God, yes of course. Coral reefs round every one,' she said.

'Nasty and sharp,' I agreed. 'I'm as near to that atoll now as I'd like to be. We only touch on the ones with mapped entrances, otherwise it's all local knowledge hereabouts.' And I thought of Hadley, somewhere out there in *Pearl*. Was he following us?

'I hope we're not making a mistake,' Clare said soberly, catching my mood. 'We must find out something useful. Pop was mad enough over the fiasco at Minerva.'

'We may not find out anything concerning managanese nodules, but I hope we'll find out something about Mark. And one thing may lead to another.' I changed the subject. 'How are you getting on with Paula?'

Clare was silent for a moment, then said, 'I thought I wouldn't like her – you know, two of Mark's popsies should be wanting to scratch each others' eyes out.'

'Don't throw that in my teeth again.'

'I find I do like her, though. I've discovered that I never was in love with Mark, it was infatuation, and when I found out what a lousy creep he could be it all died. That isn't love. Paula knew what he was and it made no difference to her – she still loved him in spite of it. That takes real love – I never had it. We're not rivals any more.'

That was a relief. Two women at daggers' point can cause a hell of a lot of trouble, and especially in a small ship.

As for Paula, she was relaxed and enjoying herself thoroughly. Easily at home among the men and for once away from both danger and professional competition, she had become yet another of *Esmerelda*'s growing assets as far as the crew went. Occasionally she sang for us in the evenings and took pleasure in her small touch of limelight. Campbell seemed to have adopted her as an unusual, but welcome, honorary niece.

When we left the main clutter of islands Geordie was able to set a course for Tanakabu without worrying overmuch about grounding. Kane was aware of this manoeuvre and again spoke to me about it. 'Where are we heading for, more research grounds?' he asked me.

I said, 'Maybe the boss wants another look at Minerva.'

He looked up at the sun. 'Making a bit too much northing for that, ain't we?'

'Or maybe he wants to have a look at Tanakabu?' I suggested, twisting the knife. It was dangerous but he'd find out soon enough.

Kane's eyes shifted. 'Has this anything to do with your brother?'

I raised my eyebrows. 'Why should it?'

'Well, old Schouten lives on Tanakabu.'

'Does he?'

'Yair, but I suppose the old bloke's dead by now. He was hitting the bottle pretty hard when I saw him. A proper old rum-dum, he was.'

I said, 'He's still alive, as far as I know.' I was tempted to play him further but fought it down.

Kane didn't say anything more, but withdrew thoughtfully, and a few minutes later I saw him heading below apparently for some more private cogitation in his cabin, which he shared with two others who were both presently on deck.

We made good time although now we were beating close-hauled against the trade wind and on the evening of the third day we were closing Tanakabu. The sun was dipping into the sea as Geordie scanned the reef with binoculars and then referred to the chart. 'We'll go in under power. The pass is a bit too narrow for comfort under sail. Stand by to hand the sails, Ian.'

He was still looking hard at the sea-pounded reef when Shorty Powell, his radio man, came up. 'I picked up a funny transmission, skipper,' he said, then glanced at me. Geordie said, 'It's okay, carry on. What was funny about it?'

'It mentioned us.'

I pricked up my ears and Geordie swung round. 'Mentioned us by name?'

'The name of the ship,' said Shorty. '*Esmerelda*.'

I said, 'What did they say about us?'

Shorty grimaced painfully. 'That's it, I don't know. I was spinning the dial and caught it in passing, and by the time I'd got back to where I thought it was the transmission had stopped. I just caught a few words— ". . . on board *Esmerelda*. She's. . . ." I tell you one thing, though. I'd lay ten to one it was an Australian talking.'

Geordie said, 'I think we'd better get Mr Campbell in on this.'

So we called him up and poor Shorty got the grilling of his life. At last Campbell said, 'Well, how far away do you think it was?'

Shorty shrugged. 'You can't tell that, not unless you've got two directional fixes on the station. But when you spend half your life listening out you get a kind of instinct. I'd say it was one of two things – a hell of a high-powered station a long way off – or a low-powered station damn close.'

'Well, man, which was it?' demanded Campbell impatiently.

'I'd say it was a low-power station close by – but don't ask me to prove it.'

'All right, thanks, Shorty. Stay around that frequency. Maybe you can pick up something else,' said Geordie.

As Shorty left and Geordie turned to his navigation again Campbell said to me, 'What do you make of that?'

'I don't make anything of it. There's not enough to go on – just that some Australian mentioned the *Esmerelda*.'

'It must have been Hadley,' said Campbell positively. 'I'd

give my back teeth to know who he was talking to – someone on land there.'

We abandoned speculation as by then we were going in through the pass. It was getting dark and Geordie was on edge. The pass was narrow and there was a dog-leg bend in it and the darkness coupled with the four-knot current made the passage very tricky. But we got through into the lagoon and dropped anchor offshore opposite the lights of a large village. A small fleet of canoes came out to meet us and soon a number of Polynesians were climbing on deck.

I had decided not to wait until morning, but to act right away. It was only early evening, perhaps the best time to see a busy doctor, and there was the fear of being followed to spur me to action. I raised my voice. 'Where can I find the doctor – Dr Schouten?' I asked.

There was an increased babble and a stocky thickset man with an engaging grin pushed his way to the front. 'These boys don' spik English,' he said. 'They spik Française. I spik English. I bin to Hawaii.'

I said, 'My name is Mike – what's yours?'

'I are Piro.'

'All right, Piro. Where do I find the doctor?'

'Oh, Schouten?' Piro waved his hand. 'He round the other side water. He in – *hôpital*. Y'un'erstan' *hôpital*?'

'He's at the hospital, over there?'

'That right.'

'How can I get there?'

'You come wit' me – I take you in jeep.'

I looked into the darkness. 'How far is it?'

Piro shrugged. 'Not far. Twenny minute maybe.'

'Will you take me now?'

'Sure. You come now.' He was suddenly cautious. 'You pay me?'

'Yes, I'll pay you.' I turned to Campbell among the jostling crowd on deck and said, 'I may as well see Schouten tonight. Tell Geordie to keep a close eye on Kane – don't let him get away. He might try.'

He said, 'I'll come with you.'

'No, I think not. But I will take an escort – Jim Taylor, I think.' I said this because he was the handiest, and grabbing him by an arm I pulled him towards me and briefly told him our errand. He smiled and nodded, and went off to find Geordie and tell him.

Campbell looked closely at me, then gripped my arm. 'Take it easy, son. Don't go off at half-cock.'

'I won't,' I promised. 'But by God I'll get to the truth.'

We went over the side and dropped into Piro's canoe, a leaky and unstable craft. Once ashore, Piro introduced us to his proudest possession – his jeep. It was a relic of the wave of war which had washed over the Pacific – and it looked it. Most of the bodywork was stripped and the engine was naked and unashamed, very like the naked toddlers who squalled and chattered, their eyes big at the sight of the strangers revealed in the flare of torches. We climbed in and I sat on a hard wooden box, innocent of upholstery, as Piro started the engine. It banged and spluttered, but caught, and Piro threw in the gears with a jerk and we were off, bouncing along the beach and swerving round a clump of palms dimly illuminated by the feeble headlight. It was very noisy. The sudden change from being at sea in *Esmerelda* was unnerving.

Piro was very proud of his jeep. 'Best car on Tanakabu,' he announced cheerfully as we winced at the racket.

'Has Dr Schouten got a car?'

'Ho, no! Doctor got not'ing – jus' stomick med'cine.'

We drove past the dark bulk of a copra warehouse and then we were on a narrow track through a palm plantation and Piro waved at it. 'These trees mine. All us got trees.'

'Has the doctor got trees?'

'Lil one lot, not'ing much. He too busy wit' med'cine and knife.'

We swerved inland and I lost sight of the sea, which seemed impossible on such a small island, but I could still hear the unceasing roar of the surf on the beaches, in between the car noises. After a few minutes we came back onto a beach and Piro pointed ahead. 'There is *hôpital*.'

In the distance was a large cluster of lights – much bigger

than the village we had left. I said, 'That's a big hospital for a small island, Piro.'

'Ho, plenny boys come from other islands – ver' sick. Plenny *wahines* too. Many lepers there, an' boys wit' swells.'

A leper colony! I felt a shiver of atavistic horror. I knew intellectually that leprosy isn't particularly infectious, but of all diseases it is the most abhorred and I didn't feel like driving into a colony.

Piro didn't seem worried though, and drove blithely off the beach right into the hospital grounds, pulling up in front of a long low-roofed shack. 'Schouten is there,' he said. 'You wan' I should wait?'

'Yes, you can wait,' I answered. 'I won't be long. Jim, don't come in with me, if you don't mind – but be ready if I call you.'

'Sure thing, Mike.' Jim leaned back and offered Piro a cigarette.

I walked up the two steps on to a long verandah and knocked on the door. A voice said, '*Ici! Ici!*' and I walked along the verandah to a room at the far end. It was an office, the door open, and a big man was seated at a desk, writing by the light of a Coleman lamp. There was a half-empty brandy bottle and a full glass at his elbow.

I said, 'Dr Schouten?'

He looked up. '*Oui?*'

'I'm sorry. I have very little French. Do you speak English?'

He smiled and it transformed his ravaged face. '*Ja*, I speak English,' he said and stood up. In his prime, he must have tipped the scales at two hundred and twenty pounds of bone and muscle, but now he was flabby and soft and his paunch had taken over. His face was seamed and lined and he had two deep clefts from the nose to the corners of his mouth, forming soft dewlaps which shook on his cheeks.

He offered me his hand and said, 'It's not often we get strangers on Tanakabu – at least not at this end of the island.' His accent was heavily Dutch but his English was as fluent as the Governor's.

150

I said, 'We just came in.'

'I know. I saw the lights of your ship as you came through the pass, and then I heard Piro's jeep coming.' He waved towards the window. 'That is why you see no patients about – sometimes they shock casual visitors, so on those occasions I keep them out of sight.'

He opened a cupboard. 'Will you have a drink?'

I said, 'My name is Trevelyan.'

Schouten dropped the glass he had taken from the cupboard and it smashed on the floor. He turned his head sharply and looked at me over his shoulder. I saw that his face had turned a sickly yellow under the tan and his eyes were furtive and haunted.

'Trevelyan?' he mumbled. He seemed to have difficulty speaking.

'Yes.'

He turned round. 'Praise be to God,' he said. 'I thought you were dead.'

I looked at him in surprise. 'Dead! Why should I be dead?'

He sat at the desk, his hands clutching the edge. 'But they said you were dead,' he said softly. His eyes were brooding and seemed to be looking at something else – something terrible.

Then I caught on – he thought I was Mark! I said, 'Who said I was dead?'

'I wrote out the death certificate – here at this desk. Mark Trevelyan was the name. You died of peritonitus.' He looked up at me and there was fear in his eyes.

I said gently, 'I'm Michael Trevelyan – Mark was my brother.'

He gave a long shuddering sigh, then his gaze dropped to the glass on his desk and he picked it up and drained it in one swallow.

I said, 'Perhaps you'd better tell me about it.' He gave no answer, merely hunching his shoulders and avoiding my eyes. 'You've said too much – and too little,' I pursued. 'You must tell me what happened to Mark.'

He was an old man, rotten with loneliness and drink and the

sight of peoples' bodies falling apart and he couldn't withstand a mental hammering. There was a stubbornness in him but also a softness at the core, and I was brutal in my approach.

'My brother didn't have appendicitis – that was an impossibility. But you forged a death certificate. Why?'

He hunched over the desk, his arms before him with the fists clenched and remained silent.

'My God, what kind of a doctor are you?' I said. 'Your medical association isn't going to like this – you're going to be struck off, Schouten. Or maybe you'll be hanged – or guillotined. A man is dead, Schouten, and you're an accessory. The best thing that is going to happen to you is a gaol sentence.'

He shook his head slowly, then closed his eyes as though in pain.

'You're an old man before your time even now, and ten years in gaol won't improve you. They'll take away your brandy and you'll scream for it. Now, what happened to Mark?'

He opened his eyes and looked at me bleakly. 'I can't tell you.'

'Can't – or won't?'

The muscles of his mouth tightened and he remained stubbornly silent.

'All right,' I said. 'You're coming with us – we're going back to Papeete and you'll tell your story to the Governor. I'm putting you under civilian arrest, Schouten. I don't know if that has any validity under French law but I'll chance it. I'll give you ten minutes to collect whatever you want to take with you.'

Something happened inside Schouten and I knew I was getting to him. He jerked up his head and stared at me. 'But I can't leave the hospital,' he said. 'What will happen to the people here?'

I pushed hard. 'What will happen to this hospital when you're in gaol? Or even dead? Come on – get your things together.'

He pushed back his chair abruptly and stood up. 'You don't

understand. I *can't* leave these people – some of them would die. I'm the only doctor here.'

I looked at him without pity. I had a cruel advantage and I had to use it – there was nothing else I could do. 'You should have thought of that before you killed my brother,' I said.

His muscles tensed and for a moment I thought he was going to jump me. I said sharply, 'You may be big, Schouten, but you're old and soft! I'm tougher than you and you know it, so stay clear of me or I'll whale the daylights out of you. I'm sorely tempted.'

His mouth twitched and he almost smiled. 'I wasn't going to attack you, Mr Trevelyan. I'm a peaceful man. I don't believe in violence – and I didn't kill your brother.'

'Then for Christ's sake, what's the matter with you? Why won't you tell me what happened?'

He sat down again and buried his face in his hands. When he raised his head I saw that his cheeks were streaked with tears. He said with difficulty, 'I cannot leave the hospital, but you must guarantee its safety, Mr Trevelyan. You see, they said – they said they'd burn the hospital.'

'Burn the hospital! Who said that?'

'What could I do? I couldn't let them burn it, could I?' What I saw in his eyes made me begin to pity him.

I said gently, 'No, you couldn't do that.'

'What would happen to my people then? I had fifty patients – what would have happened to them?'

I took the bottle and poured some brandy into a glass. 'Here,' I said, 'drink this.'

He took the glass and looked at it, then set it down on the desk. 'No. It's past time for that.' His voice was stronger. 'I couldn't help it. They made me do it – I had no choice. It was covering up a crime or losing the hospital.' He threw his arms out. 'I thought the people out there were more important than bringing a murderer to justice. Was I right?'

'What happened to Mark?' I said in an even voice.

His eyes went cold. 'You must promise protection for the hospital,' he insisted.

153

'Nothing will happen to the hospital. What happened to my brother?'

'He was murdered,' said Schouten. 'On a schooner in the lagoon.'

I let out my breath in a long sigh. Now it was in the open. All the shadowy suspicions had crystallized into this one moment, and all I felt was a great pity for this wreck of a man sitting at the desk.

I said slowly, 'Tell me what happened.'

So Schouten told me. He had more colour in his face now and his voice was stronger. His account was factual and he made no excuses for himself; he admitted he had done wrong, but all his thoughts were for his patients. It was a sad and cruel story.

'The schooner came through the pass early last year. She was a stranger, like yourselves – the only ships that put in to Tanakabu are the copra boats and it wasn't the right time for them. She entered the lagoon and dropped anchor just opposite the hospital – out there.' He nodded towards the sea.

'Two men came ashore. One was about your size, very thin. The other was a big man – as big as me. They said there had been an accident and a man was dead. They wanted a death certificate. I took my bag from the corner there and said I'd come aboard, but the big man said no, it wasn't necessary, the man was already dead, anyone could see that, and all they wanted was a bit of paper to say so.'

Schouten smiled slightly. 'I laughed at them and said what they wanted was impossible – that the body must be seen by a doctor. Then the big man hit me.' He fingered the side of his cheek and said apologetically, 'I couldn't do anything – I'm not young any more.'

'I understand,' I said. 'Tell me, were their names mentioned?'

'The big man was called Jim, the other man called him that. His name I don't remember. There was another name said, but I forget.'

'All right. What happened then?'

'I was astonished. I couldn't understand why the man had

hit me. I got up and he hit me again. Then he pulled me up and sat me in this chair and told me to write a death certificate.'

My lips tightened. It was only too probable that the big man was Hadley and the other was Kane. I'd have a reckoning with Kane when I got back to the *Esmerelda*.

'I wouldn't do it,' said Schouten. 'I asked why I couldn't see the body and the other man laughed and said it was in a mess and it would turn the stomach even of a doctor. Then I knew there was something very bad going on. I think they had killed someone, and it was someone who could not just disappear – there had to be a death certificate.'

I nodded. 'What happened then?'

'The big man hit me again and kept on hitting me until the other made him stop. He said that was not the way to do it. Then he turned on me and wiped the blood from my face very gently, and while the big man sat drinking he talked to me.'

'What did he talk about?'

'The hospital. He said he thought it was a good hospital and that it was doing good work in the islands. He asked how many patients I had, and I told him – about fifty. He asked if I was curing them and I said yes, some of them, but others were incurable. I just looked after them. Then he asked what would happen if there were no hospital on Tanakabu, and I said it would be a very bad thing – many people would die.'

Schouten caught my hand and said appealingly, 'I told him all this – I told him freely. I didn't know what he wanted.'

'Go on,' I said tightly.

'The big man started to laugh and then he hit me once again. He said, "That's so you'll take notice of what I'm saying. You sign that certificate or we'll burn the whole bloody hospital." '

He dropped his head into his hands. 'What could I do?' he said in a muffled voice.

I was angry, more angry than I've ever been in my life before. If Kane and Hadley had been in that room then I'd have killed them without mercy.

Schouten said brokenly, 'He said that he didn't care if he

burned the patients either – it was all one to him.' His eyes looked at me in slow horror. 'He kept lighting matches as he talked to me.'

'So you signed the death certificate.'

'*Ja*. I made it out as they wanted, then I signed it. Then the big man hit me again and the other man said, "If you breathe a word about this we'll know it and we'll come back, and you know what will happen to this collection of grass shacks you call a hospital." Then the big man set fire to the thatch over there and while I tried to beat it out they left. They were both laughing.'

I looked over to where there was a patch of new thatching. 'What nationality were these men?'

'I lived in New Guinea once – that is an Australian mandate and I've met many Australians. These men were Australians.'

'Did you see them again?'

Schouten nodded sombrely. 'The big man – yes. He keeps coming back. He says he is keeping an eye on me. He comes and drinks my brandy and lights matches. He has been back – three times.'

'When was the last time?'

'About a month ago.'

That would be Hadley – not a nice character from the sound of him. There were plenty like him as concentration camp guards in Hitler's Germany but the type is to be found among all nationalities. They weren't a very good advertisement for Australia.

Schouten said, 'I didn't dare tell the police. I was frightened for the hospital.'

I ran over his terrible story in my mind. 'You don't remember the other name you heard?'

He shook his head. 'Not yet, but I think it was the third man on the boat – he was not a local crewman.'

'What other man?'

'He didn't come ashore but I saw him on the deck of the schooner – a very tall, thin man with a hooked nose, very dark. I saw him only once, when the boat was coming in.'

I thought about that but it didn't ring any bells. I said, 'I'm sorry it happened, Dr Schouten. But you realize you will have to tell the authorities now.'

He nodded heavily. 'I realize it now. But I was so afraid for my patients. This is an isolated atoll – there are no police here, no one to guard against violent men. I am still afraid.' He looked me in the eye. 'What is to prevent these men, or others like them, from coming back?'

I said harshly, 'I know who these men are. They won't trouble you again.'

He hesitated and then said, 'So. I will write a letter which you can take to Papeete. You understand, I cannot leave the hospital.'

'I understand.' This would make MacDonald sit up and take notice. I would be very pleased to deliver Schouten's letter in person.

'Will you send people to guard us right away? You have promised no harm will come to us here.'

I thought that we could leave some of the lads with him while we went back, or even send a radio message for assistance before we left. Hadley would follow us back to Papeete, if he was indeed on our trail, and a couple of Geordie's stalwarts would be more than a match for him if he landed after we'd left.

Schouten said, 'The letter will not take long, but you must make yourself comfortable while I write. You would not drink with me before – will you drink now?'

I said, 'I'd be honoured, doctor.'

He went to the cupboard and got another glass, stirring the broken pieces on the floor as he did so. 'You gave me a shock,' he said ruefully. 'I thought the dead had come to life.'

He poured a stiff drink and handed it to me. 'I am deeply sorry about your brother, Mr Trevelyan. You must believe that.'

'I believe you, doctor. I'm sorry for the rough time I gave you.'

He grimaced. 'It wasn't as rough as the time the big man gave me.'

No, it wasn't, I thought, but we'd both operated on the

same raw nerve – Schouten's fears for his patients and his hospital. I felt ashamed of myself. I finished the drink quickly and watched Schouten scratching with his pen. I could see it was going to take a while, so I said, 'When will you finish?'

'To tell it in detail will take a long time. Also I do not write English so well as I speak it,' said Schouten. 'If you wait, you will have dinner, of course.'

'No. I'll go back to my ship and make arrangements to leave someone here with you, when we go back to Papeete. I'll come back later tonight or early in the morning.'

Schouten inclined his head. 'As you wish. I will be glad of a guard.' He resumed his writing and I got up to go, and then just as I got to the door, he said, 'One moment, Mr Trevelyan. Something has just come back to me.'

I waited by the door and he rose from his desk. 'You were asking about the name – the one they mentioned. The big man spoke it and the other made him be quiet.'

'What was it?'

Schouten escorted me on to the verandah. As Piro saw us he started the engine of his jeep. Schouten said, 'It was a strange name – it sounded Spanish. It was Ramirez.'

2

We had gone a mile when the jeep broke down. The roar of the engine faded and we bumped to a halt. Piro hopped out, bent over the engine and struck a match. 'She dead,' he said in an unworried voice.

I was impatient to get back to *Esmerelda*. I wanted to beat Kane into a pulp. I know that no man stays angry forever – you can't live on that plane – and I was nursing my anger because I wanted to let it rip. I intended to hammer Kane to a jelly. Jim Taylor had sensed my tension and had wisely refrained from asking me any questions.

Piro struck another match and poked experimentally into

the entrails of the jeep. Then he looked up and said cheerfully, 'She no go.'

'What's the matter?'

'No *essence.*'

I said, 'Damn it, why didn't you fill it up? Why didn't you look at the gauge – this thing here?'

'She broke.'

'All right, we'll walk – we just have to follow the beach.'

Piro said, 'No walk. Canoe along here. We walk on water.'

We followed him a couple of hundred yards up the beach to where the road turned inland and he strode to the water's edge. 'Here is canoe, sir – I take you back.'

It was only a couple of miles but it seemed longer in the darkness. We very soon saw the riding lights of *Esmerelda* in the clear air but it took an age to get within hailing distance. Some of the other canoes were still alongside and there was an air of festival on deck, with crew and locals apparently sharing their evening meal. Campbell, Clare and Paula were waiting at the rail as I climbed on board and they saw at once that I was in no happy mood. I said to Campbell in a low voice, 'Where's Kane?' I couldn't see him in my first sweeping survey of the deck.

'Geordie's been watching him. He's given him a job below. What happened, man?'

I said, 'That bastard – and Hadley – killed Mark.'

Paula drew in her breath with a hiss. Campbell said, 'Are you sure?'

'It may not hold in a court of law but I'm sure.' I was remembering the tears on Schouten's cheeks. 'I want to have a talk with Kane – now!'

'He doesn't look like a murderer.'

'Which one does?' I said bitterly. 'I've heard a filthy story. Ramirez was involved too.'

Campbell started. 'How do you reckon that?'

'Can you describe him?'

'Sure. He's a tall, thin guy with a beak like an eagle. He's got a hell of a scar on the left side of his face.'

'That does it. He was there when Mark was killed.

Schouten saw him and described him, all but the scar, and Hadley mentioned his name. He's tied up in it all right, right up to his goddam neck – which I hope to break. But first I want Kane.'

Campbell turned to Clare and Paula. 'Go to your cabins, girls.'

Paula turned obediently but Clare argued. 'But Pop, I—'

There was a whipcrack in Campbell's voice. '*Go to your cabin!*'

She went without another murmur and he turned to me.

'Clear this lot off,' I said. 'Tell Ian. Let's find Kane.'

I went down into the forecastle but Kane wasn't there, nor was he on deck. We roped in the crew and they set out to search the ship but there was no sign of him. My jaw was aching from holding it clenched for so long.

'He's skipped,' said Ian.

'Geordie – where's Geordie?' I said.

But Geordie had vanished too.

I ran up on deck to find that several of the locals were still hanging around. I shouted for Piro and he emerged from the pack.

'Can you help us find two men on the island? Can you search?'

'What men?'

'The captain and one of the crew. The captain is the big man you saw when we came. The other one is thin, tall. Stay away from him – he's dangerous.'

Piro rubbed the top of his head. 'Dan-ger-ous?'

'He's bad. He might fight – might kill you.'

Piro shrugged. 'You pay – we find.'

He dropped into his canoe with two or three of our men, and Ian was already directing the clearing of our inboard launch which was being swung over the side. Piro was shouting instructions in his own language to the suddenly galvanized locals. Campbell came up from below. 'Got a gun?' he asked me.

'I won't need a gun. I'll tear that bastard apart.'

'Come here,' he said and took me under a light. He opened

160

his hand and I saw a round of ammunition in his palm. 'I found that on the floor by his bunk – a .38 slug. Kane must have dropped it in his hurry and that means he's armed.'

'Christ, we must stop these natives making a search,' I said. 'We don't want any deaths.'

I turned to race on deck but he held my arm, pushing something heavy into my hand. 'Here's a gun,' he said. 'Can you shoot?'

I hung onto it tightly. 'I'll soon find out, won't I?' I stuffed it into the pocket of the light anorak I was wearing. 'You'd better stay here.'

'Son,' said Campbell, 'I'm not as old as that – not yet.'

I looked into his frosty eyes and said, 'We'd better make it snappy, then.' We ran up on deck and I dropped into the launch and looked ashore. Little spots of light were moving in the darkness, coming and going, sometimes vanishing and reappearing as the torches were occulted by the palm trees. 'Damn, they've started to search.' I turned to Ian. 'Kane's armed.'

'Let's go – I've got six – the rest are ashore already. They know the score.' The engine started first time off, which was a tribute to someone, and as we sped shorewards I said to the men around me, 'Listen, chaps, we're looking for Geordie. If you come up against Kane steer clear of him. Don't push him too hard – he's got a gun. And as you find the natives send them back to their village.'

Taffy Morgan said, 'What's Kane done now?'

'He's killed a man,' said Campbell coldly.

There was no more talk until the boat grounded on the beach. Piro was waiting, his face alive with excitement in the light of a torch. 'Found 'im,' he said laconically.

'Which one?' I asked quickly.

He gestured. 'The big one – up in hut now.'

I sighed with some thankfulness. This must be Geordie. 'Piro, can you call your men off – stop them? They must not find the other man. He has a gun.'

Piro made a quick sign to one of his friends, who lifted a large conch shell to his lips. The mournful sound boomed out, sending its note across the plantations. I saw the lights begin to drift back to the village.

'Let's see him.'

We found Geordie in one of the huts. His face was a dreadful mess, with deep cuts and gashes across his forehead and cheeks. Piro said, 'We found 'im in trees – asleep on groun'.'

I think he had concussion because he rambled a little, but he was able to speak to us. He had seen Kane slipping ashore in one of the many canoes and had followed in another. He hadn't had time to call anyone because he was afraid of losing Kane. He had followed as Kane skirted the village and entered the trees and then he had been ambushed.

'For God's sake, who ambushed you?'

'It – must have been Hadley. A man as big as an elephant,' said Geordie painfully. 'He stepped from behind a tree and pushed a gun into my ribs. I didn't expect that – I thought Kane was on his own – and he took me by surprise. Then he – made me turn round to face him and he started to hit me.' He was trailing off but recovered. 'With the gun. A big revolver. It was the sight that did – this. And the bastard was laughing. Then he hit me a couple of times on the head and I – passed out.'

He grinned weakly. 'Maybe he thought he'd killed me but I have a pretty hard head. I'm sorry I fell down on the job, Mike.'

'It's all right, Geordie. None of us expected anything like this. I'm only sorry you had to get it in the neck.'

His bloody face cracked in a grim smile. 'Add it to the account with my finger,' he said weakly. 'Give him one from me.'

'You'll have to wait your turn. There's a queue lining up for licks at Hadley – and Kane.' I stood up. 'I think we'd better get you back to the ship.'

Two of his shocked team moved in, gentling him up and setting off for the launch. The others began to gather as Piro called them to the hut. I spoke urgently to him. 'Is there another boat here – the *Pearl*?' I asked. If Hadley had

162

returned several times Piro was sure to know his boat. Piro's answer shocked us all, even though we were already primed for it.

'Yes, it came 'ere. It gone by *hôpital* – one, two hour,' he said.

'Well I'm damned,' said Campbell. 'He came through the pass behind us – in the dark and without lights. He's a bloody good seaman.'

'That doesn't make me love him any more,' I said.

A man ran into the hut and spoke to Piro rapidly in his own language, clearly distressed. Piro looked startled and gestured to me to come outside, where he pointed into the darkness. There was a fitful redness in the sky on the horizon. '*Hôpital*, he burn,' he said.

'Christ!'

The others crowded out to exclaim at the sight.

'How can we get there – fast – all of us?' I damned the jeep, stalled on the beach without fuel.

'Big canoe,' said Piro. 'Go fast. Faster than walk.' He ran off.

I said, 'Hadley's fired the hospital!'

Campbell looked at the glow in the sky. 'Is he plain crazy – why did he do that?' he demanded.

'He threatened to do it. No time to tell you now. We're going in canoes. Piro's gone to organize it. Now where's Ian?'

His soft Highland voice sounded at my shoulder. 'I'm here.'

'Take one canoe and go back to the *Esmerelda*. I want her down at the hospital as fast as you can make it. There's light enough – the lagoon must be safe; you just follow the beach. Just get her there.'

He said nothing but ran off towards the beach. Piro touched me on the arm. 'Come to canoes.'

Most of us could crowd into the launch and the big canoe took the rest as well as a lot of their own men – it held twenty of us. It was also leaky but by God it was fast! The rowers put their backs into it and it skimmed across the water at a great speed leaving a wake glinting with phosphorescence, and easily keeping up with the launch.

The three miles or so to the hospital took only twenty minutes, but by that time we could see that the whole place was on fire. We could see black figures running about, outlined against the flames, and I wondered how many survivors there were. I was so intent on the scene on shore that I didn't see the ship. Campbell shook me by the shoulder and pointed.

A schooner was anchored in the lagoon just off the hospital. We wouldn't have seen her in the darkness of that terrible night but for the raging fire which gleamed redly on her white hull. I shouted to Campbell, 'What should we do – go to the schooner or the hospital?'

'The hospital – we must save the patients.'

The canoe drove onto the beach, a little way below the hospital and we all splashed ashore and ran towards the fire. I saw that Campbell had produced an automatic pistol, a strange weapon with an extraordinary long, thin barrel. I took out the revolver he had given me and pounded onward, barely able to keep up with the racing Commandoes. The whole hospital was burning fiercely, the dry thatch going up like tinder and the flames streaming to the sky in the windless night.

I ran for the open space between two burning huts and came in sight of the hospital's own landing place. A boat was just moving out and I heard the sudden sharp revving of an outboard motor over the crackle of flames.

'They're getting away,' I yelled, and took a shot at them. Nothing happened – I had forgotten to release the safety catch. Campbell squatted in a half-crouch and took aim with his curious pistol, then straightened up and shook his head. 'Too far. I wish I had a rifle.'

'But we can't let them get away,' I raged.

Campbell shook me roughly by the arm. 'Come on!'

I took one last look at the boat disappearing into the darkness in the direction of the schooner *Pearl* and then raced up the beach after the others, who had already dispersed to join the rest of our crew from the launch. I heard someone shouting. 'You can't put those fires out – save the people!' and I ran across to Schouten's house.

It was no use. The place was enveloped in fire, a roaring mass of flames shooting up fifty feet into the night sky. I wondered if it was Schouten's funeral pyre, and whether he had been mercifully dead when the fires started.

I ran round the house to see what it was like at the back and stumbled across a woman sitting in the path. I recovered my balance and looked back to see that she was cradling Schouten's head in her lap. Her wails rose above the crackle of the flames. '*Aaaah, le pauvre docteur, le pauvre docteur!*'

I bent down and saw that her dress was scorched and torn. She had probably dragged Schouten's body from the house. When she saw me she gave a cry, scrambled to her feet and ran away screaming into the darkness beyond the hospital. She must have thought I was one of Hadley's bunch.

I dropped to one knee beside Schouten. He wasn't a pretty sight because he had been shot through the head more than once. His jaw was torn away and there was a small blue hole in the left temple. The right temple was gone – there was a ragged gap big enough to hold a fist and his brains were leaking out onto the path.

I rose and stumbled away, catching on to a tree for support. Then I vomited my guts out until I was weak and trembling, pouring sweat.

I had barely recovered when Nick Dugan rushed up to me, his face blackened with smoke, and took my arm to help me to my feet. 'You all right?'

'I'll – do.'

'Look, Mike – there's the *Esmerelda*. They've been quick.'

I looked across the water and saw *Pearl* getting under way and, beyond her, *Esmerelda* coming up at a hell of a lick under power, her bow wave flecked red by the reflections from the burning shore. *Pearl* was still moving slowly and I could see from the changing angle of *Esmerelda*'s bow that Ian meant to try and stop her by coming hard alongside or even ramming.

But the schooner was picking up speed under her engine and slid out from *Esmerelda*'s threatening bows. Ian changed course again to converge but just at the moment of impact *Pearl* seemed to spin smartly sideways and *Esmerelda*'s bowsprit only grazed her side. As the two ships passed one another there was a fusillade of shots from *Pearl* and an answering staccato rattle from our ship. I wondered who had guns and who was using them.

Then *Pearl* was safely out of reach, heading across the lagoon for the pass in the reef, lights springing up on board as she went. *Esmerelda* gave up the chase and turned towards the shore, and I heard her engines stop. Saving the hospital had priority and it was too dangerous to follow the fleeing schooner in the dark.

They'd got clean away.

3

Dawn revealed chaos. Trickles of smoke still spiralled skywards from the gutted buildings and the patients – the survivors – huddled together on the beach with friends and the remaining hospital staff. Piro had done a count, and the death roll numbered fourteen, not counting Schouten himself.

We were all weary, scorched and depressed.

Campbell looked about him at the scene of that damned atrocity and his face was grey. 'The bastards,' he said savagely. 'The murdering sons-of-bitches. I'll see them hanged for this.'

'Not if I get them first,' I said.

We were crouched over a couple of benches with hot coffee in our hands, brought ashore from the brigantine. We didn't have enough on board to provide adequately for everyone but we had distributed what we could, and the villagers had brought food of their own for the shocked survivors. The few men whom Schouten had trained were performing heroic feats of first aid but much more was needed. And we had received a bad shock of our own – the morning light revealed that our ship's radio had been smashed, presumably by Kane before he jumped ship. There was no way to send for help,

166

save by going for it in person. Ian, who had done wonders by bringing *Esmerelda* down the coast at night, was castigating himself for not having the radio guarded, but we persuaded him that it wouldn't have been thought necessary at the time. I hadn't even been on board to see Geordie yet, though I was assured that he was doing all right, if still confined to his bunk.

Campbell said, 'I can't see Suarez-Navarro going in for this. They're a rotten crowd, as I've told you, but this is unbelievable.'

I wasn't impressed. 'Know any English history?'

His head jerked up. 'What's that got to do with it?'

'There was an English king – Henry II, I think it was – who had a bishop as his conscience, Thomas à Becket. The legend is that the king was at dinner one day and said, "Will no one rid me of this turbulent priest?" So four of his knights went off and murdered Becket in Canterbury Cathedral.'

I scraped with my foot in the sand. 'When the king found out he was horrified. He abased himself before the Church and did his penances – but he came out on top, after all – he didn't have Becket on his back any more.'

I pointed to the burnt-out hospital. 'Suarez-Navarro have a board meeting and some plump, stuffy director says, "I wish we could do something about Campbell and this interfering chap Trevelyan." So someone like Ramirez goes out and does something, and if everything gets done – and Campbell and Trevelyan get stopped – he gets a bonus paid with no questions asked. And the dividends of Suarez-Navarro pile up, and that director would faint if he saw a cut finger so he doesn't enquire too closely into how the job was done in case he gets sick to the stomach.'

'But they didn't attack us.'

'Not directly. This has more Hadley's trademark, sadistic revenge in the meanwhile. But don't think we're not in danger now.'

Campbell looked up the beach to the patients sitting in their forlorn group. He said slowly, 'Then this wouldn't have happened if we hadn't come here.'

There was a coppery taste in my mouth. 'No. Schouten was

afraid of what would happen, and I told him he'd be all right. I said he'd be protected. What a bloody mess I've made of everything.'

We both fell silent. There was too much that could be said.

Clare came along the beach towards us, carrying a first aid kit. She looked drawn and pensive, but I was more attracted to her than ever. I would have liked to take her in my arms but something prevented me – and she guessed my intention and saw why I couldn't carry it out.

'Mike, your hands are burnt raw. I'll bandage them.'

I looked at my hands. I hadn't really noticed before but now they were beginning to hurt.

She got busy with my hands and spoke with her head down as she worked. 'Pop, I guess this is where you get busy with your cheque book.'

I said harshly, 'A cheque book isn't going to bring fifteen people back to life.'

'You men are damned fools,' she said and her voice was angry. 'What's done is done, and *you* didn't do it, though I guess you're both blaming yourselves. But the hospital is gone, and what's going to happen to the poor people here? Somebody has to do something – we can't just go away and say, Well, we didn't start the fire, even if it's true.'

'I'm sorry, Clare,' I said. 'But what can we do?'

Campbell dug his hands deep into his pockets. 'There'll be another hospital – a good one. And doctors, and good equipment. I'll endow the whole damned thing.' His voice became harder. 'But Suarez-Navarro will pay for it one way or another.'

He walked away down the beach as Clare smeared a cool emulsion on my hands. 'What's that stuff?' I asked. I had to discuss something less painful, though my throbbing hands weren't the best choice of subject in that case.

'Tannic acid jelly. It's good for burns.'

I said, 'No one else has had time to tell us what happened on board. Can you? I didn't know we had guns.'

'Several of the men have them, besides Pop's little armoury. You can be awfully innocent.'

168

'Who was doing the shooting from *Esmerelda*?'

'A couple of the crew – and me,' she said shortly.

I raised my eyebrows. 'You?'

'I'm a good shot. Pop taught me.' She began to cover my hands. 'I think I shot one – and I think it was Kane.' Suddenly her voice broke. 'Oh, Mike, it was awful. I've never shot at a man, only at targets. It was. . . .'

I was entangled in bandages but I somehow managed to get an arm around her shoulders and she buried her head on mine. 'He deserved what was coming to him, Clare. You've only got to look around you to see that. Did you kill him?'

She raised her head and her face was white and tear-streaked. 'I don't think so – the light was bad and everything happened so fast. I think I may have hit him in the shoulder. But – I was *trying* to kill him, Mike.'

'So was I,' I said. 'But my gun didn't go off. I'm not very good with guns, but I tried and I don't regret it.'

She pulled herself together. 'Thanks, Mike. I've been a fool.'

I shook my head. 'No, you're not, Clare. Killing doesn't come easy to people like us. We're not mad dogs like Kane or Hadley, but when we do come up against mad dogs I think it's our duty to try and stop them in any way we can – even if the only way is by killing them.'

I looked down at the top of her head and wished that this whole stinking business was over. It had suddenly come to me that a burnt-out hospital littered with corpses wasn't the best place in the world to tell a girl that you were falling in love with her. I would have to wait for a calm sea and romantic moonlight, with perhaps the strains of a love song echoing from the saloon.

And for the moment I was sickened of the whole chase. How Mark came to die, where his stupid treasure of cobalt lay, none of it mattered. I wanted to be done with the whole affair – bar Clare. And I couldn't get out of any of it that easily. I recognized the symptoms of exhaustion and sat up, bracing myself.

She saw the expression in my eyes and looked away quickly, but I think she read it all there. She said, 'We've got to go through with this now, Mike. We can't let Suarez-Navarro get away with it – if it is them. All this would go for nothing if we did that.'

'I know; but it won't last forever, Clare. There'll be better days coming. I'm all right now. Were any of our chaps hurt besides me?'

'Scorches, a few scrapes. None worse than you,' she told me.

'Good. We have to start getting clear of this lot, then. The local people must carry on until we can get word back.' I left her and went to where Piro was standing and was aware that she was watching me. I would have given anything to be elsewhere with her than on that beach.

I said to Piro, 'What will you do now?'

He turned a sad face to me. 'We build again. All Tanakabu people built more here – many huts. But no doctor. . . .'

I said, 'Piro, Mr Campbell there has money, more than he needs. He will send doctors and you will get a proper hospital, like the one in Papeete. But first we must go back there and tell the police what happened here. Can you write a message for me?'

But it turned out that Piro could not write, nor even sign his name, which was a pity – I wanted a witnessed account of the event to take back, but with Schouten dead there was nobody else to turn to for it.

We buried the dead in the hospital cemetery. I asked about a priest but apparently Schouten had stood in himself for such occasions. They produced a Bible and Campbell pronounced a few words, though few of the locals could understand him. He said, 'We commit to the earth the bodies of those who are the innocent victims of a dreadful crime. "Vengeance is mine", saith the Lord, but it may be He will use men like us as His instrument. I hope so.'

Then he turned and walked away down the beach, a sad and lonely figure.

Schouten was given a grave in a place apart from the others.

I thought this might be because of differing religions, but it appeared that they wished to make his resting-place special, and it was clear that they mourned him deeply. I thought that he would have a better memorial than he might ever have realized would be his lot, and was glad of it.

The islanders were already clearing away rubble, and most of the patients had vanished into other homes, when we left that afternoon. There was nothing we could find to take with us as proof of the disaster – the hospital records and all Schouten's personal belongings had been destroyed. We took photographs, though, and I included a couple of the natives gathering round Campbell and Ian to shake their hands, as proof of our friendship, and also of the crew at the mass funeral.

As Ian conned *Esmerelda* out through the pass of Tanakabu he asked sadly, 'What kind of men are they to do a thing like that? You told us they were dangerous – they seem demented, Mike.'

'They must be psychopaths,' I said. 'From what I learned from the Dutch doctor Hadley certainly is.'

Shorty Powell came on deck, white-faced, at the same time that Campbell emerged looking thunderous. 'I've got something to show you,' he said, and took me down to Kane's cabin together with Ian. On the bunk lay a brown-painted gadget which Shorty had clearly recognised and shown to Campbell.

'It's a walkie-talkie, surplus American army stock, selling for about fifteen dollars each. The range on land isn't much over five miles but on water you can keep contact for—?'

'Say about ten miles,' Shorty supplied.

'So that's how Hadley's schooner turned up so opportunely. And that's what that damned transmission was that Shorty picked up. You said you thought it was a low-powered job and very near, but who'd have thought it was from right here on *Esmerelda*?'

Campbell nodded. 'We've probably been shadowed all over the Pacific. Any boat could keep hull-down on the horizon and Hadley could have cosy chats with Kane.'

I picked up the radio and looked at it curiously. 'I don't

think Kane was clever enough to think of this himself. This bears the hallmark of organization.'

'Ramirez,' said Campbell decisively.

'Very likely,' I said. I was trying to read any further implications into the find when Paula came looking for me and Ian got back up on deck. 'Geordie's asking for you,' she said. She too looked tired, having spent all morning helping Clare on that dreadful beach, and I smiled and gave her a quick hug of friendship and support.

'How is he?'

'He'll be all right, but he's going to need medical care in Papeete, maybe stitches. I'm not a trained nurse, you know.' Considering the dangers we had drawn her into and the shocking things she had seen, I thought she was holding up amazingly well, but then I think toughness was bred into her.

'He may be scarred for life,' she added.

'A pistol whipping is a lousy thing. Damn Hadley!' said Campbell.

We found Geordie sitting up in his bunk, his eyes peering brightly at me through a mass of bandages. He'd been told about the fire and the smashed radio, but was avid for more.

'How are you feeling?' I asked him.

'Not so bad, considering. But I haven't heard the whole story yet. What happened last night between you and the doctor?' he demanded, and I realized with a start that so much had happened since that I hadn't had time to pass on Schouten's terrible story. Having made sure that he was well enough to listen, I gathered Paula, Clare and Campbell into the cabin. They heard me out in stunned silence.

'It's a bad thing,' I said heavily at the end.

'It is that,' said Geordie. 'They must be off their heads.'

I said, 'I don't think Kane's the crazy one. It's Hadley who's the lunatic, a psycho for sure. Kane's cleverer than we thought him to be, though.' I told Geordie about the walkie-talkie.

Campbell said, 'We've been played for suckers and I don't like that one little bit. But with this act I think they've outreached themselves – I have a feeling that Hadley ran amok, and even Ramirez isn't going to like it when he finds out.'

'I've been thinking, trying to put the jigsaw together, you might say,' said Geordie. 'But some of the pieces don't seem to fit.'

'Such as?'

'For one thing, you say that according to Schouten, Kane and Hadley murdered Mark, and that Ramirez was in on it. Why do you think they killed Mark?'

I said, 'I've been thinking about that. It was something that poor old Schouten said – that Hadley had laughed when he asked to see the body and said it would turn the stomach even of a doctor. What would that mean to you?'

'Knowing what we do of Hadley, it could mean torture.'

'And why should they torture Mark?' I should have felt ill at the very thought but somehow it had all become rather academic to me.

'Why does anyone torture anyone? They wanted information out of him.'

'And Ramirez was there. I think they wanted to know where the high-cobalt nodules were to be found.'

'Yes,' said Campbell. 'I've already worked that out for myself. Would Mark tell them?'

'I don't know. He'd look out for his own skin, but he was capable of being very scornful of people like them – he may not have realized that they really meant it until they got down to business, and then it might have been too late.'

The girls studied me in silence, appalled at my implication. But Geordie put it into words. 'You mean Hadley ran amok again and went too far – and he died before he could talk?'

'I think so. They clearly don't know the location, or they wouldn't be tailing us this way. So they buried their mistake, terrorized the doctor, and sent Hadley to get Mark's stuff, hoping for leads there. Hadley bungled it and let the gear slip out of his fingers – thanks to you, Paula – and so Ramirez went to England to get it back, using Kane as scout and contact man.'

'It all seems to fit,' Geordie said.

He lay back on his bunk looking suddenly exhausted, so we left him. We didn't talk about it among ourselves. We were all drained and saddened, and the trip back to Papeete was one devoid of much pleasure for any of us.

We made a quick passage and all went well until we were within about two hours of Papeete, and longing to be ashore. I planned to take Ian, Campbell and one or two members of the crew to the police as soon as we landed, leaving the others to guard the ship, especially Geordie and the girls, zealously. We had no idea where the *Pearl* might be but I wanted to run no risks. I was in my cabin when word came down for me to get on deck fast. Ian, who was acting skipper, pointed to a boat on our starboard beam. It was a fast launch and was cruising around us in a wide circle. 'Yon laddie's come up awful fast, Mike,' he said to me. 'He's up to something. He looks official.'

He handed me binoculars and I saw that it was a patrol boat, naval in style, even to a four-pounder quick-firer mounted on the foredeck. It had a number but no name, and as I looked it turned to approach us directly. 'You'd better call Mr Campbell,' I said.

The launch came up alongside and kept pace with idling engines about fifty yards away. An officer by the wheelhouse raised a loudhailer and a spate of French crossed the water.

I raised my arms to shrug violently to indicate that I didn't understand. Another man took the loudhailer and shouted in English, 'Heave to, *Esmerelda*, or we will fire.'

I looked at the gun on the foredeck. Two matelots were manning it – one had just slammed a magazine in and the other was swinging the gun around to train it just about midships.

'What the hell!' I exploded. But one couldn't argue with a four-pounder. I heard Ian giving brisk orders and the sails came tumbling down everywhere as the off-watch crewmen tumbled up on deck, Campbell among them.

'What the hell's going on?' he asked loudly.

'We're being boarded by the navy,' I said, 'in the traditional style. If we don't stop they'll open fire – the man said so.'

Campbell looked at the little gun in fascination. 'Well, I'll be double-damned,' he said. 'Pirates?'

'Not this close in. It's official.'

The sails were all down and *Esmerelda* lost way and started to pitch a little. The patrol boat edged nearer and finally came alongside, lines went across, and an officer jumped on board followed by three sailors. He had a revolver and the sailors were carrying sub-machine guns. Our men backed up, alarmed and disconcerted by all this, and I saw Campbell make a violent if surreptitious gesture to the girls to keep below decks.

'M. Trevelyan?' the officer barked.

I stepped forward. 'I'm Michael Trevelyan.'

A sub-machine gun lifted until the muzzle was pointed at my stomach. 'You are under arrest.'

I looked at him dumbfoundedly. 'What for?'

Campbell stepped forward aggressively. 'Now look here—' he began. The officer gestured and the other two sailors lifted their weapons and there were ominous snicks as the safety-catches were released. Ian caught at Campbell's shoulder and he subsided.

The officer said, 'You will learn about it in Papeete. You will please come aboard my boat. You—' He turned to Ian. 'You will accompany us in under engine. These men will stay on board with you. You will attempt nothing foolish, please.'

I looked into his cold grey eyes and realized that he wasn't kidding. I felt a sense of sick reluctance to leave the *Esmerelda* but there really was no choice, and I swung myself across without a word. I was briefly searched, and then led below to a cabin with a minimum of furnishing – a cell afloat – and once inside I heard the door being locked.

I was on my own.

4

I was pretty miserable – I didn't know what was going on, nor had I any means of finding out, though I certainly had ideas – too many of them. If only I could have talked to someone I would have felt better, but that was impossible. I wondered how they were all making out.

We went the remaining few miles into Papeete at a speed slow enough for *Esmerelda* to keep up, no doubt still under the threat of the gun. There were no portholes in my cabin and I couldn't hear much either, but the arrival at a jetty was unmistakable, and I braced myself for whatever was coming. Sure enough within a few minutes they were at the door, unlocking it, and then I was brought up into the sunshine to see that we were back in Papeete but not in our old position; instead it seemed to be a naval area. I saw *Esmerelda* tied up alongside us but there were only French sailors on deck, none of my friends to be seen. A police car was waiting for me. My legs felt like lead as I went ashore and got into it.

There was a police station, possibly the principal one, and I was taken immediately and without any formalities into another cell and left there. It was devastatingly bleak. A good couple of hours passed and then I was let out once more, this time to be escorted to a large business-like office, and to confront an angry-looking, mottle-faced man behind the inevitable desk. I stood in front of it with my escort, and another man behind us at the door. I had already decided on a plan of action, such as it was – I was going to go immediately onto the offensive. To be meek was intolerable to me and also foolish, for it might imply guilt where I certainly felt none. So as soon as the man in front of me began to speak I overrode him.

'I want to see the British Consul!'

'Sit down.'

'No. I answer no questions without the presence of the Consul.'

He slapped the table with the flat of his hand, and I was jerked back into a chair. I saw a nameplate on his desk which told me that he was one Jacques Chamant, and with a title which I mentally translated as Chief of Police. I was right at the top, it seemed. It had to be pretty bad. And I already had a ghastly suspicion as to what it was.

'I stand on no ceremony with you, Trevelyan.' Another man with more than passable English. 'There has been a massacre at Tanakabu which you started – and we will have your head for it.'

I stared at him, outraged. 'Are you crazy?'

He leaned his elbows on the desk. 'I have a dossier here on you. You came to Papeete last week and made some very serious accusations against Dr Schouten, on Tanakabu, accusations which would ruin his reputation as a medical man. You were told that someone would take steps to verify your vilifications, but that was not good enough for you. You cleared Papeete with the stated intention of sailing westward, but instead you went to Tanakabu.'

I listened in silence, in spite of my resolve.

'You got to Tanakabu and evidently had a quarrel with Schouten – and you murdered him. To cover your tracks you set fire to his house, and the entire hospital caught fire resulting in many deaths. Your crew is implicated in this as well – you are all guilty men.'

I blinked and sank down in the chair, stunned by the rage in his voice and the whole messy situation. We had made a very fast return trip to Papeete and as far as I knew there were no radio-telephones on Tanakabu, so there was only one way the police could know what had happened. I seized on a couple of things he had said and decided to make the best use of them that I could.

'Can it be that you don't know exactly how many were killed? Have you had any direct contact with the island?' I

asked rapidly. I didn't know how much time I would hav
before he had me silenced.

He hesitated and I knew I was on the right track.

'How did you get the information? Was it a man calle
Hadley – off a ship called the *Pearl*?'

That went straight to the mark – a bullseye. He coughed
oddly hesitant, and said, 'I do not see that it makes an
difference, but you are correct. Mr Hadley described th
reign of terror on Tanakabu very circumstantially. He state
that he barely escaped with his own life and that you attemp
ted to run his ship down.'

Good! I had him on the defensive already. It was I wh
should be doing the talking, not he. I sensed already th
faintest thread of doubt in his voice and pressed on.

'You say I "evidently" quarrelled with Dr Schouten. Wha
"evidence" is there? I left him after a long talk, none th
worse for it. There was a witness to that, an islander calle
Piro. He drove me from my ship. He will also attest that w
came to save the hospital when it was already burning – and s
will many others there. You have no right to arrest me. Or an
of us!'

He was listening intently and did not interrupt me. Behin
me the policemen stood like statues. I didn't understand wh
things were going my way but I was feeling stronger by th
minute.

'Why don't you study that file, M. Chamant? You've got i
down in black and white – Hadley was the man who i
supposed to have found my brother, but whom *I* say was hi
murderer – and Schouten told me so. I can't prove that now
but I can prove everything else.'

I remembered another fact and produced it triumphantly.

'I took photographs. Develop my film. It will tell you
everything.'

'M. Trevelyan, I am listening carefully. Of course we wil
check your camera, and we have already sent a police patro
boat to Tanakabu. But you still have a great deal to explain
and you are not yet released from arrest.'

I said, 'I've got plenty to tell you! That damned bastard and his mate Kane – they're the ones you want. They murdered Sven Norgaard, they murdered my brother, they murdered that poor bloody Schouten and they killed fourteen patients in his hospital – burnt them alive, do you hear – they burnt those poor wretches alive!'

Chamant was gesturing to the two policemen who heaved on my shoulders. I had lost all restraint in my anger, and was trying to climb over the table in my frenzy of trying to make Chamant see the truth. I slumped back, shaking a little and fighting for self-control. There was silence for a moment as we all contemplated my words.

'Where is Hadley now?' I asked him, trying to stay on the offensive.

He regarded me closely in silence still, then nodded gravely. He gave instructions to one of the men in rapid French, and the officer left the room smartly. Then he looked at me. 'I am not yet ready to believe you. But we will speak again with M. Hadley, I assure you. Meantime, I ask you to explain this, if you can.'

He pointed to a small box on a side-table and one of the remaining policemen brought it to his desk. Opened, it revealed four guns and a little pile of boxes of ammunition. I recognized two of the guns immediately.

'Four guns with enough ammunition to start a war, M. Trevelyan. Not a cargo for a peaceful ship, a scientific expedition.'

'Where did you find them?' But I could guess, and I was troubled. This was going to set back the progress I'd made.

'Three in the cabin of your M. Campbell. One in the possession of M. Wilkins, your captain.'

I made a weak gesture. There didn't seem to be much to say.

'You have seen them before?'

I said, 'Yes, two of them. Mr Campbell gave me that one when we discovered that Kane had gone from our ship. I must tell you the whole story, in sequence you understand. This other one he had himself. But—'

'But?'

'Neither of us fired a shot! If you exhume Schouten you'll see he was shot three times, I think.'

'Only the other two were fired.'

'Yes, on our ship – when Hadley was getting away. We did try to ram him, to stop him – to bring him to justice.' That phrase sounded melodramatic enough even for a Frenchman to gag on it, I thought.

'You will tell me the story.'

So I did, leaving out all references to our search for manganese nodules, to Ramirez and Suarez-Navarro. I thought that made it all far too complicated. I said only that Hadley, once chartering a boat for my brother and Norgaard, had quarrelled with them for reasons unknown, had murdered both of them and had implicated the Dutch doctor in his crime. I had come to seek the truth and had run into a hornet's nest. It was circumstantial and very tidy. He made notes from time to time but said little.

When I finished he said, 'You will write all this down and sign it, please. I am going to allow you to return to your ship, but you will see that you and all your crew are confined to quarters on board. There will be a police guard.'

He was interrupted by the return of the officer he had sent out, who came straight to his side and whispered agitatedly to him. They both got up to look out of the window and went on speaking in urgent undertones, in French. And somehow I guessed what they were talking about.

'It's Hadley, isn't it?'

He turned to face me.

'You've let him get away, haven't you? You've let that murderous thug walk out of here!'

He nodded heavily. 'Yes, he has apparently left. You must understand that there was no reason to hold him, after he placed the information and made a deposition. We would not expect him to leave here – it is his home port.'

Something about the way he spoke told me that he was deeply troubled, to the point of forgetting that he was speaking to a man under arrest. I could guess why. Hadley was surely known here as a tough and a trouble-maker. The police may well have had him under surveillance already, for his connections with Mark and Norgaard, and for all I knew for a score of other things. And in letting him get away M. Chamant had blotted his own copybook rather badly. I was furious and exultant at the same time.

He got himself in hand and gave instructions to take me back to *Esmerelda*, and I was only too happy to go. House arrest seemed insignificant compared to being locked up in a cell. I went on board and was not particularly bothered by the sight of armed police dotted about, a couple on deck and more on the quayside, and a little knot of spectators shifting about as if waiting for a show to begin. In fact I managed a grin and a half-wave at them as I was ushered below, to their delight and the guard's disapproval.

There was a babble of voices at my return and the same air of tense expectancy as on the dockside, only here it was tinged with anxiety and bafflement. They all crowded around me and started firing questions.

'Wait up!' I held them off goodnaturedly. 'Plenty of time – too much, if anything. First, I want a wash-up and about a gallon of coffee and some food. Who's cook?'

I headed determinedly for my cabin to get a change of clothes, leaving the others to see to my inner comforts – and was brought up by the sight of Geordie, still in his bunk in the cabin we'd been sharing all along.

'Geordie! What the hell are you doing here? Shouldn't you be in the hospital?' I was already seething at this inhuman treatment, but he waved me down casually.

'I'm fine, boy. It's good to see you. What happened to you?'

'Geordie, I'll tell you together with the rest, once I've washed and had some coffee. Are you sure you're all right?'

But in fact he looked a lot better, and I could see that his face had been professionally attended to, with neat stitches and tidier bandaging. As I stripped he said, 'They wanted to cart me off but I sat firm. There's nothing wrong with me that their pretty visiting nurse can't fix. I'd get her to take a look at you too.'

He nodded at my hands, still partly covered with burnt

181

skin, though they had started to heal pretty well on the short trip back. I completed a quick ablution and was finally seated in the saloon over breakfast and surrounded by the whole of the crew of the *Esmerelda* – bar one. It was an immense relief not to see Kane's face among the others.

I told them as much as they needed to know, reserving a few more private comments for Geordie and Campbell later.

'He's a worried man, that Chamant. Was even when he saw me, and he has to be even more so now that Hadley's skipped,' Campbell said.

'He saw you?'

'Oh yes, and the girls too, and Ian – wanted to speak to Geordie but he was unaccountably sicker just then.' Geordie, propped up on a saloon berth, winked at me, and I realized that my news had cheered everyone up amazingly. Although we, and our ship, were all technically still under arrest it was clear that we weren't in any real trouble, thanks to the various bits of evidence I had offered the police chief, and we lacked only physical freedom – not any of the oppression of spirit that imprisonment usually meant.

'Tell me about your interview,' I asked Campbell.

It had apparently been somewhat hilarious. Instead of being chastened at being caught with a small armoury under his bunk Campbell was airy and unconcerned about it, claiming that the guns were properly licensed, that he was a well-known collector and wouldn't dream of travelling without something for target practice, and that in any case only one of his guns had been fired – and that by his daughter, gallantly defending herself from attack by a shipload of murderous pirates. He was scathing about Clare's poor shooting and seemed not at all troubled by her having winged a man, only irked by her not having killed him outright. It appeared that while in Papeete, Kane had had a small bullet taken from his shoulder, ironically by the same doctor who tended to Geordie. He was not, it seemed, badly hurt, which disappointed Campbell considerably.

He was soundly reproved for not having declared the guns on his arrival and was threatened with their confiscation, but he'd wangled his way out of that somehow; and had got away with their being sealed at the mouth for the duration of our stay.

It turned out that the other gun that I had seen belonged to Nick Dugan, and he was similarly ticked off. According to Clare there had been at least two other small handguns in use during *Esmerelda*'s fight with *Pearl*, but none of them surfaced during the search that was made, and I asked no questions. I also learned that Geordie had a shotgun on board which apart from being legally licenced, had even been declared by him to the Papeete customs – and was the only gun on board that had not seen some action.

Campbell had blustered much as I had and had invoked all the powers he could think of to back his credentials, and apparently M. Chamant had done much what he had done with me – had let him speak at will, listened carefully, and had finally released him back to the ship with a fairly mild request that he write down an account of the affair. Everything pointed to our story being accepted, and indeed later that afternoon the guards began to let us all out on deck in twos and threes for some exercise, after they'd moved *Esmerelda* to a mooring buoy well away from the quayside. Things were looking up, and we all turned in that night a great deal happier than we'd been at the start of the day.

5

A senior police official came on board next morning and took formal statements from everyone on board, which took a considerable time, though some of us had written them out in advance and needed only to sign them in the official presence. My camera was removed as well, and I prayed that my photography had been up to scratch. The doctor came to see Geordie again and Campbell cornered him and asked innumerable questions about the hospital on Tanakabu, and about the possibility of getting another doctor to go out there soon.

We were all beginning to feel restless and uneasy. In spite of some relaxation, we were still confined to the ship and as they kept us battened down apart from whoever was being allowed on deck it was stifling and airless on board.

Some time in the afternoon Geordie sent word that he'd like a word with me and so I went to his cabin. He was propped up in bed and surrounded by books. His face was still heavily bandaged but he was obviously much stronger and the effects of the concussion had long worn off.

'Sit down, boy,' he said. 'I think I've found something.'

'To do with what?' I asked, though I could already guess. Several of the books were nautical and the *Pilot* was prominent among them. 'Has it got to do with those damned nodules?'

'Yes, it has. Just listen awhile, will you?'

I felt a small indefinite itch starting in the back of my skull. At the end of the terrible business on Tanakabu I had felt sickened of the whole search and had wanted nothing more to do with it. The nodules could lie on the seabed forever as far as I was concerned, and with the murder of Mark more or less exposed even the urge to lay that ghost had died away to a dull resignation. But now, deprived of ordinary activity, I couldn't help feeling that it would be interesting to have the problem to chew on again, and my professional curiosity was rising to the surface once more. So I settled down to hear Geordie out without protest.

'I was thinking of that lunatic Kane,' he said. 'He slipped up when he mentioned New Britain – the time he shouldn't have known about it. I got to thinking that maybe he'd slipped up again, so I started to think of all the things he ever said that I knew of, and I found this. It's very interesting light reading.'

He handed me Volume Two of the *Pacific Ocean Pilot* opened at a particular page, and I began to read where he pointed. Before I had got to the bottom of the page my eyebrows had lifted in surprise. It was a lengthy passage and took some time to absorb, and when I had finished I said noncommittally, 'Very interesting, Geordie – but why?'

He said carefully, 'I don't want to start any more hares – we blundered badly over Minerva – but I think that's the explanation of the other drawing in the diary. If it seems to fit in with your professional requirements, that is.'

It did.

'Let's get the boss in on this,' I said and he half-lifted himself from his bunk in delight. He'd played his fish and caught it.

I got up and went to round up Campbell, Ian and Clare and brought them back to the cabin. 'Okay, Geordie. Begin at the beginning.' I could see that the others were as pleased as I had been to have something new to think about.

'I was thinking about Kane,' Geordie said. 'I was going over in my mind everything he'd said. Then I remembered that when he'd seen Clare's drawings he'd called one of them a "scraggy falcon". We all saw it as an eagle, didn't we? So I checked on falcons in the *Pilot* and found there really is a Falcon Island. The local name is Fonua Fo'ou but it's sometimes called Falcon because it was discovered by HMS *Falcon* in 1865.'

Clare said, 'But where's the "disappearing trick"?'

'That's the joker,' I said. 'Falcon Island disappears.'

'Now wait a minute,' said Campbell, a little alarmed. 'We've had enough of this nonsense with Minerva.'

'It's not quite the same thing,' said Geordie. '*Récife de Minerve* was a shoal – exact position unknown. Falcon, or Fonua Fo'ou, has had its position measured to a hair – but it isn't always there.'

'What the hell do you mean by that?' Campbell exploded.

Geordie grinned and said to me, 'You'd better tell them – you're the expert.'

'Falcon Island is apparently the top of a submarine volcano of the cinder type,' I said soberly. 'Every so often it erupts and pumps out a few billion tons of ash and cinders, enough to form a sizeable island.' I referred to the *Pilot*. 'In 1889 it was over a mile square and about a hundred and fifty feet high; in

April 1894 there wasn't anything except a shoal, but by December of the same year it was three miles long, one and a half miles wide, and fifty feet high.'

I pointed to the pages. 'There's a long record of its coming and goings, but to bring it up to date – in 1930, Falcon was one and a quarter miles long and four hundred and seventy feet high. In 1949 it had vanished and there were nine fathoms of water in the same position.'

I passed the book over to Campbell. 'What seems to happen is that the island gets washed away. The material coming out of the volcano would be pretty friable and a lot of it would be soluble in water.'

He said, 'Does this tie in with your theory of nodule formation?'

'It ties in perfectly. If these eruptions have been happening once every, say, twenty years, for the last hundred thousand years, that's a hell of a lot of material being pumped into the sea. The percentage of metals would be minute, but that doesn't matter. The process of nodule formation takes care of that – what metals there are would be scavenged and concentrated, ready to be picked up.'

Campbell looked baffled. 'You come up with the damndest things,' he complained. 'First a reef that might or might not be there, and now a goddam disappearing island. What's the present state of this freak?'

I looked at Geordie.

'I don't know. I'll check up in the *Pilot* supplements – but they're often printed a little behind the times anyway. The locals may know.'

'Where is Falcon or Fonua-whatsit – when it's available?'

'In the Friendly Islands,' I said. Clare smiled at that. 'The Tongan group. It's about forty miles north of Tongatapu, the main island.'

He frowned. 'That's a long way from Rabaul, and that's where the Suarez-Navarro crowd is. And it's a long way from here, where Mark was.'

I said mildly, 'It's halfway between.'

He nodded thoughtfully and we all chewed on it for a few

minutes. After a while I spoke up. 'In the light of this information, I think it would be worth concentrating on Falcon – if you're carrying on, that is?' I looked enquiringly at Campbell.

'Yes, of course I am,' he said energetically. His optimistic side was gaining steadily. 'You really think this will be worth trying?'

Clare supported me. 'I was sure those drawings meant something.'

'Minerva meant two months of wasted time,' Campbell said. 'What do you think, Geordie?'

Geordie looked at me but with conviction. 'He's the expert.'

Ian Lewis waited with courteous patience. He was prepared to go anywhere, and do anything that was wanted of him. In spite of the horror of Tanakabu he was having a wonderful time, away from the dullness of home life.

The issue was settled for us while Campbell ruminated. A vagrant breeze from the open port flipped back a page or so of the *Pilot* and I happened to glance down. I looked at the page incredulously and began to laugh uncontrollably.

Campbell said, 'For God's sake, what's so funny?'

I dumped the book into Geordie's hands and he too began laughing. I said, 'It seems we looked at the wrong Minerva. Look – Minerva Reefs, two hundred and sixty miles south-west of Tongatapu – that puts them only about three hundred miles from Falcon Island.'

'You mean there's *another* Minerva?'

'That's exactly what I mean.'

Geordie handed him the book. 'They're fully mapped. They're on a plateau twenty-eight miles long. It's hard ground – shell, coral and volcanic cinders, at a depth of eighteen hundred to thirty-six hundred feet.'

'Just like Falcon Island but much, much older and well established,' I put in.

'There's no mention of nodules,' Campbell said.

'These are naval records and the navy wouldn't dredge for them. They'd just take soundings using a waxed weight to

sample the bottom material. A nodule – even a small one –
would be too heavy to stick to the wax.'

There was a rising air of jubilation in the small cabin.

Campbell said, 'Well, that does it, I suppose. We go to
Tonga.' He looked at us all fiercely. 'But this time there'd
better be no mistakes.'

So it was settled what we'd do after we left Papeete – if we
left Papeete.

6

It seemed a long time.

Apparently a patrol boat had gone to Tanakabu and returned three days later, during which time things had got a
little easier for us, but not much. All the crew members had
been allowed to go ashore in batches, but Ian, the Campbells
and I were still confined, as was Geordie for slightly different
reasons. Paula managed to be allowed ashore mainly because
she seemed to know everyone, including the policemen, but
she only went under Jim or Taffy's escort and didn't stay
ashore for long, having little faith in Hadley's having truly
disappeared.

On the fourth day we were taken ashore, Campbell and I,
and driven to the police station where we were ushered into
the same office as before. M. Chamant was awaiting us.

He was quite pleasant. 'Our findings on Tanakabu are
consistent with your statements. I note that M. Trevelyan
called off the search as soon as he found that the man Kane
was armed, which is a point in your favour. I also found that
you saved many lives at the hospital, and it is known that you
were all aboard your ship when the doctor was shot and the
fires started. Also your photographs were helpful.'

It was good news, and as near to an apology as we'd ever
get.

'When can we leave?' asked Campbell.

188

Chamant shrugged. 'We cannot hold you. If we had Kane and Hadley here you would be expected to stay and give evidence at their hearing, but. . . .'

'But you haven't found them,' I said bitterly.

'If they are in French Oceania we will find them. But the Pacific is large.'

At least they seemed convinced of Hadley and Kane's guilt, which would have come out sooner or later anyway. Hadley had been seen ashore and recognized by several of the people on Tanakabu, and it made me wonder all the more why they had stopped in Papeete to put the police on a false trail, instead of picking up their heels. But I thought that perhaps Hadley, whose mental processes were not as evident as his brutality, really thought that we would be found guilty of his crime, and so out of his way forever. It was impossible to try and read his mind. Now, if they were being hunted by the law themselves they would have less time to go after us, and we had already agreed to act as if they didn't exist, otherwise we'd get nowhere.

'You can go whenever you want, M. Campbell.'

'We're going west as we originally said,' Campbell told him. 'We're heading towards Tonga. If we see them out there we'll let the authorities know.' We were being cooperative now, wanting no further opposition to our going about our own business.

Chamant said, 'Very well, gentlemen. You may go. I will send instructions for the police guard to be withdrawn. But you will take care to be on your best behaviour for the remainder of your stay here, and I also strongly suggest that you leave these waters soon. Your family—' He pointed to me. 'Your family seems to cause trouble here, whether or not you intend to. And we do not want trouble on our hands.'

Campbell closed a hand firmly over my wrist. 'Thank you, M. Chamant. We appreciate all you have said. And now can you arrange transport back to our ship, please?'

He was reluctant on general principles but finally we got a ride back to the docks and a short run out to *Esmerelda*, to carry back the welcome news of our release. Everyone deserved a couple of days off, and neither Campbell nor I begrudged them the time. The radio had been repaired and we had a lot of planning to do before we could set sail for the Friendly Islands, one of which might be there, or might not.

Chapter Six

1

t was good to be at sea again, pounding along under the unfailing impulse of the trade wind. It would take about six days to sail to Tonga and we soon settled into shipboard routine.

Geordie was up and about. Although his face looked like the map of a battlefield he was fit enough otherwise, and took over the command from a reluctant Ian, who had gloried in his brief spell as skipper. The fresh wind blew away the last taint of Tanakabu and everyone benefited, and Kane's disappearance had lifted the last reserve of secretiveness. They were all in the know now, including Geordie's own crewmen, as we felt that it was only fair to warn them all of possible danger ahead, though none had taken advantage of Geordie's offer to pay their fares home if they wished to leave us.

And Paula was still with us. Somehow that had been taken for granted and she had fitted in so well to shipboard life that there was no sense of surprise in her having agreed to come along. She and Clare set one another off nicely.

I immersed myself in text books and charts. I wanted to study currents, so I asked Geordie for pilot charts of the area. 'Not that they'll be any great help,' I said. 'The currents might have changed considerably in the last fifty thousand years. That's why Mark worked with Norgaard – he was an expert at that sort of thing.'

'The pilot charts only have the surface currents,' said Geordie. 'Who knows what goes on under the surface?'

'There are gadgets that can tell that sort of thing, though I haven't one with me. And they can't tell us what went on fifty thousand years ago, more's the pity.' I expounded. 'Here is

Fonua Fo'ou. There's a warm offshoot of the South Equatorial Current sweeping south-west past the island. That should mean that any nodule deposits will also be laid down south-west of the island. But it's a surface current – there may be other currents lower down, going in different directions. That we'll have to check, if we can.'

I frowned at my own words. 'The thing is, have those currents changed direction in those last fifty thousand years? I don't know, but I shouldn't think so. It's not very long.'

Geordie snorted.

I put my finger on the chart. 'What I'm really worried about is this spot here. That's the Tonga Trench – our dredge will only go to 30,000 feet, and Horizon Depth in the Trench is nearly 35,000.'

'Quite a bit of water,' said Geordie dryly. 'That's over six and a half miles – a man could drown in that depth of water.'

'If the high-cobalt nodules have formed at the bottom of the Trench we're wasting time,' I said, ignoring his baiting. 'You could dredge them up, but it wouldn't be an economic proposition – it would just amount to pouring money into the sea. By the way, I haven't mentioned this to the boss. It would only cause alarm and despondency, and it might never happen.'

'I won't tell him,' he promised.

But I did seek out Campbell for another reason, and found him on deck in his favourite spot reading a book. We chatted for a few minutes about the ship and the weather, and then I said, 'Is it true what Clare said – that you're a crack shot?'

'I'm not too bad,' he said modestly if a little complacently.

'I'd like to learn how to shoot. I didn't get off a shot back there at Tanakabu, and those bastards were popping off all over the show.'

He grinned. 'What happened?'

'I think I forgot to release the safety catch.'

'I thought that might be it,' he said. 'It's obvious you don't know much about the game.'

'I don't know anything,' I said positively.

'Good. Then you won't have any bad habits to get rid of. Stick around. I'll get the pistols.'

He came back with four guns and laid them on deck: Three I'd seen and one which was new to me, but a twin of the one I'd handled. I didn't ask him where it had been hidden. He said, 'I didn't know what kind of trouble we'd be running into, so I took out insurance and brought along these two .38s for you and Geordie.'

'What about yours?'

'Oh, I like this, the .22. They're for me and Clare – she's a pretty good shot, if in need of practice.'

'I've always thought that a .22 was useless against a man,' I said.

'You're like the cops. They always think you can't use anything but a .38 or bigger,' said Campbell contemptuously. 'Look at it this way – who are the men who habitually use handguns?'

I thought about it. 'The police, the army, criminals and hobbyists – like yourself.'

'Right. Now, an army officer doesn't get much time for practice, nor the wartime officer – so they give him the biggest gun he can hold, one that packs a hell of a wallop – a .45. With that gun he doesn't have to be a dead shot. If he only wings his man, that man is knocked flat on his back.'

Campbell picked up a .38. 'Now the police get more practice and they're usually issued with, or equip themselves with, these. A nice handy gun that will fit inconspicuously into a holster out of sight, but because of that the barrel's too short, resulting in some loss of accuracy. You've got to have a lot of practice to be good with one of these.'

He exchanged it for a .22. 'With this you have definitely got to be a good shot; the bullet is small and hasn't any inherent stopping power, so you have to be able to put it in the right place. But the gun is deadly accurate – this one is, at any rate. If you meet up with a man who habitually packs a .22 steer clear of him, especially if he's filed away the front sight, because that means he's a snapshooter – a natural shot.'

I said, 'What's the range of these guns?'

'Oh, they've all got a hell of a range, but that's not th
point. What counts is the accurate range, and with any han
gun it's not very much. A guy who is an average shot will sto
a man at ten yards with the .38. A crack shot will stop his ma
at twenty yards. And I'm not talking about target practice o
the range – I'm talking about action where the other guy i
shooting back.'

He waved the long-barrelled .22. 'With this gun I'll kill
man at thirty yards – maybe a bit further.'

I asked curiously, 'You once said you had killed. Was i
with this?'

'Yes, in South America once. The jungle Indians don't lik
trespassers.'

He said no more about it, and I let it lie.

So he began to teach me how to shoot. He started with the
basic principles, stripping the guns and explaining the action
Then he showed me how to stand, and eventually how to hol
a gun.

'I'm not going to waste time with you on the classic stance,
he said. 'That's for the police and championship target boys
If you tried you'd be filled full of holes before you sighted o
your man. I want you to start with snapshooting. It's some
thing you have or you haven't – let's see if you've got it. Poin
your finger at the mast.'

I did so and he followed the line of direction. 'Not bad
If your finger had been a gun barrel – a steady one – you'
have made a hole in the mast just a little off centre. Do i
again.'

So I did it again – and again – and again. Then he gave me a
.38. 'Now do it.'

I pointed the gun at the mast and he shook his head. 'You'd
miss by a foot. Put your forefinger alongside the barrel and do
it again.'

I pointed the gun again with better results. 'You won't have
your finger there when you shoot,' he said. 'It might be cut off
by the action. But I want you to be able to point that barrel
just like you point your finger.'

He drilled me for four hours every day on the voyage to

194

Tonga. The rest of the crew crowded around at first, all asking for lessons, but Campbell declined, saying that one pupil at a time was his limit and that in any case there were no spare guns. Geordie endorsed this. Those of the crew who did have guns did a little target practice but no one had much ammunition to spare and soon they left us to get on with it.

I had to learn how to point the gun when standing, sitting, lying down and lastly, after a sudden turn. Then he concentrated on the trigger finger, making me squeeze the trigger gently without a jerk. He filed the sear of the trigger until it clicked at a very slight pressure and then made me practice a draw, snapping off the safety catch, pointing the gun and squeezing the trigger all in one flowing motion.

On the third day I fired my first shot.

Campbell set up a rough target in the bows and when I stood near the foremast and squeezed that trigger I was certain that I had missed. But he led me to the target and pointed to a hole only two inches off centre. 'You'd make a pretty fair ten yard man,' he said. 'Give me another year or two and I'll make a good shot out of you.'

He took his .22 and, standing at the same distance, loosed off six shots in as many seconds. 'Now look at the target,' he said.

He had put a neat circle of small holes round the larger one made by my bullet. 'Give me time and you'll be able to do that,' he said in reply to my honest praise.

'I doubt if we'll have time. Not if I run up against Kane and company in the near future.'

'You think we will? The Suarez-Navarro ship is still up in Rabaul as far as I know.'

'I don't think it will stay there,' I said. 'They'll be on our trail.'

Campbell suddenly seemed depressed. 'How do we know it's the right trail? We're only going on a wild hunch – a hunch that a couple of doodled drawings do mean something.'

He turned and went below, the pistols dangling heavily in his hands.

2

We raised the island of Tongatapu on the morning of the sixth day out of Papeete. Nuku'alofa, the southern port of entry for the Tongan group, is on the north side of the island, so Geordie changed the heading of *Esmerelda*.

He said to me, 'There's a paragraph in the *Pilot* that says you have to keep a sharp lookout for undersea volcanic activity and new shoals in these waters.'

I smiled. 'Sounds good from my point of view.'

'Not so good from mine. I have to skipper this ship.'

But we entered the anchorage without sighting anything unusual, tied up and settled down to wait for the port officials. Nuku'alofa was a typical Pacific island town; the wooden houses with their galvanized iron roofs forever frozen in a late-Victorian matrix. At one time it had looked as though Nuku'alofa was going to be the chief trading port and coaling station of the Western Pacific; but Suva, in the Fiji Islands, eventually came out on top, possibly for no more profound reason than that it was an easier name to pronounce. At any rate, Nuku'alofa lost its chance and relapsed into a timeless trance.

Once free to go ashore Campbell headed for the post office as usual. I went off with the two girls who were going to book in at an hotel. Clare announced that she was tired of salt water showers. 'My hair's in a mess and I can't get the salt out. It needs cutting,' she said. 'I want fresh water and luxury for a while.'

I said thoughtfully, 'It looks as though we may be based on Nuku'alofa for some time. Maybe I'd better do the same – get a room for me and see if Geordie wants one. A ship's all right if you can get off it once in a while.'

Paula felt happier here too, with Hadley a remote risk and nobody else around whom she knew either. It was a lot more relaxing for all of us than our second visit to Papeete. We arrived at the hotel and Clare said, 'My God, look at all that gingerbread!' It was a museum piece sprouting galvanized iron turrets and cupolas in the most unlikely places; inside it was pleasantly cool and dark with big electric fans lazily circulating the air.

At the reception desk we ran into trouble when we asked for five rooms – they had only three, one single and two doubles. I said to Clare, 'That's all right if you don't mind doubling up with Paula again. Geordie and I will share and your father can have the single.'

The receptionist was most apologetic. There had been an unprecedented rush on accommodation just recently. I left the desk feeling that perhaps Nuku'alofa was going to give Suva a run for its money after all.

I arranged with the girls to meet them in the lounge in an hour or so and went upstairs to soak in a hot bath, and to lay schemes for getting Clare away by myself somewhere that evening – the first chance I would have had since Papeete. When I came downstairs I found them already in the lounge with tall glasses of beer in front of them, frosted on the sides. 'That's a good idea,' I said and looked at the label on the bottle. It was Australian beer – Swan. For a moment I was back in London on a wet dull day a million years ago. 'That's Kane's favourite tipple. Maybe he'll be around for a drink.'

Clare looked past me. 'Here comes Pop.'

Campbell came over to the table with a sheaf of correspondence in his hand and the inevitable worried look on his face. Clare said, 'Have a cold beer, Pop. It's just the thing for this weather.'

He dropped heavily into a cane chair which creaked protestingly. 'I think we've come to the wrong place,' he said abruptly.

I signalled to a hovering waiter and ordered a couple of beers. 'What's the trouble?'

He unfolded a cable. 'The Suarez-Navarro crowd have moved again to Nouméa in New Caledonia.'

I raised my eyebrows, 'Interesting, but not very informative. I wonder what they're doing there?'

'I don't know but it doesn't look too good to me. According to what we've figured they don't know where the stuff is, so what the hell are they drifting round the Pacific for? It looks as though they're as lost as we are.'

Clare said thoughtfully, 'Maybe Mark gave them a bum steer before he died.'

I shook my head. 'No, if he'd done that they would have been out testing for it, and we know they haven't. But we're not lost – at least we don't think so. We're here for a purpose.'

I glanced through the door of the lounge and saw the receptionist working at his accounts. I said, 'Excuse me for a minute,' and went into the foyer where I had an interesting little five-minute chat with him, which included the passing of a discreet backhander across the counter. I went back into the lounge, sat down and took a long, lingering draught of cold beer. Then I said, 'We're in the right place.'

They all stared at me. 'How do you know? How can anyone know?'

I said, 'One Ernesto Ramirez has booked half a dozen rooms in this hotel. He hasn't turned up yet.'

Campbell looked startled and Clare let out a yelp of pure joy. Paula, on the other hand, visibly shrank back in her chair, and I made a quick mental note of that. I said, 'I thought it a bit odd that the hotel should be so full right now, so I checked up on it. Ramirez booked the rooms and paid handsomely for them in advance; he wrote that he didn't know exactly when he was coming, but that the rooms must be kept free.'

'I'll be damned,' said Campbell. 'But what's he been doing in Nouméa?'

'I think he's been stooging around in this area all the time, getting slowly closer to wherever we were, and waiting to see where we'd go without being too close, so that he could follow easily from a distance.'

'But now he is coming here, and we've not been in a day,' said Clare. 'How could he know? And why come so close now?'

'We saw several ships as we came across, and we made no secret of our destination. My guess is that he's been fed the information somehow. As to why he's closing with us, that I can't guess. But what he doesn't know is that *we* know he's coming, and we have a head start on him – we're here.'

'He must know we've arrived,' said Campbell soberly. 'He's sure to have left a man here. I'll bet they're in touch right now.'

'We're not going to be in for long,' I said. 'We'll be off dredging soon. But we could put it about that we are leaving for somewhere else – that might help draw him into the net. At close quarters we can at least do something.' It was all very dubious though, and we weren't at all sure what was happening around us.

'What kind of a ship have they?' I asked.

'Pretty much the same as ours – a bit bigger. Her name is *Sirena*.'

'Then if he leaves now it'll be over a week before he gets here.'

Campbell put down his empty glass with a click. 'Then we've got to get going as soon as we can,' he said.

I saw Geordie coming into the foyer and waved to him, and he came to the table. He was dirty and looked tired, and the half-healed scars on his face didn't make him look any better. He put a little glass pot on the table with a hand stained black with grease, and said, 'We've got trouble.'

I said, 'Sit down and have a beer.'

'What's the trouble?' Campbell asked.

Geordie sat down and sighed. 'I *would* like a beer,' he admitted. He unscrewed the top of the jar and showed that it was full of grease. He pushed it over to me and said, 'Rub some of that between your fingers and tell me what it feels like.'

I dipped up some of the grease on my forefinger and rubbed it with my thumb. It wasn't slick and smooth as grease should be but seemed gritty. Campbell reached over and tested it for himself.

'Where did you get this?' he demanded.

199

'It came from the main bearings of the winch motor,' said Geordie. 'And the grease in the bearing of the winch drum is the same – all doctored with carborundum.'

'Christ!' I said. 'If we'd have used the winch the whole damn thing would have seized up. What put you on to it?'

'Partly routine maintenance. But I also thought about what I'd do if I were Kane and I wanted to put a stop to Mr Campbell here. I wasn't looking for anything definite, mind you, but I thought I'd have a look at the winch. I never thought I'd find grinding powder mixed with the bearing grease.'

Campbell swore violently, then looked at Paula. 'Sorry,' he mumbled.

'That's all right. I know those words.'

I said, 'How long will it take to fix?'

'A week,' said Geordie definitely. 'We'll have to strip the winch right down, and that's a big job. But it's not what I'm worried about.'

'Isn't it enough?' grumbled Campbell. 'What else is on your mind?'

'I'm thinking of things Kane might have done that we haven't found yet. I don't think he got at the engine – but what else has he done?'

I said, 'He can't have done much. He was under observation all the time.'

'He got at the winch,' said Geordie obstinately.

'Geordie's right,' said Campbell. 'We can't take anything on trust. The whole ship must be checked out.'

The girls sat silent through this but I could sense their frustration matched ours. If the intention had been to foul up our operations it might have succeeded. But if it was also intended to dishearten us then Kane had read his man wrongly – Campbell of all of us was the most determined to put things right and carry on.

I drained my glass. 'Let's get to it. I kept the laboratory locked but I suppose I'd better give that a going over too.'

We went back to *Esmerelda*, rounding up crewmen along the way, and I went immediately below to the laboratory. A couple of hours' work showed nothing wrong – the spectro-scope was in order, and the contents of all the bottles seemed to agree with their labels. It was a waste of time from one point of view, and then again it wasn't. At least I knew my lab wasn't gimmicked.

Ian came down with fuel oil samples from the main tanks. 'Skipper wants these tested,' he said.

'Tested for what?'

He grinned. 'Anything that shouldn't be in fuel oil.'

I poured the samples into Petri dishes and burned them. The sample from the starboard tank left little deposit, but that from the port tank left a gummy mess on the bottom of the dish.

I went on deck to see Geordie. 'The port fuel tank's been got at,' I told him. 'I think it's been doctored with sugar.'

Geordie swore a blue streak. 'I thought we were using a hell of a lot of sugar. So that's where it went. How's the starboard tank?'

'It seems all right.'

'Kane couldn't get at the starboard tank without being seen – it's right by the wheel. The port tank is different. I remember he used to sit just about there quite often, when he was off watch.'

'It wouldn't be difficult – a pound of sugar at a time.'

'We've been sailing a lot, too. If we hadn't we'd have found out sooner – the hard way. But all the fuel we've used has come from the ready use tank in the engine room, and we just kept topping that up in port.'

Campbell came up. 'What are the long faces for?'

I told him and he cursed violently.

'We dump it,' I said. 'We can't dump it in harbour – they'd scream blue murder – so we go to sea and dump it.'

'All right,' said Geordie. 'I'll fill the header tank from the starboard main tank. We'll need some power to be going on with.'

'Nothing doing,' said Campbell. 'Kane might have been clever enough to put something else in there. Fill the header tank with new fuel from the Shell agent here.' He paused. 'It's going to be difficult. There's probably a lot of undissolved sugar lying on the bottom of the tank. When you put in new fuel you may be just as badly off.'

I said, 'I can test for sugar in water. We'll keep washing out until we're clean. How are their water supplies here, Geordie? I'd rather use fresh than salt.'

'We're lucky. In the dry season they can run short, but I think right now is okay. We'll have to pay through the nose, though.'

He thought about the job. 'We'll have to wait until the tanks dry out. Maybe I can rig up a contraption that'll pump hot air into the tanks – that should speed the dry-out.'

'Do that,' said Campbell. 'How long do you think it'll take us to get ready for sea again?'

We did some figuring and the answer was again not less than a week. Campbell shrugged. 'That's it, then. But we've lost our lead. We'll be lucky to get out of here before Ramirez pitches up.'

'He may wait until we go,' I said.

But guessing was futile, and we left it at that.

3

Next day we went to sea and pumped out both main tanks and refilled them with water from the fresh water tanks. I checked for sugar and found an appreciable quantity in the water of the port tank, so we pumped out again and went back to Nuku'alofa. We filled up with fresh water again, both in the water and the fuel tanks, much to the surprise of the suppliers, and then put to sea again.

I still found a little undissolved sugar in the port tank, so we did it all again. By this time I reckoned we were clean so we put back to port and Geordie rigged up his hot air contraption to dry out the tanks before we put in new fuel oil. A couple of days was spent on this and we used partial crews each time, spelling the others to have time ashore. God knows what stories were put about in the port, but our lads had orders to remain quiet and ignorant.

While Geordie and one team were checking the winch and its auxiliary equipment, aided by Campbell, Ian set another group to stripping *Esmerelda*. They took down all the rigging, both running and standing, and inspected everything. They found nothing wrong and we were sure we were fit for sea when they had finished. But it took time.

No more of Kane's sabotage came to light. He had carefully selected the two things which could do us the most damage – doctored grease and sugar in the fuel. If he hadn't been watched he might have got away with a lot more, and as it was he'd done more than enough.

Campbell was Napoleonic about the food stores. 'Dump the lot,' he said.

'We've no need to dump the canned stuff,' objected Ian, his thrifty Scot's soul aghast.

But Campbell insisted. 'Dump the lot. That son of a bitch was too clever for my liking. I've no hankering for cyanide in my stew.'

So on our last run out to sea for testing we dumped the food supplies, and also recalibrated the echometers against proven and charted soundings. They were all right but it was as well to make sure. The local tradesmen were delighted at our liberal purchase of fresh food stocks, and no doubt it all added to the gossip concerning the *Esmerelda*. Seven days after we had discovered Kane's sabotage Geordie said, 'That just about does it. We're ready for sea.'

'Let's hope Kane hasn't left any surprises we haven't found,' I said. 'I'd hate to start dredging and then find the bottom falling out of the ship. How's the engine, Geordie?'

He grimaced. 'Nothing wrong there. But we had to pull everything down to make sure.'

'That's the hellish thing about sabotage. Not being sure.'

When we assembled in the hotel lounge that evening Campbell asked me about the next move. 'How do we go about it?'

'I'm working on the assumption that there may be something between Falcon and Minerva. That's a distance of three hundred miles. We go to Falcon and take a bottom sample every ten miles on a direct course to Minerva. If we don't find anything, then we sample on parallel courses east and west.'

'So our first step is to find Falcon Island.'

I became thoughtful, shook my head and presently said, 'No, I've changed my mind. I think we'll start at Minerva – do it the other way around.'

They were interested. 'Why would you do that – why should it matter?' Campbell asked.

'Mark was an oceanographer and he was presumably working on the same lines as we are – volcanic theories much like the ones I've postulated. If the high-cobalt nodules are anywhere near Falcon, why should he mention Minerva at all? I think the nodules are quite a distance from Falcon, quite close to Minerva perhaps. And when Mark indicated them in his diary he thought of the source – which is Falcon – and the vicinity, Minerva.'

'That sounds logical,' said Campbell. 'But it might mean that the nodules aren't placed on a direct course between Falcon and Minerva. Hell, they could be on the other side of those reefs.'

'Or scattered all the way along,' suggested Clare. Which was also feasible.

I said, 'This is what we do. We leave here and sail due west until we hit the track between Falcon and Minerva. We turn towards Minerva and take samples every ten miles. If we don't find anything then, we come back to Falcon and on a parallel course, sampling all the way, go round Falcon and move back again further out. How's that?'

We talked it over for a while and then went in for dinner. I was glad we were going to sea again; every time we put into port something seemed to go wrong, whether it was arson, wrongful arrest, sabotage or just plain bad news.

During the meal Clare nudged me and murmured. 'Look over there.'

I looked around but couldn't see anything out of order. 'What's the matter?'

She said quietly, 'The waiters have just put two tables together over there, and laid them for dinner. There are places for eight.'

I took another look and she was right. 'Ramirez!' I exclaimed and she nodded. 'Could well be.'

We glanced towards the doorway, but saw nobody there.

'Don't tell Pop,' she whispered to me. 'He'll get mad if he sees Ramirez. I don't want us to have a scene – I want us to get him away quietly.'

'You'd better get him up to bed then – if you can. Geordie and I will check out now and go back to *Esmerelda* to push things on – we'll try and leave early tomorrow morning. You be there.'

'I can manage it,' she said.

They didn't come into the dining room while we were there, and Clare and Paula got the old man upstairs without him being aware that he was being moved like a chess piece – they seemed to be good at it, and I was hopeful that they'd handle him as well the next day. As soon as they'd gone I said to Geordie, 'We think Ramirez has arrived. We'd better pack up here.'

'How do you know?'

'Clare's been Sherlocking, and I think she's right.' I indicated the waiting table.

We went straight to the desk and settled up, taking advantage of an empty foyer, and then went up to our room to pack our gear. I took one of the two .38 revolvers which Campbell had entrusted to me and tossed it to Geordie. 'The boss says this is for you. Can you use it?'

He held it in his hand. 'Just let me get Kane or Hadley at the other end of it and I'll show you. Got any ammo?'

We split the ammunition, loaded the guns and went downstairs with our duffle bags. I was conscious of the weight of the gun in my jacket pocket and felt a bit ridiculous, as though I were impersonating a fifth-rate movie gangster. But there was nothing funny about it really – I might have to use that gun.

Halfway down the winding stairs I checked and put out my hand to stop Geordie. The foyer seemed full of people and I heard a drift of conversation. It was in Spanish.

We waited until the crowd had moved into the dining room, led by a tall, thin, hawklike man who must have been Ramirez. He tallied with Campbell's description, though I couldn't see the scar, and I felt a wave of angry nausea in my throat at the sight of him. When the foyer was empty we carried on.

We found Ian on the deck of *Esmerelda*. Geordie asked abruptly, 'Any new ships come in during the last hour or so?'

'Aye,' said Ian. 'That one.' He pointed across the water and I saw the dark loom of a boat anchored a little way out. It was difficult to tell her size, but from her riding light I judged her to be about the same size as *Esmerelda*, maybe a bit bigger but not much.

'That is Suarez-Navarro,' said Geordie and Ian stared at him aghast.

'I want the crew rousted out. I want a watch – two men on each side and a look-out up the foremast. And I don't want any extra lights – I don't want to show that anything out of the ordinary is happening. I want her ready to be moved at a moment's notice. How many are on board?'

'Most of the lads, and I can round up the others easily enough.'

'Do that, right away.'

'Aye aye, sir,' said Ian smartly and went below at a dead run.

Geordie looked across at her. 'I wonder if Hadley's over there – or Kane?' he said softly.

I said, 'They weren't in Ramirez's party in the hotel. Perhaps they're too scared to come ashore – there must be warrants out for them in every port in the Pacific by now. On the other hand, there's no reason for them to be on board her at all. Hadley's still got the *Pearl*, remember, and we've got no proof that they came here, or joined up with Ramirez after leaving Papeete.'

'True,' said Geordie glumly.

'I've got things to do in the lab,' I said. 'I have to make ready for sea. I'll see you later.'

I had been working for an hour when Geordie and Ian came in to see me. 'We've got an idea,' Geordie said. They both looked alive with something that I felt could be called mischief.

'What is it?'

'The boys think that Kane and Hadley may be across there, on Ramirez's ship. They want to go and get them.'

'Christ, they can't do that!'

'Why not?'

'You know damn well they're most unlikely to be there. This is just an excuse for any nonsense they're cooking up.'

'But suppose they are? It would solve a hell of a lot of problems. We hand them over to the police and that scuppers Ramirez. He'll be too busy explaining why he's harbouring a couple of wanted murderers to be able to follow us.'

I thought about it and shook my head. 'No, it's too risky, too damn close to piracy. Campbell wouldn't like it at all.'

'Look,' said Geordie, 'the boys are all steamed up. They didn't like your stories, they didn't like what those two did on Tanakabu, and they sure as hell didn't like the week's work they've had to put in here because of Kane. They're tired of being pushed around – some of them were shot at in Tanakabu lagoon and they didn't like that either. I don't know if I can stop them.'

I looked at the glint in Geordie's eye. 'I don't suppose you've tried too hard, have you, Geordie?'

He bristled. 'Why the hell should I? I've got scores to settle with Hadley too, remember. He gave me a pistol whipping, don't forget that. And it's *my* ship that Kane's been sabotaging, not Campbell's!'

'Suppose they aren't there after all?'

'We'll be bound to learn something to our advantage.' I noticed he was now including himself in the venture and had given up any pretence of being against it.

Ian said, 'Ach, Mike, it's all laid on. It'll be as easy as lifting

207

a trout from the stream when the keeper's having a dram in the pub.'

'Oh, it's all laid on, is it? Would you mind telling me what the pair of you have been up to?'

Ian looked at Geordie, who said, 'Well, it's like this, Mike. I thought a guard was all very well in its way, but a bit negative, if you know what I mean. So I sent a couple of boys ashore to scout around. They found a lot of the crew of that hooker in a pub, drinking themselves silly. A tough-looking mob, true, but they're almost out of it already. All dagoes.'

'And no Kane or Hadley?'

'No one spotted them. Anyway with your lot at the hotel there are precious few bodies left on Ramirez's ship.'

I said, 'They'll be keeping a watch too. Ramirez isn't a damn fool, and he knows we're here.'

'Right enough,' agreed Geordie. 'But I've gone into that too. I sent Taffy and Bill Hunter out in a boat to have a look. Bill's the best swimmer we've got, and he had a good look at that ship.' He chuckled suddenly. 'Do you know what he did? He swam right round her first, then he hauled himself aboard on the port side, had a good look round the deck, then let himself into the water on the starboard side and came back to report. That's the sort of watch they're keeping over there.'

'It would have to be done very quietly,' I mused.

'Ach, that's no trouble,' said Ian. 'We're a quiet lot.'

'Just about as quiet as a bunch of sharks. They don't make much noise either.'

'Well, what about it?' said Geordie imploringly.

'There would have to be no guns. No killing. Just bare fists.'

'Or maybe the odd belaying pin,' offered Ian gently.

'You're a bloodthirsty lot. It's a damn silly idea, but I'll agree to it – conditionally.'

Geordie grinned delightedly. 'I knew you had something of your father in you, Mike!'

I said, 'Dad would have had you court-martialled for disobedience and subordination, and you damn well know it. All right, here are the conditions. One – if you find Kane or Hadley we hand them over to the police intact to the last hair.

of their heads. We don't want to ruin our own case. Two – if we don't find them you get back here fast. We'll have to get the hell out of Nuku'alofa anyway – Ramirez will be looking for us and maybe the cops too. That means, three – that Campbell and the girls will have to be got aboard.'

Geordie's face fell. 'That means the whole thing's off. He'll never stand for it, not with the girls along.'

'He doesn't have to know about it too soon – if we time it right. You send someone up to the hotel and get him aboard at just the right time.'

'The right time being when it's too late to stop us,' said Geordie. 'Mike, laddie, you're going to have a hell of a time explaining to the old man what we're doing.'

'I'll leave the explanations until afterwards,' I said. 'I've got another condition, number four – I'm coming with you. I've got scores to settle myself.'

4

The timing was a bit tricky. We didn't know how long Ramirez and company were going to stay in the hotel, nor even if they intended returning to their ship that night. We didn't want to bump into them because then there certainly would be noise.

Again, Campbell and the girls had to be got out of the hotel under the nose of Ramirez, another tricky bit. So we made a plan.

Geordie had picked Nick Dugan to bring Campbell from the hotel. 'He's probably the best scrapper of the lot of us,' he said. 'But he's never quiet in his fighting. It's best we keep him out of the main operation, and he'll not take it well.'

I had a word with Nick and sent him off immediately. 'You've got two jobs,' I told him. 'The first is to keep an eye on Ramirez. If any of them make a move to go back to their ship, you nip down to the waterfront and flash a signal to us. Then the operation is definitely off. Got that?'

'Right.' As it turned out he was surprisingly meek.

'We'll be starting off at eleven-thirty. At exactly that tim you get into Mr Campbell's room and give him a note which I'll write. No sooner and no later than eleven-thirty – that important.'

'I understand,' said Nick.

'Have you got a watch?'

He showed me his wrist watch and, as we synchronized, wondered how many times my father had done the sam before an operation.

'I settled their bills along with mine – they don't need t stop at the desk. No porters. Get them back here as fast as yo can, and as quietly – and don't let Ramirez or any of his crow see you.'

I also had a word with Bill Hunter. 'What sort of watch ar they keeping over there, Bill?'

He smiled. 'I suppose they think they're keeping a goo one – by their standards. It's nothing to worry about, though It'll be a piece of cake.'

'Geordie tells me you're the best swimmer, so you'll g first. But you must be quiet about it or the balloon will go up Your job will be to find the quietest spot on board to get th rest of us up.'

'Not to worry,' he said easily. 'It'll be like the old times.'

As I turned away he said, 'Er – Mike. . . .'

'Yes, Bill?'

'It's good to work with a Trevelyan again.'

I was touched. 'Thanks, Bill. You don't know how appreciate that.'

At last we were ready. Six of us were going – Geordie, Ia Taffy, Jim, Bill Hunter and myself. Danny Williams was lef in command of the ship and the rest of Geordie's non-commando crew, and I said to him, 'Danny, if anything goe wrong, get the hell out of here as fast as you can, once M Campbell and the girls and Nick are back on board, even if i means leaving us behind. Mr Campbell mustn't be involved in this, you understand?'

'I gotcha,' he said. 'But you'll be all right.'

Geordie was fussing. 'Jim, got all your bits and pieces?'

'I'm okay,' said Jim. 'Stop binding, skipper.'

I stepped over to Geordie. 'What are these bits and pieces?'

'Nothing much,' he said airily. 'A few tools. Belaying pins and stuff like that. What time is it?'

I looked at the luminous hands of my watch. 'Eleven-twenty-eight.' It had been a rush to get ready but the last few minutes crawled.

'Let's go,' he said. 'It'll be a doddle.'

We dropped into the larger of our two dinghies, Ian and Taffy took the oars and pulled quietly, and the boat moved out. We rounded the stern of *Esmerelda* and Ian steered us across the harbour.

I was thinking of all the things that could go wrong and what Campbell would say when we got back, and damning myself for an idiot. I leaned over to Geordie and whispered, 'If Taffy's got that damned knife of his, tell him to leave it in the bottom of the boat. We don't want even the possibility of him using it.'

'It's all right,' he said in a low voice. 'He left it aboard – I told him to.'

It wasn't long before Ian and Taffy stopped pulling and the boat glided to a stop, rocking gently. Bill was dressed in dark clothing and all I saw of him was the flash of his teeth in the moonlight as he slipped over the side.

'Are you sure the torch is waterproof?' Geordie murmured.

'It's okay,' Bill replied. 'I'll give you a flash as soon as I'm ready.' He moved away without a single splash and we sat quietly waiting for his signal. It seemed a long time coming and as I sat there I wondered what I was doing in this Pacific harbour, contemplating an act of piracy. It seemed a long way from my office at the Institute.

I said to Geordie, 'He's a long time, isn't he?'

'Stop worrying,' said Geordie. 'We're professionals.'

I let out my breath and tried to relax on the hard thwart, never taking my eyes off Ramirez's ship. Suddenly there was a flicker of light, so faint and so quickly doused that I wondered if I'd really seen it or whether my eyes were playing tricks.

'That's it,' said Geordie softly. 'Pull together. Gently now

We moved on under the measured slow strokes of the oar until the side of the ship loomed above us. Something hit m' face and I started violently. Geordie said in my ear, 'Be still for God's sake.'

I felt him moving about and he said, always in that lov murmur that was so much more effective than a whisper 'Bill's been a good boy. He's dropped us a line. Make fas there.'

Jim, in the bows, made fast and Geordie said, 'I'll go first. He swarmed up somehow like a monkey and disappeare over the bulwarks. Ian followed and then I came up, findin that they were using a rope ladder that hung just above ou dinghy. My eyes had got used to the darkness and with th help of the waning moon and the dim glow of the riding lights found I could see fairly well. There was no one about on deck but a low murmur of voices came from aft.

Someone moved to join us and Bill's voice said, soft and unexpectedly close, 'I've copped one of 'em.'

'What have you done with him?' Geordie asked.

'Nothing much.' There was joy in Bill's voice. 'He won' wake up for a longish time.'

The others had arrived on deck and Geordie said, 'Spli into pairs – I'll take Mike. We'll do the old backward-forwar trick.'

'What's that?' I asked, trying to pitch my voice low as h had done.

'Quiet! Someone's coming. Jim and Taffy – you take him.

I watched the two figures snake across the deck and vanish into the shadows. Then I heard what Geordie's quicker ea had caught much earlier – the measured pace of footstep coming along the deck from aft. The man came in sight roun the corner of the deck-house; he was carrying a mug in hi hand, being careful not to spill it – probably coffee fo someone up in the bows.

Suddenly, to my surprise, a black shape arose quite openl

n front of him and Taffy's voice said gently, 'Well now, that's
nice thought – bringing me coffee.'

The man stopped and backed up in amazement. He was
bout to speak when something flickered in front of his face
nd he raised his hands to claw at his neck. Taffy expertly
aught the falling mug.

The man seemed to be fighting nothing. He staggered two
aces along the deck and then collapsed. I saw Jim crouch
ver him and then they both dragged him over to us, Taffy
sing only one hand.

'Anyone want some hot coffee?' he said. 'Not a drop
pilled.'

'Stop playing the fool,' Geordie growled.

'What happened?' I asked.

'It'll keep. That's two – how many more do you reckon,
3ill?'

'There were five on deck when I was here before. But I
lunno about below.'

Jim and Taffy were gagging and trussing up their victim.
Geordie said, 'We'll finish that. You lot go aft and clear up the
leck.'

They drifted away like wreathes of smoke and I helped
Geordie finish the job. The man was flaccid and quite unconscious and I whispered, 'What the hell did Jim do to
im?'

'A silk cloth with a weight in one corner. We learned that
one from an Indian instructor, old thuggee trick. But at least
Jim hasn't strangled this one – he'll recover okay.'

There was a muffled thump from aft and he clicked his
ongue. 'Someone's being careless. Come on, I want to see if
3ill's done his job properly.'

He rose and walked unconcernedly forward, not troubling
to hide. He stopped at the forehatch and tested it with his
hand. 'Bill's a good workman. No one can come from below
this way.'

He then searched about until he found what he was looking
for – the prone and unconscious body of the after watch. He
rolled the limp body over and began to tie the hands. 'Not that

213

I don't trust Bill's judgement,' he said. 'But it's nice to be saf
and tidy. You take his feet – use his shoelaces.'

It was all a little bit dreamlike. Geordie was expertly tyin;
the crewman's hands and conversing matter-of-factly as an
good craftsman might as he worked on his bench. 'Sorry t
keep you out of the fun, Mike. But you're dead inexperi
enced. You've only got to do the wrong thing once on a lar!
like this and the cat's out of the bag.'

I looked at Geordie's bulk in the semi-darkness and real
ized something I'd never thought of consciously before. H
had been trained as a professional killer, and my father ha
had a hand in his training. He had been taught perhaps ;
couple of dozen ways of putting a man out of action, tempor
arily or permanently, and he had the professional's amuse
contempt for the dilettante. I thought for the first time tha
something of Mark's ruthless streak, albeit turned in a strang
and distasteful manner, had been inherited from my father.

I said, 'That's all right, Geordie. You're doing fine. I'n
content to look and learn.'

From the stern came the lowest, breathiest of whistles an
Geordie cocked his head. 'They're finished. Let's go and se
what the bag's like.'

We went forward, walking as though the ship belonged t
us. As we went, Geordie said softly, 'Never dodge abou
when there's no need. Nothing looks more suspicious. .
mean, suppose someone's watching the deck right now – we
could be any pair of the crew.'

He slowed as he came to the deckhouse where a stream o
light splashed on the deck from the door. He peered cauti
ously round the edge of the door, then snorted. 'I might hav
known,' he said resignedly. 'It's Taffy the gutser. What d
you think you're doing, Taff?'

He stepped into the deckhouse and I followed to find that i
led straight into the galley. Taffy was sawing at a loaf of bread
'Making myself a sandwich, skipper,' he said.

'You bloody cormorant. How many did you get?'

'Three.'

'Kane? Hadley?'

'Not a sign. If they're aboard, they're below. But they'll be safe – we battened down the hatches.'

'Well, we'll unbatten them and clean up below,' said Geordie. 'It only needs one of 'em to decide he'd like a nice breath of sea air and find he can't get on deck. When you've finished your supper, Mr Morgan, we'd all be grateful if you got back on the job. And before you leave the galley clean up – and then find the flour bin and tip the salt into it.'

'Yes, sergeant,' said Taffy.

We went to the wheelhouse and found the others. Ian was unscrewing the central holding bolt of the wheel-bearing with an adjustable spanner. He looked up at Geordie and said solemnly, 'Might as well cause a bit of inconvenience while we're here.' He withdrew the bolt and casually tossed it overboard, then spun the wheel. 'They'll have a wee bit of trouble in their steering, I'm thinking.'

'Very nice, but a little premature,' said Geordie. 'Let's get the job finished first. Mike and I will take the forehatch and clean out the fo'c's'le. Ian and Bill, take this hatch here. Jim, you'll find Taffy stuffing his guts in the galley – you take amidships. Got your stuff?'

'I've got it, skipper.'

'Right. We'll all go down simultaneously. I'll give the signal – and try not to make too much noise. Come on, Mike.'

When we got to the forehatch Geordie paused. 'We'll give them a minute to get ready.' He shook his head sadly. 'That bloody Welshman.'

I looked aft along the deck. It was very quiet and there was nothing to be seen, and I thought how easy it had all been – so far. These ex-commandoes seemed to take it all as a joke, as I suppose it was to men who had tackled alert Germans. But I wasn't deceived; it was their very competence that made it seem easy.

Geordie startled me by uttering that same hollow whistle I'd heard before. 'Come on,' he said softly. 'Me first.'

He lifted up the hatch gently and went down the companionway. The forecastle was dimly lit by a single lamp and appeared full of shadowy shapes. When I got to the bottom of the steps I found Geordie fastening the door which led to the midships accommodation by means of a small wooden wedge which he took from his pocket. The door fastened, he turned to look round the forecastle. Tiers of bunks, three high, lined the triangular space formed by the bows of the ship. They pack the bastards in like sardines, I thought. There was a snoring noise and Geordie looked round quickly, put his fingers to his lips for my benefit and crept forward very gently, and then waved me forward. He was looking at a middle berth upon which was sleeping a villainously unshaven seaman. He put his lips close to my ear and said, 'Check the other bunks.'

I tiptoed round the forecastle, looking into every bunk, but found no one else. I got back to Geordie and shook my head.

He said loudly, 'All right, let's wake up the sleeping beauty.'

The man snored again, drawing back his upper lip.

Geordie shook him by the shoulder. 'Come on, chum. Prepare to meet thy doom.' The man opened his eyes and looked up uncomprehendingly and then Geordie hit him on the chin with a fist like a hammer.

He rubbed his knuckles and said, a little apologetically, 'I never like to hit a sleeping man. It seems a bit unfair somehow.'

I looked at the seaman. He was out cold.

Geordie looked round the forecastle again. 'Nine a side. They pack eighteen in here. The Board of Trade would never allow this back home. Right, let's see what else there is. The next one might be the lucky draw, Mike.'

He took the wedge out of the door and opened it carefully. We checked all the compartments we came across, even the toilets. 'Nothing like catching a man with his pants down,' Geordie chuckled.

We found nothing.

The ship rocked a little more heavily and we both stiffened but there was no hue and cry and we carried on slowly until suddenly there was a shadow at the end of the passage and Taffy came into sight. He was eating an apple.

Geordie sniffed. 'Look at that. You'd think he'd get fatter, wouldn't you? He was just the same in the army – holding the war up while he rammed himself full.' There were two cabins remaining between ourselves and Taffy and we each investigated one, with negative results.

'What did you get?' demanded Geordie.

Taffy crunched on his apple. 'Ian put one laddie to sleep – he wasn't Kane and not big enough by all accounts to be Hadley.'

'Damn! The bastards aren't here, then. We got another – that's seven.'

'One in the bows and we got two more, skipper,' Taffy said. 'That's seven on board.'

Geordie began to calculate. 'There's no less than fifteen getting boozed up ashore – that makes twenty-two. And there's eight at the hotel – that's thirty.'

'The ship's over-crewed,' said Taffy with the air of one making a profound statement.

'So is a battleship,' snapped Geordie. 'And that's what this is. They wouldn't need all this crowd just to handle the ship. Where's Jim?'

'In the engine room.'

'Good. You nip up on deck and keep watch. I don't think any of the officers will be coming back now, but the crew will, and Ramirez might come back for a check-up.'

We went aft and found Ian breaking open a desk in one of the bigger cabins. I was about to protest when I realized that it hardly mattered what we did now, short of murder. 'Ramirez lives here,' he told us.

The desk gave us nothing of interest or use and we glanced through his clothing quickly. It was elegant and extensive for shipboard life. 'Have you found our birds?' Ian asked as we worked.

'Neither of them,' I said. 'We've slipped up on this one. Campbell is going to be mad.'

Ian was disconsolate. 'My mannie wasn't Hadley. He had a black beard,' he said.

Geordie pricked up his ears. 'Are you sure it wasn't him, or Kane, in a disguise?'

'Na, na,' said Ian. 'It was too long. Kane couldn't have grown it in the time, and Hadley was clean-shaven. And it was real – I pulled it.'

I was looking down and saw Geordie peeling back the carpet, revealing a recessed ring-bolt. 'What's down there?' I asked.

'We can soon find out.' He grasped the ring-bolt and pulled, opening a trap-door. He pulled a torch from his pocket and flashed it down the hole.

'Christ!' he said, and pulled out a sub-machine gun.

We looked at it in silence, and then Geordie said, 'I told you this was a flaming battleship.'

'Let's see what else there is,' I said.

Five minutes later we were surrounded by enough weapons to start a small war. There were four sub-machine guns, fifteen rifles of assorted pattern, half a dozen pistols and a dozen hand grenades.

I summoned up a laugh. 'I wonder what Chamant would have thought of this little lot? He nearly had heart failure at the sight of our four pistols.' But I was feeling a little sick, looking at our haul and my hands, which had been fine up to that moment, were sweating slightly.

Geordie said thoughtfully, 'You were a pretty good armourer in your time, Ian. How would you put this lot out of action?'

'With the bolt-action rifles you just throw the bolts away. With the others, we smash the firing pins.'

'Why not throw the lot overboard?' I asked.

Geordie cocked his head at me. 'We'll do that too. But this mob will then do some skin-diving and I want it to be a wasted effort. Get cracking, Ian, as fast as you can. We've spent enough time here.'

We were ready for leaving fifteen minutes later after carefully dropping the useless guns over the side, with a minimum of splashing. Ian was rolling the last of the bolts he'd taken from the rifles into torn strips of cloth and stuffing them into his pockets. We were about to leave when Taffy suddenly held up a hand. 'Quiet,' he said softly.

We were very still and though I listened hard I couldn't hear anything. Taffy said, 'There's a boat coming.'

Then I heard the faint creak of rowlocks and the splash of oars. I looked anxiously towards Geordie.

'We take them,' he decided. 'We can't have the game given away too soon.' He issued quick instructions and the men spread themselves into the deck shadows. There was a soft bump as the boat reached the boarding ladder, on the other side from our own exit, and a few moments later I saw the outline of a man against the night sky. There was only one man and as he came aboard I drew in my breath sharply.

It was Kane.

'He's my meat,' I murmured to Geordie, who gave me the thumbs up. I moved forward in a crouch. Kane walked forward along the deck and just as he passed me I straightened up and gave him a tap on the shoulder. He turned and I let him have it, as hard as I could to the jaw. Ian tapped him on the head with something as he started to collapse and all in one movement, as it seemed, rolled him into a piece of canvas. Geordie looked over the railings and saw that Kane had been alone in the dinghy. 'That'll get us off the hook with Campbell,' he said with satisfaction.

'I'm not so sure of that,' I said, rubbing my sore knuckles. 'We can't take Kane to the police now. They wouldn't look at all kindly on our methods, and if they find out what we've done to this ship we're for it, right on our side or not.'

'You've said better than you know, Mike,' Geordie concurred. 'We'll leave here right away – and we'll take Mr Kane with us.'

We piled into our boat and pulled for *Esmerelda*, and as we passed under the stern of Ramirez's ship I looked up and saw her name painted there – *Sirena*. Halfway across the harbour I had a sudden thought. 'Geordie, what was Jim doing in the engine room?'

'Nothing much,' he said. Jim grinned briefly in the half-light and I was about to speak to him direct when Geordie interrupted me. 'Heave, you bloody pirates – we haven't much time.' He seemed in a devil of a hurry.

As we climbed the bulwarks of *Esmerelda* I suddenly remembered that Jim Taylor had made a name for himself as a demolitions expert during the war. I hadn't time to develop this thought because Campbell was on to me in a rage.

'What in hell is going on?'

I found I'd stopped sweating and felt very calm. No doubt the reaction would set in later. 'A little bit of direct action,' I said coolly.

Geordie was already giving orders in a quiet bellow. 'Get that bloody engine started up. Slip all lines bar the bow-line. Get that dinghy up smartly now.' The deck was astir with movement.

'You damned fools! You'll get us all gaoled,' Campbell was raging.

'Better gaoled than dead,' I said. 'You don't know what we found on that damned ship.'

'Stand by the warps,' I heard Geordie say. I heard a throb as the engines started.

'I don't care what you found,' fumed Campbell. 'Do you realise you've committed an act of piracy?'

It was lucky that the engine note drowned his voice. In the same moment Ian came running along the deck. 'Mr Campbell, sir. Yon man on the jetty – he wants a wee crack wi' you.'

We both looked ashore in alarm and saw a solitary figure standing just where our gangplank lay. It was about to be pulled inboard, but he arrested it with a gesture. It was Ernesto Ramirez.

'By God, I'll crack him!' I burst out.

Campbell recognised him at once, and I heard a buzz behind me as Nick Dugan breathed the name for the benefit of the crew. I gave Nick a sharp glance and he shook his head slightly, spreading his hands to indicate that there had been no contact before.

Campbell took my arm. 'Easy, Mike, don't go off at half-cock. Let's not compound whatever mischief you've been up to. Hold Geordie, will you?' Amazingly, as my wrath had risen so his had subsided and he seemed in complete control of himself.

He walked away to the gangplank and I shouted, 'Hold it, Geordie! There's a snag – the boss has a visitor.' I followed Campbell.

Ramirez was alone, leaning negligently on a bollard. Obviously he hadn't yet been on *Sirena* – there hadn't been time for that, and he was too composed. Campbell looked down at him. 'Well?' he asked coldly.

Ramirez smiled up at him. 'I just came to wish you farewell. I thought you would be leaving about now.' I realized that, Nick Dugan or not, he'd seen us at the hotel or he'd seen the Campbells and Paula leaving.

He walked straight up the gangplank and stepped onto the deck, elegant in his white tropical suit.

Campbell's voice was icy. 'You don't have to come on board to tell us that.'

'Maybe not, but I am here.'

To give the devil his due, he had no nerves at all. After doing what he'd done I wouldn't have had the guts to come within a hundred miles of *Esmerelda*, let alone without an escort. But he was a subtle and clever man, relying on Campbell's known sense of justice, and maybe he knew that our scruples would hold us back. Still, he had guts.

He said, 'I thought I should warn you. I have plans and I do not wish you to interfere with them. Why don't you give up and go away?'

'I'm not concerned with your plans,' said Campbell stolidly.

'You know what I mean, Mr Campbell. We met in battle before and you came off worst. And so you shall again if you do not get out of my way.' He had the Spanish trick of making gutterals out of his aitches, but otherwise his English was good. I didn't think my Spanish would be as fluent.

My mouth was dry. I said, 'Ramirez, you're a bloody murderer and I'm going to see you pay for it.'

His eyebrows quirked. 'Murder?' he queried mockingly. 'That is a libel, Mr Trevelyan. Whom am I supposed to have murdered?'

'My brother, for one,' I said hotly.

Ramirez threw back his head and laughed. 'My dear sir, I'm willing to go into any court in the world on a charge like that.' His teeth flashed. 'You have no proof, have you – no proof at all.' And he laughed again.

That was only too true. The only man who had seen him at Tanakabu was Dr Schouten – and he too was dead.

Campbell said, 'I fail to see the point of this conversation, Ramirez.'

Geordie tugged at my sleeve agitatedly. 'We've got to get away – now. Before that thing goes bang.'

'What thing, for God's sake?'

He drew me aside and said in a low hurried voice, 'Jim had a small charge of plastic explosive – he slapped it against the crank case of their engine. I wanted to blow a hole in the bottom of their boat but I wouldn't let him – I wish I had now.'

'When's it due to go off?'

'That's it – Jim doesn't know. He rigged up a time switch from an ordinary alarm clock, and you can't get those right to within five minutes or so. I thought we'd be away by now.'

'It'll rouse the whole harbour!'

'But we'd have been gone – nothing to do with us.' The urgency in his voice was an imperative. I looked across at Ramirez and said, 'I think you ought to have the privilege of cleaning your own deck.'

Geordie caught on and went immediately up to the gang-plank where Campbell and Ramirez were locked in a low-voiced, furious argument. I noticed Geordie dab his hand on the winch drum and then signal surreptitiously to Ian and Taffy. Of the rest of the crew all were spellbound except Jim, who was watching anxiously across the water. There was no sign of the girls.

Geordie placed himself squarely in front of Ramirez and was blunt in his speech. 'I'm the master of this ship – and the owner – and I'm particular about filth on my decks. I'd be pleased if you'd leave.'

Ramirez went bleak, looking carefully at his scarred face. 'Ah, the brave and foolish Mr Wilkins,' he said insultingly.

'That's me,' said Geordie. He put out his hand and smeared down the front of Ramirez's gleaming white jacket, leaving dirty trail of black oil. 'You're dirty, Mr Ramirez.'

Ramirez was so shocked at the action and at the contempt hich lay behind it that he just stood there, making no move – ut the fury grew in his eyes.

Geordie said again, 'You're filthily dirty, Mr Ramirez. I ink you need a wash – don't you, lads?'

They got the idea fast – faster than Ramirez. With a growl ey were on to him, four of them. I saw Ramirez's hand go to is pocket as quick as lightning, but Danny was faster and his and came down in a mighty chop. A pistol clattered on deck.

Then Ramirez was lifted helplessly off his feet and carried) the side. They swung him twice and then over he went, aking a great splash. Geordie wasted no time in useless riumph. He turned, picked up Ramirez's pistol and began hopping out orders again. 'Gangplank in. Don't stand there awking! Ian, get the wheel, and don't run him down. Cast off orrard. Engine slow ahead.'

Esmerelda got under way even while Campbell was still taring over the side. 'Well, I'm damned,' he said to no one in articular, while staring at Geordie. Geordie was oblivious, atching carefully out into the darkness and giving orders in a ow, carrying voice. He conned us out past the sleeping essels and the marker buoys and Ramirez's splashing pro-ress fell astern.

As we drew level with *Sirena*, anchored in the harbour, here was a dull *thump*, not very loud, which carried over the vater. At the same time there was a flicker of lights from a inghy arriving alongside. The crew returning no doubt, to nd a shambles. That would do her engine a bit of no good. ilence held us until we were well past all the shipping and breast of one of the openings in the fringing reef, and then a abble of noise got up as everyone's tongue was loosened. Ian ad to shout to make himself heard, giving orders to get some ail on her. The excitement on board was electric.

Geordie turned and grinned, his battered face alight with riumph. Raucously he began to sing at the top of his voice.

223

'*Oh, we're off to see the Ozzard – the wonderful Ozzard* (
Whiz!'

He looked very piratical because of the captured pist(
dangling negligently in his hand.

Chapter Seven

1

'You pack of damned fools,' said Campbell. 'Whatever possessed you to do a crazy thing like that?'

Ian shuffled his feet, Geordie was clearly unrepentant and I suspected we were in for a tongue-lashing, and didn't relish the thought. The lights of Nuku'alofa were falling astern as *Esmerelda* ran at full speed. Danny Williams was at the wheel and Campbell had gathered the three of us together to take us to task.

'Well,' Geordie began. 'We thought it would be a good idea to go and get hold of either Kane or Hadley and—'

'Kane! Hadley! You won't find them with Ramirez. Ramirez may be a son of a bitch but he has brains – he won't chance himself being linked with those two, not now he won't.'

I grinned at Geordie. 'Where did you put Kane, by the way?' I asked casually.

'We haven't a brig on the ship, but we're making one now. In the meantime he's under guard in my cabin.'

Campbell's jaw dropped. 'You mean you've *got* Kane?'

'Of course,' I said. I didn't say that it had been a near thing, or how close we came to not achieving our objective. 'We thought we'd hand him over to the Tongan police but circumstances – ah – preceded that.'

'What circumstances?'

'Ramirez's ship got a bit bent,' I said. 'I couldn't control the lads.' I gave Geordie a sly look – I was taking his argument and using it against Campbell.

'How bent?'

'One of us had an accident with some explosive,' I said.

225

'That thump we heard? As we left harbour? You blew u
their ship?' He was incredulous.

'Oh no, nothing like that,' said Geordie placatingly
'There's a bit of a hole in their engine crankcase, that's al
They won't be following us in a hurry.'

'They won't have to,' said Campbell. 'What do you suppos
Ramirez is doing now? He'll have got back to his ship
seething mad thanks to you fools – found it wrecked, and b
now he'll be presenting himself at the nearest police station
still in his wet clothes, claiming assault and piracy. I shoul
say that within an hour there'll be a fast patrol boat leavin
Nuku'alofa and coming right after us. And we won't get out o
it as we did in Tahiti – this time we *are* in the wrong.'

We looked at each other in silence.

'Or maybe he won't,' said Campbell slowly. 'Not after wha
I told him back there.' He jerked his head astern.

'What was that?' I said. I saw that Campbell's eyes sud
denly held the same glint that I'd seen in Geordie's earlier tha
night.

'I said the Tahitian police were very unhappy. I said the
knew about Hadley and Kane and that they had witnesse
who'd seen Ramirez with them at Tanakabu, the first tim
they went there.'

'What witnesses?'

He grinned at us. 'That's what Ramirez wanted to know.
said three of the hospital patients and a couple of staff ha
seen him. He laughed at me, but it hit home.'

'I don't know anything about any witnesses,' I said.

'Mike, sometimes you're pretty slow on the uptake – ther
were no goddam witnesses, as far as I know. But someone ha
to think fast to get us out of this jam. I told Ramirez that th
police were looking for more evidence, but that they alread
had him fairly linked with the events on Tanakabu, and that i
he went to the cops in Tonga with any kind of story about u
pirating his ship, and if we were picked up, then we'd mak
enough of a stink to get the Tahitian police down here fast.'

Geordie said, 'Now, that's interesting. We know he was a
Tanakabu – Schouten saw him.'

226

'Exactly,' said Campbell. 'And how does he know that someone else didn't see him too? He can't take the chance – he'll have to lie low. As long as the suspicions of the Tahiti police remain just that – suspicions – he'll be happy. But he won't stir up anything that will give the cops a line on him. At least, I hope not. So I hope he'll dummy up about your stupid raid.'

I said, 'He won't go to the police while we have Kane. Kane is our trump card. Ramirez wouldn't dare let Kane get into the hands of the police.'

'Mike, he's a clever man. Clever and subtle when he has to be. I wouldn't put it past him to wriggle out of that one.'

'And something else,' I said. 'Maybe the raid wasn't as stupid as you think – a bit hare-brained, I'll grant you, but worth while. What we found on that ship was as subtle as a crack on the head with a hammer.' I gestured to Ian. 'Trot out your collection of ironmongery.'

Ian delved in various pockets and brought out the bolts he had taken from the rifles. Campbell's eyes widened as he saw the mounting pile they made on the deck.

'He had *ten* rifles?'

'Fifteen,' I corrected. 'The others were automatic action. We've smashed them and dropped them over the side. Plus four sub-machine guns and a lot of pistols.'

Geordie dug into his pocket and produced a hand grenade which he tossed casually. 'There were a few of these too. I hung on to a couple.'

'Not much subtlety about that, is there?' I asked.

'And he's got twice as many men as he needs,' said Geordie. 'He isn't paying that big crew to stand half-watches either.' Geordie, too, wasn't losing any opportunity to rub Campbell's nose in it.

Campbell's eyes flickered as he watched the grenade bounce in Geordie's hand. 'For God's sake stop that. You'll blow us all up. Let's go down to the saloon and have a drink – it's pretty damn late.'

It was in fact getting into the small hours of the morning but I felt wide awake, and everyone else seemed to share that feeling, even Campbell. Only Clare and Paula, after a brief appearance on deck, had vanished below again.

'No,' I said to Campbell's offer. 'I want to talk to Kane – now. And I want to be dead sober when I do it. Is he conscious, Geordie?'

'Nothing that a bucket of sea water won't cure.'

The three of us went down to the cabin, leaving Ian on deck, to find Jim and Nick Dugan stolidly on guard. Kane was conscious – and scared. He flinched when we went into the cabin and huddled at the end of Geordie's bunk as though by making himself smaller he wouldn't be noticed. Four of us made a crowd in the small cabin, and Kane was, and felt, thoroughly hemmed in.

He looked as haggard as when I'd first seen him in London, unshaven and ill, and carried his right arm awkwardly – I remembered that Clare had shot him. His eyes slid away when I looked at him.

'Look at me, Kane.'

Slowly his eyes moved until they met mine. His throat worked and his eyes blinked and watered.

'You're going to talk to us, Kane, and you're going to tell us the truth. You might think you're not, but you are. Because if you don't we'll work on you until you do. I was at Tanakabu, Kane, and you must know that anyone who was there won't be squeamish in their methods. I'm a civilized man and it may be that I'll be sickened – but don't count on that, Kane, because there are more than a dozen men on this ship who aren't nearly as squeamish as I am. Do you understand me, Kane? Have I made myself perfectly clear?'

But there was never going to be any resistance out of him. His tongue flickered out and he licked his lips and croaked incoherently. He was still reacting to the blow over the head, a physical problem to add to his mental ones.

'Answer me.'

His head bobbed. 'I'll talk to you,' he whispered.

'Give him a whisky, Geordie,' I said. He drank some of it and a little colour came into his face, and he sat up straighter, but with no less fear in his face.

'All right,' I said deliberately. 'We'll start right at the beginning. You went to London to find Helen Trevelyan and then me. Why?'

'Jim boobed,' he said. 'He let that suitcase get away. There were the books and the stones in it. We had to get them back.'

'You and Ramirez and some of his cut-throats, right?'

'Yair, that's right.'

'But you didn't get them all back, did you? Did Ramirez know that?'

'He said – you must have something else. Didn't know what.'

'So he laid you alongside me to try and find out what I had?'

'Yair. And to pass word where you went, anytime I could.' Now he was volunteering information, and it was getting easier. Campbell and Geordie were silent and watchful, leaving the going to me. I was eager to find out about Mark but decided to lead up to that by taking other directions first, which would also serve to confuse Kane.

'You smashed our radio, didn't you?'

'Yair. I was told to.'

'And led Hadley in the *Pearl* around on our track?' We already knew this but I let him confirm it.

'Why did you tell the Papeete police that we'd burnt the hospital? Surely even you could see that we could disprove that pretty easily.'

He looked, for a moment, almost exasperated. 'That was Jim. Bloody hell, I told him it wouldn't wash. You can't tell him anything.'

I nodded and veered off on another tack. 'That time you saw Miss Campbell's drawings on deck, did they mean anything to you?'

'Eh?' He was taken aback and had to readjust his thinking. 'No, why should they?'

'You identified one as a "scraggy falcon". Why did you say that?'

He stared blearily at us. 'I dunno – did it have something to do with Falcon Island, maybe?'

We exchanged glances, and I carried on evenly.

'Go on. Why should it have?'

'I – I suppose it just slipped out. It looked like a falcon, and maybe it was on my mind, see.'

'What about Falcon Island?'

Kane hesitated and I snapped, 'Come on – out with it!'

'I dunno much about it. Ramirez, he talked a bit about Falcon Island, somewhere in Tonga it is. He said once that's where we were going after we'd got rid of you lot.'

' "Got rid of"? How was he going to do that? And why?'

'I dunno that either, Mr Trevelyan. Something about those stones you've been pulling out of the sea – those nodules, you call 'em. He had to ditch you before he could go to Falcon Island, 'cos that's where they were. My word, Mr Trevelyan, I don't know what it's all about!'

Behind me I heard Campbell let out his breath. 'Do you know exactly where they are?'

'No, they'd never let me in on anything like that, none of us except – except the top brass.'

I could believe that. Kane was much too far down the line to have access to such information, but it was a pity. I changed my tack again and suddenly shot the question. 'Who killed my brother?'

Kane's mouth twitched. 'Oh God. It was Jim – and – and Ramirez. They killed him.' He looked mortally sick.

'And you helped them.'

He shook his head violently. 'No – I had nothing to do with it!'

'But you were there.'

'I don't know nothing about it.'

'Look, Kane, stop lying to us. You were with Hadley when he went to see Schouten to get the death certificate, weren't you?'

He nodded unwillingly.

'Then you were in on Mark's death, damn you!'

'I didn't kill him. It was Jim – Ramirez fixed it all up.'

'Who killed Schouten?'

The answer came promptly. 'It was Jim – Jim Hadley.'

'And again you were there?'

'Yes.'

'But you didn't kill Schouten, I suppose?'

'No!'

'And of course you didn't set fire to the hospital and burn fourteen people to death?'

'I didn't,' said Kane. 'It was Jim – he's a devil. He's crazy mad.'

'But you were there.'

'I told you I was.'

'And you'll be sentenced as an accessory.'

Kane was sweating and his whole face quivered. I said, 'Who killed Sven Norgaard?'

Kane didn't answer for a moment, and then under the threat of our gaze he said, 'It was Jim.'

'You're not too sure about that, are you? Now, tell me again.'

'I dunno for sure – I wasn't there. It was Jim or – or your brother.'

'My *brother*?'

I could sense Geordie behind me, a restraining presence.

'The cops were looking for him, weren't they?' cried Kane defensively. 'How was anyone to know he didn't do it? He might have for all I know – I wasn't there, I tell you.'

I said, 'Tell me more about my brother. Why was he killed?'

'Ramirez didn't – didn't tell me,' he muttered.

'Don't be smart. Answer the question.'

'Well, they didn't ever tell me everything. I think he was – holding out on something. Something Ramirez wanted. I think it had something to do with those stones. I never – never killed him or nobody!'

I straightened up and said wearily, 'Well, my lilywhite friend, so you didn't kill anyone, you were never anywhere, and you're as pure as driven snow. I think you're a damned liar, but it doesn't matter. You'll be an accessory all the same. I believe they still use the guillotine out here.'

As Kane flinched I said, 'Anyone got any more questions?'

231

Campbell said harshly, 'You seem to have covered it. I can't think of anything right now. Later maybe.'

'Geordie?'

He shook his head.

'We'll be back, Kane. As soon as we think up some new questions. I think you've been lying like Ananias, and I warned you what would happen if you lied. You'd better think about that.'

Kane looked at the bulkhead moodily. 'I've told no lies.'

Campbell said, 'I wouldn't make any attempt to break out, Kane or you'll wind up deader than a frozen mackerel. You'll be safer in a cabin than outside – the crew here don't like you and they may shoot to kill if they see you, so stay put. It's better for your health.'

Outside the cabin we looked at one another bleakly. 'I could do with that drink now,' I said heavily. 'I'm sick to my stomach.'

We sat in the saloon for a while, letting tiredness wash over us and feeling the overwrought emotions of the last few hours seep away. There was too much to think about, and we all needed sleep badly. Geordie had Kane removed to a small cabin that he'd had prepared, which had been stripped of everything bar a bunk, with a padlock to the door, so that we were free to turn in in our own bunks.

Campbell said, 'I want to hear the whole story of this cutting-out expedition of yours, but we'll save it for to-morrow. And I want some ideas about Kane.'

And on that note we turned in, with the dawn already showing at the end of what had to be the most energetic day of my life.

2

The next day started late for everyone except the hands on watch, and it was a quiet and thoughtful start to the voyage. There was an air of reserved jubilation on board which was not entirely shared by Campbell or me. Over a late breakfast I spoke to Clare and Paula about the events of the previous night. 'You got back to the ship smartly,' I said. 'Well done.'

'Nick was great. But maybe not so well done – Ramirez must have seen us leaving,' said Clare.

'Not necessarily. He'll have spotted *Esmerelda* right away and knew we were here. I'm still not sure why he finally joined us. He surely didn't think we'd give up and go away, or hand over our knowledge, simply for his asking,' I mused.

Clare said, 'From what I know about him, he would prefer to bring things to a confrontation after a while. Just to see how we might react to his baiting. I don't think he's as subtle as all that.'

'Where were you during the big excitement?'

'Pop was as mad as a bull when we came on board and he found out what was going on. He was sure it would end up in trouble, maybe a riot, so he made us both go below and promise to stay there.' She giggled. 'We saw Ramirez go overboard, though – it was fantastic.'

'You cheated,' I said.

Paula said sedately, 'And we knew that Mr Campbell would give you a bawling out as soon as we left harbour. We didn't think you'd like an audience so we stayed below.'

'I think we've been forgiven,' I said.

'You've got Kane aboard, we know that,' Clare said and became graver. 'It must have been rotten having to interrogate him. Have you learned much?'

'It was rotten, and we've learned practically nothing. He is wholly despicable.'

Clare caught my hand across the table.

'Horrible for you, poor Mike,' she said and I wanted again desperately to be alone with her somewhere. At that moment, as if by pre-arrangement, Campbell appeared and our hands slid apart. Clare got up to prepare his meal.

Over breakfast, joined by Geordie, I filled Campbell in on the events of the night. When we'd finished the narrative he actually chuckled. 'My God, I wish I'd been there.'

'Pop, you know you didn't approve,' said Clare.

He sighed. 'I know, I know. But there comes a time when you have to hit out regardless of consequence. Maybe I'm getting too old and safety conscious.' He turned to Geordie. 'How long do you give Ramirez to repair the damage?'

'A hell of a long time if he has to depend on facilities in Nuku'alofa. That engine should never run again, if Jim placed his charge correctly.'

'He'll pour out money like water,' predicted Campbell. 'He'll have a new engine flown in with a crew to install it – that's what I'd do. I give him three weeks – not more than four – to be at sea again, and on our tail.'

I said, 'The sea is big. He may never find us.'

'He knows something about Falcon Island, and he can guess we do too. But let's hope you're right,' said Campbell, and raised his glass of orange juice. 'Here's to you, Captain Flint. I never thought I'd ship with a pirate crew, and I'm still not sure I approve. But you did a good job.'

He drank, then added, 'I sure hope Ramirez didn't run to the cops.'

'We'll soon find out. I've posted a lookout at the masthead with orders to watch astern,' Geordie said.

Campbell folded his hands on the table. 'Now let's talk about Kane.'

He was unhappy at the thought of keeping the man on board, for a number of sound reasons. He needed constant guarding, would require food, exercise and a check on his apparently wavering health, and was rather like a stone in one's shoe – a continuing nagging irritation that would work on everyone's nerves. 'As long as we have him with us he's a liability,' he said. 'He's told us nothing of value – I don't think he knows anything much – and he's a danger to us all every moment he's on board. So what the hell can we do about it?'

'You don't think he'd be useful as a hostage?' I asked.

They both looked at me sadly. 'Mike, he's even more worthless to Ramirez than he is to us,' Campbell said. 'They'd knock him off like a shot if they had to, without a moment's hesitation. His only value, perhaps, is in being an eventual witness should there be any police proceedings, and that could work both ways.'

Geordie said, 'It looks as though Ramirez did keep mum. A patrol boat would have caught up with us by now.'

'Maybe,' said Campbell. 'But I want to cover our butts. I want to get him to write a statement that someone on board can witness, someone not directly involved with him. One of your old crewmen would do for that, Geordie. And then I want to put him off somewhere.'

'Maroon him?' I asked. 'More pirate tricks?'

Geordie said, 'I agree with you, Mr Campbell. Let's have a look at the charts.'

He found what he was after almost immediately. Among the northern islands of the Tongan group, and not at all out of our way, lay the small islet of Mo'unga 'one. It had, according to the *Pilot*, one village and a beach where landing in good weather was possible. We tested the idea and could find nothing wrong with it, and so Geordie set about changing our course slightly while Campbell went down to talk to Kane. I didn't want to face him again that morning.

He came back presently and sat down.

'It's fixed,' he said. 'He'll write anything we want, he says, but I've told him to stick to the facts as he knows them – or says he does. He wants to save his own skin but doesn't in the least mind incriminating his great friend Jim Hadley. Lovely man. He's not well. I think a touch of fever from that shot wound, nothing that a few days' rest-cure on a tropical island won't fix. The local people will look after him for a backhander of some kind, till we can pick him up or send the cops for him. It's the only way, Mike.'

And to be truthful I would be as glad to see him off the ship as anyone. The knowledge of him being so close and yet so untouchable was something I found hard to live with.

We lay off Mo'unga 'one for a morning while Geordie and three of the crew took Kane ashore. He was willing, even eager to go, and didn't seem at all concerned as to how long he'd have to stay there. Geordie came back with news of his stolid acceptance by the local inhabitants, who were friendly

235

and incurious. They'd seen many western landing parties i
their time apparently. Geordie had asked, with many gesture
and a great deal of linguistic difficulty, if they knew anythin
of Falcon Island, and had got on best after flinging his arm
wide and imitating the action of a volcano blowing up. Thi
got grins and giggles, together with agreement that there wa
indeed just such a phenomena somewhere to the northwards
but Geordie was unable to get any closer details.

So we'd rid the boat of Kane for the second time and agai
there was a definite feeling of relief in the air. That man ma
or may not have been a murderer, I thought, but he wa
certainly bad news.

We got under way again and Geordie said at one stage
'We're almost on the track between Fonua Fo'ou and Min
erva now. All being well, we should be able to start dredgin
tomorrow – if you intend to stop for that.'

'We'll make use of every moment Jim Taylor gave us.
said Campbell. 'We might as well start. That's what we'r
here for. Come and have some coffee, Mike; I want to talk t
you.'

As I poured the coffee he said, 'You gave me two shocks i
Nuku'alofa that night. The first, when I found what you wer
up to, and the second, when you told me what you'd found
Do you think Ramirez was planning to jump us – real pirat
style?'

'From what you've told me about the strikes on your mine
I think he's capable of direct action when it suits him. Piracy i
these waters wouldn't be difficult either; it hasn't died out. It'
supposed to have happened to the *Joyita* not long ago, bu
they never really got to the bottom of that one.'

'Yes, I read about that.'

'There's plenty of piracy going on even yet, not far from
here – in Indonesian waters, down in the Bahamas – all over.
think Ramirez would jump us if it suited him. He'd obviousl
like us to lead him to the nodule deposits and then scupper u
completely. Who would ever know?'

'I think he'd like to scupper us even if he did know where i
was,' said Campbell.

'Just to get you off his tail? Yes, you could be right. But he as another problem to solve before he can do it.'

'What's that?'

'Finding us,' I said briefly.

Campbell gave that some thought. 'I can understand that. As you said that night, the sea is a big place. We should be all ight as long as we stay out at sea. It's when we put into any ort that he'll discover us again.' He drummed his fingers. But he might get lucky and find us out here anyway – and hat's what I want to talk to you about.'

I lifted my eyebrows.

'Your crew's a tough mob, and I know they can fight if they ave to – but will they? You say Ramirez has a crew of about hirty.'

I said, 'It depends on the kind of fighting. We might have leaned Ramirez out of weapons, and we might not. If he omes up against us with any kind of armament we've had our hips. If it's a matter of hand-to-hand fighting, no matter how lirty, we've got a good chance.'

'At two to one odds?'

'I've seen them in action. Admittedly it was a surprise ttack but it went off with about as much excitement as a tea arty at the vicarage. Our lot are trained fighting men, most of hem. Ramirez has waterfront scum.'

'I hope you're right. But I'd like to talk to our boys anyway. A man should know what he's fighting for.'

'They know what they're fighting for,' I said softly. 'They aw the hospital at Tanakabu.'

'True. But the labourer is worthy of his hire. They don't now the extent of what we're searching for and I'm going to ell them. There's no harm in mentioning a fat bonus at the nd of all this – whether we dredge lucky or not.'

I said, 'They'll all be about when we put the dredge over the ide. You could talk to them then.'

We had the winch made ready for dredging early the next lay, and at ten o'clock Campbell had the whole crew gathered efore him on deck. He stepped up onto the winch and sat asily on the control seat, looking down on the men.

'You know some of what this is all about,' he said to them. 'But not everything. So I'm going to tell you – officially. You know we've been dredging in a few places here and there, and I'm going to make it clear what we're looking for.'

He held up a nodule.

'This is a manganese nodule and the sea bed is covered with them. This particular nodule is worthless, but the ones we're looking for are worth a hell of a lot of money.' He casually tossed the nodule over the side.

'Now, a gentleman called Ramirez is trying to stop us. I suppose you all know that – hence the funny things that have happened in the last few weeks. Now, I want you to get this straight. Ramirez is going after those nodules for the money and so am I, make no mistake about that. The difference is that I think there's enough for all and I'm not greedy. I won't bother Ramirez if he bothers me none, but he's got a big tough crew and he seems to be spoiling for a fight.'

I had my own ideas about that statement. I was quite certain that Campbell didn't want Suarez-Navarro to have any part of the find, but perhaps on moral rather than on economic grounds.

'Now, I want you boys to know where you stand. Before you make any decisions I want you to know that whether we strike lucky or not, there's going to be a sizeable bonus at the end of this trip – you can call it danger money. If we do strike it rich, I'll be organizing a corporation to exploit the find, and I'll put five per cent of the stock aside to be divided among the crew. That may not seem much, but let me tell you it won't be peanuts. You may all end up millionaires.'

There was a babble of talk and a spate of handclapping. Geordie said, 'I think I can speak for all of us, Mr Campbell; that's a generous gesture that wasn't really necessary. We're with you all the way.'

There was a chorus of approval and Geordie held up his hand. 'There's just one more thing,' he said. 'I think Taff Morgan there will give up his bonus if he can go on double rations for the rest of the voyage.'

A ripple of laughter swept the deck.

Taffy called out, 'I don't want even that, skipper. Just give me the bastard who fired that hospital!'

The laughter turned to an ugly growl, and I pitied Hadley if any of these men came across him.

Campbell held up his hand again for silence. 'That's settled then. If any of you want to know more about these nodules you'd better ask Mike; he's our expert. And now I think we'd better get on with the job before *Sirena* shows up.'

He stepped down from the winch and the work began.

On the first drop the dredge touched bottom at 13,000 feet and when we hauled it up there were plenty of nodules in it. The crew had all seen plenty of them before but this time they were more curious. Danny picked one up and said, 'These could be valuable?'

'They could, and I hope they are. You'll be the first to know,' I said.

I took the first few samples down to the lab and began working. On deck I heard the crew securing the dredge and the bellowed orders of Geordie as *Esmerelda* got under way again. I hadn't been working long when Paula and Clare came in.

'We came to see if we could help,' said Clare. 'You'll have a lot of work on your hands.'

I rubbed my chin. Neither would be able to use the spectroscope without training, but for the rest they could be very useful. 'I hope you're good dishwashers,' I said, and waved at the glassware. 'This lot needs taking down and cleaning after every run.'

'I'll do that,' said Paula. She looked at my set-up. 'It looks like something out of one of those horror movies.'

'I'm not the mad scientist yet, although I might be if this whole thing turns out to be a bust. Clare, there's a hell of a lot of record keeping. You help your father with that kind of thing. Can you cope with this?'

'Sure. Just tell me what you want.'

I got cracking on the analysis. Working in a sailing ship heeled over under canvas wasn't anything I'd been trained for but it was surprising how much I'd learned, and I had rigged

239

up some interesting systems to cope with the movement. W
couldn't afford to stay hove-to while I assayed each time, an
in fact we'd tried it and that motion was worse. I was checkin
some rough results when I felt her slacken off and present
the winch engine started again. I knew Geordie had taken u
station for another dip over the side.

I said, 'Paula, can you start dismantling this set-up ready fo
cleaning, please? There'll be another load of nodules her
soon.'

She got to work and I turned to help Clare with the records

'There's the winch report which gives position and depth
There's the spectrograph report, together with the photo
graphic negative list. That's the quantitative analysis, an
there's a numbered half-nodule. All that lot must be file
together. This time I've written it out myself, but next time I'
call out the figures.'

I was pleased. This help on routine work made a lot o
difference and I reckoned the work would be speeded u
considerably. There was a long grind ahead – I didn't expec
to hit the jackpot at the first dip, and I hadn't. The result of th
first dredge was about average, just what the orthodo
oceanographer would expect to find in a normal Pacifi
nodule.

Clare and I went on deck to get a breath of fresh air an
were just in time to see the dredge go over the side. I watche
the bubbles rising to the surface and then we strolled awa
and sat down on the foredeck and I offered her a cigarette. A
we went past heads turned and Ian called from the winch
'Any luck?'

I smiled and shook my head. 'Not yet, Ian, but it's earl
days.'

Clare said, 'Pop told me about the questions you aske
Kane. Do you think he was telling any of the truth?'

'Not a chance. He was lying in his teeth.'

She said, 'You didn't expect him to admit to killing anyone
did you? Of course he would lie.'

'That isn't what I meant, Clare. Curiously enough, I don'
think he did kill anyone – not directly. I believed him when he

said it was Hadley all the time. I don't think Kane has enough guts to kill anyone, but I could believe anything of Hadley. I think he's a psychopath, Kane implied that even Ramirez can't control him. It won't make any difference in the long run, of course – if we get them all Kane will be as guilty as any of them, and be punished accordingly.'

'Then you think he was lying about something else.'

'That's right – but I'm damned if I know what it is. It was just something about his manner when I questioned him about Mark. There was a look of fear about him, something in his eyes I couldn't place. I think something much more terrible happened. But the outline of the story is clear enough.'

Clare shivered. 'I didn't have much sympathy for Mark – not after what he did to me – but I can't help feeling sorry for him. What a pitiful end for any man.'

I nodded. 'I wouldn't think about it too much, Clare. He's dead and beyond feeling anything any more. The world is for the living.'

And you are one of the living, I thought, looking at her. There was no romantic moon shining across the water; instead we were in the hard white glare of the tropic sun. There was no love song echoing from the saloon, just the rhythmic clanking of the winch and the throb of a diesel. I said, 'Clare, if we come out of this successfully I'd like to get to know you better – much better.'

She slanted her eyes at me. 'And if we don't come through successfully – will you just walk away and never want to see me again?'

'That's not a nice way to put it.'

'That's the way I have to put it.'

I said nothing, fumbling for the right words.

'This is rather a new experience for me,' said Clare with a warmth of humour in her voice. 'I've never had to work at it myself. Most times I've had to fend off the advances—'

'I'm not making. . . .'

' – because I wasn't sure if I liked the man, or because I sometimes thought they were after me as Pop's daughter – the

ones who never found his money a hindrance. I don't thin
that's your problem though. Or do you think that rich peopl
should only marry rich people?'

I was about to reply angrily until I suddenly realized tha
she was teasing me. Her eyes were alight with mischief – and
I thought in astonishment, with fondness. I said lamely
'Clare, there are all sorts of. . . .'

She waited but I was still fumbling.

'Complications? But we could weather them all. Oh Mike
you're an awful fool – but I love you all the more for it.'

I said after a pause, 'Damn it, Clare, it isn't the way
intended this.'

'Am I driving you to the wall, Mike? Why don't you just sa
what's on your mind?'

So I did. I said, 'Will you marry me, Clare?'

She hung her head for a moment and then looked at me. 'O
course I will,' she said. 'We'll get married by the first priest w
come across. I thought you'd *never* get to the point. Girls are
only supposed to propose in Leap Year, but I nearly had t
break that rule.'

I felt exhilarated and weak simultaneously. 'Well, I'll b
damned,' I said, and we both burst out laughing out of shee
joy. I wanted to do the obvious thing and take her in my arms
but there was too little privacy even up here, so we simpl
clutched each other's hands.

Clare said, 'Mike, let's not tell anyone just yet. Pop ha
enough else on his mind right now. I think he'll be fine about i
but I want to be sure when we tell him, and nobody els
should know first.'

I agreed with her. I'd have agreed with anything she sai
just then.

We talked a lot of nonsense until the dredge came up. I
can't remember us walking down to the laboratory – I think
we floated.

3

We dredged and dredged, stopping every ten miles on the way to Minerva Reefs. We dredged during every scrap of daylight hours and I worked a sixteen-hour day, taking my meals in the laboratory. The girls were of great service but there was still a lot of work, and I began to fear that my supplies of chemicals would soon run out.

One thing bothered me. We were being continually pestered by members of the crew calling in at the lab to see what we were doing. Not only were they anxious to see good results but I found that Taffy Morgan had organized a sweepstake on the cobalt result of every dredge. I went to see Geordie.

'Look, this is wasting a lot of my time,' I told him. 'Tell them to put a sock in it.'

He smiled slowly. 'Don't want to dampen their enthusiasm, do you? Tell you what; give me the results of the dredge each day and I'll post a bulletin.'

'That'll do it. Get the results from Clare.'

He stuffed tobacco into the bowl of his pipe. 'Campbell started something with his big talk of making us all millionaires. Do you think there's anything in it?'

'I should say he's a man of his word.'

'I'm not doubting his word,' said Geordie. 'I'm doubting whether he can live up to it. If ten to fifteen million pounds is only five per cent of what he expects to make, then I think he's expecting to make a devil of a lot.'

'He is, Geordie,' I said soberly. 'And so am I. I'm hoping that if we hit it all, it'll be big. When I've the time we'll get Campbell to talk in figures. That's going to open your eyes.'

'He's already done that.'

'He's hardly started.'

'We'll see,' said Geordie, unimpressed.

We dredged – and dredged – and dredged. Then we h[...]
shoal ground at nearly 4000 feet. Geordie said laconically
'Minerva Bank.'

'All right,' I said. 'Nice navigating. We carry out our plan
we dredge all round it. But first I'd like a sample from th[...]
middle of the shoal, as far into the shallows as it's safe t[...]
go.'

Campbell said, 'Isn't that wasting time?'

'We don't know – not until we've done it. And I'd like t[...]
know for the record – and for my own theories.'

We *were* wasting our time. We dredged at 2000 feet an[...]
came up with a bucketful of volcanic cinders, dead coral an[...]
shell. No nodules at all. The crew looked suddenly worried a[...]
the haul but I reassured them. 'I hardly expected any here, s[...]
don't worry. Plenty outside still. Now we can cross this are[...]
off the list, but I had to be sure.'

We retraced our track to the edge of Minerva Bank an[...]
started to circle it at a distance of about ten miles, dredging i[...]
deep water. Geordie worked it out on the chart. 'That's abou[...]
sixteen times we drop – say four days.'

It took us a bit longer than that, but five days later we ha[...]
made the full circle and still hadn't found anything. Campbell
first up and first down, was getting depressed again and hi[...]
fretting was agitating the crew, who'd been working manfully
'Are you *sure* we're in the right place?' he asked me, not fo[...]
the first time.

'No, I'm not,' I said sharply. I was a bit on edge too; I wa[...]
tired and not in a mood to be asked stupid questions. 'I'm no[...]
sure of a damned thing. I've got theories to offer, but n[...]
certainties.'

Geordie was more placid. 'Don't forget that our arrival i[...]
Tonga brought Ramirez there hotfoot. I think we're in th[...]
right place.'

I wished to God I knew where they were. They'd had time
I reckoned, to repair their engine, and I would have dearly
loved to know if they were out at sea searching for us at thi[...]
moment. If only we had some inkling as to how much Ramire[...]
really knew, we could be better placed to cope with him.

Campbell echoed my thoughts. 'Where the hell is Suarez-Navarro? And where are these goddam nodules? What do we do next, Mike?'

'We carry on as planned. We go back towards Falcon on a parallel track.'

'East or west?' enquired Geordie.

I shrugged and felt in my trouser pocket. 'Anyone got a coin? This is a thing that can be tossed for.'

Campbell snorted in disgust.

Geordie said, more practically, 'Why don't we do both? We use the course we came on as a centre line and zig-zag back. First sample one side, then the other.'

'That's a reasonable idea,' I said. 'Let's do that.'

So we went back, and the same old boring routine went on. The winch motor whined, the bucket went over the side with a bubbling splash and a couple of hours later came up with its load which I then proceeded to prove worthless. There were plenty of nodules but not the gold-plated ones. The crew was kept busy at keeping the decks reasonably clean and at maintenance, and we devised all sorts of games and exercises to use up spare time.

But Geordie was worrying about the maintenance of the winch gear. 'We're overworking it,' he said to me. 'We don't have time for standard maintenance. There's the cable – the lot wants a thorough cleaning and oiling. I'm scared it might break on one of these hauls if we don't check on it.'

Campbell heard him out, tight-lipped, and said, 'No. We must carry on as long as we have the headway. You'll have to do the best you can, Geordie.'

I knew what was on his mind. We had been at sea now for over two weeks and Ramirez would soon be ready to sail. While we were at sea there was a fair chance he wouldn't find us – but to put into any port would be dangerous.

So we carried on, zig-zagging back towards Falcon, fruitlessly dredging the seemingly profitless Pacific.

And then we hit it!

My voice shook as I called the vital figures out to Clare. 'C-Cobalt – 4.32 per cent.'

She looked up, startled. 'I didn't catch that one, Mike – at least I think I didn't.'

I said shakily, 'This is it – 4.32 per cent cobalt!'

We looked at each other wordlessly. At last I said carefully 'We'll assay again from that last load. More than once. Paula I want everything washed down again – cleaner than ever. And the three of us threw ourselves into a routine that was suddenly anything but boring.

The results were dotted around my first one like Campbell's bullet-holes around mine on the target. 4.38 – 4.29 – four times I tested, and every test checked out.

I croaked, 'Hell, I've got to tell Geordie. He's got to change course.'

I dashed up on deck leaving the girls thumping each others shoulders. Ian was at the wheel. 'Whoa up!' I shouted. 'We're going back to the last site.'

His eyes widened. 'You've never found something?'

'That I have! Where's Geordie?'

'He's off watch – I think in his cabin.'

I left him to supervise the change of direction and pounded below. But Geordie wasn't impressed. 'Four per cent is a long way from ten,' he said.

'You damn fool, Geordie. It's twice the percentage that's been found in any nodule before, apart from the one we had in London. We must have struck the edge of the concentration.'

'Well – what now?'

'We go back and cruise that area, keeping an eye on the echo sounder. That'll probably tell us something.'

He swung out of his bunk and put his trousers on. 'It might tell you something; it won't mean a thing to me. Thank God we've been keeping careful records of our position.'

'Come on – let's tell the boss.'

Campbell had already been told. We found him in the lab with the girls, looking at the figures. He turned as we came in, his eyes bright with expectation. 'Have we found it Mike?'

I was suddenly cautious. I said carefully. 'We've found

something. Whether it's what we hope is another thing.'

'You goddam scientists,' he grumbled. 'Why can't you ever tell a straight story?'

I pulled out the chart I had been making from the recording echometer. 'There's a ridge running along here, roughly north and south,' I said. 'The top is within nine thousand feet of the surface. We picked up our prize nodule here, on the east side of the ridge at eleven thousand feet. I'd like to sail at right angles to the ridge, striking east – this way. I'd like to see how the depth of water goes.'

'You think the depth might have something to do with this?'

'It might. It would be the natural accumulation area for the greatest volume of nodules hereabouts, rather than in the very shallowest areas – even though there's never more than one layer of thickness of nodules anywhere.'

'I thought they'd be there in great piles, humped up together.'

'Sorry, no,' I said. 'That's never been found. The best evidence from some deep-sea photographs is that there are parts of the sea-bed which are lumpy underneath the sediment layer, indicating that many more nodules might be buried there, but in that case they'd have stopped growing anyway, being cut off from their life-line – the sea water itself.'

But for the only time they were not interested in my impromptu lecture. I hastened to correct myself.

'Don't worry, the billions of tons I promised you will be there, even if it does lie only one layer thick. There are lots of things we have to find out still.'

We arrived in the vicinity of the last site with members of the crew, rather ludicrously, peering at the surface of the ocean as if it could show them anything. Geordie said, 'Right – now which way?'

I drew a pencil line on his chart. 'Follow that course, please.'

As we sailed I watched the trace of the echometer with intense concentration. The line showed a gradual deepening

247

of the water – not a sudden drop, but a falling away as thoug
from mountains into the plains. After we had gone about te
miles the bottom began to come up again from 13,000 feet.
made sure it wasn't just a local condition and then said, '
want to go back about two miles.'

'Okay,' Geordie said, and gave brisk orders. We wer
doing most of this work under engine as it was tricky for sai
and I was grateful for the continuing calm weather which gav
us the minimum of wind and ocean drift to contend with.
thought for just one envious moment of how easy it would a
be on land.

Campbell looked at my tracing. 'What do you think?'

'There's some sort of valley down there,' I said. 'We'v
come from a ridge, crossed the valley and begun to climb u
towards the opposite ridge. I want to go back and dredg
where it's deepest – it's about 13,000 feet.'

Campbell rubbed his cheek. 'Bit deep for commercia
dredging with a drag line. You waste too much time just goin
down and coming up again.'

'If the stuff's rich enough it should pay.'

He grunted. 'That's what we're here to find out.'

By now everyone knew what was in the wind and there wa
a lot of tension as the dredge went down. Ian was at the winc
and Geordie himself at the wheel, keeping *Esmerelda* o
station. It seemed a particularly long time before Ian, watch
ing the cable tension meter, slipped the winch out of gear an
said, 'She's bottomed.'

Geordie's hand went to the engine controls. Campbel
swung round, fussing like an old hen. 'Careful, Geordie, w
don't want any mistakes now.'

Esmerelda crept forward, taking the strain on the cable.
could visualize the dredge at the bottom of the abyss, scrapin
forward in utter darkness, gathering the nodules and debri
into its maw like a vast-jawed prehistoric creature.

Then the job was done and Ian had the winch in gear again
The drum started to turn and the crew began to stow the we
and slimy cable into the hold as it came off the drum. Again i
seemed to take ages and the tension increased until our nerve

airly twanged. Taffy said hoarsely, 'For God's sake, Ian, pull our finger out!'

Geordie said calmly, 'None of that, now. Take it easy, Ian – ou're doing just fine.'

Thirteen thousand feet is nearly two and a half miles. It akes a long time to haul a full dredge up from that depth, especially when you're not too sure of your cable and taking it lowly. Normally nobody took any notice until the bucket came inboard, but this time everyone's attention was riveted, and when at last the dredge broke surface there were many villing hands to swing the boarding derrick out and bring the aul in.

Geordie had handed over the wheel to Danny and he ran orward to help release the load. A cascade of nodules swept onto the deck, together with the usual lot of slimy mud. Taffy stooped and picked up a nodule. 'This doesn't look any different to me,' he said, clowning disappointment.

Ian said, 'Ye daft loon. Leave it to Mike, would you? He knows what he's doing.'

I hoped he was right.

Campbell said, 'How long, Mike?'

'The usual three hours. I can't do it any faster.'

Nor did I – in fact it took longer. The lab wasn't very big and we had enough trouble with three of us working there. Now Campbell insisted on coming in and watching, and wherever he stood or sat he was in the way. In the end I bundled him out despite his protests, but I could hear him pacing up and down n the passage-way.

At the end of three and three-quarter hours I opened the door and said, 'Congratulations, Mr Campbell. You've just become the father of a 9.7 per cent cobalt nodule.'

His eyes lit up. 'We've hit it! By God, we've hit it!'

'Bang on the nose,' I agreed happily.

He leaned against the bulkhead and sighed deeply. 'I never thought we'd make it.' After a few moments his brain started to function again and he said, 'What's the density?'

'Ten pounds to the square foot. That'll keep you busy for the next few years.'

His smile grew jubilant.

'Come up to the saloon, all of you. Let's have a drink on i' Get Geordie down here.'

In the saloon he opened the liquor cabinet and produce bottles of whisky and gin, and set about pouring drinks wit great energy. Clare and I managed to linger in the passage ju: long enough for a quick hug and kiss before joining him wit Paula, and Geordie arrived a moment later, beaming.

'To you, Mike. You've done a great job,' Campbell sai expansively.

I included them all in the toast, and we drank it with grea cheer. 'It isn't finished yet, though,' I warned them. 'We'v got to find the extent of the deposit. There's a lot of proving t be done.'

'I know, I know,' Campbell said. 'But that's detail work Do you realize we've done it, Geordie?'

'I'm very pleased for you,' Geordie said formally.

'The hell with that. I'm pleased for all of us. How abou splicing the mainbrace, Geordie – with my compliments?' H waved to the well-stocked cabinet.

'Well, I don't know,' said Geordie judiciously. 'I've still go a ship to run. The lads off watch can have a dram, but those o: duty will have to wait a while yet. There's enough buzz goin on up there as it is.' He smiled and added, 'I'm off watc' myself.'

Campbell laughed. 'Okay, join us.'

Geordie cocked his head at me. 'We're still hove-to, yo know. Where do we go from here?'

I said, 'Ninety degrees from your last course – to the south Tell the watch to keep an eye on the echometer and to keep t the deepest water they can. We'll go for about twenty-fiv miles. If the water shallows appreciably or we diverge to much off course I'd like to know at once. And I think Clar had better give you the latest bulletin, don't you?'

Clare produced a sheet of paper with the magic figures, an Geordie took it up with him. Campbell turned to me. 'Yo trotted all that out glibly enough. I suppose you've got a idea.'

'I've got an idea of sorts. We came from a ridge and dredged in the deepest part of a valley. Now I want to run along the valley to see how far it stretches each way. The echometer record will give us a lot of useful information, and we'll dredge at intervals along the course.'

From the deck we heard the sound of cheering. Campbell stopped in the act of pouring himself another drink. 'Everybody's happy.'

'Everyone except Ramirez,' I commented.

'I wish he'd sink,' said Paula, unexpectedly viciously.

Campbell frowned, then pushed the unwelcome thought from his mind; this was no time for thinking of a chancy future. Geordie came back into the saloon and Campbell pointed to the cabinet. 'Pour your own. I'm no man's servant,' he said. Geordie grinned and picked up the bottle.

I rolled a nodule onto the table. 'Geordie's a bit doubtful as to the value of this. I promised I'd get you to talk figures.'

Campbell poked at it with one finger. 'It sure doesn't look like much, does it, Geordie?'

'Just like any other bit of rock we've been dredging up the last couple of weeks,' Geordie said offhandedly.

'It contains nearly ten per cent cobalt. We don't know much about anything else that's in it because Mike's only checked for cobalt, but we know there should be a fair amount of copper and vanadium and a lot of iron – and manganese too of course. Now, I'm telling you and I speak from experience, that the gross recoverable value will run to about four hundred dollars a ton.'

Geordie was still not convinced. 'That doesn't seem too valuable to me. I thought it was really valuable – like gold or platinum.'

Campbell grinned delightedly and took a little slide rule from his pocket. 'You'd say the density would be pretty consistent over a wide area, wouldn't you, Mike?'

'Oh yes. In the centre of the concentration you can fairly well rely on that.'

'And what would you call a wide area?'

I shrugged. 'Oh, several square miles.'

Campbell looked at Geordie under his brows, then bent over the slide rule. 'Now, let's see. At ten pounds a square foot – that makes it – run to about, say, fifty-six million dollars a square mile.'

Geordie, who was in the act of swallowing whisky, suddenly coughed and spluttered.

We all shouted with surprised laughter. I said, 'There are a lot of square feet in a square mile, Geordie!'

He recovered his breath. 'Man, that's money! How many square miles of this stuff will there be?'

'That's what we find out next,' I said. I saw the two girls looking at Campbell with astonishment and something occurred to me. I said to Paula, 'You're in on this too, you know.'

She gaped at me. 'But I've – I'm not—'

Campbell said. 'Why, yes, Paula. You're one of the crew. Everybody on this ship gets in on the deal.'

Her astonishment must have been too great for her to contain, for she burst suddenly into tears and ran blindly from the saloon. Clare cast us a quick happy smile and went after her.

I could see that Geordie was trying to work out the fifteenth part of five percent of 56 million dollars – and failing in the attempt. I said, 'That four hundred dollars a ton is a gross value. We have to deduct the costs of dredging and processing, distribution and all sorts of extras. Got any ideas on that?'

'I have,' Campbell said. 'When Mark first came to me with this idea I went into it pretty deeply. The main problem is the dredging – a drag line dredge like the one we're using, but bigger, isn't much use at this depth. You waste too much time pulling it up. So I put some of my bright boys on to the problem and they decided it would be best to use a hydraulic dredge. They did a preliminary study and reckoned they could suck nodules to the surface from 14,000 feet for ten dollars a ton or less. Then you have to add all sorts of factors – processing, marketing, transport and other technical overheads – the cost of hiring ships and crews and maintaining them. We'd want to develop and build our own dredges, we'd need survey ships, and we'd have to build a processing plant.

That would happen on one of the islands and we'd get a lot of help there, as it'll mean a huge income in many ways for them, but all in all I would have to float a company capable of digging into its pocket to the tune of some forty million dollars.'

He said this in a serious and businesslike tone. Clare was apparently used to these flights of executive rhetoric but Geordie and I gaped at him. It was Geordie's first excursion into high finance, as it was mine, but I was slightly better prepared for it. 'Good God! Have you got that much – I mean can you lay your hands on it?'

'Not before this. But I can get it with what we have to show here. We'd clear a net profit of forty million in the first couple of years of operation – the rest should be pure cream. There's going to be a lot of guys on Wall Street eager to jump into a thing like this – or even take it over.'

He mused a bit, then added, 'But they're not going to. When Suarez-Navarro jumped my mines I swore I'd never hang on to another solid proposition ever again – not if they were as easy to steal as that. So I went back to being a wild-catter; in and out to take a fast profit. But this – somehow this is different. I'm sticking here. I know a couple of good joes back home, men I can trust. Between them and me, and perhaps persuading a couple of governments to take an interest, I want to tie this thing up so tight that neither Suarez-Navarro nor anyone else of their type can horn in and spoil it.'

He got up and went to a port to look out over the sea. 'Tonga's back there. They'll probably come in on the act. They'll benefit by being the ones most likely to get the processing plant built in their territory – it will be highly automated so it won't mean much steady labour, once it's built, but they'll get the taxes and the spin-off, so I should think they will be happy to cooperate. There's another thing on my mind too; nodules are still forming out there, and from what Mike says they'll go on doing so – at what he always calls an explosively fast rate. Maybe for once we'll be able to do a mining operation without raping the goddam planet.' He came back to the table and picked up his glass. 'And that's an achievement that any bunch of guys can be proud of. Let's drink to it.'

So we drank, very solemnly. I for one was full of awe at what we were doing, and I thought the others felt the same. Campbell had come up with a couple of shattering thoughts.

4

We stayed in the area for another week, quartering the submarine valley and dredging at selected spots. The material poured in and I was kept busy. A much more detailed survey would be done later – all I was aiming at was to put limits on the area and to find out roughly how rich, and how consistent it was.

Esmerelda was a happy ship in those days. Not that she hadn't been before, but the depression caused by a fruitless search had lifted and everyone was keen and cheerful. There was a lot of skylarking among the crew, although it always stopped when there was serious work to be done.

Once, when I was having a breather on deck, Paula joined me.

'I don't know what came over me the other day, Mike – you know, when Mr Campbell said I had a share in all this.'

'It is a bit of a shock when you find yourself suddenly on the verge of riches. I went through it too.'

'I never thought of being rich,' she said. 'I never had the time, I guess. I've always been on the move – the States, Mexico, Australia, Tahiti, Hawaii, Panama. Guess I was a bit of a hobo.' She looked up. 'That's what you British call a tramp, isn't it?'

'That's right.'

'I guess I was that too – in the American sense, I mean,' she said sombrely.

'You're all right, Paula,' I said warmly. 'Don't worry about it. Enjoy the idea instead. What will you do with all your new-gotten wealth?'

'Gee, I don't know, Mike. I'm not like Clare – she's used to money, but I'm not. And the way her pop talks sometimes makes my head spin, the way he juggles his millions.'

'Maybe you can go on a cruise ship to sunny Tahiti,' I said jokingly.

But she shook her head violently. 'No. I'll never go there again – I never want to see Papeete again.' She was silent for a while and we stood together companionably, and then she said, 'I think I'll go home first. Yes, I think I'll go home.'

'Where's home?'

'In Oregon. Just a small town – there aren't many big ones in Oregon. It's called Medford. I haven't been there for years – and I should never have left it.'

'Why did you leave, Paula?'

She laughed. 'Oh, it's a bromide – a cliché, you'd say. My whole life's been a cliché. I got movie-crazy when I was a kid, and when I was sixteen I won a local beauty competition. That gave me a swelled head and a big mouth – you should have heard me talk about what I was going to do in Hollywood. I was going to knock 'em cold. So I went to Hollywood and it knocked *me* cold! There are too many girls like me in Hollywood. I told you the story was a cliché.'

'What happened after Hollywood?'

'The cliché continued. I drifted around, singing in cheap night spots – you know the rest, or you can guess it.' I was saddened by the bitter resignation in her voice. 'That place where you found me in Panama – that was the best paid job I ever had in my whole life.'

'And you left it – just like that? Just because I asked you to?'

'Why not? It – it was Mark, you see. Oh, I know how you feel about Mark, I've heard you talk. All right, supposing he was a lousy no-good? I guess I always knew that, but – I loved him, Mike. And I suppose I was stupidly hoping to find out if he'd ever loved me. I always wanted to do whatever I could for him.'

I remained quiet. There was nothing I could say to that.

'Yes,' she went on quietly. 'I do think I'll go home. I alway boasted that I wouldn't go back until I was a success. I gues they'd call me a success now, Mike?' There were tears in he eyes.

'You've always been a success,' I said gently, and held he shoulders.

She sniffed a bit and then said, shaking her head briskl 'This isn't getting the glassware washed. I'd better go back t work. But thanks.'

I watched her walk along the deck and for the thousandt time I damned Mark's soul to hell. At a touch on my elbow turned to find Geordie. 'I didn't want to bust up the *tête-a tête*,' he said, 'so I waited a bit.' He nodded along the deck 'Falling for her, Mike?'

'Nothing like that,' I said amusedly, thinking how very of target Geordie's guesses were. 'But there are times when wish Mark had never been born.'

'Gave her a bad time, did he?'

'Curiously enough, he made her very happy. But he brok her heart by getting himself killed. Not that that matters - he'd have found some way of doing it, sooner or later. What' on your mind, Geordie?'

'I want to talk to you about our next move,' he said. 'W can't stay out here much longer, Mike. The winch and it components really desperately need attention. We're a littl low on water – we hadn't had time to top up completely i Nuku'alofa – and that goes for fuel too. And we've been usin an awful lot of that for station-keeping. We'll have to put int port somewhere pretty soon.'

'Yes, my lab stocks are running low too. Look, Geordie we're really finished here – I've got loads of data to work o already. Let's put it to the boss again.'

Campbell said, 'How soon can you finish here, then?'

'I am finished, virtually. This last dredge today could be it - otherwise I could go on tinkering forever.'

'That's it then. But we don't go back to Nuku'alofa, in cas Ramirez is still there, or hunting for us in that area. We'll g to Fiji – to Suva.'

I hesitated. 'That's fine, but I'd like to have a look at Falcon.'

'What for?'

I said, 'Well, it's responsible for all this.'

'A scientist to the last, eh? You're not content with finding anything – you want to know when and how and why.'

I was desperately keen to visit the island – or the site of it. I added, to give force to my argument, 'It could well give us a lead to other high-cobalt areas hereabouts. Maybe concentrations of other metals – once we find out something about the mechanism of this thing.'

He laughed. 'Okay, Mike, I guess you've earned it. If Geordie gives the go-ahead we'll go to Suva by way of Falcon.'

Geordie wasn't too certain. He pulled out his charts, measured distances, and grumbled. 'How long are you staying there?'

'Only a day or so, if that.'

'Will you be dredging?'

'There'll be no need to dredge. It's very shallow over the site. A good swimmer like Bill Hunter could go down and collect the samples I want by hand – it won't be more than a few fathoms. And he's dying to show off his talent. We could be away again in just a few hours.'

'It's cutting it a bit fine,' he complained. 'We'll be damned low on water by the time we get to Suva – and it's a good job you don't want to dredge because I really think this one was our last. We have to keep enough fuel oil for manoeuvring and for emergencies – I can't spare any more for the winch motor.'

'Away with you, Geordie. You know you hate sailing under power.'

But I got him to agree in the end. We finished with the dredge and stowed the cable for the last time. The dredge bucket was secured on deck and Geordie set a course north-ward for Fonua Fo'ou.

That evening in the saloon I said, 'I'd like to summarize what I've found. Can you stand another short lecture?'

We were moving briskly along with a helpful wind, the treasure had been found and any danger seemed infinitely remote and unlikely. My seminar settled down to hear me out in a state of contentment.

Campbell said, 'I'm getting used to being lectured to by scientists; it's sometimes boring and usually profitable.'

I laughed. 'This time it's very profitable.' I produced my charts and notebook. 'The high-cobalt nodules seem to be concentrated in a valley or depression, twenty miles wide and a hundred miles long. The nodules lie in varying degrees of richness and density.'

Clare, whom I had discovered to my pleasure to be a quick natural mathematician, said in astonishment, 'But that's two thousand square miles.'

'Quite an area,' I agreed. 'The richness varies roughly with the depth of the water, from about two per cent at the top of the ridges to a peak of ten per cent in the valley bottom – an inverse curve, if you like. On the other hand, the density varies in a different way. At the extreme north of the valley the density is only half a pound per square foot. At the other end it peaks out at fifty pounds per square foot.'

Campbell said, 'Still at ten per cent cobalt?'

'On the valley bottom, yes.'

'Hot diggety!' he exclaimed. 'A quarter of a billion bucks a square mile!' He and Clare were smiling in delight. Geordie looked dazed – the figures were so fantastic that he couldn't absorb them. Paula looked petrified.

I consulted my notebook again. 'I've worked out some rough figures. I reckon the overall average density over the entire area of two thousand square miles is about eight pounds to the square foot. The overall richness is about six per cent. Considering some of the higher figures, though, you're in for a very fine haul wherever you begin, so systematic mining will pay off.'

Campbell said, 'Those average figures of yours don't mean a damn thing, Mike. What do I care if the average density is eight pounds when I know of a place where it's actually fifty? *That's* where we start – we take the rich stuff out first.' He shook his head in wonder. 'This is fantastic – this is the damndest thing. We can prove every pound of our resources before we even start. We'll need a detailed survey, though – with you to head it up.'

'I'd be proud to,' I said. I thought of the advanced equipment and systems I could use and rejoiced inwardly.

'I'll give you the finest survey vessel ever built – with no disrespect to *Esmerelda*, Geordie. But then – you may not want to do this. You'll be a rich man.' He got up to pour us all drinks as he spoke.

'I won't be until that survey has been made and the operation started,' I pointed out. 'But you couldn't stop me even then.'

Campbell said, 'I've been thinking this thing out. I'm starting a corporation and I'm reserving five per cent of the stock for the crew. Three per cent goes to you, Mike, and two to Geordie. I'll sell twenty per cent to those two guys I know that I mentioned, for twenty million dollars and let the Goverment – any or all of 'em – have fifty per cent for another twenty million. That starts to take care of the working capital.'

Clare exclaimed, 'Pop, I'm disgusted at you. Don't think I can't add up percentages! You come out with twenty per cent for yourself and you've discovered nothing. All you've done is put up a measly million dollars or so for this expedition.'

'Not quite, Clare,' he said mildly. 'There's your cut – another five, I think. And I have ideas concerning the remaining fifteen. For centuries people like me have been taking metals out of the earth and putting nothing back. We've been greedy – the whole of mankind has been greedy. As I said the other day, we've been raping this planet.' His voice grew in intensity. 'Now we've got hold of something different and we mustn't spoil it, like we've spoiled everything else that we've laid our greedy hands on. I'm keeping five per cent for myself, sure – but the other ten will go into an independent, non-profit making organization which will push my ideas a little further. We have to find a way to take that stuff out of the sea without disturbing the environment more than we can help, and to put something back – somewhere – by way of recompense.'

'There's one way that I can think of immediately,' I said. 'There are phosphorite nodules as well. You can make good fertilizer out of them, but so far no one has thought of a way of dredging them commercially. We could get them up with the rest, and you could be doing agriculture a bit of good.'

'That's what I mean,' Campbell exclaimed. 'You've gone to the heart of it – research is what's needed.' His eyes crinkled. 'How would you like to head up a new foundation?'

'Good grief! I wouldn't know where to start. I'm a field man, not an administrator. You want someone like old Jarvis.'

'You wouldn't be an administrator – I wouldn't waste your time on that. I can hire managers, but you'd be in charge of research.'

'Then nothing would stop me taking it on,' I said, dazzled.

'That's my boy.' He lifted the bottle and inspected it critically. 'Nearly the last of the scotch. Never mind, we can get some more in Suva.'

5

I was below when I heard the engine start, so I strolled on deck to find Geordie at the wheel. It was a calm evening without a breath of wind, and there was no sound except the throb of the engine which drove *Esmerelda* over the placid sea. 'It's lucky you kept some fuel back,' I commented, looking at a steadying sail hanging limply.

'Got a few gallons up my sleeve. I always save a little more than I let anyone know. Mike, what's the depth of water at Fonua Fo'ou?'

'I don't know, Geordie. It varies from year to year. The *Pilot* gives the latest depth in 1949 as about fifty-four feet, with no sign of the island at all, but it was there in 1941 – though there seemed to have been less of it than there was reported in 1939. A shoal at the northern end had vanished in those couple of years.'

He wasn't happy with this. 'We'll have to go very canny then.'

'We've been around shoals before, Geordie. And we know exactly where this one ought to be – so what's the problem?'

'I don't like this.'

'You don't like what?'

'This weather.'

I looked across at the setting sun and then to the east. The sky was cloudless and everything was peaceful. 'What's wrong with it?'

'I dunno,' he said. 'I've just got a feeling. I don't like that yellow tinge on the horizon northwards. Maybe there's a storm coming up.'

'How's the barometer?' I asked.

'Still normal – nothing wrong there. Maybe I'm being a bit old-womanish.'

He called Taffy to him and handed over the wheel. 'Keep a bloody close watch on that echo sounder, Taff,' he said. 'By my reckoning, we should be nearly there – we've been running long enough. Ian, set a watch out. If there's nothing before dark we'll circle back and come up again in the morning.

He was more twitchy than I'd ever known him, and I couldn't quite tell why. Certainly it didn't appear to have anything to do with a possible chase by *Sirena* – we'd seen nothing and had no reason to suppose that she would find us. She'd scarcely be waiting at Falcon Island as if it were a handy street corner, I thought. And while my weather sense was not nearly as acute as Geordie's I had had my share of storms, and could see nothing in the sky or on the sea's surface to excite alarm. I didn't push him, and finally turned in to leave him pacing uneasily in the darkness, turning *Esmerelda* back on her track for a loop during the night hours.

The morning brought more of the same weather – or lack of it. It was calm, quiet and peaceful as we gathered on deck to watch for any telltale breakers while Geordie brought the ship gently back to her last night's position, and then motored slowly ahead. Presently he throttled the engine back to less than three knots. The echo sounder showed a hundred fathoms. Campbell and the girls joined us on deck and their voices were unnaturally loud in the hush of morning.

Geordie said quietly, 'The bottom's coming up. Only fifty fathoms.' He throttled back the engine still further.

Clare said, 'Is this Falcon Island?'

'Dead ahead. But you won't see anything though,' I told her. 'Just another bit of sea.'

'Twenty fathoms,' called Jim at the echo sounder. Geordie had taken the wheel again and repeated the call, then cursed suddenly. 'What the hell's going on?'

'What's the matter?'

'I can't keep the old girl on course.'

I looked across the sea path to the rising sun. The sea had a black, oily look and seemed as calm as ever, but then I noticed small eddies and ripples here and there – in an otherwise motionless seascape it was a strange and disturbing sight. They weren't large but I saw several of them. I felt *Esmerelda* moving under me, and she seemed to be travelling sideways instead of forwards. Something else nagged at my senses but I couldn't quite identify it.

Geordie had got control again, apparently. As Jim called out, 'Ten fathoms' he put the engine out of gear and as we glided to a rocking stop his hand was on the reverse gear, ready to send it home. Jim was calling steadily, 'Nine fathoms . . . eight . . . seven . . .' At six and a half Geordie touched the engine into reverse and the sounder came back up to hover at seven fathoms. Geordie said, 'This is it. As far as I'll go.' He looked and sounded bothered.

'Is Bill ready?'

Diving in six fathoms – thirty-six feet – was going to be no problem to Bill, who was already kitted up in a wet suit and aqualung, and was dipping his mask into a bucket of sea water someone had hauled up on deck. He already had his orders and they were of the simplest. He was to take down a couple of sample bags and bring me back a little of anything he could see – I didn't expect nodules, but the cinder and shell-laden bottom material would be fascinating to me. I had expected him to take someone else down with him in the accepted buddy system, but he was scathing about it and said he preferred to dive alone.

'When you want a buddy most is on the surface,' he told me, overturning most of my accepted belief at a stroke. 'You get disorientated pretty fast down there, even in clear water like this, and half the time you're not in sight of one another.'

So we'd put the smaller dinghy into the water and it was from there that Bill would launch himself into the sea. 'It won't take long,' he'd promised Geordie, and I felt sure that we could be away in an hour or so.

As he prepared to climb down into the dinghy he paused, sniffing the air, and commented, 'Someone hasn't washed their socks lately.'

That was the thing that was niggling at my mind, and recognition brought a stronger sense of unease. There was a heavy, sulphurous smell in the air. Geordie and I looked at each other and he said, 'Sulphur, Mike?'

'Well, this is a known volcanic region,' I said. 'I suppose it's always a bit niffy here.'

Ian spoke, pointing out to the horizon. 'You can almost see it in the air, skipper.' The sky low down was brightening into the dawn but there was a strange yellow tinge to it.

Bill was in the dinghy now, with Jim and Rex Larkin to row it a few yards off from *Esmerelda*. He sat on the thwart, gave the traditional thumbs-up sign as he made a final adjustment to his mask, and toppled backwards into the sea. For a few moments we could see his body sinking away from the dinghy. He had just disappeared when Geordie said hoarsely, 'Bill – stop him! Don't let him dive!'

It was too late. Several heads turned to stare at Geordie, who had suddenly gone ashen and was wrestling with the wheel, and at the same moment there was a babble of talk from the men at the bows and railings.

'For God's sake, we're spinning!' Geordie said, and I saw then what he meant.

Esmerelda was boxing the compass! Her bows swept slowly over the horizon as she twirled in a complete circle, not very fast, but with a suggestion of power in the colossal eddy that had her in its grip. And at the same time I saw a rising column of mist, darkening even as it rose, that appeared as if by magic out of the sea half a mile or so away from us. There were shouts of alarm from people, and I clung to a staunchion to steady myself as we spun about.

Almost as soon as it happened it had ceased, and *Esmerelda* was rocking tipsily, but steadying up again with the billowing steamy cloud ahead to starboard. I saw other little eddies appear and vanish on the sea's disturbed surface, and the smell of sulphur was suddenly pungent: I heard Geordie shouting but for the moment a ringing in my ears made it sound very faint and distant, and I shook my head to clear it.

'Ian! This is bloody dicey, but we've got to get an anchor down! We'll lose the dinghy and Bill both if we start shifting.'

I heard the anchor cable rattle out of the hawse pipe almost as he spoke, tethering *Esmerelda* to the shallow bottom. I could guess how reluctant Geordie would be to sacrifice his precious mobility at that moment, but it was of course essential to keep station. The dinghy rocked heavily and I saw a line being thrown to her, presumably to keep her in contact with us.

Campbell's body lurched into mine as we swung round the anchor cable, and Geordie called, 'Not enough – she'll swing into the dinghy! We'll have to get Bill up fast!' But he had gone down free-style, without a line, and there didn't seem to be any way to do it. I saw that some of the crew were swinging out the motor launch, and guessed that Geordie would use it to take up the dinghy crew into a more seaworthy craft, leaving the smaller boat in tow.

'How long will he stay down?' I asked, staring over the side. The whole surface of the water was rippling and beginning to chop.

'Not long at all,' Geordie said tensely. 'The moment he breaks surface we'll have him up out of there. With any luck there'll be enough disturbance down below to get him up

uickly. Thank God it's shallow – at least he won't have a
:compression problem.'

'What's happening?' Campbell's voice sounded as if he'd
:ked that question several times already.

I said, 'Wait a moment – I'll explain later.' I was staring at
.e column rising from the sea as if mesmerized. There was
ardly any noise but the column blackened steadily, with a
hite nimbus around it, almost like the smoke of an oily fire,
.d I knew without a doubt that if there was no underwater
isturbance to bring Bill to the surface, there was another
henomenon that would work as well – the sea would be rising
. temperature, not to boiling point, at least not here, but
:veral degrees above its normal state. I knew that I was
)oking at the beginning of an underwater volcanic eruption,
.d my heart was thudding as if my chest would burst
pen.

Geordie guessed it too, and a ripple of awareness ran
.rough the crew. Campbell's mouth hung open and his hand
:ll away from my arm. Eyes were scanning the water near us,
)oking anxiously for our diver's reappearance, and glances
ver our shoulders kept us in touch with the increasing
ctivity away on the horizon. *Esmerelda* was still rocking a
ttle roughly but there was no feeling of instability about her.
omething broke surface not far from the dinghy.

'There he is!' called Danny, pointing.

We saw the two men still in the dinghy pulling Bill in over
he thwarts, the motor launch waiting off to take her in tow
·ack to the ship, when there was a totally unexpected inter-
.uption.

Taffy Morgan shouted, 'Ship on the starboard beam!'

I spun round incredulously and pounded across the deck,
olliding with someone on the way. Out of the smoke and
team that drifted across the sea ahead of us, half shielding
.er until the last possible moment, the bulk of *Sirena* came
·earing down upon us.

Her yards were bare and she was pounding towards us full
ilt under power. I could see figures on deck, many of them,
.nd the lift of her bow wave as she approached.

265

'Goddam it! We're trussed up here for the slaughter,' Campbell said in vicious unbelief.

Geordie ran up the deck. 'Slip that flaming cable!' he bawled.

But there wasn't enough time. *Sirena* was on us, slewing and with her speed falling off at the last possible moment lay alongside us with a minimum of seamanship, relying totally on surprise to aid her terrible attack. She didn't quite make the turn and her bowsprit stabbed at us like a monstrous rapier. There was an almighty crash and *Esmerelda* shuddered violently and moved bodily sideways in the water.

I was thrown against Geordie and we both went down in a tangle of arms and legs. I scrambled to my feet, all the breath knocked out of my body, and saw hazily that *Esmerelda's* yardarm was locked in *Sirena's* shrouds.

Ramirez had rammed us. The chaos was indescribable.

There was a roar of angry voices and a flood of men poured across the deck from *Sirena*, and I saw the flash of knives in the enveloping glow of that fantastic yellow light.

Chapter Eight

1

It was a short fight and a bitter one.

In the fraction of a second before they were on to us I saw Campbell's incredulous face, his mouth open in surprise. Then Geordie roared, 'Stand together, lads!' and I was grappling with a hefty brute who wielded a long and wickedly gleaming knife.

If he had come at me from underneath I might have been disembowelled, but he used the basically unsound overarm stab. I saw the knife coming down, grasped his wrist and pulled. This unexpected assistance sent him off balance. I did a neat sidestep, more suited to the dancefloor than the battlefield, twisted his arm and pushed. He reeled into the scuppers and his knife clattered on the deck.

I looked around and all was confusion. I scarcely had time to distinguish friend from enemy before I was attacked again. I felt a cold burn sear along my ribs as the knife struck, and in desperation I hit out slantwise with the edge of my hand at the blurred figure before me. There was a choked gurgle and the blur vanished – I hoped I'd smashed his larynx.

I staggered up, clutching at a stay for support, and as I wavered about the deck I saw Campbell go down under a vicious smashing blow from a belaying pin – and then I saw the unmistakable bulk of Jim Hadley.

He had got hold of Clare and was twisting her arm behind her back and she was screaming in pain. I couldn't hear her because of the tumult around me but I saw her wide-open mouth and the glaze of terror in her eyes.

I was about to plunge across the deck when there was a staccato rattle of shots and everything seemed to pause momentarily. I took the opportunity to yell, 'Stop fighting! For God's sake, stop fighting!'

The roar began again only to be halted by another fusillade of shots. A voice called, 'Very wise, Mr Trevelyan.' Then came a rapid spate of Spanish, which I was too dazed to follow.

I called out, 'Hold it, lads! They have Clare!'

We had been defeated in less than three minutes.

Everything stopped as suddenly as it had begun. I felt the burning ache along my rib-case as only the most minor of distractions as I looked hastily around the deck. There seemed to be Spaniards everywhere, far more of them than of us, and three men lay on the deck without moving.

Ramirez stepped delicately across the deck with two armed men at his back. I had time to wonder where he'd got a fresh load of weapons from, and then he faced me. 'We meet under different circumstances, Mr Trevelyan,' he observed with a mocking smile.

I ignored him. 'Everyone all right?'

There was a low murmur and then Taffy looked up from one of the prone figures, white-faced under his tan. 'They've killed Danny,' he said in a level tone.

Over a rising growl I yelled, 'Cut it out – look at Hadley!'

There was a dead silence. Hadley had forced Clare to her knees; he had her right arm up behind her back and in his other hand he held a heavy pistol trained on the nape of her neck. Ramirez stood in front of me, nodding appreciatively.

'You have sense, Mr Trevelyan. You've lost and you know it.'

'Tell him to let her go.'

'In a moment.' He passed along the deck and came to Geordie, who stared at him impassively. 'Ah, the brave Mr Wilkins. I told you that you would regret what you did, one day.' He lifted his hand and struck Geordie across the face with a back-handed blow. A ring cut deep and blood started to drip from Geordie's mouth. He spat on the deck in silence.

Campbell moaned and tried to lift himself from the deck and Ramirez strolled over to look down at him with an odd expression on his face. It was almost as if he contemplated the defeat of an old adversary with less than satisfaction. 'Come on, old one. Get up,' he said brusquely.

Campbell got halfway up, then collapsed again.

Ramirez made an impatient noise. He pointed to Taffy, still crouched over Danny's body. 'You – carry the old man into the saloon.'

Taffy and Ian between them got Campbell up. There seemed to be something wrong with his side, as if his leg was paralysed. As he lifted his head I saw an ugly blotch of blood on his left temple, and rage rose bitter in my throat at the sight.

Ramirez gestured to Geordie with his pistol. 'You too – into the saloon. And Mr Trevelyan, you too, please. We mustn't forget you.'

A rifle muzzle poked me in the back and I walked helplessly towards the companionway. I turned my head and saw Hadley dragging Clare to her feet and pushing her forward. I wondered where Paula was.

Before we were thrust into the saloon we were brusquely searched. The man wasn't too gentle and I gasped with pain as the heel of his hand slammed against the wound in my side. He just grinned, but it was a mindless rather than a sadistic expression, I thought in that moment that there seemed to be a minimum of brain-power around – these men were mostly obedient puppets, no more than that. It might be useful, I thought, and wondered at myself.

In the saloon I helped Taffy to lay Campbell on a settee and said in a low voice, 'You're sure Danny was killed?'

'I'm sure,' Taffy said tightly. 'He was stabbed in the chest. God, the blood!'

I looked at Campbell. His eyes were open but unfocussed. I said, forcing my voice to a normal conversational pitch, 'The old boy's had a nasty knock. You'll find some water in the liquor cabinet, Ian.'

I looked around for Clare and found her coming to my side. Hadley had let her go and she was very pale but fully composed. Our hands found each others for an instance and then she was looking at the blood on her fingertips. 'Mike you're hurt!'

'That can wait. It's nothing. You'd better see to your father first.'

She went to him and began to sponge his head with a cloth dipped in the jug of water Ian held for her, her face clouded with fear and worry.

Paula was thrust into the saloon. She stumbled and nearly fell as her guard gave her a brutal shove before he took up position near the door, his rifle pointing at us. I took her arm to steady her. 'Paula – are you all right?'

'I guess so,' she gasped. 'I've still got a whole skin.' She looked round and then said to me in a lower voice, 'I saw them putting two of our men in the cable hold, Mike – and they've hauled in the motor launch too.'

'Christ!' said Geordie. He wiped the back of his hand across his mouth and looked without surprise at the blood. He did a quick calculation on his fingers and then said, 'The two on board must have been Shorty and Davie Blake – the rest of us are here or –'

Paula took him up. 'Nick Dugan and young Martin were in the launch. I saw them both. I don't know about the other.'

They were the only two who had been in the launch, and it wasn't surprising that Ramirez had spotted them and fetched them back. But there were still Jim and Rex Larkin in the dinghy, and Bill Hunter. I had a faint surge of hope – had Ramirez missed them? And if so, could they stay hidden in that misty, turbulent sea? Geordie and I exchanged a glance and then looked quickly away.

I crossed over to Taffy, who was helping Clare, and made to assist him. 'Looks as though this is an officer's party, Taffy. You'd better stay pretty quiet unless you want to join the rest of the boys – they're in the cable hold.'

He nodded. 'I'll be all right,' he said, and rubbed the back of his neck in a curious gesture as if he had been hurt there.

One of the men with rifles said in Spanish, 'No speaking! Be silent, all of you.' I pretended not to understand and started to speak, but this time the gesture that went with the repeated

270

struction was clear, and I subsided. I had time to assess the
situation now.

Neither Ramirez nor Hadley had actually entered the
saloon with us – there were only the two armed guards. We
were seven, and in the cable hold there were possibly four men.
Danny lay dead on the deck – I could barely make myself
think about that – and three were, with any luck, still at large.

I decided to try a gamble.

'It will be all right to let us speak,' I said in the best Spanish I
could muster. 'Mr Ramirez will permit it.'

They glanced at one another, and one of them shrugged. I
had guessed correctly – they were so accustomed to being
given orders that they would accept this one even from me,
spoken as it had been with an air of authority. I turned to
Geordie and told him what I had said in Spanish, with a wary
eye to the rifles, but to my relief the guards gave no further
sign of stopping us.

Geordie said, 'What happens now?'

'That's not up to us. Ramirez has the next move, and I don't
like to think what that will be. We can't do much while they're
around.' I jerked my head very slightly in the direction of the
guards.

'Seven here, four below,' Geordie murmured. He had done
the same arithmetic that I had. 'And three – somewhere.'

I looked at Campbell who seemed to be recovering.
'They're a murderous lot of bastards, aren't they?'

'I wish I'd given Jim his head when he wanted to blow a hole
in *Sirena*,' said Geordie viciously.

'Wishful thinking won't help us now. What bothers me
most is that I think that's what they may be going to do to us.'

He shook his head irritably and we all lapsed into silence.
Clare came over to me, unbuttoned my shirt, and proceeded
to patch up what luckily proved to be no more than a skin
graze, though it hurt me more than the slight wound war-
ranted. I thanked God that we kept small first aid kits all over
the ship. As she worked I felt her hands shaking just a little,
and I grasped them to try and reassure her, but it was a
wretched attempt.

271

There was a lot of movement on deck and a great deal of shouting. Ian looked up at the deckhead speculatively. 'I'm thinking they're having trouble, skipper. There's a hell of a tangle at the masthead.'

That was all to the good. The longer they took to separate the two ships the more time we would have to think of a way out of this mess. I looked at the guards and felt very depressed. They looked as though they'd murder their grandmothers for two pesetas, and they'd certainly have no qualms about shooting us if we tried anything.

It was nearly an hour before anything happened. We used the time to some little advantage; all of us achieved better control over ourselves and Clare brought her father to a degree of coherence. He had a pretty bad concussion – his speech was affected, although his thinking seemed clear enough.

'Goddam sonsa-biches,' he said indistinctly. 'Why d'you quit, Mike?'

'Hadley had Clare,' I said briefly.

'Haaaah,' he sighed, and sagged back on the settee. 'shoulda lef' her behind,' he muttered. 'Never lissen to woman, Mike.' He closed his eyes and turned his head away and Clare and I exchanged worried looks across his head.

'It's my fault,' Geordie burst out. 'I should have kept the lads up to scratch. We should have kept watch. We shouldn't have been surprised like that.'

'Shut up, Geordie,' I said. 'That won't get us anywhere. There's no blame – not on us. We weren't looking for trouble.'

'Aye,' said Ian softly. 'Yon Ramirez has a lot to answer for.'

Presently there was a rattle at the door and one of the guards opened it. Out of the corner of my eye I saw Taffy slide into a corner, half-hidden behind the settee, and then Ramirez came in, as elegant as ever. 'I trust you are comfortable,' he said solicitously.

'Let's not have any blarney,' I said bluntly. 'What's the next move, Ramirez?'

He smiled, and seemed to be enjoying a huge joke.

'Why, I have to introduce you to someone,' he said.

He leaned out of the door and beckoned to someone in the passage. He turned back to me and said, 'I told you once that you shouldn't make libellous statements that you couldn't substantiate.'

The man who came into the saloon was about my size, dark and heavily bearded. He carried my laboratory notebook in one hand.

Ramirez said, 'An old friend for you. I think you all know Mr Mark Trevelyan.'

2

As I looked into Mark's eyes I think my heart seemed to miss three full beats and I felt the hairs bristle on the nape of my neck. It isn't often that one is confronted by a dead man – especially a dead brother.

There was a sound as of a long-pent breath being released throughout the saloon and then the silence was total. Ian was the first to stir. 'That's the mannie I found. . . .'

His voice tailed off as Mark switched his eyes to him. 'Ah, Ian Lewis. So it was you who clobbered me, was it?' he said pleasantly, and then his voice hardened. 'You'd have done better to stay in your Highland hovel, you Scots peasant.'

The whole pattern of events of the last few months had suddenly been shuffled like the pieces in a kaleidoscope, to present an entirely new picture. It was no wonder that Ian hadn't recognised the bearded man he found on our raid on *Sirena*; he had last seen Mark as a boy. I might have recognised him, but I hadn't taken the trouble to look. We weren't looking for a dead man that night in Nuku'alofa.

I looked round at the others. Their expressions were a mixture of amazement and slowly dawning comprehension. Clare gave Mark one long, measured look, then made a small contemptuous sound and turned back to her father. Campbell took her by the wrist protectively, never taking his eyes off Mark. He said nothing.

Ian was furious and showed it, while Geordie merely stared speculatively at Mark under lowered brows. Paula had made a sudden move as if to go to him, but she shrank back and hid in the shadows at Geordie's back. Taffy didn't show himself at all.

Of them all, Mark was watching me. 'Hello, Mike,' he said soberly.

I said, 'Mark, for God's sake – I—'

He was urbane where I was dumbfounded. He lifted the notebook and some papers in his hand. 'I've been rooting about in your laboratory. So kind of you to have done the preliminary survey for me. I couldn't have done it better myself.'

He dropped the papers on the table.

Ian looked at him with black anger in his eyes. 'I wish that I'd hit you a bit harder,' he said harshly.

Mark smiled at him but said nothing. He picked up my notebook again and flicked the pages with one hand. 'We seem to have struck it rich, Mike. There may be billions in all this, don't you agree? A pity you wasted your time but never mind, you saved me a bit of work.'

I spoke through a dry throat. 'You're a bastard, Mark.'

'Oh, come on, Mike. Aren't you maligning mother?'

He looked around. 'And who else have we? Yes, Wilkins, isn't it? What's it like on Tyneside these days, Geordie?'

Geordie showed his disgust. 'A bit cleaner than this saloon.'

'We will have our little jokes,' said Mark lightly. 'And my dear old boss, Mr Campbell, the fallen warrior – and Clare. I'm sorry you had to be here, Clare.'

She refused to look at him and said nothing. It irked Mark and he shrugged petulantly, turned away and peered behind Geordie. 'And who's the young lady sitting in the shadow?' he asked. 'I didn't know you were such a one for the ladies, Mike.'

He moved round the table and stopped suddenly. His face

went very pale. 'Paula!' he whispered. He turned his head quickly to Ramirez. 'You didn't tell me she was aboard.'

Ramirez shrugged. 'Just another woman,' he said casually. For an instant they glared at one another and I had an insight into their relationship.

Paula stood up. 'Mark – oh Mark! I thought you were dead. Why didn't you come to me, Mark? Why didn't you trust me?'

Ramirez laughed softly.

Mark actually looked troubled. 'I'm truly sorry,' he said. 'Sorry you had to be on this ship.' He made a curious gesture as though wiping her away, and a prickle ran up my spine. In that one sudden movement he had rejected us all – wiped us out of his world.

Paula took a step forward. 'But Mark, I. . . .'

Ramirez snapped out a curt phrase in Spanish and one of the guards lifted his rifle. The meaning was unmistakable.

Paula stopped dead and looked at Mark with the comprehension of horror. His eyes flickered and he looked away from her and she slowly fell back into a chair and buried her face in her hands. I heard the racking sobs that shook her, and saw Clare move to put her arms round her shoulders.

I had to force myself to speak calmly. 'We all thought you were dead. Why did you do it?'

'I had to die,' he said. He perked up – the change of subject took his mind off Paula. 'The police were after me and getting a little too close, so I conveniently killed myself.'

I suddenly knew another black truth. 'You did kill Sven Norgaard, didn't you.'

He turned on me. 'What else could I do?' he said defensively. 'The bloody fool wanted to *publish*. Him and his bloody scientific integrity – he wanted to give it all away, billions of dollars that belonged to me – to *me*, do you hear that? I made the discovery, didn't I?' His voice tailed off, and then he added softly, 'I *had* to kill him.'

The silence was murderous and we all stared at the ego-maniacal horror that was my brother. He straightened up and said, 'And then I killed myself. The police would never look for a dead murderer. Wasn't that pretty clever of me, Mike?'

'It was stupid,' I said flatly. 'But then you always were a stupid man.'

His hand crashed on the table and we all jerked at the sudden violence. Only Ramirez watched him unmoved and dispassionate. 'It wasn't stupid!' he yelled. 'It was a damn good idea! But I'm surrounded by bungling idiots.'

'Like Kane and Hadley,' I said.

'That's right, them,' he agreed, suddenly calm again. 'Those damn fools gave me appendicitis, of all things. I could have killed that madman, Hadley – there was no need to invent extra details.'

'I'm sure you could,' I said. 'But it was you who bungled it. You should have told them precisely what to say.'

He betrayed for the first time his lack of authority. 'It had nothing to do with me,' he said sullenly. 'Ernesto fixed it.'

I shot a sidelong glance at Ramirez. 'So he's a bungler too?'

Ramirez smiled sardonically and Mark said nothing. I went on, 'You bungled again when Hadley let your papers and the nodules go. You should have taken them with you – that was bad planning.'

'They got them back though.'

'Not quite, Mark. I had a nodule still – and I had your diary.'

He reacted to that with white-faced fury, then subsided and nodded thoughtfully. 'You were lucky. You read it?'

'Oh yes,' I said casually. 'A simple code, really.' And watched him swallow his ire yet again as item by item I did my best to undermine his self-confidence. Then he suddenly laughed.

'That lunatic, Hadley. But you all thought I was dead anyway. And poor old Ernesto here was getting all the blame. That was really funny.'

Ramirez, who had been leaning negligently against the bulkhead, suddenly straightened, his face cold. 'This is a pointless conversation,' he said shortly.

Mark said, 'Let me have my fun, old boy. It isn't often a corpse can hold an inquest on himself. I'm getting a kick out of it.'

Ramirez looked at him contemptuously. 'All right. It won't make any difference,' he said dismissively. I knew that he was only waiting for word that his crew had separated the two ships before he did what he was going to do – and I had a good idea what that was.

I rubbed my ear – there seemed to be something getting in the way of my hearing, and Ramirez's voice had seemed to vibrate in a curious way. The ship creaked and rocked uneasily, and I wondered what was really happening outside. But it was also important to me to hear what my brother had to say, and I pushed the thoughts that were bothering me to the background.

'My inquest,' Mark said again. 'Let's develop this interesting theme.'

'Yes, let's do that,' said Campbell suddenly.

I turned to find him sitting up on the settee, waving away Clare and Ian. 'Let's do that,' he repeated, and I noticed that his voice was stronger and his speech clearer. 'Let's consider the burning of a hospital and the murder of a doctor and fourteen of his patients.'

Mark flinched. 'I didn't do that. It was Hadley again.'

'Hadley again,' I said caustically. 'You sound as pure as Hadley's pal Kane.'

'You condoned it,' said Campbell relentlessly.

'It was *nothing* to do with me. I didn't even know about it until afterwards. That man's beyond controlling.'

Ramirez had picked up my injudicious reference to Kane and was looking at me enquiringly. He was very acute.

'You have spoken to Kane again, Mr Trevelyan? He was supposed to come to me in Nuku'alofa, but I didn't see him there.'

I tried to make the best of my slip. 'Yes, we've spoken to him. He's told us a great deal too – enough to condemn the lot of you, so think carefully about what you're planning, Ramirez.'

'Might one ask where he is?'

'Where you won't find him, and all ready to sing like a bird.'

He looked thoughtful and did not speak again for a moment, and Campbell, sensing a faint opening, was quick to take advantage.

'What were you planning to do with us? It won't work now you know.'

'You speak stupidly,' Ramirez said. Mark watched us fascinated, all his boasting silenced. He'd shocked us but he'd failed to impress us, and now things were taking a turn that he didn't like. It was slowly becoming obvious to me that in spite of Mark's almost insane posturing, it was Ramirez who was the more powerful of the two, and possibly the more dangerous.

Campbell said, 'You've decided that you can't leave us alive, haven't you? That would be too much to expect. You've already killed some seventeen people – another dozen or so won't make any difference. But you won't get away with it. We have covered our tracks, Ramirez, and for another thing your own crew will talk about all this, sooner or later.'

It was a bold try and I had never admired Campbell more.

Ramirez threw back his head and laughed. 'My crew – those morons?' He gestured to the stolid guards. 'Those oafs? They do what I tell them and nothing else. They have no mind of their own – I am the only brain they have. And who would believe them if they talked? They have never understood what it is all about, not one of them. Besides, that can be taken care of too.'

'A series of unfortunate accidents?' asked Campbell sardonically.

'Regrettable, isn't it?'

I listened to this ghastly conversation with a feeling of unreality. Ramirez was prepared to kill us without compunction. What was more, he was equally prepared to kill his own crew as well. I could just imagine how it would be arranged. The men would be well paid, split up and dispersed and then there would be, as Campbell foresaw, a series of accidents. A man found dead in a harbour here, a fatal car smash there, until the whole crew was disposed of.

'All right,' Campbell was saying. 'You still won't get away with it. Quite apart from Kane's evidence, you don't suppose

I haven't made my own arrangements, do you? My agents have sealed letters which will be handed to the police if I don't turn up somewhere soon. There's going to be one hell of an investigation if I go missing.'

'You're an old fool,' said Ramirez brutally, the gloves off at last. 'The barometer has dropped three points in the last hour, there's a storm coming up and that thing out there is going crazy. You're going to be lost at sea – the lot of you. We will not be anywhere near here. There will be no proof – no proof of anything.'

Campbell shuddered and Clare pulled a little closer to him. Watching Ramirez, I was fascinated by a movement outside the port light behind his head. Nobody else had seemed to see it, too appalled and horror-stricken by the finality in Ramirez's voice. I saw Taffy, crouched at the end of the settee, fumble again with that curious gesture at the back of his neck, but his eyes never left Ramirez.

Campbell said slowly, 'Ramirez, you're a bloody-minded butcher.'

Ramirez spread his hands. 'I don't like killing for killings' sake. I'm no Jim Hadley – he was stupid back on Tanakabu and I abhore that, putting pleasure before business. I kill only from necessity. But when I do, whether it's seventeen or seventy lives doesn't make much difference. Lives are cheap, my friend, when there are large stakes. I consider my measures necessary.' He was as cold as a snake.

I switched my gaze back to the port and caught my breath. There was a face out there. An eye winked.

Bill Hunter was back on board.

He was a hidden ace that Ramirez must not become aware of. I cautiously lifted my hand to my mouth, coughed, and then made a slow downward movement, being careful not to jerk. I didn't want to catch anyone's attention. The eye winked again and the face disappeared.

Campbell was still speaking, desperately searching for arguments to persuade Ramirez not to go ahead with whatever plans he had for us. Again there was that vibrancy in my ears, a curious beat in Campbell's voice as though there were

279

some sort of aural interference, some note so low as to be inaudible. Not far away there was a sound as though an engine were letting off steam. *Esmerelda* shuddered and the noises on deck increased suddenly.

Ramirez interrupted Campbell, turned and to my horror strode over to look out of a porthole. I tensed but then he turned back and spoke again, and I realised he'd not seen anything untoward.

'Whatever is going on out there will serve its purpose,' he said coolly. 'As soon as these idiots of mine have parted the two ships we go our separate ways. You won't have far to go – a mile or so straight down. We will tow you into deep water – or point your nose into that thing out there.' He turned on Geordie. 'We have borrowed an idea from you, Captain. We will set an explosive charge against your hull, and that storm out there will do the rest.'

Geordie ground his teeth together but said nothing.

Somebody ran across the deck over our heads and a voice called out. Ramirez cocked his head and glanced upwards. 'It sounds as though they are about ready.'

I heard a clatter of heavy boots on the companion steps and there was a thump on the door. At a gesture from Ramirez one of the guards opened it and Hadley came in. He looked at us with an oafish grin that didn't reach his pale, cold eyes and bent to whisper to Ramirez, who immediately turned to look out of the porthole again. I thanked God that Bill had kept out of sight. Or had he?

Ramirez turned back. 'Which would you choose? Deep water or Falcon Island? There seems to be increased activity over there.' He smiled and said to Mark, 'This is lucky, you know. Where else should a survey ship be wrecked but in investigating Falcon Island a little too closely at the wrong time? Keep our friends happy for a little while.'

He turned on his heel and left the saloon, followed by Hadley.

Geordie watched them go and then transferred his attention to Mark. 'You're a poor specimen of a man,' he said with contempt. 'What makes you think I'm going to sit back and let ou wreck my ship and murder my crew? If I'm going to be illed I might as well take you with me.' He began to rise from is chair. With Ramirez's departure a curious change had ome into the atmosphere. It was as if we could all recognise hat where Ramirez had real authority and total amorality, Mark had only his ego and his self-seeking veneer of toughness over a very insecure personality.

As Geordie started to rise Mark snapped out a command in panish and the guards' rifles lifted to the ready. 'Be careful,' Mark said. 'They are trained killers.'

'So am I,' said Geordie with menace. He continued to rise lowly and Ian started to get up as well.

Mark spoke again in Spanish and one of the guards casually red his rifle, apparently without aim. The noise was appalling and we flinched back as splinters flew from the bullet as it truck the cabin sole just by Geordie's foot. He hesitated and spoke sharply. 'Cut it, Geordie – you haven't a chance. You an't move faster than a bullet.'

Geordie glared at me under his lowered brows but I made a quick slashing gesture with my hand and, taking a chance, winked at him. His brow smoothed and he sat down again, as lid Ian. Both were watchful, and I knew that I had succeeded n alerting them.

There was a sustained racket from overhead. Geordie said, They're making a muck-up of it out there, aren't they?'

'Mind if I smoke, Clare?'

I put my hand into a pocket and stopped as a rifle barrel urned and the muzzle pointed unwaveringly at me. 'For God's sake, Mark, can't I even have a cigarette?'

He looked amused. 'Smoking's bad for you, Mike. Go ahead – but you'd better have nothing but cigarettes in your hand when you pull it out.'

Slowly I withdrew my hand as he spoke to the guards again. The rifle barrel drooped a little and I opened the packet and but a cigarette in my mouth. And at that moment I saw Bill's ace at the port once more. The sound of the rifle had brought him back, as I'd hoped it would.

The saloon door opened and there was a brief exchange

between one of our guards and a man outside, and then closed again. Clearly Ramirez too had sent to ask about th shooting. I put my hand to my pocket again and said to th man with the rifle, '*Fósforos*?' He made no sign and I ma aged to get the matches out without being threatened.

I lit the cigarette and said, 'Look, Mark. You know ever body cooped up in this saloon. Some have been your friends others have been more than friends – a lot more. In God name, what kind of a man are you?' I found it hard to speak him without my voice betraying me.

'What can I do?' he asked petulantly. 'Do you think I wa to see you all killed? It's out of my hands – Ramirez is i control here.'

Clare's voice was cutting. 'He washes his hands – the ne Pontius Pilate.'

'Damn it, Clare, you don't think I want to see you at th bottom of the sea? I can't do anything, I tell you.'

Campbell said, 'It's no use, Mike. He wouldn't do anythin to save us even if he could. His neck's at stake, you know.'

This was my chance. To speak to Campbell I had to ha turn away from Mark and the guards in a natural fashio 'He'll join us anyway,' I said. 'Ramirez has got what he want now. He doesn't need Mark any more – he only needs to tak my notes with him – and I'm damn sure he'll want to rub ou *any* witness to all this – including Mark.'

I was printing on the back of the cigarette packet with th stub of pencil I had taken from my pocket with the matches The words, as large as I could make them, were 'CABL HOLD'. I drooped my eyelid at Campbell and he caught o fast. He shook his fist at Mark to divert attention and starte acting up a little. 'You damned murderer!' he shouted.

'Shut up,' said Mark venomously. 'Just shut up, dam you.'

I held up the cigarette packet towards Campbell and said 'Take it easy. Have one?'

'No, no,' he brushed my offer aside, but the job was done and Bill had had a clear vision of my message over Campbell' shoulder. I hoped to God that he had good eyesight. Clar aw the message too and her eyes widened. She bent her head ver the still prostrate Paula to hide her expression. I saw er whisper in the other girl's ear, apparently still soothing er.

I said to Mark, still playing for time, 'Why the hell should e shut up? We've got nothing to lose by telling you what we hink of you. I'm sickened at the thought of you being any kin ɔ me.'

Mark's jaw tightened and he said nothing. I had to goad im into speaking. I risked a glance at the port, and saw that he face had gone, to be replaced with a hand. The middle nger and thumb were joined in a circle. Bill had got my nessage.

Whatever happened now I had to give him time to act on it. Jow he knew where the rest of us were and might be able to lo something about it. I wondered if he was alone or if Jim nd Rex were still with him. It was a slim chance but it was all ve had. I reckoned that the only thing we could do to help was ɔ get at Mark in some way – and in his highly nervous state hat might prove deadly dangerous.

I said, 'What put you on to us? The sea's a big place, Mark. 3ut of course you always knew where that high-cobalt nodule ormation was, didn't you?'

'I only knew approximately. I wasn't the only one doing ɪssays on that damned IGY ship, and I couldn't get at all the nformation I wanted.' His sullen tone implied that such nformation should have been his by rights, which was typical ɔf him, but I was on the right track in getting him to talk about ɪis own cleverness. Few genuine egotists can resist such an ɪppeal.

'Who had the bright idea that found us here, then? We ɔuld have been anywhere. We could have been a hundred niles from here. You couldn't know where we were.'

He laughed. 'Couldn't I? Couldn't we? I know you like a ɔook, Mike. I knew that you'd find that deposit given time to ɪurvey properly – so I gave you that time. And I knew that ɔnce you'd found it you couldn't resist investigating the ɔource. I knew you'd *have* to come to Fonua Fo'ou, to Falcon.

Ramirez couldn't see it, of course. He can be a stupid man at times. But I convinced him that I knew my own brother. We've been hanging round here for two bloody weeks waiting for you to turn up.'

I said, 'How did you get tangled with Ramirez?' We already knew the answer to that one but it kept him talking.

'Campbell there couldn't finance me and Suarez-Navarro could. It was as simple as that. Who else should I go to but them? They'd just shown that they weren't too scrupulous by what they'd done to his mines, so they were just what I wanted.'

'And then they led you into murder. You had to kill Norgaard.'

'That was an accident,' said Mark irritably. 'All Sven was doing was tying up loose ends. We were waiting for the hue and cry to die down, and then Suarez-Navarro were going to provide us with a proper survey ship to find this stuff.' He thumped the papers and notebook. 'Meantime that damned fool decided that he wanted to publish. You see, he didn't know much about Suarez-Navarro and that's the way I wanted it. We had an argument – he was a pretty excitable chap – at first in words, and then it came to blows. The next thing I knew was that he'd cracked his head open on the coral. But I didn't mean to kill him, Mike. I swear it. All I ever wanted to do was to shut him up.'

'All you ever want to do is to shut people up,' I said flatly. 'How do you go about shutting up a good scientist, Mark? It seems to me that the *only* way is to kill him.'

I was cold inside, chilled by his amoral egocentricity. Everything he had done was justified in his own eyes, and everything that had gone wrong was the fault of other people.

Mark waved me aside. 'Hadley knew, of course. He was my liaison with Ramirez. They helped me to cover it up, but somehow the police got onto it.'

'My God, you think *I'm* naive,' I said. 'Look, Mark, I wouldn't be surprised if Ramirez didn't tip off the police himself. It wouldn't matter to him – he was in the clear. He arranged for your "death" and that was that. But he had you

284

eatly wrapped in a package from then on, and you couldn't
o a thing without his say so.'

'It wasn't like that,' Mark muttered.

'Wasn't it? Even when the first plan went wrong and
Hadley was implicated in your so-called murder Ramirez
rasn't worried. That's why he laughed his damn head off
rhen I accused him. He knew that all he ever had to do to
lear himself and Hadley was to produce you, and you can be
ure he'd do it in such a way that would earn him the
ongratulations of the law.'

'What do you mean by that?'

'He'd produce you dead – or dying, Mark – just so you
ouldn't talk. And the police would pat him on the back for
apturing Mark Trevelyan, the murderer of Sven Norgaard,
nd maybe the mastermind behind the killing of Schouten. By
God, I was right when I called you stupid. You'd really got in
ver your head, hadn't you?'

He was angry and baffled, and I could see that my attack
ad hit home; doubt was in his every action.

Campbell said, 'It doesn't make any difference now. Mark,
ou're for the deep six along with the rest of us. Ramirez will
ee to that.'

Geordie laughed without humour. 'Do you think you can
rust Ramirez?'

Mark thought deeply and then shook his head. 'Maybe
ou're right,' he admitted, and I don't think he had often used
hose words in his lifetime. 'But it still makes no difference.
'ou want me to help you, but I can't. You'll never beat him –
nd if you did I'd still be wanted for murder. I'd rather stick to
Ramirez and take my chances. He still needs me.'

I wanted to try and tell him how wrong he was, but
omething else had finally penetrated to my consciousness.
'here was a whistling sound in the distance – high pressure
team was escaping somewhere. Mark looked out of the
orthole and what he saw over the water made him acutely
nhappy. 'Damn them, what are they doing on deck?' he
nuttered. 'This is no time to be hanging around here.'

His nervousness increased and he conferred with one of

the guards in a low voice. An argument seemed to devel⟨ as the guard answered back, but Mark overbore him. Wi⟨ a black glance and a reluctant shrug the guard opened t⟨ saloon door and went out.

I looked at Geordie with hopeful eyes and he nodde⟨ grimly. The odds were improving, but anything we trie⟨ would have to be done before the guard returned. Geordie⟨ hand crept towards the heavy glass ash tray on the table an⟨ then relaxed near it. He couldn't throw it faster than the guar⟨ could shoot – but he was ready if a chance came up. We we⟨ all sitting tensely.

There was a reddish reflection in Mark's face as he we⟨ again to look out of the porthole. Evidently things we⟨ stirring on Falcon. I said, 'What's going on out there, Mark⟨

His voice was strained. 'It looks as though Falcon is goi⟨ to bust loose.'

I felt suddenly colder. Mark and I were possibly the on⟨ two people on either ship qualified to have any understandi⟨ of what that might mean. I said, 'How close are we?'

'Maybe a quarter of a mile.' He straightened his back an⟨ added, 'It's happened a couple of times this week already. It⟨ never amounted to much. A great sight, but that's all.' But h⟨ was not convincing.

We were much too close to Fonua Fo'ou. To Ramirez an⟨ Hadley it might seem a good safe distance, especially if the⟨ had been watching pre-eruption patterns all week, but Mar⟨ and I knew better. We knew what volcanic eruptions cou⟨ do.

No wonder Mark was scared. So was I.

He looked at the remaining guard, hesitated, and the⟨ spoke to him. The guard shook his head vigorously, and a⟨ Mark started to leave he stepped in front of the door an⟨ raised his rifle.

Campbell said ironically, 'What's the matter, Mark⟨ Doesn't he trust you?'

The whistling and belching suddenly increased an⟨ *Esmerelda* lurched, her joints squealing a protest. We swu⟨ round, still locked with *Sirena*. There was a sudden blast of a⟨

286

rid sulphurous smell in the air. Mark's eyes darted from the
ard to me and our glances locked as tightly as the ships.

Mark said sharply, 'He doesn't want to be left here alone
ith you lot. I must wait for the other guard.' He crossed to
e porthole and looked out again and I felt bile rise in my
roat.

Geordie said, 'What the hell's the matter . . .?'

He didn't have time to finish. *Esmerelda* gave another great
rch and went over almost on her beam ends. I slithered
elplessly towards the side of the saloon and jarred my head
gainst the table as I fell. There were sounds of bedlam above
ecks.

The ship righted herself and we fell back in a jumble of
odies. I heard Campbell groan; it must have been hell for
m in his condition. Geordie was up first. He grasped the
htray and hurled it at the guard, and then leapt the length of
e saloon. The guard tried frantically to retrieve his rifle from
e deck where it had fallen. He had his fingers on the butt
hen Geordie kicked him with precision in the jaw and his
ce disappeared into a bloody ruin.

Ian had gone for Mark and any trace of his normal High-
nd gentleness had vanished. His face was a mask of rage.
eordie had grabbed the rifle and turned it on Mark. They
nverged on him, but Mark managed to evade them both
d scrambled towards the saloon door.

There was a curious flicker in the air and he slumped, his
and clapped to his right hip, and I saw blood welling between
s fingers.

I had raised myself to go after Geordie and a shouted word
f protest was already on my lips, but as Mark fell both Ian
nd Geordie came to an abrupt stop, the momentary blood-
ust dying from their faces. All eyes were on the gleaming,
loodied blade on the floor beside Mark.

'Who threw the knife?' I demanded.

Taffy came from the far end of the saloon. 'I did.' He saw
e look that sparked in my eyes and added hastily, 'I
ouldn't have killed him, Mike – even though he deserves it. I
now where to put a knife.'

'Well, you'd better come and get it,' I said.

He came forward to take it from the deck and carefu[l]
wiped it on his trouser leg. Clare was looking at him ashe[n]
faced, but Paula had already pushed forward to Mark's sid[e]

I said, 'I saw you searched like the rest of us, Taffy. H[ow]
did you hide the knife?'

'I had it dangling down the small of my back on a piece [of]
string. It's an old trick but they fell for it.'

For the moment the crisis was passed. I looked anxiou[sly]
out to sea. There was a haze of steam in the near distance a[nd]
beyond it the swell of sullen black clouds still rolled skywar[d]
The sea was choppy, with little eddies swirling here and ther[e]
and around the fringe of the steam there was a white roil [of]
froth. The smell was fitful and nasty. Closer in, I saw o[ur]
motor launch swinging astern with nobody on board h[er]
There was no sign of Bill, nor of anyone else on deck.

In the saloon Ian was helping Campbell back onto t[he]
settee with Clare to lend him a hand. Paula was bandagi[ng]
Mark and Geordie was searching the prostrate guard.

Taffy was missing.

'Geordie, where's Taffy?'

'Danny Williams was a special mate of his, you know.'

'Damn it, we need team work, not singleminded heroics[.]'

'Easy now,' Geordie said. 'Taffy never was a good tea[m]
man, but he's deadly on his own. He'll do a hell of a lot [of]
damage.'

'All right for him, but we need a plan of action urgentl[y.]
Taffy's loose and Bill is somewhere on deck, and with lu[ck]
Rex and Jim are with him. Maybe they've been able to [do]
something. And there's us – three men and a rifle.'

'Four men,' snapped Campbell, getting to his feet. 'And [if]
those sons of bitches haven't searched our cabins there'll [be]
guns in them.'

He met my eyes with a cold blue glare. He was right; he[']d
be no good in a brawl but give him one of his target pistols a[nd]
he could be deadly. Clare looked from her father to me an[d]
there was something of the same hard wildness in her face.

'I'm coming with you,' she said.

'Clare, you can't. . . .'

She cut in decisively. 'I'm a pretty good shot too, remember? Better than you, Mike. You're going to need all the help you can get.' She was determined to stay close to me and her father, and she was right. We would need her. And if it came to the worst, for her as for the rest of us, death by a bullet was preferable to drowning, clawing for air in a scuttled ship. My throat closed up with fear for her but I couldn't argue with her decision.

She moved to the liquor cabinet. Several bottles had broken in the roll, and she picked one up and stared at the jagged edges. She said slowly, 'I've seen them do this in movies.'

I thought that she could probably never use it, but it gave her some confidence. Geordie actually chuckled from the doorway. 'That's the stuff,' he said. 'Come on. We haven't much time. Me first, then Ian. Mike, you bring up the rear.'

Paula was bending over Mark. She met my eye and shook her head slightly. Mark lay back with his eyes closed, though whether he was unconscious or shamming it was impossible to guess. 'Okay, Paula, you stay here with him,' I said.

Geordie opened the door and slipped out.

One by one we followed him cautiously into the passageway. He hadn't gone more than a few feet when he stopped, stepped over something and then moved on. It was the body of our second guard. He must have been on his way back to the saloon when he met up with Taffy. His throat was cut in a gaping gash and the front of his shirt was sodden and dyed scarlet with blood. Clare swayed a little as she looked down and I took her firmly by the arm and pushed her past.

We moved ahead to Campbell's cabin and went inside to find that it hadn't been searched. Campbell took his valise from the bottom of the wardrobe and unrolled it, looking satisfied and stronger with every movement. There were three guns in it, his own and Clare's, and the one Geordie had taken from Ramirez back in Nuku'alofa. Father and daughter quickly loaded their weapons and Clare discarded the jagged bottle with obvious relief.

In our cabin Geordie and I found our two pistols untouched, and as we loaded them Campbell nodded with approval. 'Now we've a fighting chance,' he said.

We crept on without interruption to the after companionway. Geordie climbed up cautiously, then ducked back. There was a man standing above on the deck silhouetted against that yellow-glowing sky. He was holding a rifle. Geordie laid his own weapon aside and moved slowly up the steps. Then he motioned me to follow – Ian was the professional but, being much slighter than the Scot, I had a better chance of reaching the deck simultaneously with Geordie.

Geordie leapt swiftly up and took the guard from behind, one arm swinging round his neck and the other grabbing the rifle. I scrambled after him and clubbed the man with the butt of my gun. He collapsed in a heap.

We dropped him down the companionway like a sack of potatoes. With a grim smile Geordie said to me, 'You're learning, laddie.' We followed the body down again.

We now had three rifles and a small assortment of hand guns. The odds were getting better all the time. Geordie, making his disposition of his troops, said, 'Mike, I want us to take a look at Falcon. You come with me. Ian, cover our rear. Mr Campbell, you and Clare keep watch down here, and shoot anybody who tries to come down that passageway – as long as they aren't ours.'

We slipped quietly on deck and I got my first full look at Falcon. The yellow glow seemed to be diminishing but there was a lot more steam, and sheets of a rain-like substance were falling to one side of the troubled area. In the middle of it all the dense black smoke billowed upwards with fleeting streaks of red intermingled in it. The sea there was heaving and broken, but the ships were still in an area of almost untroubled ocean, save for the hurrying turbulence on the surface. The whistle of high-pressure steam was deafening, a bad sign, and the smell was gut-wrenching. I stared in utter fascination.

But once on deck Geordie was more concerned with his

hip. He looked up at the foremast. 'Christ, what a mess! They haven't cleared her yet.'

In the dazzle of sunlight looking upwards I could see that he two masts were almost separated; they now seemed to be ocked only somewhere high up. The taller *Sirena* leaned over *Esmerelda* at an angle and there was a hellish tangle of lines, broken spars and general debris scattered everywhere. The motor launch still hung astern but from where we stood there was no sign of our dinghy.

'They're still busy,' Geordie murmured. 'We'll make for he winch. We can hide there while we try to open the cable old.'

There was nobody at the wheel but ahead I could see knots of men at the foot of each mast. Some were up the masts working to free the wreckage, and I hoped to God they were too occupied to look down and spot us.

'We'll have to chance it,' Geordie said, and gestured to Ian o follow us. We ran forward in a crouch, keeping to the shadow of the deck house. At the end of it Geordie paused, caught my arm and pointed. There was a slight movement in he shadow of the winch drum, and to get there we would have to further cover.

'Bill – or Taffy,' he breathed.

A hand came out into the light and fumbled with the fastenings of the hatch cover. Ahead the men on board *Sirena* seemed to be watching the attempt to clear the mast or ooking back towards Falcon, and there was a good chance hat they wouldn't see a man if he moved stealthily across the deck. A wild dash would be suicide.

The disembodied hand was still working on the hatch cover. 'I'm going to undo the other side,' I said quietly to Geordie. 'Cover me.'

A rumble came clearly across the water from Falcon cutting hrough all other noises, and the red flashes of light in the black cloud suddenly flared higher. Voices were raised in alarm and there was a stampede of running footsteps. The diversion was well timed and I slid along the deck, clutching or the edge of the hatch, and pulled myself to lie close

291

alongside. Groping for the catches, I saw that my companion was Bill Hunter. I had released one catch and was attacking the other when there was the sharp crackle of gunfire and thunder of feet. Ian and Geordie were on their knees, firing at *Sirena*'s men who were pounding aft towards us.

A contorted face loomed over me, the butt of a rifle poised over my skull. I jerked to one side and it slammed into the deck. Then I heard the distinctive 'spaat' of Campbell's target pistol and my assailant grew a third eye in the middle of his forehead and crashed on top of me.

I shoved his body aside and grabbed for the hatch. The second catch came free and Bill and I heaved the cover up and flung it open. Four men came boiling out of it, ready for blood.

Geordie screamed, 'Aft! Get aft!'

We all tumbled down behind the deckhouse. More shots rang out and Ian scored a hit. The rest of *Sirena*'s crew retreated back to the mast as covering fire came from on board their ship. It seemed to come from their deckhouse, but it was hard to tell in the confusion. Geordie looked us over counting heads and to my intense pleasure the face of Jim Taylor was amongst them. At least one of the dinghy crew was safe, which gave me hope for Rex Larkin. Bill gave me a quick thumbs-up sign.

Sporadic fire came from *Sirena*. There was at least one sharpshooter up the mainmast, and Geordie ducked as a bullet sent splinters flying just above his head.

'This is no good,' he said. 'There's not enough cover, and we're running out of ammo.'

Then came the methodically spaced shots from Campbell's pistol. There was a scream from the yardarm and a dark figure fell, all spinning arms and legs, to *Sirena*'s deck.

Geordie got us moving aft, leaving Nick and Ian to cover our retreat. In the companionway Campbell was reloading the pistol as we swarmed below. His lips were curled back in a fierce grin. He motioned us aside curtly and aimed at the yardarm, crouching to steady himself in the hatchway. Another body plummetted down, this time into the sea.

'That's the lot,' Campbell said. He looked drawn and white nd near the end of his endurance. In the passageway Clare as standing with her pistol held in a steady hand. The alarm her face subsided when she saw us. I caught and held her riefly.

The men gathered below and there was a swift redistribu-on of weapons. Nick lifted a brawny fist. 'I won't need a n,' he said. He was holding a huge stillson wrench.

A few more shots came from above but they died away, and short time later Nick and Taffy reported that *Esmerelda* was ear of enemies below decks at least. With the exception of y brother.

Jim and Geordie went to reconnoitre the forward com-nionway, after a brief word with Campbell. Somehow he ersuaded the Canadian to stay back in the saloon with Mark, aula and Clare, and I forebore to ask him whether he'd done by tact or threat. I was deeply relieved, either way.

'They've retreated – they're all aboard *Sirena*.' Geordie as back with a report. 'I didn't see any sign of Ramirez, but adley's all over the place, bellowing orders. He's making a ght foul-up of the job too. We're still locked on, damn em.'

'What about Falcon?' I asked.

'The same as before – it's pretty fierce out there. But we've ecked the engines and there's no sabotage there, thank the rd. We're going to have to get clear of *Sirena* and away oody fast as soon as we can. But how?'

We all looked at one another, desperately searching for eas.

Geordie swung round to Hunter. 'Bill, how did you get ack on board? And where's Rex. Is he okay?' Bill didn't ow about Danny yet, but I'd seen his eyes scanning our unch and he looked grim. It took him a moment to reply.

'I'm sorry, skipper – we lost him. We saw some of *Sirena*'s t take over the launch. They held guns on our lads and threw em a line to haul them in. They hadn't seen us, so I got Rex d Jim here to slip over the dinghy side and we swamped her. m and I got back on board okay, up our ladder, but we had

293

Rex between us and when *Esmerelda* lurched over he – let g
God, Geordie, I—'

'You did your best. It's another one to chalk up
Ramirez,' said Geordie curtly. I left them together and we
up to take another look at Falcon, feeling sick and depresse
The launch still bobbed at the end of its line, but somewhe
under that twitching sea lay our dinghy and one of o
crewmen.

The distance to the belching gout of smoke seemed les
Either we were dragging our anchor, which was very like
with the disturbance under her hull and the extra weight
Sirena alongside, or the area of eruption was enlarging – a
even more alarming prospect. There was even more stea
than before and I longed to know what was going on behi
that red-lit misty curtain. I would have very much liked to a
Mark's opinion.

I went back down to Geordie. 'We've got to get out of he
before Falcon really starts acting up.'

He looked across the sea. 'It's weird, I'll grant you, but is
that serious? Lots of observers have seen eruptions at s
before now. And Mark said it's been going on for da
already.'

'This is just an overture,' I said. No time now to begin
lecture on undersea vulcanology. 'I don't think we should
around when the finale's being played.'

'Oh, I want out too, make no mistake. But we've got
closer problem than Falcon right now – our friends out ther
I wish to God I knew where Ramirez was, and what he
planning. Bill, could you see any sign of tampering with o
hull? They've threatened us with explosives.'

Bill shook his head. 'No, skipper. At least not that I'
seen.'

My warning about Falcon seemed to have passed Geord
by – it was something quite out of his experience. He was st
wholly concerned with unshackling *Esmerelda*, and certain
for the moment he was right.

I asked, 'What the hell can we do?'

'Well, whoever's in command over there – Ramirez

adley – will want to get free as much as we do. They're in anger just as we are. And I don't think they'll find it so easy retake us now, or blow us up as they threatened. Knowing amirez he may be prepared to cut his losses.'

'And try another time?'

'Another time isn't our problem right now. Let's solve this he first.'

He was right, and we waited in silence, aware that a plan as forming in his mind. At last he said, 'I reckon we should all a truce. If we send a man up the mast they won't fire at him they know why he's going up there.'

'What's the good of sending one man up? They've had a ozen men up there for an age and they haven't been able to chieve much.'

'I've got an idea about that,' Geordie said, and passed the ord for Jim to join us. 'Got any more of that plastic xplosive, Jim?' he asked.

Jim shook his head. 'No, I only had the bit I used on their ngine.'

Geordie pointed to the masts. 'See that yardarm – where 's tangled with rigging? Could you blow it off if you fastened hand grenade on each side of the spar?'

I stared at him, but Jim was already immersed in techni-alities. 'It would be a bit tricky, skipper. Grenades aren't xactly meant for that sort of thing.' He peered at the spars oubtfully. 'It's steel tubing.'

'Of course,' said Geordie. 'If it was wood they'd have nopped it through by now. Steel halliards too.'

'I dunno,' said Jim honestly.

'It would weaken the spar though, wouldn't it?' Geordie ersisted.

'It wouldn't do it any good, if that's what you want.'

'Hell, come down to brass tacks. Suppose I have the engine oing and put a strain on the yardarm after the grenades are lown, do you think that would do the trick?'

'I reckon it might,' said Jim slowly. 'It would be a nice job to lace the grenades right.'

Geordie had trapped him neatly.

'You'll have a go then? You're our expert.'

Jim grinned. 'I'll give it a bash – if they don't shoot me.'

'Good,' said Geordie briskly. 'We'll take care of that pa[r]t of it. You gather together what you need and I'll get tho[se] grenades. I knew we'd find a use for them. Mike, you'll be th[e] best man to negotiate. Try to settle terms for an armistice wit[h] that bunch of pirates.'

I wondered if Ramirez would realize that if he let us go h[e] might never catch up with us again. We would forever be [a] threat to his freedom, and he might never agree to such term[s.] There seemed to be too many imponderables. And there wa[s] Falcon. . . . We were very vulnerable – underarmed, unde[r-] manned, and in no position to dictate terms. And then [I] thought of Clare, and how precious she had become to m[e.] Whatever else, I was determined that she should survive, an[d] to hell with the rest.

I crawled into the wheelhouse, keeping below windo[w] level, and raised the loudhailer.

'Ahoy, *Sirena*!' I shouted. 'Ahoy, Ramirez – can you he[ar] me?'

A shot was fired at the wheelhouse. I heard the smash [of] broken glass and a small shower of it fell near me. There wa[s] shouting and then silence. The only sound came from th[e] ships as they creaked and groaned together and from th[e] hissing of the volcano behind us.

'*Sirena*! Ramirez! I want to talk to you.'

My knuckles were white round the loudhailer. The silenc[e] was finally broken by a harsh voice. 'Well?'

'Is that you, Ramirez?'

'Yes. What do you want?'

'That volcano – it's going to erupt at any moment. Hell, it['s] *started*.'

'I know.' He sounded frustrated and I almost smiled wit[h] relief. He'd cooperate.

'We have an idea.'

'What can you do?'

'We want to send a man up the foremast. We can clear tha[t] rigging.'

His voice was full of suspicion. 'How can you do that?'

I did not intend to tell him our plan. I called, 'We have an expert here. We want you to guarantee that he won't be shot at.'

There was an even longer silence this time. Someone tapped me on my shoulder and pushed a note into my hands. It was from Geordie and read, 'Got to slip the anchor. Quiet as possible. Good luck.'

The silence was broken by Ramirez. 'All right, *Esmerelda*. We don't shoot.'

I called, 'Ramirez, if our man is shot at you'll be dead within the hour. Every man here will make you his personal target.'

'You terrify me.' Was he laughing? 'You can send your man up the mast in five minutes. I will arrange things at this end.'

I crawled out of the wheelhouse and joined Geordie, who had Campbell beside him. Geordie said, 'We heard that. What do you think?'

'I think he'll hold off,' I said. 'He's in as big a jam as we are and he knows it. And he must accept that we do have more expertise aboard here than he has.'

'It's not your neck,' said Campbell sharply. He was right back on form. 'Jim will be an Aunt Sally if he goes up there.'

'It will be his decision,' Geordie said. 'I've got some lads up in the bows to slip the anchor. They've timed it in with that, to cover any noise.' He nodded towards Falcon.

I said, '*That* makes this really urgent – it scares me to death.'

Jim had joined us and was listening gravely as Geordie explained. Then he said, 'All right, I know the odds. I'll have a go.'

I said, 'We've got three minutes left. At one minute I'll call Ramirez again.'

We waited, huddled in the corner of the wheelhouse. The minutes ticked by as we listened to the ominous rumbling and hissing from the sea. I turned to Geordie. 'We're only forty odd miles from Nuku'alofa – a fast boat could reach us in a couple of hours. Surely that would be some protection for us. What's the chance of getting off a radio message?'

Geordie's voice was bitter. 'The radio was the first thing they smashed. It's fated. Shorty's trying to whip up a spare transmitter out of the wreckage, but he says it'll take time.'

There was one other faint hope, the possibility of the pall of black smoke being seen and investigated. But we knew only too well how few ships there were in this locality. None of them would be very fast – and as soon as any sensible skipper came near enough to see what was happening the chances were that he would keep well clear. Every track of thought seemed to lead to a dead end.

I crawled into the wheelhouse again and took up the loudhailer.

'Ramirez!'

'I hear you.'

'Our man's going forward now. In the open. He has a bag of tools with him. No shooting!'

'No shooting,' he agreed. 'I have told my men.'

I watched through the window as Jim walked to the foremast, a satchel slung round his shoulder. He climbed the mast steadily. Almost all our crew were watching from various hidden vantage points, several with rifles or pistols handy. Jim reached the yardarm, paused, then swung the satchel in front of him and put his hand inside. He'd have to clip his way through some of the tangle first. On board *Sirena* there was no one in sight; like us, they were staying in cover.

There was a sudden lurch of the two ships as an eddy caught us. I was braced and swaying with the movement, hoping to God that Jim had a firm handhold and that he wouldn't drop a grenade. Suddenly from *Sirena*'s wheelhouse came a babel of voices, and a second later Hadley came running on deck, into full view. He was laughing, and he carried a sub-machine-gun. Swiftly he raised it and fired a burst at the foremast.

Jim toppled from the yardarm, falling with limbs awry to slam with a dull thud across the starboard bulkhead. If the bullets hadn't killed him, then that fall would surely have done so.

There was an angry roar from *Esmerelda* and guns began firing. Hadley stepped back into the shadow, still laughing, and sprayed the rest of the magazine across our decks. Splinters flew on deck at the madman's feet but he seemed to dance away from the bullets and vanished into cover.

Hadley's blast had shattered the rest of the wheelhouse windows. I catapulted myself out of there towards Geordie and Campbell. Geordie was speechless with rage and grief. Campbell was snarling. 'The goddam maniac!'

'I'll have his guts,' Geordie said stiffly.

The firing from our crew died away and I saw faces staring, stunned by the horror of what they'd seen. Two men broke cover to go and collect Jim's body. No one shot at them. Slowly I followed the others below for a council, and found Clare waiting for us in the passageway, white-faced and rigid. She came and clung to me and I held her tightly, and for a moment the only reality seemed to be my love for her.

'Dear God, Mike – Pop – what happened up there?'

'Jim's been killed,' Campbell said shortly.

'They've got a raving maniac over there,' I told her. 'Hadley – he's lost all control.'

'I'll kill him,' said Geordie.

'Geordie, wait! This isn't a war and you're not some bloodyminded general who doesn't care how many men he loses to the cause. We've lost Danny and Jim – and Rex – and other men are wounded. We haven't a hope of getting aboard *Sirena* – we'd be massacred.'

'Hell, what other way is there?' he asked, still spoiling for a fight. There was a growl of approval from most of our crew. I felt as they did, but I had to stop them.

'Look, Hadley's run mad and there's no knowing what he'll do next. But I'll bet those Spaniards over there are even more scared of him than we are. I think Ramirez will have him dealt with, for their own safety.'

Geordie's face was still shuttered and frozen. He wasn't going to listen. Then Campbell said, 'Don't forget we're drifting now. You slipped the anchor.'

299

And that brought Geordie fully to his senses. He frowned, and it was an expression of worry that was far healthier for all of us than his glare of bitter hatred. 'Christ, yes! We could drift right into that thing. We've got to get the foremast right out of its housing, clear the shrouds, the lot. Dump it all overboard. It'll hamper *Sirena* if she tries to give chase. Taffy – Nick—' His voice rose in command.

The men gathered round, grasping their weapons and waiting for him to order them into battle. Instead he began to give firm orders for freeing *Esmerelda*, and they recognized the urgency and sense in his voice. The fighting craze began to leave them all.

I turned to Clare. 'Are you all right?' I asked quietly.

'Better now, darling.'

But even now there wasn't time for more than that one quick moment of comfort. 'Where are Paula and Mark?' I asked her.

She nodded towards the saloon. 'They're still in there. He's not too seriously hurt. He was sitting in a chair the last time I looked in. But he won't give us any trouble, Mike. I've never seen him so subdued.'

'There are all the signs that Falcon will get rougher soon. I want you to get both of them up on deck – it'll be safer than staying below. And stay with your father, Clare. Keep them all together.' I kissed her and then she went into the saloon without a word.

Geordie and the men had gone up on deck and I followed. On board *Sirena* there was frantic activity as men wrenched and struggled with equipment at the base of the foremast. A similar scene was being enacted on our ship. There was no shooting, and of Hadley there was no sign. With any luck they had killed him themselves. I had a brief glimpse of our motor launch, still attached and dancing wildly astern, of the litter strewn on deck, of Jim's body being passed below. I started to go forward and make myself useful.

And then Falcon blew.

There was a mighty roar as thousands of tons of water exploded into superheated steam. A bright flickering glare

hone on us and the sunlight was dimmed as a pillar of steam
scended into the sky.

The first wave reached us in less than fifteen seconds. As I
taggered, grabbing for support, I saw it racing down towards
Esmerelda, silhouetted against the raging furnace. It was a
monstrous wave, rearing mast high, creamed with dirty grey
pume and coming with the speed of an express train.

I crouched on the open deck, trying to flatten myself into
he planking.

The wave broke against *Esmerelda*. She heaved convul-
ively and ground against *Sirena*. There was a rending crash
nd I thought that both ships must have been stove in. A flood
of near scalding water washed over the deck, and I writhed as
felt it in the stab wound in my side.

Then the wave was past us and the ships dipped in the
fterwash, creaking and groaning in every timber. There
vere four more huge waves, but none as high as the first. I
taggered to my feet, feeling the ships' curious writhing
motion on the water.

The waves had done what we had failed to do. *Sirena* was
dipping and bobbing in the water about fifty yards away from
us. *Esmerelda* was free, and she had no foremast at all. It had
been plucked out by the roots.

But every time *Sirena* rolled there was a crash which sent a
hudder through her. I stumbled to the side and looked down
nto the water. Our foremast hung there, still tethered to
Sirena's mast by a cat's cradle of lines and spars. As I watched
a surge of water sent it slamming against her hull like a
battering ram and she shivered from stem to stern. She
vouldn't stand much more of that treatment.

I fell over a body lying in the scuppers. Nick lay there with
blood oozing from a wound in his forehead, but as I turned
him over he groaned and stirred and opened his eyes. He must
have had a constitution like an ox because, in spite of the
massive contusion, he began to struggle to his feet at once.

I shouted, 'Let's look for the others!' and he nodded. We
urned and then stood frozen in amazement as we caught a
glimpse of Falcon.

There was *land* back there. Land that glowed a dull red sh
with fiery gold streaks and which surrounded the pit of He
itself – a vast incandescent crater which spewed forth red ho
cinders and streams of lava. Falcon was building an islan
once more.

The sea fought the new land but the land was winning
Nothing could stop the outpouring of that huge gaping re
mouth, but the sea did its best, pitting water against fire, an
the result was an inferno of noise. There was a great ear
splitting hiss as though all the engines of the world wer
letting off steam together, and under that a rumbling bas
from the depths of the chasm.

Great gouts of fire leapt up from the crater, half hidde
behind the red mist, and the water boiled as it encountere
from the blazing heat of the new Fonua Fo'ou. There was th
sound of surf pounding along a reef, but such surf as none o
us had ever seen before. Mighty columns of tephra, all th
pent-up material that Falcon could fling into the air from
its huge maw, seethed and erupted in spasms, hurling ash
magma and boulders high into the sky. A hazy brown clou
of fragmentary pumice hung over all, obscuring the sun.

Esmerelda was pitching as helplessly as *Sirena*. Black
figures moved on both decks, outlined against the red glow o
Falcon, and I felt a great leap of relief. For a moment it ha
seemed that Nick and I were the only two creatures alive.
hoped to God that Clare was safe.

Nick's eyes were glazed, not in fear but in awe. He wa
tougher and far better trained for danger than I, but I had on
great advantage. I knew what was happening across th
water, and my knowledge helped steady me. I shook hin
roughly and consciousness crept back into his face. He
breathed deeply and then led the way across the littered deck.

On *Sirena* a ship's boat dangled from one davit. Clearly
some of the crew had tried to get away, but those terrible
waves would have made nothing of their chances. One of the
falls had parted and the men must all have been tipped into
the sea.

As we made our way forward, incongruously, it began to

302

snow. The flakes came drifting from the sky, featherlike, to settle everywhere. I brushed one from my shoulder; it was a flake of ash. The air was becoming poisonous with fumes, the increased stink of sulphur and the worse stench of sulphuretted hydrogen. I looked at the sea. It was bubbling like a mud pool. Great fat bubbles were coming up from the sea-bed and breaking on the surface, adding a dangerous smoke to the haze of steam. I realised with sick horror that we were not drifting closer to the source of the eruption – it was expanding under the sea, coming to meet us.

3

There was a shattering roar from Falcon as a second vent opened, only a few hundred yards away from the two ships. The waves this time weren't as massive as before; this was a smaller vent. We clung to handholds during the first swamping rush of hot steamy water and then emerged gasping into the foetid air. Nick was nursing one arm and my rib-cage was alive with pain, but we'd survived. Figures struggled to their feet on our foredeck, and I recognised Ian's bulk among them, and then Geordie.

Sirena lurched and wallowed in the turmoil of the sea. Then she began to spin as *Esmerelda* had done when we first reached Falcon. The eddy that caught her moved on and after a few turns she steadied up again, still dragging the wreckage of our mast.

A plume of water suddenly shot up from the sea not ten feet to starboard and drops of warm gritty water fell on my head. Another waterspout shot up a little further out, and then another. It was for all the world as if we were under shell-fire.

The whole angry sea was pock-marked as though by a mighty rain. It was a welter of spouting water as rocks from Falcon's second vent, hurled high in the air, fell vertically and straddled the two ships. Smoke wreathed about us and steam coiled everywhere.

The falling tephra didn't straddle for long. There was a crash from midships. Splinters of wood leapt into the air to mix with the hail of ash and burning magma. As we stumbled forward we found a ragged hole on the galley roof and a huge glowing ember beginning to eat its way through the deck planking inside. Already small flames were starting to flicker and gnaw at the woodwork.

'Fire, by God!' Nick said. 'How the hell do we cope with this?'

The answer was dramatic and swift. With a booming roar another vast wave engulfed us. We emerged miraculously still intact to find the embryo fire completely doused at the cost of a drenched and sodden galley.

At last we managed to join some of the others. By clinging to anything stable enough we were able to steady ourselves. Of cuts and bruises there were plenty, but everyone was on their feet again. Except Geordie who'd vanished. I caught someone's arm.

'Geordie – he was here. What's happened to him?'

'Gone to try and start the engine,' Taffy bellowed in my ear.

A moment later there was a steady rhythmic throb underfoot as our engine started, and the sound gave me a wild surge of hope.

A warm rain, condensing steam mixed with the slippery and treacherous ash, was falling all around us. The acrid stench was still heavy in my nostrils and the banshee sounds of the ships' timbers mingled with the high-pitched whistlings and rumbling from Falcon's new orifice, threatening to pierce our eardrums. A fresh rain of tephra assailed us. Three or four larger flaming rocks crashed down on *Sirena*'s deck, a couple on ours. *Sirena* was almost level with us and her rails were lined with men. Several of them jumped, some into the sea itself, some trying to reach our decks.

'Bring lines!' Ian yelled; and I pounded after him to the ship's side as he and Nick began throwing them over the rails.

ne man battling in the water seized a trailing end and Ian
ad Shorty dragged him on board. Nick threw another line
at. *Esmerelda* was buffetted by a sudden wave and his feet
id across the ash-strewn deck. He cannoned into me and we
oth crashed down against the railing.

All the breath was knocked out of my body and for a
oment I blacked out. Then I started to struggle to my feet, in
ne to see Nick about to topple clean over the ship's side into
at raging sea. I got him in a tackle around his knees and
restled to keep him on deck, but the slippery footing and his
wn weight were proving too much for me. He seemed to be
nconscious.

Then another wave poured down across both of us, tipping
smerelda the other way and doing what I couldn't manage,
rcing Nick's body back inboard. We slid away from the
ilings together, half submerged in the gritty water that
scaded down over the deck.

I landed spitting and spewing up sickly-warm sea water.
ands helped me to stand up, and one of them was Clare's.

'Mike – are you all right?'

She was trembling and so was I.

'I'm okay. How's Nick?' I was still panting and spluttering.
ut I was comfortably aware that our engine was still running,
nd Geordie was backing us steadily away from *Sirena*.

Clare gave me a fierce hug and I winced.

'Mike – you're hurt?'

'Don't worry, it's really nothing. But go carefully with
ose hugs for now.'

Campbell limped up to us, his face blackened with smoke,
is clothes scorched and sodden. He and I exchanged a look
ver Clare's head and he smiled briefly.

'How's Paula?' I asked him. 'And Mark?'

'Both all right. We haven't lost anyone else,' he said grimly.
he boys pulled two Spaniards aboard and two others
mped across.'

Taffy was helping Nick to his feet. Apart from his arm
hich was obviously crippled and the abrasion on his face
ere seemed to be little wrong with him. Again I marvelled at

his strength. Taffy said, 'We've sent all the Spaniards belo
and Ian's got 'em locked in our homemade brig.'

I said, 'Surely they aren't a danger to us now?'

'Well, there could be trouble,' said Taffy. 'We've got—'

A stunning crash interrupted him. The hail of ash a
magma had died down briefly, but now it started up again as
fresh pillar of smoke and steam boiled skywards from almo
dead ahead of us. Our ship rocked wildly as another barra;
of waves hit us. *Sirena* reemerged from this last assault on fi
in several places. We heard men's voices faintly through th
uproar.

I'll lay odds that Geordie Wilkins must be the best seam;
ever to put his hands on a wheel. With consummate skill ar
an astonishing use of gear and throttle he edged *Esmerel(*
nearer and nearer to the doomed *Sirena*, to aid the strick(
men. As we closed in we saw that one of Falcon's barrag(
must have sheared through the rigging and brought down t}
main gaff. Struggling men lay pinned to the deck. Others we
trying frantically to release them, but the fires were closing i
eating their way along the deck timbers.

Clare screamed, 'Look – Ramirez!'

A man was staggering across the deck of *Sirena*. Obliviou
to the cries and struggles of his crew he never took his ey(
from *Esmerelda*. Through the smoke as it was lit by ;
occasional red glare I saw that he was carrying a rifle. His tor
clothing appeared scorched and blood-stained, and his fac
was a mask of smoke, blood and fury. He had crawled like ;
deadly spider from its crevice to use its poison for the la
time.

I don't know if he had given up all hope of surviving and w;
bent only on revenge, or if his mind had given way. I didn
believe that cold intellect, so unlike Hadley's unreasonir
savagery, would break as easily as that. But there was ;
implacable singleminded purpose about him that was terrif}
ing.

He aimed the rifle across the water.

I flung myself down shielding Clare – I had no idea who ł
would choose for a target – and I heard the gun fire, sharp an

risp against the background bedlam. It was followed almost instantly by a terrible grinding roar, louder than anything we had heard before. We staggered to our feet in time to see Falcon play its most horrible trick.

It was Geordie, intent on his delicate steering, who first saw the danger. I don't know if he'd even been aware of Ramirez. *Esmerelda* sheered off violently as he spun the wheel so that we turned in a half-arc as fast as the one in which the eddy tide had taken us. Then he pushed the throttle in until the engine was pounding at maximum speed, to carry us away from the arena.

Behind us I saw *Sirena* jar to a sudden halt and Ramirez flung across the deck. The ship rose grotesquely in the air and tipped over on her side, looking like a small sailing boat stranded by the tide. But this was no sandbank. It was a bed of writhing red-hot lava. The sea recoiled from it in a tempest of steam.

In that last fraction of a second Ramirez rolled back down the deck, his clothes a mass of flame. He was flung straight overboard into the raging lava bed and vanished instantly. *Sirena* went up like a funeral pyre, before banks of smoke and steam rolled across to blot her out of our sight.

4

The rain of fire from Falcon continued. In all we were hit by four of those fiery bombs. An exhausted and shell-shocked crew was kept busy dousing fires, using the hoses for the biggest, buckets for the rest, and praying that we would not run out of fuel. The hoses worked only as long as the engine continued to run. And we knew that there wasn't the slightest possibility of rigging sail.

Even with the engine at full speed there were times when *Esmerelda* began to drift back towards Falcon, caught in the grip of a cold water current as it rushed in to replenish the

vaporized water. An occasional eddy swung her round by th
bows and Geordie had to take her out in reverse.

It was three hours before we were well clear of Falcon,
mad jumble of fire, steam, smoke and lava falling mercifull
astern of us. Geordie had been spelled at the wheel by Ian an
Taffy; the rest of us had managed to extinguish the fires, hu
the worst of the debris overboard, and bring some fain
semblance of order to the ship. We took turns to collapse wit
exhaustion. Clare worked steadily taking care of burns an
wounds.

Some parts of *Esmerelda* were in better shape than others
By a strange miracle the launch still clung to our coat-tails
though we had no time to stop and haul her up on davits.
found to my great relief that my notes and the bulk of th
lab files were in order, though most of the apparatus wa
wrecked. It was better to work on things like that than t
dwell on the last appalling few hours. But there were a coupl
of matters that had to be taken care of, that could not, for al
my wishing, be put off much longer.

Mark was still on board and had to be dealt with.

And so was Hadley.

Taffy had started to tell me, just before Falcon blew its top
Hadley had been one of the two men who had leapt to ou
deck, and was being held in the brig with the other men from
Sirena. It was dismaying to know that he was with us, but fo
me the most serious problem was Mark.

He and Paula had stayed together in the saloon during th
whole of the encounter with Falcon. Now I had to face him.
pulled myself to my feet and went wearily below. Paul
looked up as I entered and her face, like everyone else's, wa
drawn and shadowed.

'Are we safe yet, Mike?' she asked.

'Pretty well. You should both come up on deck and ge
some air. It's remarkably peaceful up there now. Paula, than
you for standing by.'

She smiled a brief acknowledgement and she and Mark go
up together. He was very pale under the heavy beard, an
limped a little, but he seemed fairly strong. He had sai

thing as yet. I led the way on deck and they followed in
ence, numbed by the sight of so much damage. Nobody
oke to Mark, but more than one of the crew reached to pat
ula's arm or give her a quick smile as she went by.

We stopped outside the deckhouse, a shattered and burnt-
t shell. They stood together looking astern at the now
stant ascending cloud of smoke.

'I wish I'd seen it,' Mark said. He sounded wistful.

'It was fantastic, but too close for comfort,' I said. 'I'm
ing to tape my impressions as soon as I can. There's a lot to
 learned from such close-up observation. Do you know
hat happened to *Sirena*?'

'Clare told us,' Paula said, and shuddered. Mark seemed
moved. He was not going to be overtaken by conscience as
sily as that. I didn't mention Hadley or the other prisoners.

'Mark,' I said abruptly, 'I have to talk to you.'

'I'll go,' Paula offered.

Mark took her arm and held it. 'Stay with me,' he said. She
as the only one he could be sure was on his side, and he
eded a friend at court. He turned to me and a hint of the old
rogance was back in his voice. 'What's it going to be? One of
ur little lectures on decency?'

I felt grim and tired. This wasn't going to work.

'For God's sake, Mark, ease off. I'm not going to lecture
u – it was always too late to get you to listen to reason. But
e have to work something out before we land, or before
meone sights us.'

I wanted above all things to lie down, right there on the
ck, and sleep for a week. I was physically beat up and
xhausted, but the onus of Mark was a heavier burden. I
ished I could have had Clare to stand by me, as he had
aula, but I wasn't going to bring her into it.

We stared at one another in stalemate.

My jumbled thoughts were interrupted by a bubbling
ream. The sound came from below. Taffy and a couple of
e others dived down the companionway, and Ian came past
 at a run. I made a move to follow but then held back,
aving it to the professionals.

I said, 'I think it's one of the Spaniards. He must be hu...
poor devil.'

'What Spaniard?' Mark asked.

For answer there was a crash from below, and Hadley bu...
into view through the burnt-out galley and onto the de...
where we were standing. He had a kitchen knife in his hand...
backed away from his red-rimmed crazy eyes as he came at n...
like a bull.

I booted him on the shin but it was like trying to stop...
truck. He leapt on me in a bear hug that jarred excruciating...
on the knife-graze in my side. His knife hovered near n...
throat. Desperately I clawed at his face as we fell. Hadl...
landed on me with all his weight but thank God his knife-ar...
was pinned beneath us. I chopped viciously at his throat a...
he choked. His grip loosened. I jerked a knee up into h...
crotch and broke free.

But Hadley recovered fast and rolled over onto his fee...
Agile for his bulk he leapt on me as I gasped for air. He pinn...
my arms and I felt the breath being squeezed from my lun...
and a rib cracked agonizingly. Blackness surged in front of n...
eyes.

Suddenly he lost his balance and we both crashed to t...
deck. Nick, crawling up from behind, had seized Hadley...
ankle and had yanked his foot out from under him. I roll...
free and Hadley got the full force of a bullet from Ian's gun...
his belly.

Astonishingly he regained his feet and swooped for t...
knife which lay on the deck. For a near-fatal instant we a...
stood paralysed. With an unearthly bubbling scream of ra...
and agony he plunged towards Mark and the knife flash...
viciously in the sunlight.

Mark flung Paula aside and met the attack full on. The kni...
sank into his side and he collapsed without a sound.

The weapon fell to the deck. Hadley took two staggeri...
paces backwards, clutching his stomach, and then in a fu...
back arch he went over the railings into the sea.

Silence hung in the air after his fall.

I stood shakily clutching my ribs and breathing in sho...

inful gasps. Clare and Bill Hunter were first at my side.
hen Campbell went to help Paula, she brushed him aside
d ran to Mark, who was still lying on the deck. But he was
nscious and trying to sit up.

Geordie arrived at a run and a babble of voices told him
hat had happened. Taffy said harshly, 'My fault, skipper. I
t the bastard out. We heard a man screaming and I thought
meone was in pain in the brig. I went in with Bill but Hadley
ent through us like an express train.'

Bill said, 'No wonder that poor devil was screaming.
adley had near taken the arm out of his socket; to get us to
en up.'

'He was quite mad,' said Ian soberly.

To dispel the air of gloom Geordie said briskly, 'Well, he
ied and he failed. And that's the last of them. The others
n't make any trouble. Now, lads, back to work. We're not
me and dry yet.'

They dispersed slowly. Geordie turned to me and said
ftly, 'The last of them – bar Mark. What are you going to do
out your brother, Mike?'

I looked at him bleakly.

'I don't know. First I must see how badly he's hurt. But I
n't just hand him over to the police.'

'I don't think you've any choice, laddie.'

'I guess not. But it's a hell of a thing to have to do.'

Clare, her arm comfortingly firm around my rib cage,
aited in silence for me to come to a decision. I said,
Geordie, I have to talk to him alone. Take Paula with you,
lare. Look after her. God knows she's had enough to cope
ith. Keep everyone away from us for a while, would you?'

'I'll do that,' Geordie said.

Clare gave me a smile of compassion and warmth and then
alked back to the deckhouse. Mark was sitting propped up
gainst the railing with Paula as always by his side. I waited
ntil Clare took her gently by the arm and the two girls went
elow to join Campbell. I wanted to speak to Mark, perhaps
r the last time, with no one to act as a shield between us.

He looked stonily at me as I squatted beside him.

311

'How is it?' I asked.

He shrugged his shoulders. 'Not good,' he said breathlessly. He was sheet-white and his eyes were cloudy.

I said, 'Mark, thank you for saving Paula.'

'Don't thank me. That was my business.' He did not want to hear praise from me. 'I told you that man was off his rocker.'

'Well, he's out of it now. Ramirez too. Which leaves only you, Mark. And puts me in a devil of a fix.'

I expected his usual sneering retort, but instead he surprised me. He said, 'I know that, Mike. I've caused you a lot of grief, and I'm sorry. I'm likely to cause you a lot more as long as I live.'

'No, I—'

'Which won't be long. I'm no doctor, but I know that much.'

'Mark, we'll be back in port pretty soon and you'll be in medical hands. We may even be sharing a ward,' I said, trying to speak lightly. Mark was sombre and less arrogant than I had ever known him, and I was dismayed.

'Don't be a fool, Mike,' he said with a touch of his old acerbity. 'You're going to have a million questions to answer as it is. It's not going to make things easier for you if you suddenly turn up with your long-lost, murdered, murdered brother, is it?'

I knew that he was right. I foresaw nothing but trouble for both of us. I shrank from the thought of turning him over to justice, but I could see no other way. Mark let me think about it for a while.

'Mike, I have one chance, just one, to make things easy for you. I've never done anything for you before. You have to give me this one chance.'

I said slowly, 'Dear God, what can I do?'

He pulled himself more upright and swayed a little. Then he said, 'Mike, I'm going to die.'

'Mark, you don't know—'

'Hear me out.' His voice shook. 'Remember, Mike, I'm already a dead man. Without me you have every chance of coming clean out of this. There will be nobody to contradict our story. You were sailing to meet up with Ramirez on a survey expedition, and got caught up in the shambles of Falcon. By now the world will know it's blown. There'll be scientists overflying, ships coming to look, the lot. You know that. Your stalwart fellows can wipe out all traces of a gunfight. And you can persuade those Spaniards you've got on board to shut up.'

He drew in a harsh breath. He was drenching in his own sweat.

'Christ, do I have to spell it out for you? I'm not going to recover. I can do one thing for you, if you'll help me now.'

I asked, knowing the answer, 'Help you to do what?'

'Help me to die.'

I had known. 'Mark, I can't kill you.'

'You won't need to.'

Something glittered in front of my eyes. It was the kitchen knife Hadley had used on Mark, bloody at the tip but winking in the sunlight. I swallowed, a hard lump in my throat.

'What – do you want me to do?'

'Get me over the side, into the sea. It'll be as quick for me as it was for Hadley.'

Silently I got up and began to pace the deck. He watched me carefully, saying nothing, giving me time. This was the only completely unselfish thing he would ever have done in his life. But he gave me a dreadful choice.

At last I came back to him.

'All right, Mark. God forgive me, I'll help you.'

'Good.' He became brisk. 'Don't let anyone see us. The story will be that I climbed over on my own, after you'd gone. I would do that, but I need your help.'

There was nobody in sight. Geordie had done his work well.

I could find nothing else to say. Mark gave a short hard cough and his head drooped, and for an instant I thought that he had already died, sitting there. And then he raised his head and looked me in the eye. For the only time in my adult life our gazes locked without antagonism.

It took only a couple of moments. I got him over to the

railing and we both looked down into the sea where the bow-wave ran along *Esmerelda*'s side. I remember thinking how quiet it was.

He hooked one leg over the rail and I helped steady him as he lifted the other across. For an instant I held him.

'Goodbye, Mike,' he said clearly.

I let go. He fell backwards and disappeared into the spray. I turned blindly away and with my head in my hands huddled down by the side of the deckhouse.

After a while I stood up shakily. It was done. And I must go and talk to some of the crew. Not to Paula, not yet. But I must give Mark's plan a chance to work. I turned to leave.

The knife had gone from the deck.

I stood for a moment riveted, a flood of thoughts pouring into my mind. Then I swung round to look at the deck where Mark had been lying. There was still no knife, and now that I came to think of it, very little blood.

In two strides I was at the rail, looking aft, my thoughts erupting as the volcano had done. The motor launch which had been running in tow was gone, and the painter dangled loosely over the stern. Across the water I thought I could see a tiny dancing speck, but I couldn't be sure of that, or of anything.

Slowly I walked aft and hauled in the painter. The end of it had been cut across, newly-severed and just beginning to fray.

There was fuel in the launch and iron rations, for it had always had the function of a lifeboat. There were fishing lines, blankets, flares, a first aid kit. There was everything needed for survival.

I stood at the railing, alone as I'd asked to be, and bade my brother a final, ironic farewell. And yes, I wished him luck.

Desmond Bagley

— a master of suspense —

'I've read all Bagley's books and he's marvellous, the best.'   *Alistair MacLean*

THE ENEMY   £1·50
FLYAWAY   £1·65
THE FREEDOM TRAP   £1·50
THE GOLDEN KEEL   £1·35
HIGH CITADEL   £1·50
LANDSLIDE   £1·50
RUNNING BLIND   £1·50
THE SNOW TIGER   £1·50
THE SPOILERS   £1·50
THE TIGHTROPE MEN   £1·50
THE VIVERO LETTER   £1·50
WYATT'S HURRICANE   £1·50
BAHAMA CRISIS   £1·50
WINDFALL   £1·75

FONTANA PAPERBACKS

Gerald Seymour

writes internationally best-selling thrillers

'Not since Le Carré has the emergence of an international suspense writer been as stunning as that of Gerald Seymour.'   *Los Angeles Times*

HARRY'S GAME   £1.50

THE GLORY BOYS   £1.95

KINGFISHER   £1.75

RED FOX   £1.75

THE CONTRACT   £1.50

ARCHANGEL   £1.75

FONTANA PAPERBACKS

Alistair MacLean

is first book, HMS *Ulysses*, published in 1955, was
utstandingly successful. It led the way to a string of best-
elling novels which have established Alistair MacLean as
e most popular adventure writer of our time.

FONTANA PAPERBACKS

Helen MacInnes

Born in Scotland, Helen MacInnes has lived in the United States since 1937. Her first book, *Above Suspicion*, was an immediate success and launched her on a spectacular writing career that has made her an international favourite.

'She is the queen of spy-writers.' *Sunday Express*

'She can hang up her cloak and dagger right there with Eric Ambler and Graham Greene.' *Newsweek*

FRIENDS AND LOVERS £1.75
AGENT IN PLACE £1.95
THE SNARE OF THE HUNTER £1.50
HORIZON £1.75
ABOVE SUSPICION £1.50
MESSAGE FROM MALAGA £1.75
REST AND BE THANKFUL £1.75
PRELUDE TO TERROR £1.75
NORTH FROM ROME £1.50
THE HIDDEN TARGET £1.75
I AND MY TRUE LOVE £1.75
THE VENETIAN AFFAIR £1.75
ASSIGNMENT IN BRITTANY £1.75
DECISION AT DELPHI £1.95
NEITHER FIVE NOR THREE £1.95
THE SALZBURG CONNECTION £1.95

FONTANA PAPERBACKS

Geoffrey Jenkins

Geoffrey Jenkins writes of adventure on land and at sea in some of the most exciting thrillers ever written. 'Geoffrey Jenkins has the touch that creates villains and heroes — and even icy heroines — with a few vivid words.' *Liverpool Post*. 'A style which combines the best of Nevil Shute and Ian Fleming.' *Books and Bookmen*.

SOUTHTRAP   £1.50
A BRIDGE OF MAGPIES   £1.50
SCEND OF THE SEA   £1.50
HUNTER-KILLER   £1.50
A TWIST OF SAND   £1.35
A RAVEL OF WATERS   £1.50
THE UNRIPE GOLD   £1.75

FONTANA PAPERBACKS

Fontana Paperbacks: Fiction

Fontana is a leading paperback publisher of both nor
fiction, popular and academic, and fiction. Below ar
some recent fiction titles.

- ☐ THE SERVANTS OF TWILIGHT Leigh Nichols £1.95
- ☐ A SEASON OF MISTS Sarah Woodhouse £1.95
- ☐ DOUBLE YOKE Buchi Emecheta £1.50
- ☐ IN HONOUR BOUND Gerald Seymour £1.95
- ☐ IN SAFE HANDS Jane Sandford £1.95
- ☐ SHARPE'S ENEMY Bernard Cornwell £1.95
- ☐ A WOMAN OF IRON Sheila Holland £1.75
- ☐ FAIR FRIDAY Peter Turnbull £1.50
- ☐ THREE WOMEN OF LIVERPOOL Helen Forrester £1.95
- ☐ FRIENDS OF THE OPPOSITE SEX Sara Davidson £1.95
- ☐ KNAVE OF HEARTS Philippa Carr £1.95
- ☐ THE SECOND SALADIN Stephen Hunter £1.95
- ☐ ECHOES OF WAR Joan Dial £1.95
- ☐ MAKING WAVES Liz Allen £1.95
- ☐ GLIDEN-FIRE Stephen Donaldson £1.25

You can buy Fontana paperbacks at your local bookshop o
newsagent. Or you can order them from Fontana Paperbacks
Cash Sales Department, Box 29, Douglas, Isle of Man. Pleas
send a cheque, postal or money order (not currency) worth th
purchase price plus 15p per book for postage (maximum postag
is £3.00 for orders within the UK).

NAME (Block letters) _____

ADDRESS _____

_____

While every effort is made to keep prices low, it is sometimes necessary to increase them at sho
notice. Fontana Paperbacks reserve the right to show new retail prices on covers which may diff
from those previously advertised in the text or elsewhere.